Praise for

The Shell Collector

"This is a beautiful story full of love, loss, and second chances. A collection of vivid characters, an inspiring setting, and heart-held hope for a better tomorrow."
—DEBBIE MACOMBER, #1 *New York Times* bestselling author

"As an avid shell seeker, I enjoyed this tale of surprises deposited among the tides, with its underlying message of finding just the shells we are meant to discover. A tender story of faith, love, and friendship that will warm the hearts of beachgoers and lovers of the sea."
—LISA WINGATE, #1 *New York Times* bestselling author of *Before We Were Yours* and *The Book of Lost Friends*

"A touching story of hope and renewal—proof that you can find more at the beach than shells."
—SHEILA ROBERTS, *USA Today* bestselling author

"An amazing emotional story of putting one foot in front of the other, of overcoming heartache, and of learning to live— and love—again. You'll cry—and smile—and you'll close the book with a very full heart."
—LORI FOSTER, *New York Times* bestselling author

"Nancy Naigle is at the top of her game with *The Shell Collector.* A compelling cast of characters—all acting in accord with their best lights—tackles the issues of loss and grief with wit and grace. 'The Wife' is my favorite new character. An uplifting, hopeful page-turner that shouldn't be missed!"
—BARBARA HINSKE, author of
the Rosemont series and *Guiding Emily*

"A touching story about love, loss, and healing, *The Shell Collector* gives you all the feels. I enjoyed spending time at the beach collecting seashells—and pondering the encouraging messages inside them—right along with the characters. Don't miss this uplifting, faith-affirming read!"

—BRENDA NOVAK, *New York Times* bestselling author

"*The Shell Collector* is a beautiful, emotional story about the glorious sunrise that can come after a dark night, about surviving loss and finding hope and joy again. Amanda, Maeve, and the entire cast will break your heart and then heal it all over again. I loved every word."

—RAEANNE THAYNE, *New York Times* bestselling author

"In *The Shell Collector*, Naigle takes readers on a hopeful journey of healing after unimaginable loss. A tragic past, lovable characters, and a charming small-town setting align for a meaningful beach read. Don't miss this tender tale full of wisdom and insight!"

—DENISE HUNTER, bestselling author of
Bookshop by the Sea

"*The Shell Collector* is utterly charming. Naigle's story of restoration, love, and hope is a perfect read any time of the year. The characters are fun if not a bit quirky, and the setting evokes so much peace. Well done. I loved it."

—RACHEL HAUCK, *New York Times* bestselling author

"*The Shell Collector* is an unforgettable story of love, hope, and healing. This inspiring novel has found a place in my heart."

—JANE PORTER, *New York Times* bestselling author

"*The Shell Collector* gives voice to the profound truth of grieving and learning to come alive again. Nancy Naigle beautifully shows how love can come in so many different forms, as long as you're open to the unexpected miracles life has to offer. In her own words, "Life is rarely predictable if we're doing it right."

—ERIN CAHILL, actress

Books by Nancy Naigle

Adams Grove Novels
Sweet Tea and Secrets
Out of Focus
Wedding Cake and Big Mistakes
Pecan Pie and Deadly Lies
Mint Juleps and Justice
Barbecue and Bad News

Boot Creek Series
Life After Perfect
Every Yesterday
Until Tomorrow

Seasoned Southern Sleuths Mystery Series
In for a Penny
Collard Greens and Catfishing
Deviled Eggs and Deception
Fried Pickles and a Funeral
Wedding Mints and Witnesses

Stand-Alone Titles
Sand Dollar Cove
inkBLOT
Recipe for Romance
Christmas Joy
Hope at Christmas
Dear Santa
Christmas in Evergreen
The Secret Ingredient
Christmas in Evergreen: Letters to Santa
Christmas Angels
Mission: Merry Christmas
A Heartfelt Christmas Promise
Christmas in Evergreen: Tidings of Joy

The Shell Collector

The
Shell Collector

A Novel

NANCY NAIGLE

WATERBROOK

THE SHELL COLLECTOR

Published in the United States by WaterBrook, an imprint of
Random House, a division of Penguin Random House LLC.

WATERBROOK® and its deer colophon are registered trademarks
of Penguin Random House LLC.

LIBRARY OF CONGRESS CATALOGING-IN-PUBLICATION DATA
Names: Naigle, Nancy, author.
Title: The shell collector / Nancy Naigle.
Description: Colorado Springs: WaterBrook, 2021.
Identifiers: LCCN 2020045095 | ISBN 9780593193594 (paperback) |
ISBN 9780593193600 (ebook)
Classification: LCC PS3614.A545 S54 2021 | DDC 813/.6—dc23
LC record available at https://lccn.loc.gov/2020045095

Printed in the United States of America on acid-free paper

waterbrookmultnomah.com

2 4 6 8 9 7 5 3 1

First Edition

Interior book design by Virginia Norey

This story has been pressing on my heart to be told since the year I lost my husband, but I just couldn't bring the words to the page until recently. Wishing you unexpected strength in your most difficult times.

The Shell Collector

1

It was her nerves, not the December chill in the air this morning, that made her shiver as they sat on the tailgate of his pickup truck. She pushed her palm beneath Jack's warm hand. He'd be leaving shortly. She readjusted her position, hoping he hadn't noticed the fear racing through her right now. The last thing she wanted was Jack distracted by worry about her.

He scooched closer, wrapping his arm around her.

She nestled against his chest. *A safe place.*

Behind them, squeals of excitement from an overzealous game of ring-around-the-rosy filled the air as Hailey and Jesse climbed up on Jack's seabag. One following the other, they leaped as if they were ten feet off the ground. Round and round in the truck's bed, their eight-week-old English bulldog, Denali, chased them, nipping at their heels before tumbling unsteadily over his own paws.

They'd celebrated Christmas early since Jack had to ship out. She'd been dreading this day. While she'd been worrying, her husband was obviously shopping for the ultimate gift: the puppy. Since Jack was a Marine to his core, the breed shouldn't have surprised her. She had to admit that at this age, the bulldog was absolutely adorable. That droopy face and those wobbling folds of skin made them laugh, and that was what they needed.

Denali jumped on, chased, and chewed on everything in his path. At the moment, that happened to be the dangling orange grosgrain ribbon hanging from Hailey's left braid.

"Denali! No." Not even four years old yet, Hailey had already mastered that command, and they'd only had the puppy for six days.

The black-and-white pup cocked his head but hesitated only a beat before leaping into the air again.

"No!" Hailey pulled her hands onto her hips.

"That poor dog will think his name is No," Amanda whispered to Jack.

"At least they're letting him walk today. They carried him around so much those first two days that I was afraid the passive pooch would forget he had legs and could run."

"I know, right?" It would be like having another toddler in the house. *Put the puppy down. Don't pull his tail. No, don't feed Denali your lunch. Denali, don't bite. Don't chew. Don't.* Trying to conceal her sigh, she said, "It'll be interesting."

That puppy was going to be a handful, and if he grew into all those wrinkles, he'd be one big dog. At least Jack would return well before then.

But all those worries, and the stress of the pup on top of it, fell away when she turned and saw how the lines at the sides of Jack's eyes crinkled as he watched their children play. His smile still made her insides tumble. She reached for his hand and squeezed it.

He tugged her closer. "Livin' the dream," he said with a playful bump of their shoulders.

She nodded in agreement, but an icy lump in the pit of her stomach settled right on top of that warm, loving feeling. This wasn't the first time she'd seen him off, but it was different now that it wasn't just her.

The kids' cheeks and noses were red from the cold, despite

the fact she'd bundled them in so many layers they could barely raise their arms. The crazy frigid temperature wasn't normal for this part of North Carolina. Jack had suggested they say their goodbyes at home, but she didn't want to miss one second with him before he had to leave.

Vapor from Amanda's breath hung in the air like smoke as she watched the other Marines starting to move out.

Jack slid down from the tailgate and stood in front of her. As if he'd read her mind—*her worries*—he placed his hands on her shoulders and then pressed a kiss to her forehead. "I love you."

She couldn't help but smile. *"Forehead kisses mean the most."* He didn't have to say it out loud now; he'd told her that the day he'd asked her to marry him. She'd never forget it or that feeling. Safe. Loved. Protected. *Everything will be okay.*

She rested her cheek against his shoulder.

"You've got this," he whispered softly.

"I know. I know." But she didn't, really. She was trying so hard to be strong for him. She looked up into his deep-blue eyes. His dark hair and lashes stood out even more against the blasé tan, brown, and gray camouflage uniform he wore today. Both Jesse and Hailey had his eyes.

He looked anything but afraid. In fact, excitement twitched in his smile. Alive with the anticipation of what was to come. Proud to be a Marine.

Her heart raced. She already missed him.

"And we've been talking to Jesse and Hailey about it. They'll be fine," he said.

She knew better. "Hailey asked me this morning if we could have you make pizza tonight."

He sighed. "Okay, I guess you were right. Maybe she's too young to really understand."

She shrugged. "She's your baby girl. She adores you. She misses you every day even when you're here."

"I adore all three of you."

She kissed him on the cheek. "Goes both ways."

Amanda tugged her coat tighter, dipping her chin into the warmth of her white infinity scarf. Six months. They'd been lucky it hadn't been a twelve-month deployment. *Be thankful.*

They sat quietly until Jack lifted her chin and brushed a strand of her hair back from her face. His eyes held her gaze.

"My beautiful wife. I love you." He leaned in close. "Don't worry. Time will fly. I promise." He rubbed his freshly shaven cheek against hers, then nuzzled her. "I'll be home before you know it." Then he made an animated growling noise against her neck.

She curled into herself, laughing as his breath tickled her skin. In the middle of that laughter, they both knew it would feel like forever. "Hurry."

"Enjoy it, because when I get back, we'll have a lot of time to make up for." He raised an eyebrow. "I will miss you like crazy."

She looked away, trying to ignore the swelling loneliness. Across the parking lot, other Marines moved toward the buses.

He inched over, blocking her view.

She lifted her gaze.

The calm in his voice soothed her, if only for a moment. "It'll be summer. We'll take the kids to the zoo, Carowinds, and the water park. And it'll be beach weather. You know how I love chasing you through the waves."

"No fair." She swatted at him playfully. "You always catch me."

"You love it."

"I do. You're right." He'd proposed to her at the beach not all that far from here, and they'd gotten married in that very same spot the following summer. A private ceremony with her best friend, Ginny, and his best friend, Paul, to witness their vows to each other. Her parents still hadn't forgiven her for not doing the big church thing. Instead, they'd had the minister from the chapel on base perform the private ceremony. It was small and perfect. A meaningful promise rather than a party. She'd never apologize for that.

Jack leaned against her and made that stupid growly noise again that always made her laugh. And she did. Laugh, that is, because the truth was, it was every silly, stupid, playful, romantic thing this guy did that made her love him like no tomorrow.

She squeezed his hands, wishing she could blink and spring forward six months.

Standing tall, he repositioned his hat. It was time to leave.

Amanda followed Jack's line of sight as he turned and looked at the four buses nose to tail at the end of the parking lot. In red script, "Holiday Tours" covered the side of the white buses as if all these folks were going on a fun excursion. But this wasn't a holiday. And it was definitely a different kind of tour. A tour of duty. The irony wasn't lost on her.

A loud "Oohrah!" carried across the parking lot. All that the guys seemed to notice was they'd have a plush-seated ride down to Florida to start this endeavor. She couldn't blame them for their excitement about that. It sure beat the rough ride of a convoy, and for that she was thankful.

Marines huddled with their loved ones, working in those last instructions, promises, and kisses. Saying goodbye was never easy.

"Come here, Hailey-bug." Jack held his hands out, and their daughter ran into his arms. "I've got to go. I need you to be a good girl for Mommy, okay?"

"I'm always good."

"Yes, you are. I'll be back soon." He touched his finger to her nose. "Boop."

Hailey giggled, but then her lower lip protruded and her chin quivered. "No, Daddy."

"I have to go," Jack said. "Remember, we talked about it. You'll have Denali to keep you company while I'm away. Teach him lots of tricks. I can't wait to see how smart he is. You'll be such an excellent teacher."

"Stay, Daddy." Tears welled in her blue eyes. She looked so much like Jack. "I need you."

"I have to travel for work. We can count down the days together."

Amanda pulled in a stuttered breath, trying to contain her own tears as she watched Hailey and Jack. She picked up Jesse, holding him so tight she could feel his heartbeat against her own.

Jack took Amanda's hand as he held Hailey. "I have to come back," he said to Hailey. "I promised your mom an anniversary trip to Denali. Right, Mom?"

"That's right." Amanda nodded. They'd been saving for the trip since the day they married.

Hailey clung to Jack's neck. "I don't want you to go."

Amanda saw the sorrow in Jack's eyes. He hated to see his baby girl sad, and this was heartbreaking.

"She'll be fine," Amanda said, trying to reassure him. "We'll all be fine and waiting for you."

Hailey lifted her tiny hand in the air and extended her pinkie. "Promise."

"Pinkie promise," Jack said, then set Hailey on the ground.

Hailey looked up at him, sniffling tears. "Who's gonna teach Denali not to poop in my room again?"

"You will," he said. "You're smart, and Mommy will help."

Of course I will. The puppy had been Jack's idea. A surprise to all of them. Mostly her, because she'd have flat out vetoed getting a dog. She had enough to worry about with Jack not being around for six months. Now she had a puppy to train on top of it all. She wished Jack had at least talked to her about it first, but then he loved surprising her.

As if Denali could read her mind, the chunky pup lumbered over to the edge of the tailgate and flopped down with an exaggerated sigh.

"You're irresistible." She already had her arms full with Jesse, but she pulled the puppy up too.

"Woof." Jesse pointed his finger toward the dog, which Denali immediately nipped.

"Ow!" Jesse jerked his hand back but then laughed and put his finger in the dog's mouth again. "Woof you, Nali."

"Careful," Amanda said, flashing a tired look in Jack's direction.

"He'll figure it out," Jack said. "He's all boy. A few scrapes and cuts are nothing for boys like us." He ruffled Jesse's hair, then took the puppy from Amanda and placed him in the truck bed and closed the tailgate.

"Yeah, he's definitely your boy." She stood and shifted Jesse to her hip so she could slip her free arm around Jack. "Thank you for the surprise. The kids love the addition, and I will too. It won't be the same as having *you* here, but Denali is a good second best."

"Don't let Denali steal my pillow," Jack warned.

She shrugged playfully. "We'll see. Just hurry home."

Across the way, a few of the wives stood talking. She could hear them already planning a girls' day out and weekly get-togethers. Amanda had been part of some of those conversations before, believing it made the time go by faster and easier for those left behind.

Jack took Jesse into his arms.

Jesse simply said, "Bye." His favorite new word. Jack whispered into his ear, and to whatever Jack was saying, Jesse just kept repeating, "Bye."

He put Jesse down next to Hailey. "I love you both." They hugged his legs.

"This is it, babe," he said, pulling Amanda into the group hug.

"I love you, Jack."

"I love you. I'm already counting the days. This is a good thing I'm doing. We're doing."

"Honorable. Amazing. I know." Her throat grew tight. "I love you for it, but I hate it. I miss you already." She took Hailey's hand. "Come on, Jesse. We have to let Daddy go." Jesse looked up at Jack and then waddled over to her without a word.

Jack heaved his duffel bag over the bed rail to his shoulder, reaching for her hand one last time.

She squeezed his hand, trying to smile through tear-filled eyes. Her thumb traced his wedding band. Her heart hung in her throat as her fingers slipped from his strong hand.

Watching his long, familiar strides, her breath caught with every step as he moved across the parking lot toward the other soldiers. Proud, and ready to fight for freedom.

Butterflies danced in her stomach.

"We can be brave together," she said, hoping saying it out loud would make it true.

Hailey started wailing, which made Jesse cry. She knelt and held them close. "Wave to Daddy. Make funny faces." Hailey and Jesse sniffed back tears, then started mugging. Anything to keep them from crying. "We'll go get hot dogs to take home for lunch when we leave here. Deal?"

Jesse flapped his hand. "Bye."

Hailey, with tears falling onto her cheeks, held Amanda's gaze. "Daddy has to come home."

"Yes, he does, honey. We will plan lots of things to do. He's going to be home just as soon as he can be."

She turned and watched as the bags were loaded onto the bus, and then the guys. Once Jack cleared the door, she couldn't see him through the tinted windows.

"Come on, let's blow Daddy one more kiss before we go." They all raised their hands to their mouths and blew kisses. She had no idea if he'd even seen them, but he'd know. He always knew.

She put the kids in the back seat of the truck and buckled them into their car seats. Denali was standing with his paws on the tailgate. She lifted the chubby fellow and stuck him on the floorboard under the kids' feet.

As she closed the rear door, she saw one of the gals from the women's group heading toward her.

She didn't have that much strength right now. A pedicure or a game of bunco wouldn't change that Jack was gone and would be for quite some time. Although she'd been one of them in the past—the wives supporting those who had husbands away—and she knew firsthand their intentions were honorable, she just couldn't do it today.

Amanda hopped into the front seat and cranked the truck, pretending she hadn't seen the woman. She drove off with a slight pang of guilt, mostly because she lived in base housing too. They were neighbors. No way would she be able to avoid these ladies for long. They were determined to help one another, and that was a blessing. Amanda realized that. But right now she was sad, and she wasn't ready to let go of that yet. She needed to muster every smile she could to put on a brave and happy face for her children. That was her priority.

Rain fell, and from the looks of the sky, it was settling in for a while.

She stopped at the drive-through to pick up hot dogs for lunch and then drove home. Thankfully, Hailey and Jesse seemed exhausted by the morning's events too. Jesse was already asleep in his car seat. When they got home, Amanda woke them up to get them inside. They ate hot dogs and then all climbed into her king-size bed, even Denali, and watched cartoon reruns.

She hugged Jack's pillow to her heart, hoping the scent of his aftershave wouldn't fade anytime soon. Once Hailey and Jesse fell asleep, she cried quiet tears. She missed Jack already, and he probably hadn't even made it out of the state yet.

2

Two years later
Whelk's Island, North Carolina

Our character is often most evident in our highs and lows. Be humble at the mountaintops, be strong in the valleys, and be faithful in between.

—MARC CHERNOFF, *Getting Back to Happy*

Becoming a single parent had never been the plan. Sure, Amanda was aware that marrying a Marine carried a certain amount of risk and sacrifice, but their love was big and true. She'd worried more about how much she'd miss him while deployed than the remote chance he might not come home. Those teensy percentages happen to someone, though, and it had happened to Jack. And her.

Still, after all this time following Jack's death, more than two years now, there were mornings Amanda woke up with her arm flung over the other pillow, reaching for him. Each time, reality tore at her tender heart. She remembered the way his morning stubble prickled her fingertips, and the curve of his smile when her touch accidentally awakened him. She clenched her fingers into a fist. *Please don't let that memory ever fade.*

Everyone said time would make the loss more bearable.

If she'd had a twenty-dollar bill for every time someone told her that, she'd be a rich woman. She'd lay odds that whoever started that rumor had never lost a husband.

The first year, she'd been on autopilot; friends and family had leaned in whenever she faltered. The second year, as she came out of the fog, that support system had faded away. Time had healed them, so they'd moved on, leaving her to find her own way.

That's when reality settled in and every part of her life had a gaping hole that Jack had once filled. No one had warned her the second year was even worse. It would have been nice to know in advance.

The third year would be better than the last. She'd promised herself that. So this morning she lay there summoning the strength to get started.

As usual, Jack's voice filled her mind. *"You can do this. You're a strong woman. Stronger than you know."*

He'd convinced her of that, until he was no longer there. He'd been her strength all along.

She never remembered it being this hot in early July before. Amanda took in a deep lungful of the humid Whelk's Island air. Loneliness hung from her like a wet sweater—oddly heavy and cold—in the middle of summer.

If she could turn over and never wake up again, it would be fine by her.

That's not an option.

Two tiny hearts depended on her: Hailey and Jesse. Three if she counted Denali, and he needed her too.

She pulled the covers back and sat up. Stretching her arms to the ceiling, she looked around her bedroom. The real estate agent had called this house a cottage, but that made it sound more glamourous than it was. Bungalow was probably more fitting.

There was an advantage to the place being in poor condition. Price, for one, but it also gave her the freedom to go a little wild with decor and paint colors. Years of sand had ruined the hardwood floors, so she let the kids help her whitewash them. They'd even written messages of hope and love and dreams across the thirsty boards before painting them. It would forever be their family secret. The project made the house feel more like home.

Despite the fact there were still boxes stacked in the corner of her room even after having lived here over two months now, she and the kids were finally getting into a good routine.

It was liberating to have no history in this town. Gone were those side-glance looks of condolence from the other Marine wives. The are-you-okays. It might be true that those looks had just been in her head, that people weren't giving Jack a second thought after two years. That's what Mom had said, but honestly, was that any better? To think Jack had been completely forgotten was heartbreaking too.

Her phone rang. One glimpse at the screen confirmed what she'd already suspected: Mom. *Please don't push today.* She hesitated answering, but with each ring, she realized that waiting to talk to her wouldn't make it any easier.

"Hello, Mom. How are you this morning?" She made herself smile. She'd read somewhere that an actual smile on your face came through over the phone. If that would convince her mom she was doing okay, it was worth a try. *Fake it 'til you make it.*

"I wondered if you'd answer. You must never keep your phone with you."

Which was Mom's passive-aggressive way of letting her know that she suspected Amanda had been ignoring her calls, but Amanda refused to let her bait her today.

Mom rambled on. "Anyway, the house down the street went on the market this morning. Huge backyard and one of those big swing sets with a slide and a fort. You know we have the best school district here. I already called the agent, so I can go see it this morning at ten. I'll video-call you."

"Why would I do that? I just moved."

"But this is better. You'd be here with family. We've talked about this."

"Mom, thank you, but no. I'm not coming back to Ohio. My life is here now. Jack and I want to raise the kids in North Carolina."

"But Jack isn't there."

She pulled her hand to her heart. "Yes. I'm fully aware. Every day I'm reminded of it. But I have to do this on my own. Why can't you have faith in me? I need to do this. It's important to me."

"Well, those kids need more than just you. We're their grandparents."

"I know, Mom. I totally agree. Come visit. Y'all can sleep in Hailey's room. She sleeps in Jesse's most of the time anyway. The beach is great. You can see for yourself we're doing fine."

"You know your father won't leave. He's got all those things going on."

Amanda sucked in a breath. *All those things?* Like what? Mom had a million excuses why they wouldn't come down to visit. Amanda was tired of begging them.

"You shouldn't let this house get away. It's perfect. Homes in this neighborhood don't go on the market often. Somebody has to die to get one."

"Somebody died?" Good grief, that's all she needed—to live with someone else's ghost.

"No, it's a saying. Look, if you're worried about the money, we can help you. The cost of living is cheaper here. It would be so much easier for you. Please—"

"Thank you. I know you mean well, but I'm where I need to be."

Her mother let out an exhausted sigh. "Well, then I suppose I must call and cancel that appointment. I don't know why you can't at least try. We worry about you. You're our daughter. This is hard on everyone."

"I'm doing the very best I can. I start teaching in September. Everything is all set."

"Well, that's another thing. Here you could work part time, or not at all. You wouldn't have to go back to teaching. You could live off the insurance until the kids are older."

Teaching wasn't what Amanda wanted to do. When she'd uprooted the family and moved here, the plan had been to start her online store selling herb-infused salts prepared at her house. She and Jack had set some money aside for the venture. She wished she'd done it sooner, while he was still around, but the kids were little and the timing never seemed right.

She'd paid a contractor to cordon off a space for the sole use of her business as soon as she'd closed on this place, only to then find out she couldn't run the food business from her home with Denali on the property. That had been a devastating discovery and a huge waste of money. She'd thought Mom would console her, but instead it fueled the arguments to get her back to Ohio.

"I guess we shouldn't complain since you'll be using your college degree," Mom said.

"Right." Like she hadn't heard about that a hundred times since she had Hailey. "Thanks, Mom. Kiss Daddy for me. I've got to go. Something's on the stove." She hated lying, but these calls left her feeling uncertain, and she wasn't strong enough for that today. "I love you, Mom. Bye."

No doubt things would be easier in Ohio, but her mom

would put herself in the middle of everything, and finding a way to move on without Jack was something Amanda needed to do for herself.

She tossed her phone aside and made her bed, brushing the cover free of wrinkles.

Instead of keeping the masculine blue color scheme she and Jack had shared, she'd decorated this room in beachy tones of taupe and a sassy fruit-punch pink. Jack would never have agreed to the girlie combo, but it made her feel happier. Even if the moments were few and far between, they were coming more often now than they had.

"Good morning," she said to the gerbera daisy on her night-stand. Its magenta petals brought joy every day. *If you talk back, I will have a problem.*

Next to the flower sat a conch shell. She'd bought it at a garage sale for a dime. That was the day she'd started house hunting for a home at the beach. Not just any beach. The beach where she and Jack had gotten married.

She picked up the shell and held it to her body. Since she first laid eyes on it, the shell made her feel powerful and able to come up with solutions that otherwise seemed impossible.

The weather was so hot that even at night the house didn't cool off. She shook her hair from her face and stretched to the sky. She'd once read somewhere that stretching when you got up was a sign of being healthy. That was a good enough reason to give it a try.

Amanda's feet stuck to the humid floor as she walked down the hall. She poked her head inside Jesse's room. Even though the ceiling fan was on, both kids had kicked off their sheets. Hailey was still fast asleep, hugging the stuffed lop-eared bunny she'd gotten for Christmas two years ago. Jesse was wiggling—a sure sign he'd be up any minute.

She walked to the living room and sat on the couch, pulling her feet up underneath her for a few minutes of quiet. She closed her eyes and took in slow, deep breaths.

I'm thankful for the security the teaching job will bring.

I'm thankful for this humble house. It's becoming a home, and we're safe here.

The kids are stronger than I'll ever be. I'm so lucky, and they keep me going.

And then that was it because Jesse came tearing down the hall, his bare feet slapping the floor. He jumped over poor Denali, who'd practically dug a hole while trying to scramble out of the way.

Have I ever finished a list? I'm grateful for so many more things.

"You're awake!" Jesse struck a squatty sumo stance.

Amen.

He ran over and threw himself at her. "Love!"

"Good morning, my little man." She hugged him tightly.

He smacked a wet kiss on her cheek. This was their special time each day. Hailey wasn't an early bird, but Jesse greeted Amanda with enthusiastic smiles every single morning.

It would be hard to switch gears when school started, but she didn't have a choice. She'd been frugal with the insurance money. Hopefully, with some clever planning, someday she'd still be able to do something with her herbs.

Jesse belly-flopped onto the couch next to her.

"I love you," she said.

"I love you ten and five." He burst into a fit of giggles as if ten and five was the biggest number in the world.

She pulled him close. He smelled of baby shampoo and sweet dreams. She blew her lips against the side of his neck, making him laugh. His chubby legs kicked in the air.

He wriggled free to climb down on the floor and kiss Denali on the head. "Good boy."

The dog let out a sigh and licked Jesse's hand. It was amazing how much Denali had grown from that tiny eleven-pound puppy to this fifty-two-pound solid hunk of love. The handsome black-and-white bulldog now took up most of the doorway when he sprawled out. His chest was so wide that he looked like he could stop just about anything. Well, except on the days Hailey dressed him up in her tutu. Denali really was the perfect dog for them. *Yes, Jack, you were right.*

Hailey came down the hall, her eyes still half-shut. "I wasn't ready to be awake. Jesse, you always wake up too early."

He shrugged. "My eyes just pop open. I can't help it." His expressive face tickled Amanda. He was so committed to getting his point across.

Amanda raised her hands, fingers wide, mirroring him. "Me too. We must be twins."

He cocked his head. Then he burst into a fit of giggles. "You're Mommy."

"Yes, I am. The luckiest mommy in the world to have you two." She wrangled both kids in for a family hug. "It's supposed to be cooler today. Want to take Denali down on the beach?"

"Yes!" They both bounced, which excited Denali. He leaped up, then nudged his nose under Hailey's hand for more attention.

"Go change into your swimsuits, and I'll pack breakfast to take with us."

Jesse took off for his room, but Hailey started filling a tote bag with cups and plastic takeout containers. She was planning to design a sandcastle worthy of a princess.

"You have to carry that over the dune, Hailey-bug. Don't make it too heavy."

Hailey gave the bag a test lift, then removed a couple of things. She raised it again. "I can carry this much."

"Bring it back too?"

Hailey took one more thing out, looking satisfied.

"Good deal. Go put on your swimsuit and bring a hat."

Amanda made peanut-butter-and-banana sandwiches, cut into fourths, the way they liked them, then tucked them and frozen juice boxes into her bag. She'd quickly figured out how to eliminate carrying a cooler. Even a small one was too much to lug over the dune with everything else they required for a few hours on the sand.

"Y'all ready to roll?" Amanda called out.

Both kids came skidding down the hall.

"Rollin', rollin', rollin'." Jesse marched through the kitchen, wearing his western straw hat and stars-and-stripes swim trunks.

Amanda hoisted the straps of her beach chair onto her back, then grabbed her tote bags. The kids ran past her out the front door with Denali. They waited for her at the gate of the white picket fence that outlined the perimeter of their postage-stamp lot.

She unlatched the gate. Hailey and Jesse, holding hands, started running up what they liked to call the mountain. It had been the perfect spot for watching the fireworks display earlier in the week. The kids were fascinated by the colors even if the bangs scared them every single time. Independence Day was a milestone for her, too, this year. She'd have to be brave, stay strong, and endure.

They made it over the dune in record time and unloaded everything far enough back from the waterline that the tide wouldn't force them to move, something they'd learned the hard way after chasing towels and toys into the surf one afternoon.

Amanda spread out a sheet. "Let's eat breakfast before you play, okay?"

Hailey and Jesse each nibbled on a quarter of a sandwich but were more interested in getting down to the water.

"Is this enough for now, Mom?" Hailey asked.

Jesse climbed to his feet.

"Sure. Go play," Amanda said. "I'll save these for later."

Hailey grabbed her bag of tools and ran down to the water. Jesse and Denali caught up to her and began digging like crazy. Sand flew in the air, left and right.

Denali ran halfway up the beach with his tongue hanging out but then turned and went back for more. The kids squealed and giggled as he chased them in and out of the ankle-deep surf.

The pooch tuckered out quickly and sprawled out on the sheet next to Amanda. She poured water into a bowl for him, which he ignored, but then he gave her a lazy wink she took as a thank-you.

Hailey ran back up, settling her hands on her hips. "Mom, make Denali come play."

"Give him a break, Hailey-bug. Look, he's worn out." The dog's tongue lolled out to the side.

"Okay. I'll show Jesse how to draw hearts and flowers."

"Excellent. That sounds fun." Amanda dug through her beach bag and pulled out two spoons. "Here. You can use these."

"Yay!" Hailey jetted off toward the surf, a willing Jesse following her wherever she went.

They moved near the water, and Hailey started giving orders. She was bossy for a six-year-old, or maybe all six-year-olds were. Amanda didn't really have anyone to compare her to. But fortunately Jesse didn't seem to mind being bossed about. He'd been born with a chill personality. Never crying. In fact, for a while she'd wondered if something was wrong with him. He was so different from Hailey. Amanda hoped he'd never change.

Watching them work so diligently together always made her heart happy.

A flash of color caught her attention. Down the beach a tall elderly woman wearing a skirt in a kaleidoscope of gem colors kicked her feet through the surf. She grabbed the edge of her wide-brimmed hat as she hopped over a crashing wave that soaked the hem of her skirt.

Amanda wished she could feel that carefree.

She watched as the woman crossed in front of where Jesse and Hailey were playing. Just then, Jesse pointed at the woman. In an instant, he was on his feet, running toward her.

Amanda jumped up. As she tried to get momentum in the soft sand, Jesse reached for the long tote hanging from the woman's shoulder.

Lord, if he tugs that woman into the water, what will I do?

3

Maeve twirled around like a waterspout to keep from falling. It wouldn't be the first time she'd been hung up in a blob of seaweed or someone's towel that had been stolen by a wave because she wasn't paying attention to where she was walking. She'd been focused on the horizon—the magical spot where the deepest parts of the sea met with the sky. Her arms flailed, but she caught herself.

A little boy with royal-blue eyes framed by dark lashes stared up at her with one hand still clutching her shell bag, and his eyes as wide as silver dollars. She wasn't sure who had been startled the most, her or him.

She squatted to get to his eye level. People had always complimented her on her icy-blue eyes, light blue like the North Carolina sky, but his were like sapphires, bluer than she'd ever seen before.

"Hey there, buddy." The bottom of her skirt floated around her legs like a colorful jellyfish. "You scared me."

The little boy let go and leaped back next to a girl with the same bright eyes. "What's that?" he asked, his finger pointing at Maeve's bag.

"That's where I keep all the treasures I find for safekeeping."

A woman with long blond hair ran toward them, panic on her face.

"That your momma?" Maeve nodded her way, trying to calm her.

"Yes ma'am." The little girl took her brother's hand possessively.

A wave came in, churning foam and spray into the air.

"I'm Hailey. This is Jesse."

"My name is Maeve."

"Maeve," Hailey repeated. "That's a very pretty name. You look like a mermaid. Do you live in the water?"

Maeve noticed that the way her skirt floated in the water did look peculiarly like fins. "Being a mermaid would be pretty special, don't you think?"

With an emphatic nod, Hailey said, "I do."

"Would you like to see some of my treasures?" Maeve let them look inside her bag. Jesse reached in and pulled out a large scallop shell, his mouth forming a perfect O.

"Pretty neat, isn't it? And that's not even the best of 'em," Maeve said.

The woman raced to Maeve's side. "I'm so sorry." The woman huffed, leaning forward to try to catch her breath. The dog that was following her had lost interest and was now biting at the waves, his tiny stub of a tail swirling in a circle so fast it looked like he might helicopter above the water.

"Thank goodness you didn't fall," the woman said, exhaling. "Jesse, you can't do that, sweetie."

"He's fine. He was curious about my bag. They're both delightful." She offered the young woman a smile. "Really. It's okay."

"Thank you. I'm Amanda Whittier, their mother." She seemed to collect herself. "This is—"

"Hailey and Jesse," Maeve said, completing her sentence. "Yes, they politely introduced themselves."

"Her name is Maeve," Hailey explained.

"I see." Amanda turned her attention from Hailey to the woman. "So nice to meet you, Maeve. I've seen you walking the beach before. We're new to the area."

"Yes, I know." She stood and leaned in. "I'm a lifer. Born and raised here. I know everyone." Maeve paused, expecting Amanda might explain her connection, but she didn't.

Maeve finally said, "If you need to know anything, just ask. I can recommend restaurants, mechanics, a church. Whelk's Island is a wonderful place to live."

"We love it." Amanda placed her hand on Jesse's shoulder. The dog lay in the wet sand.

"That's Denali," Hailey said, pointing to him.

"He is quite handsome." Maeve turned her attention back to Amanda. "It's great that you chose Whelk's Island. We need young families like yours to move in to keep this town alive."

"These two are pretty lively twenty-four seven," she said with a laugh. "We live in the first house on the right."

"I know that house. It's been empty a long time."

"It's a work in progress, but we're slowly getting settled in."

"It's a wonderful location. Protected by the dune, and kind of tucked away in your own little oasis. What brought you to our town?"

Amanda stammered. "Well, I . . . We needed a change. I . . ." She looked off, then back at Maeve. "I love the beach, and it's beautiful here."

"It is." Maeve suspected there was more to that story, but she didn't push. Instead, she pointed to where the land began to curve around and rise higher. "That's my place. I'm sure we'll see lots of each other on the beach. I'm out here every day." She delicately tapped Hailey and Jesse on the head.

"That's a big house," Hailey remarked.

Unlike the other houses around here that sat close to one another, hers sat alone. It did look big from here. Three levels above the stilts, and a walkway on the top floor with a wonderful view. Yes, it looked quite grand from a distance.

"I grew up in that house," Maeve said. "It sat empty for years after my folks died. Like yours, it took some work. That makes it even more special, don't you think?"

"Definitely," Amanda said with a smile. "We love a project."

Maeve had a feeling that even simple tasks became a project when there were two littles at your feet, but then she'd never had any so she wouldn't really know. "When I lost my husband, I moved back. A lot of house for one lady and her old dog, but it's home."

"Your dog can come play with Denali someday," Hailey offered. "Like a playdate."

"I'm not so sure my dog is up for much playing anymore. He's like me: old."

Hailey propped her hands on her hips. "You're not old. You're fun."

"In all my eighty-one years, I don't think I've ever had a nicer compliment. I'll tell my sister, Judy, you said so." Maeve lifted her chin. "She thinks I'm old as dirt. She wants me to come live with her."

"You're eighty-one?" Hailey's eyes bugged out. "You don't look that old. Is that in mermaid years?"

"You really don't," Amanda said.

"Well, thank you, both, but I am, and my dog is old too."

"What kind of dog do you have?"

"Mine's just an old mutt. The veterinarian said she thought he was a schnauzer-beagle mix."

"A schneagle. They are so cute," Amanda said.

"He's not really that cute at all, but he's sweet. I didn't even want a dog, but that sister of mine said I needed one. She also said he was a senior dog that would never find a home if I didn't take him. I figured I'd appease her since the thing probably wouldn't make it to the end of the year, and here I am seven years later and that dog will probably outlive me."

"Oh no." Amanda lifted her hand to stifle a laugh.

"It's true, but we've grown to really enjoy each other."

Hailey tugged on Amanda's arm. "Maeve collects stuff in her pretty bag while she's walking on the beach."

"Treasures!" Jesse jumped, inadvertently splashing the entire side of Maeve's long flowing skirt. The brightly colored fabric hung heavy and wet.

Amanda winced. "Sorry."

"Don't be. It's the beach!" Maeve lifted her foot in the air and stomped the water, splashing them all.

Jesse's drenched face struck an awkward expression, and then he dropped his hands to his knees and belly-laughed.

Hailey reached for Amanda's hand. "Mom, I want to collect sea treasures just like she does."

Jesse touched Maeve's tan leg, jabbering so fast she only understood about every other word, but she saw that his gaze was intent on her bag.

"Please?" Amanda seemed to remind him.

He pressed his lips together, then looked up at Maeve, dimples deep into his cheeks. "Please can I see more shells?"

Maeve lowered her bag to the sand. "Go ahead. Rummage around and pick out your favorite."

Jesse picked up a tiny corkscrew-shaped shell. "I like this one. It's funny looking."

"That's a neat shell, isn't it?" Maeve placed her finger on the sharp point at the top. "It's called an auger."

Jesse's tight grip made his fingertips whiten. "Ogger."

"Right. An auger is a drilling tool that construction workers use to dig holes. See how it's shaped? When it spins, it moves the dirt out of the way and makes a deep hole."

His eyes sparkled. "I like dirt."

"I bet you do."

Hailey extended a finger toward the biggest shell in the bag. "I like that one."

Maeve reached in and handed it to her. "That's a lightning whelk."

"Lightning?" Hailey held it out as if it might shock her.

"Not that kind of lightning. It won't hurt you."

Hailey closed her hand around it, testing to be sure. Satisfied, she asked, "Where did it come from?"

"Whelks are kind of like snails. They build their shell, making it bigger as they grow. I guess this one died, or maybe he moved away. The tide brought the empty shell in last night."

"It's beautiful. Now place it carefully back in her bag," Amanda said.

Jesse put his shell back in Maeve's bag too. "Thank you." He marched off in a circle around Maeve, happier to be splashing.

Maeve tidied her bag. "It's been nice chatting with you. I wish I had more time, but I've got to run. I like to be at the courthouse for the town council and zoning meetings. You should come check them out sometime. It's a great way to be on top of what's happening in this town." She turned to leave.

"Bye." Hailey waved. "I hope we see you soon."

Maeve walked away, hoping the same.

Maeve changed into a sundress and flats and walked over to the courthouse. It wasn't but a few blocks away but seemed farther in this heat.

The Whelk's Island courthouse was no Taj Mahal. Just a long two-story saltbox with white pillars in front. She climbed the three steps and walked inside. The air-conditioning was a welcome relief.

She nodded hellos to the regulars and the mayor as he walked by. "Good morning, Maeve. You're looking well."

"Thank you, Mr. Mayor." Maeve slid into her favorite spot in the second row. She'd learned to sit near the end so she could leave without bothering anyone if she got bored or fed up. Truth was, her temper flared now and again at some of the foolish things people tried to pass in this town. If she didn't stick up for Whelk's Island, there'd be no telling what shape this city would be in ten years from now.

The meeting was called to order, and Maeve stood for the Pledge of Allegiance. She loved this part. It made her proud that Whelk's Island still placed importance on the pledge. In other parts of the country, people were abandoning it in public and schools, and she didn't like that one bit. She placed her hand over her heart. "I pledge allegiance to the flag of the United States of America." Pride swelled inside her as the voices united and lifted in the room. Good people, doing good things. "With liberty and justice for all."

The harrumph of everyone sitting back down at the same time was followed by the roll call. A silly process when it was easy to do a quick head check, but that was politics. Lots of rules for rules' sake.

There wasn't much on today's agenda that really needed her attention, but she'd listen and speak up if necessary. After all, can't complain if you don't offer your reasons. She was rich with opinions.

Several consent orders followed, including one for the Friends of the Library proclamation, as well as the hundredth anniversary of the American Legion Auxiliary. She clapped wildly, proud of her friends and neighbors for their good works.

When the floor opened for general public commentary, she recognized the dashing young man with the compelling blue eyes who owned Paws Town Square walking to the podium. He was fit but had brains to match his rugged good looks. He'd proven he was a smart businessman, and this council hadn't made it easy. They gave him a fight from the word go. In the beginning, no one wanted him to bring his business to this town. She'd stood up for him because his plan included repurposing the vacated Lowe's building. Ghost box, he'd called it. It was overgrown and an eyesore. She was glad he'd hung in there until everyone saw it the way he did.

The man stood at the podium, then addressed the council.

"Good afternoon. Paul Grant. Paws Town Square, Whelk's Island. Mayor, council members, and others here today, I wanted to provide an update now that we're fully operational. It's been a long road to get here, as you well know. This is our second location, and the third is now underway in Jacksonville, Florida. We're delighted with the enthusiasm of the local community using the dog park and trails, and we're nearly booked to capacity the entire summer, which exceeded our expectations on year one. I wanted to share a couple key measures that show the good we're all doing, because without the support of this council, and this town, this would not have happened."

He drew their attention to a slide projected on the wall. "In the Whelk's Island location, we already have fourteen retired military working dogs going through rehabilitation. The twelve-week program will prepare these dogs to be reunited with their original military handlers. There are over twenty-five hundred active military working dogs in our armed forces currently. They serve our country as soldiers, and upon return, like our men and women, they need special handling to address issues like PTSD or injuries sustained while working in combat zones. We're proud to be part of that solution."

He took in a breath and spread his stance. "We currently

have thirty veterans working in different roles at this location. Without the hard work of this town council and committee, we would've never been able to accomplish the four cornerstones of our mission: to reunite military working dogs with their handlers; to support our veterans, both human and canine; to self-fund these efforts; and to give back to the community. It's an honor to be able to do this here on Whelk's Island, which I now call home."

The mayor smiled. "You certainly came through on all fronts, Mr. Grant. Your tenacity was hard to ignore."

Paul had been accused of that before. Heat rose to his cheeks. "We've put new discounts in place for locals, and tourists can reduce their kennel bills by simply visiting their animals during their stay. Hopefully, that will make this feel like a pet-friendly town and even more appealing to travelers."

The assistant town manager said, "The business has great eye appeal as tourists come into town too."

"Thank you." Paul twisted his papers in his hands. "Your support has given us a wonderful template to help expedite these efforts in other cities across the nation."

With nothing else on the agenda, a motion to adjourn followed and everyone made their way to the exit.

Maeve shortcut across the room to catch up with Paul. "Sir? Excuse me. Paul?"

"Yes ma'am." He turned.

He looked even kinder up close, but he still had that tough Marine appearance. Strong and capable.

"Hi. I'm Maeve Lindsay. I wanted to congratulate you. Your hard work is really admirable, and I'm glad you picked this town to set up shop."

"Thank you, ma'am." His smile was easy, genuine. "I appreciate you standing up for the plans in the early zoning meetings. I remember you."

"To take a tired and decaying building on the outskirts of town and transform it into a beautiful and functioning part of the community is appreciated, Mr. Grant. But doing so to fund good works—sir, that is a gift." She placed her palm on his heart. "Truly a gift. I hope to come out and see Paws Town Square in person one day. It's a little farther than I walk, but I'll get a friend to take me."

"Thank you. Believe me, it's not only a pleasure but a dream come true." His heavy brows tilted. "It's very dear to my heart. You let me know when you come. I'll drop everything and give you a personal tour. You rarely miss a meeting, do you?"

"Can't leave everything in their hands. Sometimes they need an old lady's advice."

His laugh was nice.

"Well, thank you," he said. "I'd be happy to arrange transportation when you come visit if you need it." He reached into his pocket and handed her a card. "Call me."

She took the card. "Careful, now. I might take you up on that."

"It would truly make my day if you did." The words came across as sincere. "Please do."

"That's very kind," she said. "I know it doesn't mean much, but I'm very proud of you. I wanted to meet you and thank you personally for helping bring something positive to Whelk's Island. I was born and raised here. I love this town, and that old shopping center was just a mess."

"Hopefully, other businesses will be inspired to consider ghost boxes now."

"Wouldn't that be great? Honey, I won't keep you. Thanks for giving an old gal a minute of your time. You have a nice day." When she squeezed his arm, his bicep was as solid as a coconut.

Maeve walked out of the building satisfied for doing her

part. She did love these meetings. It was way better than sitting in front of a television, watching something that meant absolutely nothing. Why didn't more people care about what happened in their town?

Walking home, she thought about how Paul must feel knowing he was responsible for helping two groups—animals and veterans—who'd served our country and fought for our freedom.

Only a very special man would recognize that need and be able to find so many ways to contribute.

4

As Amanda went over the dune, it made her happy to finally see the outside of her house shaping up. The overgrown yard had been wrangled into something close to order. Goodness knows they'd had enough barrel fires to get rid of the debris. So many that the kids considered gathering brush a precursor to hot dogs and s'mores for dinner . . . again.

The freshly painted front door, the same color as the geraniums she'd planted, added life to the place.

"Doesn't our home look pretty today?" Amanda said out loud.

Hailey gave a halfhearted "yep" as she tried to catch up.

The day the real estate agent showed them this house, Hailey and Jesse had been hesitant to go inside. She couldn't blame them, but she'd felt an immediate kinship to the place. Like her, it had seen better days but now seemed sad. Unloved. Unwanted. Uncared for. The sellers hadn't even tried to put lipstick on the pig, but a Marine sticker on a surfboard and a dirty old postcard of Mount McKinley in Denali National Park on the closet floor were all the signs Amanda needed to know this was where she was meant to be. She and the house would take the journey to restore their futures together, and they were off to a good start.

The kids took turns dancing under the cool water from the spigot before going inside.

"Mom, it's hotter in here than it is at the beach," Hailey complained.

And she was right.

"Everyone put on shorts and sneakers," Amanda said. "I've got a plan."

She changed too and then piled Hailey and Jesse into the car. As she drove down the old beach road, she noticed a whole display of fans blowing red streamers in the hardware-store window. "What do you think about that?"

Hailey and Jesse perked up. "That looks cool!"

Cool was exactly what she had in mind. The kids hadn't complained one bit up until today, but summer was showing its strength. Amanda had underestimated how miserable it could be with no central air in North Carolina. This was nothing like the lake in Ohio when she was a kid. Not having AC had been no problem back then. She couldn't afford air-conditioning with the price she'd paid for the house, and she'd thought they could get through one summer without it. That clearly wasn't going to work.

She parked in front of the store and they went inside. An hour later, she had the two box fans she'd gone in for, and the owner had even hooked her up with a great deal on a used AC window unit for the kids' room.

She drove home and sent Jesse to bring his little red wagon around to the car.

He kicked up sand while running through the yard and came back with the metal wagon clanging behind him.

She lifted the AC unit out of the trunk and placed it in the wagon. The two box fans were light, so she stacked them on top.

"Okay, let's roll these up to the house." She took the handle and let the kids push from behind. Jesse's cheeks were puffed out and red. "Breathe, Jesse. You don't have to push too hard. You might knock me over." That was unlikely, but he sure did put his all into everything he did.

She propped the air conditioner in the children's bedroom window and plugged it in. To cover the gaps on each side of the small unit, she cut cardboard strips, covered them in a heavy trash bag to waterproof them, and then duct-taped them into place. For good measure, she pounded a single nail above the sash to keep the window from sliding out of position. She'd sleep better knowing there was no chance of that thing falling on the kids.

"Ready to try this thing out?" Amanda held her hand at the power button.

"Yes." Jesse walked over and put his finger on top of Amanda's. "I'll help."

"Here we go," Amanda said. The old window unit chugged, sputtered, and then revved up like a race car before it started blowing icy-cold air into the room.

Jesse loved the noise. He hopped and waved his hands in the stream of air.

"Mom, this is so cold!" Hailey closed her eyes and stood like a statue in front of the unit. "I think it could blow snowflakes!"

"It's heavenly." Amanda picked at her shirt, letting the cool air sop some of the dampness from her. "This will feel so good."

"It's kind of loud," Hailey said.

"Maybe now you won't hear Jesse when he wakes up early." Hailey grinned. "I will like that."

"I thought you would. Come on." They all left the room,

and then she closed the door behind them. "Now for the fun part. You two open the fans for me while I get the windows ready."

The kids wrestled with the boxes in the kitchen while she worked to pry open the windowsill in the living room. It had been painted shut, but after wiggling it, she finally got it free. Unfortunately, the sash wouldn't hold. It kept sliding back down. She found a paint stick in the hall closet to hold it up until she could get the fan in place.

Hailey and Jesse thrummed on the empty boxes, singing a mishmash of nursery rhymes and country songs. She let them entertain themselves while she slid the fan into the window frame, just about guillotining herself in the process.

Once the fan was snugly in place, Amanda went about setting up the other one across the way, near the kitchen table. She positioned it to blow the hot air outside, creating a steady flow through the house. It was a trick Daddy had used when it got hot.

Refreshing air moved through the house, bringing instant relief. She went back into the living room and started singing into the spinning blades. "Aaaaaa-aaa-aaa-aaa-aaa-aaah."

She couldn't resist testing her old robot voice, so she bent toward the fan and her words reverberated as if they were in a blender. "Thaaa-aaa-aaank goo-ooo-oodness this fee-eels soo-ooo gooo-oood."

Hailey and Jesse abandoned the boxes and rushed to her. "What are you doing?"

"Singin' in the fan." Holding a fake microphone, she leaned in closer and continued. "Just singin' in the fan. What a glorious morning. I'm singin' in the fan."

Jesse retrieved his cardboard box from the kitchen and started drumming to the song, sort of.

Hailey joined Amanda and sang along.

In a fit of giggles, Amanda announced, "I expect a concert after dinner tonight."

"Every night!" Hailey played an air guitar and belted out the words to "Twinkle, Twinkle, Little Star" in the fan.

That night Amanda moved one of the fans to her bedroom. She slept better than she had in weeks and even rolled out of bed an hour before Hailey and Jesse got up. By the time they showed their faces, she was already cooking breakfast.

The kids came running into the kitchen together. A first. "Good morning!"

"Great to see my two favorite children so happy."

Hailey pulled her hands to her hips. "We're your *only* children, Mom."

"Thank goodness." She kissed them both. "You're just in time. Jesse, you can separate the tortillas. Hailey, how about you tear up some spinach leaves."

Jesse's fingers worked the tortillas until they were about the furthest thing from round. She might have to stack two together to keep the eggs from falling through them, but it was a delight to see him trying so hard.

Hailey handed the bowl of spinach to Amanda. "Here you go, Mom."

"Perfect." Amanda dumped the bowl of spinach into the eggs and sprinkled cheese across the top, placing the lid over the pan so it would all melt together. Then she poured cups of milk and set them on the table.

"Okay, we're ready. Forward march. One at a time." Her little soldiers grabbed their plates and tortillas and stood in line. Jack had started the tradition, and it still made her happy. She wondered if the kids even remembered why they did it. Did they think of him on these mornings too?

She scooped egg mixture onto the tortillas, and Hailey and Jesse raced back to the table to roll them up.

She made a plate for herself and joined them. As soon as she sat down, they all bowed their heads. They sang, "Thank You, Jesus, for our food. Many, many blessings."

Their faithful voices buoyed her.

Amen.

"Need some help rolling yours, Jesse?"

"No ma'am." He gobbled from one end, eggs falling from the other.

He'd figure it out someday.

Hailey giggled but didn't scold or correct him. "Let me know if you want help, brother."

"You're a good sister," Amanda said.

Jesse shrugged, then scooped the eggs back into the tortilla with his fingers and tried again. This time he held a hand over the end and looked proud of himself when nothing fell to the plate.

They'd gone through a tricky phase for a while when poor Jesse couldn't make a mistake without Hailey putting him down or boasting about herself. Amanda was glad they'd gotten past that.

"I can't wait to collect shells," Hailey said.

"Me too." Amanda was happy about anything that didn't require a bunch of gear to carry. "Go get changed. I'll get some snacks ready."

As soon as the kids were dressed and everything was packed, they paraded out of the house, with Denali at their heels.

"All present and accounted for. Let's do this." Once she had Denali's leash attached to his red collar, she opened the gate and they all raced over the dune for the beach.

Maybe it was the low cloud cover this morning, but the ocean sounded so much louder today. She had a feeling it would be a brief stay the way the wind was whipping. The kids ran in circles at the shoreline, letting Denali chase them until he needed a break and ran to lie by her feet.

She got up and met them at the water with their pails. "Y'all ready to find some shells?"

They began scouring the sand. She knelt down and picked up a handful of tiny vibrant-colored shells. Most of them were broken, but a purple one caught her eye. She tucked it inside her pocket while the children quickly filled their pails with shells at every step until their buckets got heavy. When she looked up, she noticed they'd walked farther down the beach than they'd ever gone before.

"Let's head back," Amanda said.

Denali lay down in the sand.

"We can't leave him," Hailey whined.

"He'll catch up." At least she hoped so. There was no way she'd be able to carry him.

"Do you want to stop and go through your shells? Lighten the load by getting rid of a few?"

Jesse lugged his bucket with both hands. "Can't. They're treasures."

"Let me help you with that." She carried his pail the rest of the way to their beach towels, where the kids dropped to the sand and dumped their shells. "Do you think we need to keep all of these?"

Jesse pulled his shells closer. It was crystal clear he had no intention of letting any of his go.

"I don't know." Hailey scooped some shells into her hand. "Most of them looked prettier when I first found them." She dropped a couple in the sand, then picked up one of them, a sparkle in her eye. "I already forgot I found this one." She twisted the scallop shell in the air. "It's like a ruffly potato chip."

"Half of the fun is looking for them, right? If we collect all of them, there won't be any for others to find. Maybe we should only keep a couple seashells each day. What do you think?"

Hailey's eyes narrowed. "How many?"

"Pick out your very favorites, and then we'll decide together."

Hailey sorted through hers.

Jesse inched closer, pointing out the ones he liked best of hers, and then finally he moved a few broken fragments from his pile to her discards.

As the kids worked, they sipped on the juice boxes Amanda brought. She took the novel from her tote bag, not expecting to get through but a page or two, but as she'd been telling herself for two years, any progress is progress. And that seemed to apply in all cases.

She'd read straight through to the end of the chapter before the kids finished sorting shells.

"Should we throw the shells we're not keeping back into the ocean?"

"That's a great idea."

They scooped up the discards and ran to the water's edge, dumping them into one big pile, then raced back.

"Want to see my best shells?" Hailey asked.

"I do." Amanda leaned over. Hailey had kept five: the big scallop shell, two twisty-looking shells, a pink one, and another that was black. "They are all pretty. I bet it was a hard decision."

"Mm-hmm."

"How many did you save?" she asked Jesse.

"One." He held up a finger.

"Where is it?"

He looked around, then brushed the sand with his hand.

"Oh no." He pulled his arms up, making tight fists, and ran toward the water where they'd dumped the shells. Amanda jogged behind him. Bless his little heart.

He squatted, leaning over his knees to look through the pile. His lower lip protruded. He brushed his hand through the shells again. Amanda's heart tugged as he searched in earnest. Finally, he lifted a shell in the air.

"This one!"

It was a pretty bluish color and twisty. "I love it."

"Me too." He blew her a kiss.

"All right, then. Let's go home and eat some lunch."

As they walked back over the dune, she looked toward Maeve's house. Amanda was sorry Maeve hadn't been there today to see the kids so excited about collecting shells. She had a feeling their new friend would have taken delight in it.

The three of them walked through the soft sand until Hailey stopped in the middle of the path.

"Mom, look!" Hailey dived for the large shell sitting right on top of the sand. She lifted it into the air. "It's so heavy."

Jesse ran to Hailey's side. "Pretty."

It was large and perfect. "Let me see," Amanda said.

Hailey dusted the sand from the shell and handed it to her. "Look! There's something written inside it."

They walked this path every day. Amanda was surprised they hadn't seen it before. Then again, they had never been looking for shells until now. The wind must have blown enough to uncover this one from the seagrass where it sat.

"What's it say?" her daughter asked.

Amanda read the words to herself and then aloud: "*All the art of living lies in a fine mingling of letting go and holding on.—Havelock Ellis*"

"Who is Have Lots?" A thoughtful look crossed Hailey's face. "He must be really lucky."

"Havelock Ellis. That's the person who first said that."

"Did he write it in our shell?" Hailey always had to have all the answers.

"No, I don't think so." The quote hung in her mind. *Living lies?* No, it wasn't about *living lies;* it was about how the art of living was achieved. It was such a simple quote, but it grabbed her, provoking her. How was someone supposed to recognize what to let go of and what to hold on to?

She thought of Jack's shirt still hanging on the back of her dressing-table chair as if he might grab it and put it on tomorrow. Some nights she still slipped it on before she climbed into bed. Certainly, after two years, any scent of him had to be long gone, but she swore she could smell him when she wore it. *I couldn't.* Letting go of that meant letting go of Jack.

She tipped the shell up, reading it again.

Why am I taking this so personally? It's a random find.

"Can we keep it, Mom?" Hailey asked.

"We sure can." The quote rolled in her mind.

Trekking those last thirty feet over the dune was like crossing the finishing line of a marathon. The kids were dragging, but she felt the world brighten more every time she saw their house waiting for them. She opened the gate, and Denali ran through, followed by Jesse and then Hailey. More than a house. The latch clicked behind them. *Home sweet home.*

"Where should we put our keeper shells?" Amanda asked.

"Can we have them in our rooms tonight?" Hope hung in the air. "For a while," Hailey begged. "Just until we get too many?"

It was hard to say no to them. "Yes. If you want to. That seems fair." She had no intention of leaving hers outside either.

Jesse placed his on the corner of the flower box that Amanda had hung over the hose bib. "Mine."

As they ran ahead to go inside, she took the purple shell from her pocket. *Help me stay focused on the beauty around us.* She placed it next to Jesse's treasure.

She prayed Hailey and Jesse were adjusting to life as well as it seemed despite her own daily inner battle. She carried the big shell inside, reading the quote once more.

5

From Paul's office at Paws Town Square,
he had nearly a panoramic view overlooking the dog park,
pond, and myriad walking trails. Because the facility was
meant to also serve as a rehabilitation-and-training center,
each of the hiking paths had multiple rest stops, including
water fountains and benches. The outside trails had them,
too, but with the humidity, not many people cared to use
them this time of year.

His leather chair screeched against the ceramic tile floor as
he leaned his arms forward on his desk. Memories from his
Marine career filled a shelf on the bookcase otherwise piled
with nonfiction, reference books, and binders of information
on projects completed and pending. A few of his personal belongings were on that shelf. He walked over and picked up the
picture of him, dressed in fatigues, with his partner Gunner,
one of the best bomb-sniffing dogs the Marines had. He located more IEDs than any other dog and had the medals to
prove it. The hardest part of leaving the Marines had been
leaving Gunner behind, but the powers that be weren't ready
to let him retire at that time.

Paul's life had changed a lot in the past two years. There was
a time when he'd thought he'd be an active-duty Marine until
his hands began to weather with age and they forced him to
retire. But now there were no more combat boots and no daily

salutes. The expectations hadn't changed that much, though. He still put his needs and wants second to his new mission: to help his fellow service members, including the military working dogs. For that, there was honor.

He'd danced with death, been taken prisoner, protected his country, and helped shape another round of new recruits along the way. He made friends and lost the best of them. Those losses had forced him to make a change. Who would've thought that at the lowest point in his life, he would come up with the greatest opportunity of all?

A double knock came from his open door. His assistant poked her head inside. "Hey, Paul. I have those packages ready for you. Do you want me to run them down to the post office?"

"No, thank you. I can take care of it. I have a couple other errands to run today." He walked over to get the packages. "Thanks."

"Don't forget that conference call in an hour."

"I'll be back in plenty of time," he assured her.

Her lips pursed as she pointed out the window toward the view of the park below. "When are you going to slow down long enough to find yourself a nice gal to share all this with?"

"Me? Never gonna happen," Paul said, then winced. He hadn't meant it to come out so abrupt, which left him feeling the need to explain. "There's not a woman out there who could put up with the likes of me." He took in a breath. "I met my one true love. It just wasn't meant to be, and that's that. Mission impossible."

"Sorry, boss. I won't press, but for the record, I don't believe that."

She was plucky—he had to give her that. "Thank you, but I've found my life's calling now. I'm married to my work. She might not be all that pretty, but she's all I need."

"You need to look out that window again. She's pretty. Real pretty. High maintenance as heck, but beautiful. You made sure of that."

"Yeah, I guess I did." Paul laughed. He could've gotten away with a lot less and served his customers just as well, but the ambiance got people in the door, and the service kept them happy.

"Okay, I'll get out of your hair." She walked out of the room, and Paul moved over to the window. His assistant was right. It was beautiful. The greenery and flowering trees and plants below soothed his soul. *What more could I need?*

A Lynyrd Skynyrd song played in his mind.

That's what I get for asking questions. "I always need Skynyrd."

He dug the keys from his pocket and headed downstairs.

It wasn't even four miles to the post office. On a cooler day he could've walked or jogged, but with less than an hour to spare, he took the truck. He got behind the wheel and hit re-dial on his phone for Tug's Diner as he backed out. "Can I get two hot dogs all the way for Paws Town Square? I'll be by to get them in about twenty minutes."

Those hot dogs were his weakness. He ate them for lunch at least twice a week, something he used to avoid completely, but they were quick, cheap, and easy, and Tug made homemade chili and toasted the buns. He could already taste them.

The Whelk's Island post office was the tiniest one he'd ever seen. The original for this town, it was a historic landmark. According to the locals, the compact building had once sat right in the middle of a sandy field, but the town had eventually grown up around it.

The teeny structure had withstood years of hurricanes, and when the city planner recommended relocating it to an up-dated building, the townspeople wouldn't stand for it. Instead, they compromised and allowed an external makeover.

The worn and rotting pillars had been replaced with new composite material that would never need painting, and where there used to be lapboard was all vinyl siding in soft yellow with glossy white trim. It looked like a kid's playhouse to him.

He parked his truck at the curb and carried the packages inside. The interior boasted the original wooden counter, and vintage brass twin-letter-combination post-office-box units lined the walls.

"Hi there!" Maeve walked toward him with a stack of mail in her hands.

"Hello, Maeve. We meet again."

"And so soon," she responded. "How are you?"

"Doing great. Just mailing some packages." Paul jostled the boxes in his arms.

Her eyebrows darted up. "You can't tell me you don't have someone who could do that for you."

"I do, but I like to get out. With the tourist season in full swing, I haven't been jogging on the beach like I usually do. I get a little stir-crazy, but it's too crowded out there for me."

"Oh gosh, I wouldn't go to that end of the beach if you paid me. You should park at my place and access the beach from my house. I'm right up the street."

"Really?"

"Of course." She wrote down the address for him. "I walk from there to Tug's Diner and back almost every morning. I'm the big blue stilt house in the curve. I don't even have a car, so there's always room to park."

He thought for a moment. "I know which house you mean. That's a hike. You walk that every day?"

"I do."

"Good for you. My buddies and I used to surf that pier."

Her mouth sprang into a smile. "Seriously, make yourself at

home. It's a great stretch of beach to run. Or walk, in my case. I'd love it if you would."

"I'm going to take you up on that sometime," Paul said. "I've been using the trails at Paws Town Square, and they're nice—don't get me wrong—but there's really nothing like the ocean air and the sound of the waves crashing at your feet to get your head in the right place."

"From your mouth to God's ears. We both know that's true." She started out the door, then paused. "Is that your big blue truck?"

"It is."

"Looks like you." She waved a hand over her head. "See you around the beach soon, I hope."

He watched her walk out, then took his packages to the counter, where a postal worker wearing a name tag—Ruthie—stood.

"I see you've met our resident beachcomber," she said.

"Maeve? She's great."

"Yes. Everyone loves Maeve. She used to help decorate this place on all the holidays. She helped the Master Gardeners club with the planting, too, only she never was good with plants, so she'd just drop shells alongside all the flowers. Kind of her thing. She loves seashells."

"Who doesn't? Nice lady too. She was a real supporter with the city when I was trying to get all my plans approved."

"She's one you want to have on your side. She's a pistol, that one. Rain or shine, she's out and about. Walks everywhere. It could be raining buckets or a hundred and five in the shade and she'll show up."

"Doesn't really surprise me."

"Nothing she does surprises me." Ruthie chuckled as she weighed and labeled Paul's packages. "That all for you today? No stamps?"

"No, thank you. That'll do it." Paul took his receipt, then walked out to his truck. As he drove down the road, he saw Maeve walking. He slowed and pulled over to the curb. "Need a ride? It's awfully hot out today."

Maeve shook her head emphatically. "I'm fine. I like it this way."

Sixty-six-degree air blew from the AC across his face as he rolled up the window. If Momma were alive, she'd beat him with her flip-flop for not insisting Maeve accept the ride, but he didn't think Maeve would take too kindly to that.

In his rearview mirror, he could see her still plugging along.

The blue-and-white sign for Tug's Diner came into view. He whipped into a spot along the curb in front and got out, then dropped the tailgate and pulled a hand truck to the ground. He stacked four boxes on it and rolled them into the diner through the front door. Thankfully, they didn't have too big a crowd right now.

Tug must've seen him drive up. "Is that The Wife's food you ordered for me?"

"And treats too. They weren't on back order after all."

"You didn't have to deliver that stuff," Tug said. "I would've picked it up."

"No need. Gave me a reason to get a couple of those awesome hot dogs you make."

"You don't need a reason for that."

Paul rubbed his belly. "Yeah, I have to be mindful, else I'll look like I have a load of laundry on my washboard stomach."

"I think you're a few hot dogs away from that, son." Tug waved him toward the back exit, which led to a gazebo where a huge cage hosted his African gray parrot. "Mind wheeling that back here? I've got storage under her cage."

Paul pushed the handcart out the back door.

The Wife sang out a greeting: "Oh, Pauly. Hello, Pauly." She stretched out her charcoal-gray wings to their full span of eighteen inches, then settled down and cocked her head with a click.

"I taught her that," Paul said to Tug. "The last time I was here."

"With a vocabulary of over four hundred words, she could say whatever she wants, but she learns what she wants to learn. Just like a woman." Tug pulled out a huge wad of cash from his front pocket and started peeling back twenties. "I appreciate you ordering those supplies for me. Saved me a ton of money."

"No problem. I'm glad you thought to ask."

"Well, I owe you."

"No, you don't. Just keep on making those delicious meals so I don't go hungry."

"You got it." Tug led them back inside, where he grabbed one of the to-go bags lined up by the register. "Here you go. On the house today."

"Thanks, Tug. I'll see you tomorrow night."

"I don't think you've missed a fish night since you came to town."

"Doing my best to set a record. Plus, your counter has the best view of the beach in this town." It was true. Unlike most diner counters, which faced the grill or wall, the one at Tug's Diner was in front of a wide span of windows that looked out over the deck to the water. Paul had mulled over plenty of problems here while trying to open Paws Town Square. There was a peace in this place that he'd never experienced anywhere else.

He loved this town and every single person in it. He wished he could stay and work from here long term, but duty called and he was best boots on the ground, where the projects were.

He jumped into his truck and did a U-turn to head back to

work. Darn if he didn't pass Maeve still walking up the road. "You go, girl." He waved, unsure if she'd even notice him, but she threw her arm up in the air in an enthusiastic reply.

He hoped she would take him up on the offer of a tour.

Back at Paws Town Square, he swung into his parking spot, then jogged up the stairs.

"You're back." His assistant glanced at her computer. "And with fifteen minutes to spare. You *are* good."

"What can I say? I love a challenge." He pulled up the reports he needed for the conference call, then settled behind his desk to devour those hot dogs.

6

That night, Amanda stood in the living room against the front doorjamb. Her hand grazed the screen, sending a resting moth off in flight. The leaves on the trees swished, although she couldn't feel even the teensiest breeze. A lightning bug twinkled right in front of her, then more of them. They lit sporadically, like lazy Christmas lights in gold.

Even though the dunes rose as high as her house, she could hear the muffled sound of the waves when she stood silent. It soothed her, and for a moment it was as if she were completely alone in this world, in a good way. Safe and at peace. She let her eyes close, enjoying the moment.

These were precious days. At the end of the summer, she'd go to work again. A new schedule would replace all this relaxed fun. Responsibilities would nip away at the time she had to spend with Hailey and Jesse. At least by teaching at her daughter's school, she might get to see her during the day, but it would be harder knowing Jesse was under someone else's care. He wouldn't have the same benefit of being with her full time like Hailey had at his age.

She hated to shortchange Jesse. A second time. First losing Jack, and now losing her time.

Those thoughts made her heart hammer. *Don't have a heart attack. You're all they've got.* The words were so clear they could have been said from right behind her, but they weren't a stranger's voice. Nope. Not Mom's, like it used to be when she was younger. No, these days it was Jack who spoke to her. It had scared her at first. Was she going crazy? Or worse, was Jack so worried she couldn't make it on her own that he couldn't rest? That wasn't Jack's style. He trusted her. No. He was walking those streets of gold, doing good just like he had here. He'd probably signed right up to be her guardian angel. *Thank you, Jack. I wouldn't trade the time we had together for anything.*

This life here on earth was for her to figure out now without him, and she'd never thought she'd have to do that. But she would, no matter what it took.

No one—not her mother or father, not even Granny Lee, who she'd loved to pieces—had ever made her feel like Jack did.

That wasn't true. God did, but He'd taken Jack. That was a whole other struggle.

She shook her head, trying to flick away those hurtful feelings. She refused to ask why. She knew it wasn't personal, but it was hard to understand how that could have been the plan all along.

It seemed like it had been forever since Jack had held her in his arms, but the pain of him being gone was as fresh as the dew on the grass outside every morning.

Another season had passed. Now with summer racing by, a new job and Hailey in school this fall, it would be winter again. Dread filled her as she considered the next holiday without Jack. Those thoughts made her want to run out the door into the darkness.

Denali pawed at her leg, startling her. She hadn't even heard him come up. She opened the door and stepped out onto the porch with him at her heels. After lowering herself to the step, she put her elbows on her knees and rested her forehead in her hands.

The AC unit in the kids' bedroom window whirred. She

wondered if it bothered any of the neighbors. It sounded like a freight train out here. But it was doubtful anyone else had their windows open.

From where she was sitting, she could reach the watering can she'd left on the railing this morning. She lifted it and gave her plants a sprinkle. Flower boxes filled with herbs hung from the long porch rails. Some of them she'd transplanted from her garden back home, and some were new. Like the rosemary. She'd never grown it before, but she'd been drawn to the Christmas tree–shaped bush adorned with tiny ornaments while shopping for supplies at the hardware store. The smell was so inviting, almost too perfume-like to believe you could cook with it. She'd been delighted to find that it brightened every dish from beef, chicken, and fish to potatoes. She and the kids had experimented with lemon rosemary cookies and cake, too, with surprisingly good results.

She grabbed a pair of scissors from the stoop and snipped fresh herbs from the plants. Tending to them had been her salvation. Before Jack died, she'd made herb-infused oils and salts for hours. It had become a hobby with purpose. She'd never been one to want to have a junk room full of crafting supplies like many of her friends had. Scrapbooking, quilting, even knitting required more gear than she cared to accumulate. At least with the herbs, she could cook with them, even provide nutritional value, and that appealed to her.

Less is more. That had always been her motto.

She snipped a few more sprigs to hang up and dry. The lemon balm and lavender looked pretty, and they had healing properties. *Can't get enough of that.*

How bad would my life be if I didn't have a porch full of these plants? Calming lemon balm. Lazing lavender. Oregano for respiratory issues. Dill, basil, sage, mint, parsley, and thyme all had their roles too.

She lifted the clippings and let them rest on her arm against her body, not wanting to crush them.

"Come on, Denali." He followed her inside, where she separated the sprigs on the counter.

Last weekend she'd stopped at a garage sale on her way back home from the grocery store. Among the yard full of household items, there'd been a huge over-the-couch-size painting in an ornate frame, marked thirty dollars. The picture itself was horrible: dark muted colors smudged together with a stormy look that couldn't be anything but bad mojo. Who would want something so ominous in their house?

That was probably why it was still sitting there so late in the day. The frame was worth more than the painting would ever be. She offered ten dollars, and the woman looked grateful to have a bid at all.

Amanda had walked away with that huge painting, and the first thing she'd done when she got home was rip the canvas from the frame. She rolled it up and smooshed it deep down in the big trash bin outside. With the kids' help, she went to town scrubbing the years of collected dust and grime away from the frame.

Surprisingly, it cleaned up nicely. A much lighter color, with almost a golden shimmer to the stained wood. All it needed was a coat of gloss over it.

"It's pretty, Mom." Hailey already had very clear opinions on decorative items.

"I think so too." She stood it up and leaned it against the pump house to dry in the sun.

Later, she hauled the half-empty bucket of polyurethane from the shed. She brushed two coats on the frame while the kids and Denali raced through the backyard, their playful giggles like background music.

She dragged an old roll of chicken wire that she'd found in

the shed when they moved in. It had long ago lost its shine. She'd almost thrown it out a couple of times, but she was glad she'd resisted the temptation. It would be perfect.

She measured the frame, then rolled out enough chicken wire to cut a piece to size. Her kitchen scissors wouldn't do it, and she hated to ruin them by trying. She went back into the shed and rummaged through Jack's old toolbox. She pulled out a chisel and a hammer. It only took one swift bump with the hammer to separate the delicate wire.

Thump-thump-thump. She made her way through every octagon and then attached the wire to the back of the frame with a few well-placed paneling nails.

Hailey and Jesse walked over and squatted beside her. "What are you making?" Hailey asked.

"Guess!" Amanda loved playing the guessing game with these two. Their minds always surprised her.

"Jail!" Jesse held his hands up like he was behind bars.

"Oh no. What are you in jail for?"

"Too many cookies."

"What? Have you been sneaking my cookies?" she pretended to be mad.

"No, I ate Sissie's."

She glanced over at Hailey. "He didn't steal them. I let him have them."

Amanda picked up an imaginary gavel. "I release you from jail." She banged the gavel three times, then pretended to toss it over her shoulder. "You are free to roam the yard."

He lifted his hands in the air, then took a lap around the grass.

She picked up the framed wire, pleased with the results. "Y'all can help me hang it."

They followed her inside like baby ducks on a windy day, rushing to keep up with her.

She held the frame up to the blank wall near the door. "What do you think?"

"Okay," Jesse said.

"It needs a picture." Hailey pulled her hands to her hips.

"Well, I thought we could turn this into a project. Once a week we can cut herbs, tie them with pretty ribbons, and hang them here to dry."

"So, then we can make yummy salts?"

"Exactly. Or with the lavender, we could make potpourri so everything smells pretty."

"I love that."

"I'll teach you both how to tie a bow too."

"Yes." Jesse fist-pumped. Oh how Jack would've loved Jesse's spunk. It may have been the product of too much television early on, but now that they were at the beach, there was a whole lot less television—proving Jesse's personality was growing and he was more like Jack all the time.

Amanda lifted the frame into place, then positioned the kids below it, letting them steady it above their heads. They looked like they were in a lineup. She marked the spot for a couple of nails. It was nice that the wood lap of this old house made for easier hanging than the crummy drywall at the old house. She tapped in two nails, then hung the frame. Shabby chic was definitely becoming her thing, and she wasn't about to apologize for it.

Smiling at the memory, Amanda hung some of the fresh herbs on the frame. Clipped together there, they should dry quickly. She hadn't worked on a new combination for her salts in a while. With all the plants she was growing, she was motivated to get started again even though the business had flopped before she ever got it underway.

Savory thyme, oregano, basil, and the teeniest bit of rosemary filled the room with a pleasing aroma. Changing one element made a completely different experience. Not just the scent, but the taste too.

She treated each combination as an experiment, carefully cataloging every measurement and result. She loved the scientific part of it. Coming up with recipes was just as much fun, although Hailey and Jesse didn't really have the adult palette she needed for input.

She spread out the leftover clippings on her cutting board. Then she took the mortar and pestle Jack had given her for Mother's Day the year Hailey was born, and she ground the mixture of herbs. There was an art to knowing how much to mix them. In the beginning she'd pulverized them, thinking they needed to almost dissolve into the mixture, but they lost their aroma and flavors that way. She closed her eyes, enjoying the sound of the tool against the mortar. She inhaled, adding a sprig of this, a leaf of that, until she stumbled upon just the right mix.

Working the herbs into the salt was her favorite part. She let the new combination rest while she neatened the house to prepare for another day tomorrow. After stacking the books on the coffee table, she picked up the small hardbound one that her friend Ginny had sent her after they'd buried Jack. She still hadn't read it. She should, if for no other reason than that her friend spent her hard-earned money on it. Amanda opened the front cover and read the inscription written inside.

> *Amanda,*
> *I have no idea what to say or possibly do to help make this okay for you. It's heartbreaking. I'm grasping at straws here. I hope there is one tiny soothing moment amidst these pages somewhere that you can cling to. One breath of solace at a time.*

I'm so sorry this happened to you.
I'm always just a phone call away. Any hour. Anytime.
　　　　　　　　Ginny

Amanda folded the cover against the inscription. She'd read that note countless times since Jack died, but it read differently tonight. *It didn't happen to me; it happened to Jack. I was just collateral damage.* Broken, and she would never be the same.

"Be grateful," Mom had said after reading an article about the healing powers of gratitude. Everyone had an answer, something to try. It was exhausting, really.

I have things to be thankful for. She wasn't an idiot. She was just sad, and didn't she have a right to be sad?

She had their children. She had shelter. She'd been provided for. Yes, perhaps modestly so, but she had enough. She was grateful for all of it, but that didn't dissolve the grief and there were just as many opinions on that.

She'd read about the five stages of grief or DABDA. Three stages of grief: Coping. Grieving. Surviving. In the end, all the books said the same thing: it was hard, and everyone's experience was different. And that was probably why she never bothered to read any of them to completion, because, really, all she wanted to know was that there was hope.

It was nice that Ginny had bought her a book with God's worldview, although she wondered if she had read any of it before picking it out. Ginny had never been one to go to church unless it had been following a Saturday-night sleepover at Amanda's house.

She flipped open the book to a random page and started reading.

Stop surviving each day, and thrive in your life.

That was sound advice. It was true she'd kept her focus on one day at a time, but some big-picture thinking would do her good. She might tape that quote to her mirror.

She flipped through a few more pages until the first line of the chapter caught her eye.

It's okay to decline offers.

Now you're talking, she thought.

You don't owe anyone an explanation. "Thank you, but I'm busy" is a perfectly acceptable response. People don't have to know that what you're busy with is taking deeper breaths and silencing irrational thoughts. They might understand; they might not. Just thank them for the invitation and encourage them to ask again next time. I promise that you will feel like saying yes again one day. Only you can decide when that is, and that is okay.

She gave the book a nod of approval, and rather than tossing it back on the table as decor, she carried it to her bedroom. *Maybe I'll read a page a day,* she thought as she stretched out on her bed.

Amanda flipped to the back cover. There an attractive dark-haired woman smiled back at her with a list of accolades five lines long.

Oh yeah, easy for you to say. If I can get through this and look even half as confident as you are, I'll be doing good.

7

Maeve hadn't slept a wink, and for the life of her, she didn't know what was keeping her awake. She'd tossed and turned until she finally gave up trying.

She slid the bedroom patio door open and stepped out onto the deck. The humid air hung so thick she playfully grabbed for a handful of it. There was no breeze tonight. Earlier the sky had been dark beneath a heavy curtain of clouds. She couldn't even see the waves crash against the shoreline then, but now the nearly full moon cast light over everything, almost sparkling as it danced on the moving water.

Her dog, Methuselah, tapped across the room, hopping over the threshold as if it were a hurdle. She needed to get his nails trimmed. Sometimes when they got long, as they were now, it sounded like he was marching through the house in flip-flops.

He sprawled out on the deck and let out a sigh.

She sighed too.

Sleepless nights frustrated her. Something was at the edge of her mind. Whatever it was, she wrestled with it, wishing it would become clear. But it remained just out of reach.

She glanced over her shoulder at the clock in her bedroom. There was still an hour and a half until sunrise. If she got dressed and walked up the beach to the diner, Tug would probably be there by the time she arrived.

Maeve put on an orange T-shirt and stepped into a flowered skirt. She felt graceful like a dancer when she wore it, enjoying the way it swished across her shins. The gauzy fabric made it a good option on hot days, plus the material dried quickly, which she considered to be perfect for beachwear. She picked up her sandals and walked outside.

Bugs hung around the front-porch light like stragglers at an after-hours party. She swooshed them away and went downstairs.

She hadn't even made it to the water, and her skin was already damp from the humidity. Once her feet hit the cool sand, she breathed easier. She lifted her arms in the air, feeling free all alone out there.

She and Tug had been through a lot over the years with him being Jarvis's closest friend, the best man at their wedding. *Her* closest friend too. She'd now spent more years with Tug than with Jarvis.

Tug had never married. His high school sweetheart, Willa, had begged him to marry her, but he never did make an honest woman of her.

Maeve never had liked Willa. She was a constant complainer, and that didn't sit well with her.

When one of Tug's customers kicked the bucket, they'd left Tug their African gray. As soon as Tug learned there was at least another thirty years in that bird's minimum expected life span, he'd decided to jokingly rename her The Wife.

When Willa heard about that name, she didn't see the humor in it.

The Wife didn't make a secret of what she thought about Willa, either, and to this day Tug swore he had nothing to do with it. But Maeve could picture Tug sitting in front of the bird with a picture of Willa, training it to respond, and she rather enjoyed the image.

Whenever Willa showed up at the diner, The Wife would say, "Time to go" or "You're not gone yet?" or Maeve's favorite, "*I'm* Tug's wife for life."

Maeve had seen Willa pitch a fit over that more than once. She didn't come around much anymore. She finally realized Tug wasn't going to marry her and had taken up with a man from up north.

Tug loved that crazy bird. He was known for threatening to leave her to anyone who gave him a hard time. "She'll outlive me, and I'm going to bequeath her to you." Truth was, he'd spent weeks working with a lawyer to come up with a plan for what to do with The Wife if something should happen to him.

Maeve climbed the access stairs from the beach to the restaurant. It was warm enough that Tug could leave The Wife out here on the gazebo all summer, and this morning was no exception. She sat in the corner of her tall cage, preening her bright-red tail feathers.

"Good morning. How's The Wife today?" Maeve asked as she slipped on her sandals.

The bird flapped her wide wings and bowed her head. "I'm good, good, good, good, good. Rise and shine!"

"You're always such a pleasure in the morning."

The African gray perked up, bobbing her head high and low. "Good morning. Love you."

"I love you too." Maeve opened the cabinet under the cage and grabbed a couple of bird treats. She pinched one between her fingers and poked it through the frame.

The Wife took the cracker from her. "Mmm, mmm, good. Breakfast time."

"Or at least coffee," Maeve said.

"One sugar, one cream." The Wife followed the order with a series of five clicks, sounding quite pleased with herself that she'd remembered.

"You always remember."

The bird bobbed her head up and down again and then turned her back to Maeve and stretched, displaying her pretty tail feathers.

"You're such a show-off." Maeve shook her finger at the bird.

"You love me."

"That I do." Maeve reached through the cage, and the bird bent her head forward so Maeve could give her a little scratch. Too bad Methuselah couldn't speak. It'd be nice to have two-way conversation with him, even if sometimes it didn't make sense.

The smell of fresh coffee lured Maeve inside.

"Thought I heard The Wife up and at it," Tug said. "What are you doing here so early?"

"I don't know. Couldn't sleep."

"Everything okay?"

"Yeah. You know how sometimes a thought is right there at the front of your mind?" She took a stool at the counter. "Like you're forgetting something, or there's something you should take care of? I have no idea what it is."

"I hate that." He grabbed a coffeepot and filled a heavy white mug for her. "You're always welcome here before business hours. Glad you came."

"Thanks." She added one sugar to her coffee, and Tug topped off his.

"Gonna be a hot one today."

Idle chitchat never did sit well with her. "It's summer. What do you expect?"

"What do I expect?" Tug took a slug of coffee. His cup rattled on the counter when he set it down. "Customers, tourists with sunburns, random thunderstorms to cool things down, and lots of fresh fish. The wahoos are running big-time."

"You know I love what you can do to a fish. I might have to come for dinner one night this week."

"I'll save you the best seat in the house."

"Sounds good." She lifted her gaze to the water beyond the bank of windows. The sun was beginning to poke the tippity top of its bright-orange rim over the horizon. "So, what's the latest?"

He leaned his large forearms on the counter. There'd been a time when he had muscles like Popeye. Now they weren't sculpted, but they were still big. "Well, rumor has it down at the campground there was a group of naked campers. A whole club of 'em." Tug shook his head. "Now why on earth would anyone want to run around with the sand fleas and prickly briars in their nothings? That's just a recipe for disaster."

"Beats me. Did the police arrest them?"

Tug shook his head. "Gave 'em a warning. I heard they packed up and left, asked for a full refund. Nobody told them they had to leave, just had to put on some pants. I wouldn't refund them, but you know how McDuffy runs his campground. He's a softy."

"My goodness. How do you even talk with people like that? I think I'd have given them their money back to avoid the awkward conversation. Good riddance."

Tug snickered. "I heard they were all senior citizens too. Must have been a sight."

"I guess." She drank the last of her coffee, and Tug poured her another.

"How about a crabmeat-filled crepe? Does that sound good?"

"Fresh blue crab?"

Tug pulled off his ball cap, revealing the flaming tips of his ears beneath that shock of white hair. "Of course. You know me better than to ask that."

It was meant to be a little jab, because everyone knew Tug *only* served fresh crab. He hated it when people asked, and she loved it when his ears got red like that. "I'm in."

"Good." He washed his hands, then went to work on breakfast for the two of them. "Heard there's a guy wanting to open a workout venue here on the beach."

"Here, or over on the public access?"

"Right below the diner there."

"Like Muscle Beach?" She'd seen that in the movies once. "Why would someone want to do that?"

"I heard the guy trying to schedule an offshore fishing trip with Captain Aubrey the other day. The guy told Aubrey he's taking it to the town meeting for approval next week."

"I don't like it," Maeve said. "There'll be trash and a bunch of people making noise. Tourists on the private beach too."

"Could mean more customers for me. Can't say that's a bad thing."

That was true. It wouldn't be half-bad for Tug. "Would there be equipment out there?"

"No idea."

"If not, I guess mostly they'll just be jogging the shoreline, trampling my shells."

"Or stirring up ones still below the surface."

"Okay. Yeah, maybe." She didn't want to be one of those cynical old ladies, but darn if it didn't come easy lately. "Why can't more businesses be like Paws Town Square? They serve a need for the community and help others too. Plus, it transformed that horrible eyesore of the empty building. Now the entrance to Whelk's Island looks welcoming. In fact, it looks more like the courthouse than the real one." She laughed. "Won't Mr. Muscle Guy be surprised if he pulls up to Paws Town Square thinking it's the courthouse only to be met by a bunch of dogs running around!"

"Yeah, that place does look a lot nicer than our real court-house." Tug flipped a crepe in the air.

Maeve let out a quiet, "Impressive."

Tug looked pretty pleased with himself. He slid the slip of a pancake onto a plate, then filled it with a fluffy layer of crab-meat and a drizzle of his famous milk gravy. He put another on a second plate, rolled it, and slopped it with another bit of gravy before setting the plates on the counter in front of them.

She inhaled. The natural salt from the crab teased her senses, and that rich gravy had her stomach growling. "That smells very good."

He never prayed, but he always paused for her to have her own little silent moment. She bowed her head and silently thanked God for her food and many blessings. Then she added, *And thanks for Tug. He's been a true friend. A real best man. Amen.*

When she opened her eyes, he was smiling at her almost as if she'd said those last words out loud.

At the same time, they plunged their forks into the meal before them.

"Here goes nothin'." Tug took a hearty forkful and shoved it into his mouth.

Maeve took a bite. "Oh yeah." She lifted her other hand to her lips. She was raised better than to talk with her mouth full, but this was too good to wait. "So good."

"Just what I was hoping. Love it."

"I vote for this to be on the menu."

"At least a special when the crab is in season."

"Even better than crab benedict."

Tug's bushy brows disappeared under his mop of hair, usu-ally hidden by his ball cap with the diner logo on the front. "That's a real winner, then."

"Didn't I already say that?"

From out in the gazebo, The Wife called out, "Winner, winner, chicken dinner."

"The Wife seems to agree," Maeve joked.

"She loves me. What can I say?" He paused between bites. "Hey, I'm going to the town council meeting tomorrow. You're going, aren't you?"

"Try to always make it," she said.

"The hearing should be interesting after them naked campers, the workout guy, and I hear there are a couple other businesses trying to get in before the season is over. Meet you there?"

"Maybe I will."

"Can't complain if you don't say your piece." He chewed, watching her. "People always listen to you."

"I'll think about it."

"Always thinking," the bird sang out, followed by a whistle that sounded a little like a fizzling firework.

Maybe it was just as well Methuselah couldn't talk. That would get on Maeve's last nerve eventually. Since Jarvis had passed, she'd learned to like her quiet life. Actually, it had taken about ten years to feel that way, but finally it had crept in like a comfort.

Tug walked over and unlocked the front door of the diner. A few regulars spilled inside, taking their usual seats at the counter and in booths. The tourists were easy to recognize, always fumbling around trying to figure things out and asking a bunch of questions.

Maeve sipped her coffee, enjoying the clatter and conversation. It kept that needling feeling of something on her mind at bay, and that was a relief.

"Are those shells from around here?" A woman dressed in a

Whelk's Island T-shirt and white jeans pointed toward the shadow boxes on the wall. "Someone down at the surf shop told me about those shells yesterday. She found one." The woman clomped across the diner floor in what looked like flip-flops on top of two-and-a-half-inch wooden platforms. Not exactly beachwear.

"Really?" Tug handed her a menu. "Yes, those have all been found around here."

"How'd you get them?" Her head bobbed with each word, but her short overbleached hair didn't budge.

Tug moved closer, pointing to the shell and news article framed right next to the woman. "Well, some were in articles in the local paper here. I talked the people who'd found them into selling them to me so I could display them with the news-paper clippings. *Beachcomber* magazine picked up a story about that one. And when folks heard I was hanging them in the restaurant, well, they just started sending them to me. It's kind of cool. I mean, something nice like that happening right here in our backyard. People who find them say the shells al-ways have the right message at the right time."

"How is that?"

He shrugged and wiped down the counter. "Just happens that way. Some things are meant to be. Some think its divine intervention. I don't know. I like how happy it makes people when they find them. Who cares how?"

Her mouth pulled to one side, almost a smirk.

Maeve noticed the young woman's bad attitude.

"Are they always found at the same place?" the woman asked.

"Are you a reporter?" Tug slung a towel over his shoulder.

"No. Just wondering."

"They've been found all over the island. Heard one was

found over in Beaufort one time. Someone sent a shell from St. Augustine, Florida. Can't say if it was carried home by a tourist who'd visited here, though. Could be from all over, for all I know."

The woman scanned the menu.

"What can I get you this morning?"

"I'm not usually a breakfast person. Do you have a protein shake?"

He sputtered at the comment. "No. I could make you an egg-white omelet. Plenty of protein in that."

"Okay. I'll have that and a glass of water."

Maeve slid off her stool and approached the woman. "So, you were over at the surf shop? Were you talking to Kimmy, the owner? Is she still working? I'd think she should be having her baby anytime now."

The woman turned to Maeve. "Hi. Yes, at the surf shop, but actually I talked to her mother. She said her daughter is in the hospital, getting ready to have twins."

"Oh my. I hadn't heard. Twins?" Maeve lifted her chin and motioned toward Tug. "Twins. Little Kimmy is having twins. Did you know?"

"Yeah. Heard something about it."

Of course he knew. "I can't believe you didn't tell me."

Tug was whisking eggs in a bowl. "I forgot. Becky mentioned it when she was here last week. She's been having some trouble with swelling."

"Swelling? Becky or Kimmy?" Maeve asked.

The young woman spoke up. "Her daughter was on bed rest, but now they have her in the hospital as a precaution. Becky said she found that shell on the beach right after they put Kimmy in the hospital."

For a tourist, that woman was a bit of a know-it-all.

"Becky must be worried." Maeve hadn't spoken to her in quite a while.

"She couldn't stop talking about that shell. Like it was a sign or something. Then she was telling me about how lots of people have found them around here."

"What did it say?" Maeve asked.

"The shell?"

"Of course the shell." Maeve pasted what she hoped resembled a polite smile on her face. That last comment had most definitely come out with a tinge of judgment she'd meant to contain.

The woman rolled her eyes. "Something about someone showing up and treasures. That's not the point."

It's exactly the point. Maeve's heart picked up its pace. Caffeine or concern, she wasn't quite sure. She'd known Kimmy since she was a tyke learning how to skimboard out in front of the beach house. Such a tomboy, but she'd turned into a beautiful young woman and now a mother.

Maeve looked over to Tug. "Did you hear that? We should probably stop by and check in on her."

"We should." Tug flipped an anemic-looking omelet into the air.

"Do you really think those shells just show up? Like out of nowhere?" The woman's arched brow and sassy tone made it clear she didn't.

Maeve pondered how to answer such a question. "Sometimes you have to trust things for what they are." She looked the woman square in the eye, daring her to make another brash remark. "Just believe."

With that, Maeve strode out of the diner, her belly full, her heart full. And as she walked by the big parrot cage, The Wife said, "You better believe it."

"Oh, I do." Maeve nodded, and The Wife did too.

"Bye-bye."

Maeve stopped at the top of the steps and took off her sandals.

A little sand between the toes stomps out the woes.

That uptight woman back there needed to kick off her shoes and take a long walk on the beach.

8

Paul and his newest employee, Chase, walked into Tug's Diner. The beautiful environment that Paws Town Square was becoming known for was all credit to Chase. He knew his stuff about landscaping, and he'd been an incredible asset to the quick start-up on this second Paws Town Square location. Former army, Chase had a hard time adjusting to civilian life, but he'd found his niche. Now they were working on three more sites together.

"Two specials, Tug," Paul said as they grabbed two seats at the counter.

"Good morning, Paul." Tug waved from across the way. "You got it."

"And coffee. Lots of coffee."

The waitress slid over with two mugs and filled them before Tug could even respond. "Got 'em," she said.

The woman sitting to Paul's left pushed her omelet around on the plate. She had that look about her, like someone who sent back every meal for it being wrong somehow. Or one of those letter-writing complainers.

She lifted her gaze.

"Good morning," Paul said.

"If you say so."

He turned to Chase and gave him a sorry-I-asked look.

Chase shrugged and snickered.

The woman leaned forward, bypassing Paul, to speak to Chase. "So, what do you think about shells popping up out of nowhere with quotes on them? Think it's possible, or a marketing ploy?"

Chase had that deer-in-the-headlights look. The kind a husband gets when he realizes there's no right answer.

Paul turned to the woman and extended his hand. "I'm Paul."

"Stacy," she said.

"Nice to meet you. You have something against the shells?"

"I think it's bunk, and who needs to be spreading lies?"

"Who are you to say they are?"

"Look, I'm just saying I think it's probably some kind of marketing ploy to get tourists invested in things around here or romanticize the place. Like something out of one of those Nicholas Sparks novels. It's dishonest."

Paul should drop it, but he couldn't stop himself. "What's the harm if it's real or not? The only one putting all their attention on it seems to be you. Just let it go."

Stacy let her fork drop to her plate and pushed it forward on the counter. "Let me guess. You're a business owner in this town too."

"I am, but I also found one of those shells before I had a business here."

She leaned her elbow on the counter, spinning on the stool toward him. "Is this guy for real?" she asked Chase.

"He's a solid guy."

"Really?" She cocked her head. "What's your business?" she asked Paul.

Chase chimed in. "Paws Town Square."

"I love that place. I'm keeping my dog there. It's so nice that I get a discount for visiting him each day."

"I'm glad you're happy with the service," Paul replied.

"Oh yeah," she said. "Top-notch."

"Well, if I hadn't picked up that shell, I might not have made it through the planning meeting for my business and we might not be having this conversation. So why don't you just let people believe what they want to believe?"

"Like some kind of divine intervention?" She made it sound sordid.

"I have no idea," Paul said, "but what I do know is it gave me what I needed that day, and for that I'm thankful. Whatever it is, there's no reason for you to cause a ruckus in here and ruin it for everyone else."

She slapped the counter. "Well, Mr. Tug, I believe I've been called out for bad behavior in your establishment. I apologize."

Tug's wild eyebrows rose into his hairline. "Apology accepted."

She dropped a twenty-dollar bill on the counter and stood. Then she stepped between Chase and Paul and put a hand on each of their shoulders. "Sorry I ruined your breakfast. Thanks for giving me a good place to keep my dog while I'm in town."

And with that she walked out, not saying another word.

The family at the table in the corner clapped, and so did another couple at the counter.

Tug walked over and slid two platters in front of them. "Order up."

"This looks good," Chase said.

"Paul, if that was your version of flirting, I think you need a better approach, or a better wingman."

"You offering to be my wingman?" Paul teased.

"Sure!"

"No, no, I was kidding. I'm perfectly fine alone." He grabbed for the Texas Pete and sprinkled it over his eggs.

"No one is perfectly fine alone," Tug said. "Ask me. I'm alone. I know."

The waitress dipped into the conversation. "You've got The Wife, Tug."

"I'm The Wife," the bird called out from the deck. "Let me go!"

"What was that?" Chase sat taller in his chair, looking out over the counter to the outside area. "You some kind of pirate with wenches tied up out there?"

"No." Tug cleared the dishes where the woman had been sitting and cleaned the area with a white towel. "The Wife is my bird. She'll outlive us all. Just as much trouble as a woman, but with none of the benefits. She doesn't even clean up after herself, much less me."

"You call her The Wife?" Chase chuckled. "That's priceless. What's your real wife think about that?"

"Never had one."

"Never?" That surprised Paul. Tug always seemed like a real charmer to him, always chatting up the local ladies.

"Nope. For a long time I was too hardheaded, and then the only one worth having won't have me. Here's some good advice: never settle for second best, especially in affairs of the heart."

"I'll drink to that." Paul lifted his cup of coffee in a pretend toast. "Words to live by. I met my soul mate, but she married someone else. That was the end of that."

"It happens."

"I don't fret much about it. I have an awesome company to run that's doing good things. Keeps me busy."

"Too busy to think about her?" Tug's skepticism hung in the air.

"Oh, I think about her. She made it clear I wasn't to ever contact her again. I'll tell you this, though. If I saw her today, I'd hand you the keys to the building and the codes to the banking accounts for a second chance with her."

"See. I knew it."

"But that won't happen. So let's all just be happy with what we've got."

"Were you serious about finding one of those shells?" Tug asked. "You never told me about that."

"Guess I never gave it much thought. The shell served its purpose and it was over, but that woman's attitude kind of struck me wrong. I had to say something. I found the shell when I was on my way into the zoning meeting. Things weren't going well. It was an important meeting, and I was nervous about the outcome. A wrong decision could've set me back months or even disabled the whole project. I've kept that shell in my glove compartment ever since."

Tug didn't look surprised. "Those messages are always so spot-on. I'm Tug, by the way," he said to Chase.

"Sorry. Where are my manners? Tug, this is Chase. He's the one who is transforming Paws Town Square into a tropical and lush getaway. I'm lucky to have him on the team."

"Good to meet you. Hope to see you in here more often." Tug wiped his hand on his towel and shook Chase's hand. "I've got to check on my other customers." He moved across the room.

Chase sat back. "So, Paul. What's the whole story? With the girl? You don't think about looking her up?" He shrugged. "Things change. People change."

"There's no hope for that situation. The promise I broke stole her joy. Stole mine too. It's why I left the Marines and how I found my commitment to serve this cause. It's all working the way it's supposed to."

Chase's lips twisted into a cynical smile. "I don't know about that. Nothing is as good as when it's shared with someone you love. Even the bad times. I thought my wife had written me off for forever, but after I got in this program with you, everything changed. I'm just saying not to shut that down completely. If not her, maybe another."

"You talk too much," Paul said. "Have I told you that before?"

"Yeah. Plenty of times. Probably won't be the last either."

"Why do I know you're right about that? Come on. Let's get back to work."

Paul paid the bill, and when they got back in his truck, the first thing Chase did was drop open the glove box and rummage around. "Hey, you really do still have it." He held up the calico scallop shell. "You weren't lying."

He wasn't even sure why he'd kept the creamy-white shell with the maroon blotches. It wasn't all that pretty. The inscription read,

> *If you don't give up, you still have a chance.*
> *—Jack Ma*

"I never lie."

"But you broke a promise."

"That was totally different." Paul revved the engine and pulled away from the curb. "I never lied about anything. I promised something that was out of my control." *I didn't have a choice.* But the words from inside that shell tumbled through his mind, hitting him as strong today as it had the day of that meeting. Was there always a chance? "You can put that back where you found it, man."

Chase tossed the shell back into the glove box.

Paul turned up the radio, trying to drown out the feeling that the real purpose behind that shell hadn't been fulfilled. *I'll just hang on to the keepsake awhile longer.*

9

Maeve was up to her ankles in ocean water when she spotted something in the sand that looked extra special.

Could it really be light-pink sea glass? Most sea-glass charts placed pink at the rare end of the spectrum. Her own experience had been the same. She bent down and plucked the glass from the rushing water. The smooth piece was slippery between her fingers. She held it up, admiring the pink hue. Very subtle against the sky, but in the sand it appeared even more pink. The tide slurped the water back out. Just beyond her foot, she spotted another one.

What were the odds of finding two pink pieces of sea glass at the same time in the same place? She'd been doing this a lot of years, and this had never happened before. She rushed to pick it up before the ocean could reclaim it. She snagged it right as the water rushed back, then she looked at them both, holding one in each hand.

A roll of laughter came from deep within her. *Twins!* She shuffled the sea glass in her palms. *Twins, indeed. Together and strong.* That had to be it. She could picture two matching baby girls sitting in the sandy water in ruffled-bottom bathing suits under Kimmy's watchful eye, coordinating frilled hats protecting their delicate skin from the sun's rays.

Excited by her find, she forged on. By the time she got back home, the rest of the town was finally beginning to awaken.

Inside, she placed the two pieces of sea glass on a coaster on the living room table for safekeeping. She wasn't quite sure what she'd do with them, but she'd give them to Kimmy at some point.

Maeve filled a bowl with kibble for Methuselah and took it outside. She sat down, watching him crunch through his breakfast. Her thoughts turned to Kimmy again and her babies. Funny how she still saw Kimmy as a child even after all these years.

Maeve and Jarvis had tried—they had—but when it didn't happen, they'd decided that was God's will and that was okay too. They focused on their relationship, and it was a good one. But then she'd never thought she'd be alone for so long, and now—now there was no one to pick up where she'd leave off. Not that it was all that important, but it was something. Her something.

She loved this beach.

All this change bothered her. She wanted this place to live on the way it was now for many years to come. Who would tend this stretch of shoreline when she couldn't anymore?

From here she could see that the tide was almost all the way out. There were probably starfish sunning there right now. At that moment, she thought she saw a dolphin fin. She lifted the binoculars she kept on the deck and scanned the water.

Tug had given her the high-powered binoculars the Christmas after Jarvis died. He'd said that Jarvis had been researching what kind to buy for her. She didn't know if that was true or if Tug had just been trying to be nice, but she'd really enjoyed them all these years.

She turned the adjustment on the binoculars, bringing things into focus.

Beautiful, miraculous, awe inspiring. Even though she couldn't see every detail, she marveled at what she knew was happening beneath the surface.

The waves lapped out a little farther. Like her, the tide kept showing up.

Movement down the beach caught her attention.

Light sparkled from the shiny aluminum pole of a colorful umbrella. Her new neighbors were back on the beach.

She watched for a good long while, taking joy in their activity. The children raced to the water's edge, then back up to show Amanda what they'd found. Shells. Had to be shells. Or maybe that was wishful thinking. Delight danced in her heart at the possibility of them taking up her special hobby.

She adjusted the focus on the binoculars and watched again.

A pang of guilt for spying like a common Peeping Tom crept upon her. She lowered the binoculars and set them aside.

"Now isn't this rude? What has come over me?"

Methuselah looked up at her and gave her a half bark.

"That all you have to say?"

He cocked his head.

"You'll never be The Wife."

Methuselah seemed to take exception to the accusation, turning and walking down the ramp to the lower level.

She pushed herself up from the comfortable chair and smeared sunscreen on her arms and face. She went into her sunroom, where she kept all the best finds, and pulled a few special items from her desk drawer. Before going over to the beach, she tossed a ball for Methuselah and he carried it back to her a couple of times, then finally lay on top of it.

"Already? Really?"

She rarely talked to Methuselah like this, and he didn't seem to quite know what to make of it. His ears pulled up high on his head. Poor thing was a mismatch of styles and texture. Part beagle. Part schnauzer. Part who knew what else. Those ears looked like they could spin and lift him off the ground.

But Methuselah didn't even bark. Rarely did. "Why am I talking to you?"

Eager for conversation? Is that what has nipped at me all day? She looked back toward Amanda and the kids. Her heart giddy-upped as she anticipated the discussion that might happen between her and the two shell seekers.

She picked up one of her shell bags to take with her in case she ran across any more treasures while she was out, then grabbed a smaller one she'd made a long time ago. Too small for what she was looking for, but perfect for someone else. She walked along the dune line, then down to the water.

She watched Hailey and Jesse lift shells in the air, squealing all the way back up to where Amanda had settled. Sand kicked from the back of Hailey's feet. Jesse was more like a bulldozer trudging through, instead of on top of, the sand.

Maeve stopped at the tide line, where a moment ago those two had made their discoveries. A small pile of shells lay there like a pyramid. *The discards.* She ran her big toe across the pile, then leaned over and picked one out of the rubble, a special one they'd missed. She rescued the giant tun. It wasn't perfect, but even so, it was pretty rare. She couldn't wait to give it to them.

Maeve looked up from the shell.

Amanda was waving her arm high in the air. "Hello!" she called out as she got to her feet. She started toward her with Hailey and Jesse at her side.

"We were just talking about you," Amanda said.

"Were your ears itching?" Hailey asked. "That happens when people talk about you."

"Nope. But they were tickling. Were you saying nice things? I think nice things just tickle."

Hailey's mouth dropped open. "That must've been us, then."

Jesse lifted his bucket at Maeve's side. "Look!"

"My. You have found some really good stuff."

"Mm-hmm." His cheeks pouched with pride.

"I found this one in the pile here." She handed the giant tun to him. "This is a pretty cool shell."

"I like this." His head bobbled in appreciation. "Thank you."

"We're doing your hobby," Hailey announced.

Although for her it wasn't a hobby. More of a way of life. She'd become a bit of a hoarder of shells. A shell collector gone cuckoo. But that wasn't a point of contention. Instead of commenting, she stooped down to see how they'd done.

They took turns showing her their favorites.

"It so happens that I brought something for you, Miss Hailey."

"For me?"

Maeve nodded. "For you and your brother. Just different things."

She pulled the smaller version of her shoulder bag out from under her own and handed it to Hailey. "It's a bag. Like mine. Only Hailey-sized."

Hailey grinned. She slipped it over her neck and shoulder like Maeve had hers. "I'm Hailey-sized."

"Yes, you most certainly are."

"Help me put my shells in here." Hailey glanced over at her mom and then rephrased the demand. "I meant to say, Can you *please* help me put my shells in this bag?"

"I thought you'd never ask," Maeve said, winking at Amanda. "You are such a kind and polite young lady. That makes you fun to be around."

"You're fun too."

"Thank you."

"How did you know I wanted one of these?" Her eyes were wide and clear.

Maeve delighted in the little girl's energy and excitement. "Just a lucky guess. So, what are you going to do with all those shells?"

Hailey finally looked up and grinned as though she'd found the winning answer. "We'll look at them."

"Of course."

"But before we go home, we try to pick out three to take back with us."

Maeve tapped her finger against her lips. "That's hard."

"It is." The little girl nodded slowly, the words lingering.

Jesse splashed through the water in front of Maeve.

"I brought something for you too, sir."

He froze in place, his eyes widening with interest as he straightened. "A present for Jesse?"

"Sort of." She dug down into her shell bag and pulled out a length of leather that held a single shark's tooth. The tooth wasn't sharp, as the tide had worn the edges smooth, but it was impressive nonetheless. "Look. This big tooth used to be in a shark's mouth."

Jesse put his hand above his head like a shark. "Shark. Shark."

"That was so thoughtful, Maeve," Amanda said. "What do you say, Jesse?"

"Thank you. Please."

He took the necklace and tried to put it over his head. Amanda stepped in to help. Jesse took a victory lap with the shark tooth around his neck. "I like this," he said.

"I'm glad." Maeve walked over to where Hailey busied herself with a mound of sand. "Can I help?" she asked.

"Sure. You can help Jesse make a wall." Hailey scooped more sand together. "I want it to be a big castle."

Jesse and Maeve worked together to form a wall in the time that it took Hailey to patty-cake one tiny mound. Amanda finally joined them, behind their sandcastle hedge of protection.

"Nothing's going to get past that wall to ruin my castle," Hailey said. "We're totally protected."

"As you should be." Maeve lifted a handful of wet sand and let it slip through her fingers, building up the height of the wall drip by drip. Jesse tried to mimic the move. "Would be nice if it were this easy to protect ourselves from anything that could go wrong, wouldn't it?"

She looked at the two happy children and then into Amanda's eyes. They seemed to be smiling, but inside there was something troubling her. A sadness hung behind an invisible veil.

What is your story, Amanda? Can I help? Just give me a clue.

But Amanda turned away, busying herself by placing shells on the top of the turrets her daughter had just built. "Beautiful, Hailey. Best castle ever."

Maeve let out a deep breath, not allowing herself to get stuck on wondering what was wrong but rather to enjoy the company.

Jesse looked up at her as if he'd heard everything that had just played through her mind. He lifted his sandy hand and patted her on the leg. "Good job."

Just then Amanda got up and started folding towels. "I've got to get these two back up to the house and feed them," she said to Maeve. "Would you like to join us?"

"No, but thank you so much. Maybe another time." Maeve stood. "I'm off to catch up with a friend."

Hailey and Jesse jumped up and swished the sand from their bodies, then waited for Amanda to dry them off.

Maeve enjoyed watching the choreographed routine the family went through to leave. By the time they were done, everyone was dry and they were ready for the trip back over the dune.

Even after all these years, she remembered how long those hikes over the dune had seemed when she was their age. It may as well have been the Sahara Desert to cross in the blazing heat.

She watched the trio disappear toward their house before she set off down the beach. She needed to stop in at the surf shop this afternoon and check on things. It was hard to picture Kimmy as a mother, much less Becky as a grandmother, even though she was plenty old enough to be one. She still remembered when Becky would sit on the beach watching little Kimmy skimboard for hours. That child was no bigger than a whisper, but she had the energy of a school of porpoises. It seemed like yesterday.

A teensy bit of envy chewed at her about the shell Becky had found. It was strange how shells found their way into the hands of exactly who needed them, at just the right time.

Suddenly Maeve realized what had been nipping at her. She didn't know how much longer she'd be around to enjoy Whelk's Island, or her friends, old and new.

Shaking off the thought, she walked through her back gate and showered off her feet under the spigot at the bottom of the stairs. Methuselah met her there and then followed her up the stairs, hanging close as she fixed herself some cheese and crackers before walking over to the surf shop.

Traffic was busy on the beach road today. Word was getting out about where the locals shopped and ate, and although it was great for merchants, it was changing the pace of this part of town.

As soon as Maeve entered the store, the smell of surf wax

and suntan lotion washed over her. A group of girls were trying on bathing suits in a fit of giggles while Becky helped a
young man with a surfboard. Maeve recognized the logo on a
yellow-and-lime-green board as one of Kimmy's sponsors.

All the medals and surfing-championship trophies Kimmy
had won lined the shelves around the shop. She was a celeb-
rity around these parts. Maeve was pretty sure it was a surf
competition in California where Kimmy had met her husband.

Maeve wondered if he was the one interested in creating a
Muscle Beach kind of workout place here on Whelk's Island.
That would make sense. Perhaps she'd skip that town meeting. She'd hate for her opinion to play any part in Kimmy and
her family not reaching their dreams.

She wouldn't be here forever, anyway.

"Maeve?" Becky had walked up to her. "I thought that was
you. It is so good to see you. It's been eons. You look great."

"Thank you. I see you're holding down the fort here."

"Doing my best. I don't know how Kimmy does it, keeping
so many details about all this equipment in her head like she
does. Frankly, I'm not sure I'm even helping."

"I'm sure you are. How is she?"

"You must've heard." Becky's signature red-lipstick smile
faded. She pushed back a wayward strand of hair. "I'm trying
not to worry."

It didn't look to Maeve like Becky was succeeding. "Someone at the diner mentioned something about her being in the
hospital. Twins?"

"Yes, twins. Can you believe it?" She blinked as if she were
still trying to believe it. "Doesn't run in either of their families. Surprise!"

"Very exciting. Does she know if they'll be boys, girls? One
of each?"

"No. She didn't want to find out. The doctor assured her they're healthy, and I guess that's all that matters. She's been on bed rest, though, and you know how hard it is to keep Kimmy still. They finally put her in the hospital to manage her blood pressure, but I can't help but worry about my little girl." Becky glanced around, then took Maeve by the hand. "Oh gosh, did you hear? I found one of those shells. I've always silently wondered over the years if that was a real thing."

She tugged Maeve toward the counter. There, next to a bucket of colored zinc to protect the real sun warriors from skin cancer, sat the shell.

Almost fluorescent pink inside, the big conch looked polished.

Maeve reached out and touched it. The words had worn in places, but she could still make them out:

I can't wait to be with you,
but until then know that I'm gathering
treasures and stories to share.

Becky clutched Maeve's arm. "Isn't that crazy? I mean, you can practically hear Kimmy say something like that." Becky's face lit up as she picked up the shell, cradling it in her thin hands. "I was a basket case until I found this. It made me feel so much better about the whole situation."

Maeve leaned in and gave Becky a squeeze. "That does seem to fit the current circumstance."

"What kind of shell is it? I knew you'd be able to tell me."

"It's a conch. Quite easy to find down in Florida, especially these with the pretty pink inside. Once in a while we'll find them around here, but often they've had a rough trip. They're seldom in this kind of shape."

"Won't it be cute in the nursery? It'll be such a neat story to tell them. Kimmy's been so anxious for those babies to be born. I can't wait to hold them and squeeze them." Becky looked like she could burst from all the joy.

"You're going to be a wonderful grandmother." Maeve hugged her, then paused. "I have to ask. Where did you find the shell?"

"That's the craziest part. I'd gone down to the pier to give Kimmy's husband, Nate, an update on her condition, and while I was waiting for him to paddle in, there it was, right in the sand by the pylon. It was the bright pink that caught my eye."

"Right there at the pier? That's amazing." Maeve was surprised she hadn't seen it herself.

"Some people are such skeptics. This lady yesterday just about accused me of writing the message myself. I told her this wasn't the first shell someone had found around here."

"Don't let her bother you. That shell was found by the right person at the right time. Everything is going to be fine. I just know it." *It is a wonder how those shells make their way into the hands that need them most.*

She looked up at Becky, knowing how precious Kimmy was to her. "May I leave a little note for Kimmy?"

"She'd love that. You know how much she adores you. You were one of her biggest fans when she was actively competing."

Maeve wrote a note wishing Kimmy well and reminding her how lucky the twins would be to share her love for the beach and the ocean by living on Whelk's Island. "Let me know when she's accepting visitors. I'd love to see her. I'm so happy for the whole family."

"Thank you, Maeve. I'd better get back to those customers and see if I can salvage a sale to pay for those twins. They require a ton of stuff."

Maeve walked out of the surf shop with joy bubbling in her heart. Kimmy would be fine. The heavenly shade of pink in that shell only confirmed what she'd been thinking since she found her own pink treasures down on the beach earlier: twin girls.

Whelk's Island was growing, and in a good way.

10

That evening, Amanda rearranged the kitchen. There was no reason not to use the space she'd had built for her business. They could use the room for a homework station for Hailey or more storage. She regretted not having done enough research and planning to pass the inspection required for a cottage food business in the first place.

Rookie mistake. Jack would have never missed that detail.

Dried herbs had seemed like such an easy option, and she loved working with them. Even though she'd made certain she could partition Denali's access from the kitchen area she planned for her business, it was a direct violation for him to be in the house at all.

She thought of rehoming Denali, but she couldn't deprive the kids of him. Jack had specifically picked out that dog for them. It was their last gift from him. She wouldn't give up her dream, though. Somehow, someday, she'd figure out a way to make it happen.

The kids were still playing in their room, so she took advantage of the extra time to package dried herbs, then jar some of the new salt she'd made. In a couple of weeks, she'd try it on a few dishes.

She hoped for good results. If nothing else, her family ate well. She was proud of herself for not letting her kids live on hot dogs, chicken nuggets, and macaroni and cheese. That in itself was a win.

Jack used to tease her that she'd have inventory to supply the world before she ever sold the first jar if she didn't start advertising them. The plan had been to take the different mixes to the farmers market as a testing ground, but that was the summer Jack never came home. Another year had passed since then, and here she was still experimenting.

She lifted her chin as she often did when she spoke to Jack. "I'll sell them one day."

It wouldn't be this year, but she'd find a way to rent a space that met the state requirements. For now, she could give the salts as Christmas gifts to the new friends she'd make at work. And she'd concentrate on designing the website. Those were things she could do now, and maybe even build up some early reviews and clientele.

The thought of new people in her life warmed her. She picked up one of the jars. Elegant yet simple. She and Jack had looked through the catalog many times before making a decision. Even coming up with the recipes to test each new flavor was backed by hours of thought and methodical measurement. A flash of a memory—Jack sitting there, pretending to be nervous about trying yet another dish. Then slowly savoring each bite as serious as a judge on one of those cooking shows.

She put a lot of work into coming up with good recipes to use her herbal salts in, and Jack had been a big part of that. She sank into the loving memory for a moment. Enjoying it. He'd always been her biggest cheerleader.

Recipe cards! Why hadn't she made that connection before? She could offer a monthly subscription service. *There are opportunities here. No, I won't give up the dream, Jack.*

Amanda grabbed a notebook and jotted down the ideas.

How she wished she'd been able to make it happen this year. *Everything will fall into place when it is supposed to.*

She climbed on the step stool and tucked the new batch in the cupboard. Jars filled the shelves of the double cabinet.

She took three different jars down from the cabinet shelf: one sweet, a citrus, and a savory blend. She placed them on the counter. They might make a nice gift for Maeve. If she cooked. She couldn't really picture the older woman dawdling around in the kitchen in those snap-up cotton shifts old ladies wore. No, Maeve, even on the beach, was always in vivid colors. Gauzy flowing fabrics that moved like the surrounding weather. She seemed like a free spirit who loved nature. Someone who'd pick lazing in a hammock outside over a day in the kitchen wearing an apron.

There was something about Maeve that made Amanda want to learn more about her.

Maybe it was the confidence with which she moved. Her independence. Or the dedication to what she loved—being on the beach, rain or shine. Or simply that she'd been kind enough to stop and chat with Hailey and Jesse. Maeve hadn't been the least put out by their interruption. In fact, she'd seemed delighted, charmed even, by them. Amanda loved how Maeve had stomped her foot into the surf and splashed Jesse back. So unexpected and playful. Amanda wished she could be that carefree and spontaneous.

Smiling at the thought, she fashioned a ribbon around bunches of lavender, rosemary, and thyme and wrapped them and the herb-infused salts in a length of unbleached muslin for Maeve. She'd deliver them later. But now it was getting late and she needed to put the kids to bed.

After Hailey and Jesse had brushed their teeth and changed into pajamas, Amanda knelt next to the bunk beds and squeezed her eyes tight. Her two angels started their prayer.

"Now my lay me . . ."

Those little voices grabbed her heart. Such a big job to do all the right things by them, by herself. *Don't let me mess them up. Some days I can barely take care of me.* As usual, Jesse yawned before they could get through the whole thing. There were a few times when he'd been fast asleep before Hailey said amen.

She kissed them each on the forehead. "I love you with all my heart."

She let out a breath with the click of the bedroom door.

We're all safe. I made it through another day.

As Amanda climbed into her own bed, she thought of the message in the lip of her shell: *"All the art of living lies in a fine mingling of letting go and holding on."* Jack's shirt hanging on her chair still tethered her to life these days.

I'll know when it's time.

She quietly recited her prayers, adding one new name to the list tonight. *Maeve.*

Maeve had been so distracted thinking of Kimmy and her soon-to-be arrivals that she nearly missed Amanda and the kids leaving the library.

"Hello!" Maeve said. "What a nice surprise."

"Hey. Hailey was just talking about you again."

"Really?" Maeve rubbed her ear, teasing with Hailey.

"Good things," Hailey said.

"She checked out a book about North Carolina shells so she could learn about them."

"You are absolutely precious," she said to Hailey, who beamed.

"There are a lot of pictures in here too. I'm going to try to collect one of everything."

"My. That will be quite the adventure. It could take a long time."

"Will you help me?"

"Of course. I'd love to."

"I got *Clifford the Big Red Dog*." Jesse lifted the book in the air, showing it off. "Ruff ruff bowwow."

"My daddy used to read that to me when I was a little girl," Hailey said with all the confidence of a teenager rather than a six-year-old. "I told Jesse it's a good book. He's going to love it." She leaned in, lowering her voice. "Hopefully, Mom can do the voices right. Daddy was so good at it, but he's not here."

Hailey glanced at Amanda, almost as if she were worried her mom may have overheard.

Maeve wondered what the rest of the story was.

Amanda's cheeks were as red as the brightly colored dog on the cover of Jesse's library book. She lowered her head, looking everywhere except at Maeve.

"I'll do my best." Amanda sounded playful, but Maeve caught the overzealous tone that didn't ring quite sincere.

Amanda swallowed so hard that Maeve thought the young lady might choke. *Poor thing. I recognize the hurt behind those pretty eyes.* "Everyone tells a story in their own special way. I bet it will be different but every bit as special."

Hailey seemed to think about it for a second. "You're probably right." She reached for her mother's hand.

"Thank you, Hailey." Amanda brushed her hair back over her shoulder. "Why don't you and your brother go sit on a bench over there in the reading garden and look at your books. I'll be there in a few minutes."

Hailey took Jesse's hand and together they ran through the gate.

There was a nervous laugh, followed by a sigh, and then

Amanda turned and faced Maeve. "It's not easy when a marriage ends. The kids—"

"They're resilient, and yours are just fine. More than fine. I can feel their joy from a distance. Don't you worry."

"Well, I . . . we moved here for a fresh start."

"You made a wonderful choice." Maeve eyed her, wishing she'd tell her more. She'd always been a good listener, but it was harder to listen when folks wouldn't share the words. "Whelk's Island is a happy place. Sure, it's gotten busier over the years, but the true locals are a rare and wonderful lot. This community still embraces old-fashioned traditions, and I have a feeling you're going to fit right in and be very happy here."

"I sure can use some happiness. I'm so tired of being sad."

"Honey, unfortunately no life is free of sadness, be it from pain, loss, illness, or . . . well, you get the idea. It's all a necessary part of a life well lived."

"Seems like there'd be an easier way."

"Not our place to say, is it?"

Amanda raised her eyes. "All in His time. Is that what you're going to say?"

"You know as well as I, but the ocean is a great stabilizer. I think being here helps make things easier to understand. Some people think that when life is good, it's like the tide flowing in and when it's bad, it's like the tide going out. I don't personally see it that way."

She glanced over at Amanda's children. They hung close to each other, heads down, enjoying the books. "Want to know what I think? I believe we need both the good and the bad, just like the ocean needs the fluctuating tides."

"Balance." Amanda said it barely above a whisper.

"If the tide only ever came in, we would drown. Well, I guess technically we could live on boats, but you know what I mean. When the tide goes out, we get to appreciate the treasures it reveals. And when it comes in, new life is washed ashore. There's beauty in both."

"Like your shells." Amanda's head cocked slightly to the left.

The metaphor had landed on her the way Maeve had suspected it might.

"Exactly." Maeve took in a breath of satisfaction.

"If we only had good, we'd never appreciate how good it was. I understand that. But sometimes the bad outweighs the good by so much." Amanda bowed her head again.

"Sometimes it feels like that. I've sure been there, but as the journey continues, you will always find balance. That I promise you. You're still very young. There is a lot more good coming your way. Be patient, and believe."

"I'm glad we crossed paths."

Maeve gulped back an unexpected rush of emotion. "My goodness, you have no idea the joy meeting you and your children has brought me. You know, I never had children of my own."

"Really? That surprises me. You're so wonderful with them. Especially Jesse."

Maeve couldn't hide her delight. "Hailey is like talking to an adult, if that's what you mean, but I love deciphering Jesse. He's such an animated little communicator."

"He's a good boy." Amanda glanced over at her children, a look of love in her eyes.

"You're a good mother. I can see that."

"They make it easy." Amanda stood there quietly.

Maeve started toward the reading garden, not wanting to intrude on whatever was going through Amanda's mind just then.

A moment later, Amanda fell into step behind her. They walked into the garden, which was really a series of raised flower beds, each containing a tree surrounded by flowers the local master gardeners maintained for the library. Curved cement benches were placed throughout. It was quite cozy, even if it was just a small space between a couple of buildings.

Maeve sat on the bench adjacent to where Hailey and Jesse sat on the ground. They flipped through his book on the bench as if it were a table. Amanda peered over them.

"Hi, Mom." Hailey turned the page. "I'm telling Jesse all about the story."

"She used to be able to recite the whole book by heart," Amanda said to Maeve. "If we tried to end the story early or skip a part, she'd call us out on it."

"I can picture that," Maeve said.

Hailey sat back on her heels in a fit of giggles. "I did that?"

"You sure did."

Hailey reached out and touched the end of Maeve's big toe. Her eyes lifted, like a frightened doe, as if she hadn't realized she'd actually done it.

Maeve took pleasure in the precious child's curiosity. Hailey's skin was beginning to tan, making her blond hair look even lighter in contrast. Maeve wiggled her toes, and Hailey's giggle rose into the air like the wings of colorful butterflies, sending waves of delight through Maeve. This is when not having children was the hardest—these magical moments that she'd missed. She'd convinced herself all this time that her marriage to Jarvis had been full in other ways, but at this moment, she was certain there wasn't anything quite as delightful as that kind of laughter.

Completely uncontrolled. Unpracticed. Unpredictably touching.

Hailey stretched out her leg next to Maeve's, then pointed her toes. Each tiny toenail had been painted hot pink. It wasn't a perfect job, although it probably had started out that way. The sand had done a number on them.

"What color polish is on your toes?" Hailey asked. "It's pretty. So shiny and see-through. Maybe kind of silverish, but not glittery."

Maeve mused at her intent thought on the subject. "No polish." She wiggled her toes again, adoring the laughter that it brought on like a light switch. "Naked toes."

"Naked? What?" She covered her mouth like the word *naked* was naughty. Perhaps it was, in some contexts. Better to leave that one alone. It had been a long time since she'd been around young children. My, what a treasure. The real kind. Human, breathing, learning, loving. Maeve loved the delight these innocent minds came up with. "I don't paint my nails."

"Not your fingers either?"

Maeve extended her hands, showing her. "No ma'am."

"I'm not a ma'am. I'm just a little girl."

"Oh you most certainly are. Ma'am isn't about age; it's about respect. I respect you, Hailey."

Hailey sat taller. "Wow. That's really good, right?"

"Very good."

"Mommy paints my fingernails and toenails. Sometimes we go to the fancy place with the shaky chairs. It feels good, but it takes so long." She brushed her hand across her brow. "Hours!" She dropped her hand and the drama. "Is that why you don't have yours painted?"

Maeve slowly shook her head. There'd been a time when she dressed up her nails for Jarvis, but it had been a constant battle against nature. Then one day as she rushed to repair the chipped color before they went out, he'd said to her, *"Couldn't you be doing something better with your time? I really don't care whether your toes are decorated."*

It had struck her as so odd. Offended at first, she couldn't believe he'd have so little appreciation for her attempt to look her absolute best for him. Then he'd pulled her into his arms and said, *"I love you just the way God made you. You don't need to add one single thing."*

She could still remember how much that had meant to her. She loved him even more that day for it.

Maeve looked at Hailey. "Sometimes things are perfect the way they are, even if they aren't perfect. What do you think?"

Hailey pressed a finger to her lip, truly considering this. "Your nails look so pretty and shiny."

"I'm sure that's from the sand."

"That's crazy."

"No, not really. Think about it. Sand is coarse. Actually, it's teensy leftovers of rocks and minerals."

"That doesn't help your toes shine."

"Actually . . ." Maeve took three pieces of sea glass from her pocket and held them out for Hailey to see.

Hailey straightened to a stand. "Wow! They look like diamonds and rubies. What are the green ones, Mommy?"

"Emeralds." Amanda glanced over at Maeve.

"Where'd you get them? At the jewelry store?"

"Nope." Maeve shook her head. "They are sea glass, and they come in even more colors than that. I found them right out there on the beach."

Hailey stretched taller as her body tensed with excitement. "Really?"

"Yes ma'am. Which one is your favorite?"

She mulled over the options before finally picking up a green one.

"Years and years ago, that was part of a broken glass bottle."

"Like trash?"

"Yes, actually it was. This color could be as old as three

thousand years ago but most likely is from the 1940s to the '80s, when soda became popular. They used to bottle lemon-lime soda in bright-green bottles. That broken piece of glass starts out sharp, but when it's in the sand, the water pushes it back and forth, wearing away all the sharp edges. Eventually, all the ridges smooth until it becomes frosted like this one."

"That's why your naked toes are so shiny like they are painted?"

"I suppose it is."

Shock resonated from Hailey's lips to her eyebrows. "Mom, I want to have naked toes from now on. Okay?"

"Fine by me. Maybe I'll try that too. It does look pretty."

"We can be as pretty as Miss Maeve." Hailey's head bobbed up and down.

"That is the nicest compliment anyone has ever given me. You made my day. Thank you, Hailey."

"It was an accident, but you're welcome." Hailey flung herself into Maeve's arms. "I'm glad I made you happy. I wasn't even trying."

11

Thank goodness Amanda had let the kids pick out a few extra books at the library this week. With the high temperatures and humidity, she'd become accustomed to a daily thunderstorm, and that was no problem. She'd started planning the indoor activities around the weather. Good thing, too, because it ended up being nearly three days straight of rain.

They were all beginning to have cabin fever. She'd done her best to keep them busy. They worked on crafts, colored, and even did a science project that turned out to be more of a magic trick with a balloon, water, and duct tape.

She stood at the screen door, the rain falling so hard that it looked like water boiling on the sidewalk. Thunder rolled across the sky.

An hour later, a stream of sunshine flooded the kitchen.

"Hey, guys, it's raining with the sun out," Amanda called to the kids. "I bet we can find a rainbow if we look."

She heard their feet slapping the wooden floors as they ran toward the windows.

"It's sunshining!" Jesse ran in circles in the house. "Beach!"

He belted it out with such enthusiasm that at first she wasn't sure if he was hurt or happy. She raced to catch up to him, but his toothy grin was all she needed to see.

"I know." She grabbed his hands and danced in a circle with him. "Finally. Hooray!"

"Can we go to the beach? Please?" Hailey ran down the hall. "The sun is back."

"About time," Amanda commiserated. "I think we're overdue for a good beach day."

"And shells!" Hailey threw her hands in the air.

Jesse ran toward his bedroom. "And fun!"

They changed into their swimwear and loaded up their beach gear. The dune was so much easier to walk over after the rain had packed it down. Amanda wondered how much it would cost to run her hose up the dune to water it down when it got so dry and deep that it was like tilling rather than walking. It was probably farther than it looked, but she'd spring for another hose if it would make a difference.

They made record time getting over the dune. It had helped that she'd figured out the bare minimum to bring and still be comfortable. She'd left her chair behind today, opting to sit right down on the sheet. One less thing to carry.

The turbulent waves churned from the storm, tossing white foam into the air. She wasn't sure if it was the sunshine or the way the beach seemed to mute the waves when she was lying directly on the damp sand that lulled her body into relaxation.

A seagull swooped over. She heard its cries, like laughter, as it joined up with its colony near the water.

Hailey and Jesse danced in the sand, raising their hands toward the birds.

Amanda spotted Maeve walking down the beach toward them before the kids did.

Maeve waved and altered her path from the water to where Amanda was sitting. "Good to see you."

"You too. I was beginning to think the sun was never coming back out."

"Oh, July is like that sometimes." She put her hand on top of her hat, shifting it back a smidge.

"Miss Maeve!" Hailey and Jesse raced across the beach, skidding to a stop near the sheet.

Maeve bent forward to get down to their level. "Well, hello there. How are you two today?"

"Better now that there's no rain so we can come out and play."

She raised a finger in the air. "But sometimes good things happen when you're stuck inside."

"We colored and read books." Hailey folded her arms across her chest. "We took some naps, but the days were so long. It felt like forever."

"Well, I made something for each of you." She pulled her shell bag forward and dug into the front pocket. "One for you, and one for you." She handed them each something.

Jesse held whatever it was in the palm of his hand, staring at it.

Hailey held hers by the fishing line tied to the top of it and let it dangle. "It's Denali!"

"I'm glad you could tell."

"It's Denali made out of shells," Hailey said. "See it, Jesse?"

Jesse swung his ornament in the air as he barked.

"I thought you could keep them by your bed at night. They can help bring you good thoughts and happy dreams."

"I love it." Hailey wrapped her arms around Maeve's waist. "Thank you."

"Me too." Jesse pushed his hand forward, handing his gift to Amanda.

As she took the shell dog from him, she noticed the woman

who'd been sitting across the way with her husband and toddler earlier. She was trying to wrangle the child, an umbrella, and a bag full of toys as the man walked over the hill ahead of them carrying only his cooler.

What a jerk. Amanda sat up on her knees. "Maeve, could you watch these two for a quick second? I want to give that gal a hand."

Maeve seemed to register the situation. "Of course."

Amanda ran over to the struggling woman. "Hey, let me help you with that. Boy, it takes a ton of stuff to keep the kids over here, doesn't it?"

The woman gave her a blank stare at first, then let out a sigh. "Thank you. Thank you so much."

Amanda helped her stack the things inside one another to make it easier to carry, and then the family toddled off. By the time they reached the top of the dune, the woman had caught her breath.

"Thank you. I've got it from here. That was really kind of you."

"No problem. You'd have done the same for me. I'm sure of it." She wished there was something reassuring she could say to her. "Have a great rest of the day." But she doubted the woman was in for much of a treat when she got back. Why were some guys like that?

Amanda walked back over to her little spot, where Jesse was yammering to Maeve, who looked intent on pretending to comprehend what he was going on and on about.

"Thanks. Sorry. I just know how much of a hassle that can be by yourself." She looked at her children's sweet little faces. "I've been so blessed. These two are so easy."

Yes, it's been a season of unwanted change, but things could be worse.

Before she sat down, Amanda hung the ornaments from one of the spindles of the umbrella. "That was so thoughtful. These are adorable."

Maeve bent down and sat on the sheet with Amanda. "It also kept me sane the past few days. I have to cut my walks shorter when it's a downpour like that. It gave me something to do."

"So you still walk on the beach in the rain?"

"Every day. No matter how hot or cold or wet. I love how the weather and time of day change the landscape of things, and the crazier the weather, the better the treasures. Of course, I have to plan around the weather if it's lightning, but there's always a little window of opportunity every day, if you're flexible."

"I don't mean this to sound disrespectful, but I hope I have your energy when I'm your age." *Actually, I'd like to have it now!*

"Ah, but I don't have two babies to tend to. That seems like it would be exhausting. And no disrespect taken. I do love staying active. It's part of what gives me purpose."

"Purpose." Amanda hung her head. She hadn't been able to get the lie of omission from the other day out of her mind. What kind of friend would she ever be if they started this friendship on an untruth?

Amanda pushed her hair back over her shoulder. "Maeve, I owe you an apology. I wasn't completely honest with you about something. I don't even know why."

"Oh, goodness. Well, I'm sure you had your reasons."

"No, not good ones." She rubbed her hands together. She'd tucked her wedding band in her jewelry box, thinking it would be easier if no one knew her situation. All part of the charade. "I . . . I moved here thinking I could leave something behind. That by being here where no one knew what I'd been through that it would be easier."

Maeve didn't say a word.

Amanda took a breath in trying to find the words. "It's not easier. It's different, but . . ." She pressed her lips together. "You've been so nice. The kids really like you, and I enjoy talking to you too. I don't know why I didn't tell you—" She swallowed hard. This was so much harder to explain than she'd thought it would be.

"Whoa. Slow down. Honey, you don't owe me anything. You tell me whatever you need to as you feel you are ready. Some things are personal. You never have to apologize for that."

"I wanted you, well not just you, but everyone . . ." She was babbling. For a moment, she closed her eyes and looked for strength. "I even told the real estate agent that I was in the middle of a divorce. I'm not."

"Are you married?"

"Yes." She glanced down at her empty ring finger. "No. Not anymore. Well, yes, forever. My husband passed away two years ago." She looked at Hailey and Jesse playing in the sand. "We don't talk about it much. I was so tired of being introduced as Amanda, followed by the stage-whispered 'She's widowed' as if that were my last name. It tore at me over and over. I'm sorry I wasn't up front with you about it, but I can't stand people looking at me like I'm going to break down into tears." Her own body defied her at times, like now. Her eyes tingled. "And yes, I might some days."

"It's okay."

"No, it's not. I should've been honest when Hailey mentioned Jack at the library, and I'm sorry." Amanda reached for Maeve's hand. "I want us to be friends."

"We are."

"I mean real friends. Like you call me and let me know if we can do something for you. Anytime. I mean it."

"Thank you."

"Like when I make a big pan of spaghetti but it's too much for us, it's okay because you can join us or I can drop some off to you. Like that."

"I do love a good spaghetti. I'd like that very much."

"Jack." She suddenly wanted Maeve to know everything about him. "That's my husband's name. He was such a good father. A great husband and provider."

"I'm sure you miss him very much."

"I do. So much. People say it gets easier with time, but if that's true, I haven't gotten there yet. The first year was a blur. The second year was worse. Now . . . it's . . ."

"You're so young. I'm sorry that happened to you. To your family."

They sat quietly for a moment.

"The pain." Maeve shook her head. "Losing a spouse is losing half of yourself. Your better half in some cases even. The pain of that loss is inevitable. It's going to happen to every couple at some point. One of you is going to lose the other."

Amanda sniffled.

"Grief changes shape but doesn't really ever go away, leaving a scar behind that affects everything we do. But, Amanda, the suffering is optional. Don't let your grief turn into suffering. It's a whisper-thin line there."

"I'm not sure I understand. Aren't they the same thing? Kind of action reaction?"

"Not exactly." Maeve's words were so gentle that Amanda wished she would pull her into a hug. "Amanda, I would never compare what we've been through. You have children. You're so young, and you have a wonderful, full life still to live ahead of you. I lost my husband a long time ago, but I was nowhere near as young as you."

Amanda raised her eyes to meet Maeve's gaze.

"I was so sad. Then mad. Mad at him. Then mad at God." Maeve's eyes glistened. "That kind of anger makes you react irrationally. It's a release. A way to cope. Not that any of it makes sense at the time."

"It doesn't make it right, though." Amanda felt the understanding in Maeve's words. "I was so unkind to Jack's dearest friend—well, *our* dearest friend before Jack passed. I took out my anger on him. I blamed him for Jack not coming home. They'd enlisted together, had a spoken oath that they'd protect each other. But he didn't, and I hated him so much that day. For letting Jack down, then not being there for me."

"Don't beat yourself up. It's the grief making you do things you'd never do. People understand." Maeve's words eased the pain, a little.

"No. I called him on the phone one night, shouting at him, making him promise he'd never contact me or the kids again. I threatened him. I made a momma bear look like a puppy that night."

"We protect what we love. When that's disturbed, everything topples." Maeve sat quiet for a moment, then seemed to shift her focus on something off in the distance. "It's survival, Amanda. I sat around in a blind stupor, wishing I'd die so I could be with my husband, Jarvis. But that didn't happen. It took me a long time to live again. Friends tried to convince me to move forward, but honestly, just waking up each day and remembering to breathe in and out was almost more than I could bear. The more they told me to move on, the more I wanted to hold on to the past. Surviving is hard work."

"Yes." Amanda swallowed a sob. "Exactly. Jack was my everything. I loved him with every bit of my heart."

"We don't have to understand any of it, Amanda. We only have to keep living." Maeve offered her an easy grin. "Don't you hate it when people say stuff like that? Makes no sense. Death never does."

Amanda traced her finger through the sand. "For a while it almost killed me when those sweet children would look at me. They have his eyes. I felt guilty every time I turned away from his eyes in them. I know that sounds awful."

"It sounds honest."

Why did I tell you all that? I must sound like a horrible mother. "I hope they never felt that."

"I'm sure they didn't."

"Now I treasure the chance to see him in their eyes, but it's still hard."

"Here's the thing I learned: There is a difference between grief and suffering. You see, suffering is solitary, but you share your grief with good people. It's the way you release the pain and adjust to the loss."

"But that's just a big downer. We lived on base. Jack was a Marine. He was supposed to be gone six months, but he didn't come back. It got so every time I saw one of the other wives coming over, I felt like an anchor. I was weighing down their happiness and stealing their joy. I'm sure I was a constant reminder of the loss they potentially could face too. Who wants to be around that?"

"But see, that's not how most people view it. Good people want to be of service. Listening and being there for others. Even those ubiquitous casseroles are their way of helping. If we don't let them do that, they feel powerless. Then nobody wins."

Amanda groaned. "The casseroles. Oh my gosh."

"I know, I know. You can only go through so many casseroles. I fed the birds with them. I mean, who thinks one person can eat a nine-by-thirteen casserole in a week? Let alone a half dozen of them!"

"Yes. It's an obscene amount of food that arrives, and the last thing you want to do is eat."

Maeve nodded. "They want to help. They want to do their part, and sometimes those casseroles are all people can think of to do."

"I guess I can see that, but it's so hard to be constantly reminded."

"You moving here to pretend Jack hadn't been the best part of your past—that's suffering. Suffering is solitary. It's a barrier to processing your loss. You've lost something, Amanda." Maeve pulled her fists to her heart. "I've experienced how deep and heavy that can feel."

A tear slipped down Amanda's cheek. "I have to be strong. For the kids."

"Yes, you do. No question about that." Maeve looked out over the water. "I can't imagine how that must be. All I had was me, and that was hard."

"I know the five stages of grief and that it ends with acceptance. I accept Jack's not coming back, but I still hurt so much."

"I know you do, but you don't have to do it alone. Talk to someone. A good person won't let you suffer." She placed her hand on Amanda's. "Can we talk about this? Can I be your person?"

"My good person?"

"I'm an excellent listener. I won't ask or push. Just let me be there for you as you're ready. Don't make the mistakes I made. I wasted so many years buried in suffering."

"Thank you so much." The tears streamed down her cheeks now. She blotted them with her free hand. "I'm sorry."

"Nope. Don't apologize. Tears are healing. There's scientific proof that emotional tears reduce pain. Maybe that's why the ocean is so good for us—all that salt water. Let those salty tears fall, my dear."

Amanda laughed, but the tears didn't curtail.

Maeve leaned forward and wrapped her long arms around her. "You're going to be okay. Better than okay. Just keep things simple. You'll see. Each day will be better than the last."

A weight lifted ever so slightly from Amanda, anxiety and sorrow falling away into Maeve's arms.

A long moment went by.

"You sit right here and you cry as long as you need to. Get it out. Be thankful." Maeve's hand rubbed along Amanda's back. "Smile. Laugh. Grit your teeth and say bad words if that's what it takes. I'm going to go down and spend some time with Hailey and Jesse." She leaned back, looking into Amanda's face. "You okay?"

She nodded.

"I'm going to walk down there with them. Don't worry. Don't even think about us or look our way. You be here, with your thoughts. With Jack. Whatever it takes. Take all the time you need. Deal?"

"You don't have to—"

"This is the part where you have to let me help you grieve. Let *me* have a purpose. I have absolutely nothing else more important to do. Please?"

"Yes. Deal."

Amanda looked on as Maeve made it to where the kids were playing. They jumped around as Maeve started talking. Her hands moved in the air, and it looked like the children were absolutely captivated by her.

A loud sob broke from Amanda's chest as she let it go.

12

Amanda lay on the beach with her eyes closed. She could hear Hailey's playful shrieks in the distance. *Jack, did you send Maeve?* She licked her lips and sniffed back the tears. *She's an angel, right? I mean, who walks the beach like that and can make people smile with a shell?*

But Jack didn't answer.

She scooted out from under the umbrella. Puffy clouds moved across the sky, giving way to spots of blue. She and Jack used to watch the changing clouds and identify shapes in them. Sort of like an inkblot test. They'd lie in the bed of his pickup doing that for hours. Keeping score, of course.

A tear slid down her neck. She hated for the kids to see her cry. They didn't deserve the burden of her sorrow. She pulled one of the frozen juice pouches out of her bag, wrapped it in her beach towel, and placed it over her puffy eyes, gathering herself.

Thank you for Maeve.

The kids' giggles rose above the crashing waves. How long had it been since she'd had even just a few minutes to not worry about them? She sat up and took a sip of water, then lifted her phone to see how bad her eyes looked. Thank goodness her image in the selfie frame didn't look too bad. She lightly tapped at the puffiness around her eyes. Totally passable once she put on her sunglasses.

But she did feel better. Thankful. Grateful. Ready to tackle the rest of the day.

She got up and brushed the sand from her legs, then walked down to meet up with Maeve and the kids.

They were having quite the little party down there. They hadn't even noticed her approach.

"How's it going?" she asked.

Hailey jumped in front of the project, legs spread and arms wide. "Don't look yet!"

"It's a secret surprise!" Jesse ran over and grabbed Amanda's hand, tugging her back toward the sheet. "Not yet, Mommy."

"We'll see you in five minutes." Maeve waved and gave Amanda a thumbs-up.

Amanda cross-stepped, backing away slowly. "I'll wait up there. Come and get me when you're ready."

"No peeking," Hailey said sternly.

"No problem." Amanda made it to the sheet and sat down. Laughter came out of nowhere. *Me time.* When was the last time she really had me time? *Thank you, Maeve. A hundred thank-yous.* She put her hands on her legs and closed her eyes, determined to sit there with her mind empty of any thoughts until the kids came to get her.

The weight of her body shifted, her center of gravity lowering as the stress release allowed her to really relax. She did find herself peeking a couple of times, curious what they were up to. But it felt good to be free of any responsibility, even for a short time.

Oh yeah. I could definitely get used to this.

"We're ready, Mommy." Jesse ran up to her. "Come on. You have to see."

She scrambled to her feet and jogged alongside him to where Hailey and Maeve stood.

"Sorry we took so long," Maeve said with a wink.

"Well, the best projects take time. No problem."

"Ready?" Hailey looked at Maeve and then they both stepped aside.

A castle rose from the sand. A series of tall slim buildings, all different heights and bridges connecting them. It was an entire city. Indeed, they had been busy.

"How did you do that so fast?" Maybe she'd been up there longer than she realized.

"Maeve taught us how to make drip castles." Hailey stuck her foot out with her toe pointed and arms wide. "It's so amazing."

"It sure is."

"We dug a long trench from the water to a pond in the middle of our city," Hailey explained.

"The waves filled it up instead of destroying it," Amanda said. "I bet I can guess who was in charge of digging it." Jesse was a master at it. Fast and deep. Just his style.

Jesse jumped in the air. "Me!"

"Look how tall your castle is. It must be five stories high. Like an apartment building."

"Princesses don't live in apartments, Mom."

"Of course not. What was I thinking?"

"Look," Hailey said to her. "Come on, Jesse. Let's show her how we did it. Just like Maeve taught us." They both knelt and took a scoop of watery sand in their hands and began releasing it just a little at a time. Drip by drip, the sand piled upon itself.

"That's really pretty impressive." Amanda looked over at Maeve. "Very cool."

"Best part is you can leave all those buckets and boxes behind and still be able to make a castle. Right, Hailey? It's called keeping it simple."

"Yes ma'am." Hailey ran around to the backside of the castle, where there was a drip-sand fence. "Know what's back here?"

"Horses?"

"No! A doghouse for Denali."

"Of course. You have thought of everything."

"Maeve helped."

"Thanks, but you two really did all the work. I just supervised."

Amanda turned to Maeve. "Thank you. For this. They are having a blast. And for the time. Oh my gosh, this is better than a day at a spa. And thank you for being a friend. I'm sorry I kind of dumped on you. Forgive me?"

"Don't be silly. You did no such thing. I'm so delighted. This has been the best day I've had in a very long time."

Hailey stepped between them. "Does that mean we can play tomorrow too?"

"I'm always available to supervise and give a little castle-building advice."

"And shells," Hailey added. "You know everything about shells."

"So it would seem." Maeve pushed her hat back on her head. "Don't you love the beach after a couple good rainy days?" She inhaled deeply. "You can really smell the salt in the air once the pollution gets blown to bits."

"What's pollution?" Hailey's nose wrinkled.

"Bad stuff in the air, like smoke and car exhaust." Amanda hadn't noticed until Maeve had mentioned it, though. "Yes, you're right. We also appreciate how much easier it was to get over that dune today. Sometimes that deep sand is a real killer."

"Especially on the walk back," Maeve said. "Am I right?"

"You are." Hailey inched closer to Maeve.

The tide was coming in. The water lapped at their legs above their ankles now. "When I was a little girl," Maeve said, "it was such a long walk to the beach. The dunes were taller back then, and our house was so far away from the beach that some days I thought I would never make it back. Over the years, the tides have taken a toll on the coastline. I don't know if that's how nature means it to be or it's some by-product of our human impact on things. I like to believe the ocean realized I was getting older and too tired for that hike and so it met me halfway."

"So when we're old, we won't have to walk this far either?" Hailey asked.

"Probably not."

"That's very, very good." Hailey threw her hands in the air. "I'm going to like that very much."

"Me too." Jesse jumped up and then landed in his favorite superhero stance.

"I'm going to walk on down the beach." Maeve picked up her shell bag and hung it over her shoulder. "I hope I'll see you here tomorrow."

"We'd like that," Amanda said. "I usually pack a lunch. Will you join us?"

"That sounds wonderful."

"Noon?"

"I'll see you all right here tomorrow. I may even catch you on my way back if you haven't already gone home for the day."

Hailey waved as Maeve turned to walk on. "Don't fall in our pond when you come back," she yelled through cupped hands.

"I'll keep a lookout." Maeve swished her feet in the water as she walked away.

It had been a good day. Amanda looked at Hailey and Jesse, who'd returned to sitting in the water, dripping sand into tall piles. Connecting one to the next. It was like Jesse's first

Christmas when all he wanted to do was sit in the box that Hailey's Barbie Dreamhouse had come in and make truck noises rather than play with all the toys they'd so carefully picked out for him.

Keeping it simple. That's going to be our new motto.

The next morning, Amanda busied herself in the kitchen. She looked forward to Maeve joining them for lunch on the beach. It was nice to have someone to chat with who knew more than she did. Not just about the area but about life.

On the kitchen table, she'd set out a platter with grapes, cheese cubes, strawberry slices, and melon balls for the kids to make their favorite caterpillar kabobs for lunch. They loved assembling them, and she thought Maeve might get a kick out of them. She chopped veggies and mixed them with cream cheese to spread on tortillas, then rolled the tortillas up and sliced them into pinwheels. They looked pretty sitting in the container. Then she made a couple of PB&J sandwiches and cut them into fourths. It would be a nice little assortment.

She stopped and looked at everything on the table. Clearly, simple was not in her nature, but the kids loved her fun recipes. She'd have to find other places to simplify.

Hailey climbed into a chair at the kitchen table and ran her hand through her hair. "Are we making caterpillars?"

"You noticed."

"We love eating caterpillars!" Jesse climbed into the seat next to Hailey and rose up on his knees. Slowly, he extended a hand, his eyes wide, like he was going to sneak a strawberry.

She pretended not to notice, then spun around and scared him. "Are you stealing caterpillar faces?"

He sat back on his heels in a fit of giggles. "Maybe."

"There's plenty. You can have one, but don't ruin your appetite. We're going to Tug's Diner for breakfast."

Hailey and Jesse locked eyes, then squealed. "Pancakes!" No matter where they went out to eat breakfast, these two were a sure bet for pancakes. It didn't matter that they'd had some at home yesterday.

They made short work of the caterpillar-kabob project, lining each loaded skewer in a plastic container. "We have a whole army of caterpillars. Think we have enough to share with Miss Maeve?"

Jesse leaned over as if he were counting, but he couldn't count. Finally, he nodded. "Yes. She doesn't look like she eats much."

That struck Amanda as funny. Maeve wasn't skinny, but she was tall and lean. She was surprised Jesse had even noticed.

"Okay, get those teeth brushed and put some clothes on so we can go eat. I'm hungry."

They jumped up and were down the hall without a moment's delay.

Amanda changed into a yellow sundress and slid her feet into a pair of flip-flops, then herded the kids out the door.

They piled into the car and pulled out of her driveway. At the stop sign, she waited for the traffic to clear, then turned right. It wasn't that far to Tug's Diner, but it made her nervous to have Jesse and Hailey on the sidewalk so close to the traffic on this road that moved faster than the posted limit most of the time.

Parking at Tug's was tight. She'd heard it was a popular hot spot with the locals. Someone pulled out of a spot, and she whipped in. Lucky break.

The walkway to the diner looked more like the ramp to a

pirate's ship the way the thick ropes hung between pylons along the deck boards. The smell of bacon and sausage wafting through the air made her think it might be worth a playful sword fight to get inside.

A waitress greeted them with menus as they walked in. "There's a table open right over there, ma'am."

"Thank you." They went over and sat down.

All of a sudden Hailey belted out, "Mom, look! They have shells like the one you found."

"Shh. Indoor voice, Hailey." But she followed her daughter's pointed finger, and sure enough there were several shadow boxes holding all different types of shells containing messages.

She studied the box hanging over their table. The shell in it wasn't big like the one Hailey had found. It was flat and about the size of a peanut butter jar lid that looked sort of like a scallop shell. The frame was deep and the shell took up half of it. On the other half, a handwritten note was mounted with those paper corners used in photo albums. There was no date on it, but it had the look of having been there a long time.

> *Dear Tug,*
> *Your restaurant has been our favorite for the ten years we've been coming to Whelk's Island. My wife and I can't make a trip to that town without a night there. We'd always thought the shells decorating the walls were a clever marketing ploy. We were shocked when we found a shell containing a message in front of our beach house on our last trip. We decided it should be kept in the restaurant, where other people could enjoy it too. Enclosed please find the shell, and a check to cover the framing.*
> *Keep up the good eats.*
> *Stan and Margie Fuller*
> *Charlotte, NC*

Inside the scallop shell was the quote:

Stay away from negative people. They have a problem for every solution.—Albert Einstein

From their table she could make out a couple of the other shadow boxes. One shell read, "Happiness comes in waves." Not all the shells had such poignant messages, though. She laughed as she read the next one. "Sunburn is the way others know you're a slow learner . . . and a tourist."

Suddenly Amanda felt silly for thinking her shell had been special. They were probably mass-produced in China and sold for ten bucks in the souvenir shop.

The waitress came over and poured her some coffee.

"Thank you."

"Y'all decide what you want yet?" She reached across the table and turned one of the menus over. "Kids' menu is right here. Mine love the octopus."

"Octopus?" Hailey looked horrified.

The waitress snickered. "It's yummy. A big ol' pancake with bacon tentacles." She flailed her arms to the side like a sea creature. "Even has a fruit face, and the syrup is blue like water."

"Mom, can we? Pretty please and thank you?" Jesse asked.

Amanda couldn't say no to *that*. After all, she was feeding them caterpillars for lunch. "Looks like we have a winner. What do you recommend for me?"

The waitress leaned back, placing the end of her pen against her lip. "Hmm. Healthy or hungry?"

"Something splurge-worthy."

"Tug's sausage milk gravy over biscuits. To die for. How about a couple strips of bacon on the side? We have the best bacon around."

"Sold." Amanda stacked all three of the menus up into a pile and handed them to the waitress. "Milk for these two. I'll stick with coffee."

"Gotcha covered."

"Oh, and . . ." Amanda tried to catch her before she got too far away.

The waitress spun back around, her pen to the ready.

"These shells. Are they part of some kind of local legend?"

The waitress brightened, beginning to talk with her hands. "Oh yeah. Been going on for years. The article down there near the door"—she pointed toward the front of the restaurant—"was from the local paper here, from like twenty years ago. Funny how the shells just show up out of nowhere."

"It's kind of nice. I was reading this note. So mostly tourists find them?"

"No. People from around here too. Maybe more locals. I don't know, really, but it's been a thing since as long as I can remember."

"That's neat."

"Yeah. I'd like it if I ever found one. People say they are life changing." She slid her pen behind her ear.

Amanda couldn't help but peek back at the one about sunburn.

The waitress followed her line of sight and laughed. "Yeah, well sunburn can cause cancer. It was like a PSA. The tourists, man, they get burnt slap up. It's dangerous. You think people would know better."

"Touché."

"I'll get this order right in. Won't take long." She reached into her apron pocket and set two packs of crayons and coloring pages about the size of index cards on the table in front of Jesse and Hailey.

The kids compared pictures, traded, and then started coloring the postcards. Amanda stood and walked over to look at another shell near the glass cases filled with T-shirts and to-go desserts. That shell was really tiny and almost green, the writing in it so precise:

What is your personal gift?

What was the point of a message like that? *Gift?* She couldn't sing, paint, or even type. A wife and mother? Anybody could do that.

"What's yours?"

The voice took her by surprise. She swung around to see Maeve standing there. "Maeve?" She hadn't heard her walk up. "Hello."

Hailey and Jesse ran up, squealing hellos to their new best friend.

"Good morning. How did you find my very favorite restaurant?"

"Mommy drove us here," Jesse stated.

"I heard it was a local favorite," Amanda offered.

"I'm a local. It's my favorite. I guess you'd be right. Plus, the owner is a good friend of mine." Maeve waved over Amanda's head. "Tug, say hello to Amanda, Hailey, and Jesse. They moved into the house at the dunes."

Amanda turned to look.

Tug's eyes lit up. He threw a welcoming hand in the air. "Yes, glad to have you. I heard we had new neighbors." His white ball cap had the diner logo on it. He had that aged tan beachboy look to him. The kind with the dark, leathery skin who loves the outdoors and never gives up being outside as long as they live. "Nice to meet you. Folks call me Tug."

"Hi, Tug. Nice to meet you too."

Hailey said, "I'm having octopus for breakfast."

"You'll love it. It's a crowd-pleaser."

"I hope it doesn't taste like fish sticks, because that would be pretty yucky for breakfast."

"If you think it does, then I'll fix you something else."

Hailey raised her eyebrows, liking the idea of being catered to.

"I'm sure it will taste great," Amanda assured Hailey.

"I see you were catching up on our claim to fame," Maeve said. "The shells?"

"We fou—"

Amanda twisted Hailey around toward the table. "You and your brother zip on back to our spot. I'll be right there." She turned and smiled, glancing back at the shells on display. "Yeah, the stories about the shells are so interesting."

"So, what's your gift?"

"Mine?" Amanda sputtered. "I don't have one."

"Sure you do. Everyone does."

She shrugged. "I got nothin'. What's yours?"

"I'm an excellent listener. Took me a long time to realize that. Turns out it's a rare gift too. Who knew?"

It was true. Maeve had proved that yesterday. Most people were so busy thinking about their response that they didn't half listen to a conversation these days.

Tug leaned out over the counter. "She doesn't forget anything either. Ever."

Maeve shot him a look. "Don't mind him. We've been friends forever. He was the best man in my wedding."

"Still am the best man, if you ask me."

"No one asked you," Maeve said as she and Amanda walked toward the table where Hailey and Jesse sat pushing sugar packets around the table like cars. From somewhere beyond the room came a voice, "Who asked you, Tug?" followed by a cackling laugh.

"What was that?" Hailey raised up in her seat.

"That's The Wife," Maeve said with a look over her shoulder toward Tug. "Tug, you want to introduce them to her?"

He wiped his hands on his apron, then came around the counter. "I've got a minute. Let me take you to meet The Wife."

Hailey and Jesse looked at Amanda and then Maeve as they all fell in line behind Tug and headed toward the back door.

"The Wife is a parrot," Tug explained as he led them out to the deck.

There sitting in a cage in a gazebo, a dark-gray-feathered bird with a bright-red tail stared at them, then followed up with a resounding, "It's about time. Where've you been?"

The kids' mouths dropped wide, and then they scrambled toward the cage.

Tug said, "Say hello to our new friends."

The bird bobbed her head up and down and made a car-alarm noise.

"That wasn't very polite," Tug reprimanded her.

"Hello, cuties." The parrot lifted her black beak in the air, seemingly pleased with herself.

Amanda watched as Hailey and Jesse interacted with the bird. They were having a whole conversation. Tug treated The Wife to french fries for being playful, and the kids loved it.

"What's a dog say?"

The Wife let out a series of barks. Jesse chimed in. "Bow-wow. Woof."

The parrot laughed—which only made the kids laugh more—and then imitated an ambulance before yelling, "Help! They turned me into a parrot!"

Tug led the kids to the end of the porch and let them throw fries into the air for the seagulls. The birds swooped in, bringing more over until there had to be twenty of them angling for a snack.

"He shouldn't do that," Maeve said. "Those seagulls will quickly become a menace."

"He looks like he's having fun."

It was comical to see the old man leap into the air and spin around, tossing taters in the air. Even funnier to see Hailey and Jesse trying to copy the moves.

"He is. Silly old bird himself is what he is. Then again, who am I to judge? He talks to the birds." Maeve shook her head. "Me? I got so lonely after Jarvis died that there for a while I talked into a recorder every day just to have someone listen. It was ridiculous." Almost as if she meant to be musing to herself, she said, "I wonder where all those tapes are. I should get rid of them. It could be embarrassing should I die and someone come to clear out the house and find them. I might have rattled on about people in this town. The good and the bad."

Amanda doubted that anything on those tapes could be bad. "Seems to me like everyone just wants the best for the town and their neighbors."

"You're right. For the most part, that's about it summed up. We need some uplifting hearts like yours among all us old beachcombing curmudgeons."

"Oh, stop. You're not a curmudgeon."

Tug walked over with a big grin on his face.

"I was referring to him." Maeve shot him a look.

"She loves me," Tug said as he led the group back inside to their table. Maeve didn't take a seat but stood nearby.

"Someday she's going to admit it." Then he added, "Meanwhile, I just keep slinging hash. Feeding her breakfast and hoping she'll tell me."

"No luck yet?" Amanda watched the two of them. The banter was easy and fun. She wasn't sure if it was more like brother and sister or a romance brewing, but either way it seemed to be in good fun.

"Not yet. But I'm not giving up." Tug adjusted his ball cap.

Hailey motioned to Tug and curved her finger in the air. "C'mere."

He leaned down where she was sitting, and she cupped her hands to the side of his head and whispered—well, it looked like a whisper, but darn near everyone in the place heard her— "If you like her, you're supposed to give her flowers and chocolate."

"That's what I've been doing wrong? Guess that's why it hasn't worked."

Hailey nodded, quite sure of herself.

"Don't waste your money buying me flowers," Maeve said. "Never was a fan of them."

Tug lifted his brows and smirked. "I'd have gotten her if old Jarvis hadn't asked her out first," he said to Amanda. "I'm way more charming."

"No one was more charming than my Jarvis," Maeve said.

"Your order's up," the waitress called out from behind the counter.

"Y'all better eat before it gets cold," Maeve said. "I'll see you over on the beach later."

"You're still going to meet us for lunch, aren't you?" Amanda asked.

Maeve walked over to the back door. "Absolutely."

"We already made a fun meal and packed it," Jesse shared.

"I can't wait." Maeve waved and said goodbye to Tug on her way out.

Next time she and the kids would find a safe route and walk here to eat. The exercise would do them all good.

13

When Maeve got back to her house, she pulled out her journal. Not a decorative one with a lock and key like the diary she wrote in as a child, just a simple spiral notebook she bought when school supplies went on sale. She had a mess of them stacked on the bookshelf. As she scrawled the date across the top line of the page, she noticed the last entry. It had been a while since she'd written.

There'd been a time when journaling had been her lifeline. An outlet for the words she wanted to convey about her emotions and health. It all went down in here—times in her life when she desperately needed strength, and prayer didn't seem to be enough. She'd spoken the prayers, then recorded them in these journals. She wasn't entirely sure why she kept them around. It wasn't like she wanted to go back and revisit those days.

Then again, the notebooks were full of everything that had ever made her who she was. The best and worst moments of her life.

She'd sat down today to simply write one sentence about having met Amanda, Hailey, and Jesse. What she ended up with was three pages about it. She smiled as she wrote each memory, right down to the drip-castle building and their re-action to meeting Tug and The Wife.

She closed the notebook with a sigh, then tucked it into the end of the stack on the bottom shelf of the bookcase. All the rest of the volumes were spiral in, only the page edges showing, tattered and wavy from the changing humidity in the house through the seasons. It didn't matter, though, because those pages represented time. Someday when she couldn't remember, maybe she'd read them all again.

The ladies at the church had been the ones who'd inspired her to start journaling again. They'd given her a beautiful leather-wrapped diary. Long leather laces tied around it. Her name had even been embossed in gold on the front.

Of course, she'd never written in that one. It was too pretty to use. It still sat there on the end table as decoration, but seeing it had willed her to write sometimes.

She picked it up, the fine leather supple in her hands. So much had come as a result of this gift, yet no one would ever realize it by looking at it. She unwrapped the leather laces and bent the journal between her hands, thumbing the empty pages. Softened gold lines and the brown outline of a compass in the top corner skittered as the pages flipped.

Still carrying the leather journal, Maeve gathered a couple of things from the backyard, then opened the side gate and set out across the sand to meet with Amanda and her kids for lunch.

The sun warmed her shoulders. She was still a good hundred yards off when Hailey and Jesse screamed out her name.

"Miss Maeve!" Their hands in the air, they sprinted toward her like they'd been waiting forever for the reunion.

Choking back a joyful sob, she crouched to catch them as they flung themselves into her arms. "My goodness!" She laughed as Jesse tangled in her skirt. "That is a greeting."

"We've been watching for you."

Jesse's hand clung to hers. His skin was as soft as the leather-bound journal she still held tight against her body.

Hailey slipped her arm around Maeve's waist, tugging on her until she knelt down. Hailey hugged her neck, the young girl's fingers gently patting Maeve's skin at the pace of a tiny heartbeat. The sudden outpouring of love made her almost lose balance for a moment, as if the surrounding air had become so light that they swirled.

"Wow. I was excited to see you too!"

"I'm sorry." Amanda had come over in the midst of the welcome. "They can be a lot of energy sometimes."

"No. I'm not complaining. It was so sweet."

Maeve watched as Amanda looked at her children like they were a miracle. She'd said she wouldn't ask or push, but she wondered about all the details between Amanda and Jack.

"We've been collecting shells. We'll bring them up to show you," said Hailey. The brother and sister fled back to their sand fort to play.

Amanda and Maeve walked up to the sheet tucked in the sand.

"I hope you don't mind if I ask, but how long ago did you lose your husband?" Amanda asked as she sat down.

Maeve sat, too, and pulled her knees up. "I lost him in 1995." She looked at the beautiful young woman sitting there. "We were married longer than you are old."

"Jack and I were only married for five years when he . . . when he didn't come back."

"The length of the marriage doesn't make it hurt any less." Maeve clamped her hand to her wrist around her knees, leaning back. "Jarvis was a good man. Everyone liked him. He worked on all the boats around here. Back then Tug was a commercial fisherman. That's how the two of them became friends."

"Must be neat to live in one town your whole life."

"I wouldn't know any different."

"My parents can't understand why I don't want to move back to Ohio now. I haven't lived there in years. It's not home anymore."

"I'm sure they're worried."

"They think I need the support system I'd have there."

"They might be right." Maeve shrugged. "Only you can make that decision. Honestly, having been through it, my experience is nothing makes it easier. It's a process. Sometimes a very long one. Everyone is different, and you can't shortcut it."

"I try not to get frustrated with them about it, but if they're really all that worried, why don't they come here and help me?"

It wasn't Maeve's place to answer that question, if indeed it were one. "You could visit them to reassure them. You don't have to move there to do that."

"It's hard to travel with two kids, and then there's Denali. What would I do with the dog?" She took in a breath. "I'm being hardheaded, aren't I?" She closed her eyes for a moment, drawing strength. "Maybe because it's the only thing I can control."

Maeve nodded slowly. "Well, traveling with two young ones could be a challenge, but they seem well behaved. I think you could do it if you wanted. Just a short visit. Not long enough to regret it."

Amanda shot her an I-can't-believe-you-just-said-that look.

"And as for your dog—"

"No, I'm not leaving Denali with you. He's a huge handful, and he's so strong."

"Oh, honey, I wasn't about to take that on." She threw her hand in the air. "Do I look crazy?" She wagged her finger in front of Amanda. "Do not answer that."

"No, you don't look crazy! I'd never say that. Or think it."

"Paws Town Square recently opened in town. I sat through

all the zoning meetings, and they get dicey at times, but it looks like it must be a great place to kennel your pets. As I understand it, they do outreach to soldiers with PTSD and work to reunite military working dogs with their handlers or place them in forever homes after rehabilitation. It's much more than a pet-boarding business. They find these worn-out vacant buildings—"

"Ghost boxes? I read something about that the other day. There are so many of those big-box stores that have either gone out of business or been abandoned in favor of building new, bigger locations, leaving the old ones to fall to pieces."

"Yes, well, this company figured out the way to leverage those wasted spaces to a lot of people's benefit." Maeve tried to remember the details from the town council meetings. "They update the facade and transform ugly parking lots into dog parks and running trails. I hear it's really quite beautiful. They have indoor and outdoor walking trails that people can use with their pets for a very fair fee. And locals get a discount. So there you go. You might have an option for Denali."

"I might. I'll have to check into that. I probably should take the kids to visit their grandparents. They haven't seen them since . . . in a long while." She lowered her gaze.

"Maybe it's time." Maeve smiled. "It'll all work itself out eventually."

"Everyone says that." Amanda shook her head.

"Everyone is different. For me, at first I was in disbelief, then sad. So sad." She placed the palm of her hand against her heart. "See? All these years later, I still get choked up. Jarvis promised he'd always be there for me. I never expected he might abandon me, and that's exactly how it felt. With no warning I was left alone. After I climbed out of the pit of devastation, I got fighting mad. At him. At everyone."

Amanda took in a breath but didn't say a word.

"I wasn't pleasant to be around during that time. Intellectually, I knew it wasn't his doing, but he worked hard. Too hard. I was always telling him that." She could still picture him so clearly. Sweating under the hottest sun. The way he'd nudge his ball cap up on his head and readjust it. He'd loved working on those boats. One hundred degrees and humidity so high he was wet before the sunrays hit him, or so cold she was afraid he'd get frostbite. That's why those who earned a living with their boats relied on him. They trusted he wouldn't let them down.

"He had a heart attack out there working. Fine one minute." She snapped her fingers. "Gone the next. Just like that." She looked over at Amanda. "It took me a long time to forgive him. I knew it wasn't really his fault, but I'd warned him he was working too hard." Maeve moistened her dry lips. "I was so mad that I sold the house he'd built for me. Not my brightest move, in hindsight." She turned toward her home, which rose up from the dunes. "That's how I ended up back in the house I grew up in."

"So for you there *was* some solace in going back home, even if it was by way of moving into the house you'd grown up in."

"Hadn't really thought of it *that* way." She pondered for a moment. "No, it didn't make me feel any better. Mostly I'd acted out of anger. I regret having let our house go. That was a stupid move on my part."

"I bet it was beautiful."

"No, not at all." Maeve laughed. "Kind of looked like a boat, if truth be told. But then, everything Jarvis built did. He was a shipwright. But he'd built that house with love in his heart, and we were happy there."

"How long did it take before you felt like yourself again?"

She wished she knew the right thing to say. *What kind of friend would I be if I just told her what she wanted to hear?* "You're not going to want to hear this."

"It's been over two years. I'm still a mess."

"In twenty-six years, I've never felt like I did with him. I don't think you ever get over it."

Amanda blinked, seeming to do the math in her head.

"I'm happy," Maeve continued. "At peace. I love my life. But it's . . . different. At first I blocked out everyone."

"I can understand that."

"The ocean was the only friend I let in for a long time. The waves greeted me, and that was all I wanted. Even in hurricanes, I'd come out here. Selfishly, there were times when I was out here in extreme weather, praying the sea would grab me and sweep me away so I could be with him again." The memory of that desperation washed over her. A tear slipped down her cheek. "I wanted to die so badly that I gave up, believing that if I lay in bed long enough, it would be over. I'm not sure how many days I lay there, still waking up each morning mad at the world."

"I'm so sorry I didn't know you then." Amanda's hands were at her heart. "I'd have been there for you. My heart aches to think of you broken. You seem so resilient."

"Broken is exactly how I felt. There was one night in particular. The full moon hung high in the sky, slashing across my face through the curtains. I was worn out, weak from not eating, but that light beckoned me. I walked out to the dock behind our house." She lifted her hands. "I can still almost feel how shaky my limbs were. I made it to the edge of the dock and sat on those splintering boards. My feet dangled in the water. It was cold sloshing against my toes." The icy memory made her shiver. "Two of Jarvis's boats still sat tied up there, ready to go out. Two other boats sat in different states of repair. Out of the thin air on that moonlit night, I took action. I went back to the house and took a special shell down from the mantel, where it had been since we found it one weekend. I held it for a long time, reflecting on all the good times, tears streaming as fast as the memories came."

Maeve took in a breath. "His foul-weather gear still hung there at the back door. I put it on." She wiggled her fingers. "The sleeves dangled well past the tips of my fingers, but I marched out to his boat with that shell in my hand as if I were going to war.

"Over the years," Maeve continued, "Jarvis delivered boats down to Florida or north as far as Massachusetts, and I loved riding with him out into the Gulf Stream. He never was one to putter along the intracoastal waterway. He loved the ocean."

Amanda's eyes shimmered. "You shared that love."

"We did. That night, I boarded the *Almost Heaven* and stood behind the wheel. The thirty-four-foot center console had been a good vessel for Jarvis. He'd made the money to remodel the house on side trips taking tourists out fishing on that boat."

"You went out on the boat? At night?"

Maeve nodded with a snicker. "I did. Started it up and eased out into the sound under that full moon. I pushed the throttle forward and let the boat run free. I was crying, but I was going so fast the tears didn't even hit my cheeks." She blinked, as if reliving the moment.

"Oh my gosh. Maeve."

"I know. It was a little crazy."

"A lot!"

"I finally stopped the boat and drifted until morning when the sun rose. I'll be honest, a hundred plans came together and fell apart over those hours. Eventually, I leaned over the side of the boat, holding that shell, then dropped it overboard."

"For Jarvis." Amanda's sigh was almost a cry.

"The splash was followed by a gulping sound as the water filled the hollow of the shell and it sank to the depths. I watched it disappear. Gone. Like Jarvis." Her pause hung with heavy sorrow. "I sat out for hours that day, but late that afternoon I motored back and docked the boat. I packed away the foul-weather gear, opened all the windows in the house, and cleaned it top to bottom. It's the day I started over."

"It's so hard to go on." Amanda brushed away a tear on her chin. "To know what to cling to, and what things are anchoring me to a past that—"

"Grief will tear you out of the frame if you let it, Amanda. Until I got my focus off of me and started looking for my purpose, I was a mess." She'd almost forgotten she had the journal with her. "I brought you something. It was a gift to me when Jarvis passed. The ladies at the church gave it to me. It has my name on it, but I thought you might still like it." She handed it to Amanda.

"It's gorgeous."

"It is. I never could bring myself to write in it. Isn't that silly? I use twenty-five cent spiral notebooks instead, and I've kept that up. You should see the stack of cheap notebooks on my bookcase."

"That's funny." Amanda pressed the journal between her palms.

"It inspired me to write down my thoughts, so it was probably the best gift I ever received. Sometimes you just have to get the words out into the world. Like talking to the wind, the sea, the sand. Anyway, I hope having it might bring you some inspiration to try that. It couldn't hurt."

"Thank you. This is such a thoughtful gift." She set it aside, her hand resting on top of it as she looked down the beach. "Thank goodness I've got those two." Her eyes seemed lasered in on the children covered in sand, smiling, making memories as if they didn't have a care in the world. "I can't figure out how to keep Jack's death from lingering inside them their whole lives."

"Be careful, Amanda. Just like my only life purpose wasn't to be Jarvis's wife, yours doesn't stop at being a mother."

Amanda straightened, a flash of hurt in her eyes.

"It's a very important role," Maeve added quickly, "but there's more to your life. You have to share your gifts, and you'll do some of that through your children, but we are meant to share them more broadly."

"Gifts again? I don't have time for anything but them." She lifted her chin toward the kids. "I don't have anything left. No gifts. No energy."

"Quit looking like I've asked you to walk the plank. Seriously, everyone has gifts. We just don't always see them in ourselves as easily."

"Well, then it's a good thing we've become friends, because if there's a gift in here somewhere, you're going to have to help me find it. It's likely to be quite a treasure hunt."

They laughed easily.

"I can do that," Maeve said. "Challenge accepted."

Jesse raced from the water up to Amanda. "Mom, we're starving. Hailey told me to ask if we can please have lunch now."

"Sure. I bet Maeve is starting to get hungry again too."

"I am." Maeve rubbed her tummy, and Jesse mimicked her.

Without another word, he went to get his sister. The two of them ran back, Hailey easily winning the race.

Amanda opened a series of plastic containers.

"Would you look at this spread!" Maeve leaned in taking a closer look.

Hailey's pigtails bobbed. "We helped make it."

"You did? What is this?" Maeve pointed to the fruit-and-cheese kabobs.

"Caterpillars!" Jesse sat next to her, so close that he was practically on her lap.

"Ooh. You eat caterpillars?" She scrunched her face. "I don't know about that. I'm not a bird."

"Not that kind of caterpillar. It's really food." Jesse's dimples pressed deeper into his cheek when he laughed.

Maeve pretended to be unsure. "Are you positive caterpillars aren't bird food?"

"Nooo. You'll like it. I promise."

Hailey and Jesse started singing the blessing, and Maeve wasn't sure if she'd ever heard anything sweeter.

Jesse grabbed a caterpillar and bit the grape from the end. "See!"

"I do." She picked up a skewer and did the same, making overenthusiastic approving sounds. "You're so right."

As quickly as they'd become hungry, Hailey and Jesse were full and excited to go play some more.

"How do you keep up?" Maeve couldn't imagine being surrounded by that much energy all day, every day.

"I don't. Believe me." Amanda blew out a short breath. "My financial situation is forcing me to go back to work this fall. I'll get a little break once in a while then."

"What will you be doing?"

"It wasn't the original plan, but I'm going to teach. It'll allow me to keep the same hours as Hailey while she's in school. I need to start looking for a day care for Jesse since the school doesn't offer pre-K."

"What was the original plan?"

Amanda managed a shrug. "Well, I was going to start selling herbal salt. It's something I've done for a while, as a hobby, but we'd saved money for me to start a business. Nothing fancy. Online. Anyway, I thought I was going to do that and regulations got me all twisted up. It just isn't feasible right now." Her words were riddled with disappointment.

"I'm so sorry," Maeve said. "Well, don't give up. It's all about timing. Things have a way of working out at the right time."

"Good advice. Thanks." Amanda rocked forward. "Right now I'm focusing on getting used to the idea of being separated from Hailey and Jesse while I work. I've never left them with anyone."

"Never?"

"Not since Jack." She shrugged. "Well, except for yesterday when you were down with them on the beach."

"Honey, trust someone. You need the break. They do too. You can't do it all alone."

"I can if I have to."

"But you don't have to. There's always someone in the wings who can help."

Amanda didn't argue, but she didn't look convinced either.

Maeve studied her. "Have you ever said you needed help?"

"To who?"

"Doesn't matter. The wind. The water." She picked up a handful of sand and let it fall. "The sand."

"Why?"

"I don't know. I'd think admitting it would be a start. Try it."

Amanda's brows pulled together. "You want me to say it right now?"

"Why not?"

Tentatively, she spoke the words. "I need help." She felt her forehead wrinkle in protest. "No I don't. I take it back. My kids are great. Okay, yes, once in a while some help would be nice."

"You need a break. That's why families have two parents. It's not a one-person job. It takes a village and all that. Listen to me acting like I'm the authority, and I've never even had children. Even my dog I got when I was an adult and he was already housebroken. I haven't raised anything."

"Well, the advice seems sound. It is exhausting."

"If nothing else, why don't you at least let me give you . . . let's say an hour." The sudden burst of excitement inside her surprised Maeve. "Let me visit with them to give you time to read or think or nap while you are out here on the beach once in a while. Just a chance to not pay attention at all."

"A whole hour? That does sound nice."

"Then we'll give it a go. I'm not trying to get in your business." *Or maybe I am, and I don't even know why.* "I just think . . ." How could she articulate it? "I've been alone a long time. I'm not complaining. Once I figured out how to live again without Jarvis, my life changed. I still love and miss him every day. Our reunion someday will be so wonderful. My heart soars when I think about it, but his time wasn't my time. If I can help you find that peace more quickly, save you even a bit of that struggle, then I'd consider that quite a gift."

"A gift." Amanda's lips pulled up at the corners. "Oh yes, that would be a real gift."

"Good. I'm going down to teach your precious angels how to defy gravity. Your hour of freedom starts now. Enjoy." Maeve stood and walked away, hoping she dragged some of Amanda's baggage along with her.

14

The next four days were sunny and clear. All three of them were getting so tan. *We don't look like tourists anymore.*

Amanda couldn't say for sure if it was the escape Maeve had treated her to or the extra exercise from walking the beach every day now, but she'd never felt more at peace.

That night as she walked through her house locking doors and turning off lights, she realized she wasn't sad.

Tears, happy ones for a change, tickled her lashes. She tipped her chin to the ceiling.

I'm grateful for all the things we've found joy in right here in our backyard.

I'm thankful that I had the strength to uproot my precious children and move here.

Thank You for bringing Maeve into our lives.

I do need help sometimes, and I'm ready to accept that.

Other than the day she and Jack had gotten married on the beach, she had no ties to this place, but already she felt more stable here.

I thank You for the continued blessings.

She'd been driven here by a need to survive, and now the days were filled with good things and new possibilities. The kids were eager to make friends, and Hailey was excited about starting school in the fall. For the first time, Amanda wasn't afraid to let go of them for a few hours each day.

It'll be okay.

On Sunday morning she woke up knowing Sundays would be different from now on. Since the week after she laid Jack to rest, she'd steered clear of church. It was time to correct that. This morning she got them all dressed in their good clothes and went to the church that was a short two blocks away. Rather than explain why they hadn't been to church in so long, Amanda acted as if this was part of the plan. To her relief the kids didn't ask a single question about it.

They slid into the end of a row near the back only a minute before the service began. Jesse squirmed a lot, and Hailey was so quiet at one point that Amanda thought she'd fallen asleep. When Amanda leaned forward to check on her, though, Hailey's eyes were focused, almost trancelike, on the cross on the wall. The look on her face was so sweet. Whatever was going on in Hailey's mind at the moment, it was soothing.

I'd give anything to know what you're thinking, baby girl.

Jesse swayed to the music every time they got up to sing a hymn. Once he learned some songs, he'd enjoy it even more. Hailey picked up on the chorus, singing along with her. The words came back, and when the pastor spoke the benediction, Amanda found she wasn't ready for the service to be over.

The first few notes from the organ filled the air, almost vibrating as everyone stood and edged toward the center aisle to leave. The postlude song carried familiar tones that comforted her.

Most of the people offered a few words to the ushers as they left. Her stomach churned, causing an acrid taste at the back of her tongue. Her sweaty palms slipped against the tiny hands that clung to her.

Please don't ask me anything.

"Welcome. It's so nice to have you here with us," the pastor said.

"Thank you." She braced herself for the questions, but they never came. Just a kind smile. And that was it.

Why do I expect the worst?

Hailey waited by the car door for her to unlock it when a little boy walked over to her. In his light-blue button-down shirt and glasses, his hair slicked over to one side, he looked like a miniature financial adviser. All he lacked was a calculator.

"Hi. I'm Matt." He lifted his hand in an awkward hello, his feet shuffling as he spoke.

"I'm Hailey, and that's my brother, Jesse."

Amanda turned, noticing the proud mother and father who stood watching from across the way. She smiled at the couple, resisting the urge to rush her kids into the car and speed away.

"Are you going to elementary school this year?" the accountant continued. "I'm gonna be in the first grade."

"Me too," Hailey offered eagerly.

Matt dropped the backpack from his shoulder to the ground and unzipped it. "I brought this in to show everyone at children's church today. I got it when I was on vacation at my grandma's house last week." He pulled out a huge shell. The twisted shape with the tall spire and knobs around the top looked very similar to the one they'd found. "If you put this to your ear, you can hear the ocean no matter where you are."

Hailey hesitated as she reached for the shell, then held it to her ear. Her eyes lit up. "No way."

Amanda wished she'd been the one to show Hailey that. Why hadn't she thought to do that with the one they'd found?

"It's pretty cool." Matt seemed pleased with himself.

Just then his mother and father walked over.

Oh no! Amanda had relaxed too soon, but she pasted a smile on her face as she tried to decide how to answer questions about Jack. Lie and tell them she's divorced? That had been the plan all along, but then she'd been unable to live with the lie to Maeve. And she was in the *church* parking lot, for goodness' sake.

"Hi. We're Matt's folks. I'm Matthew, and this is my wife, Nikki." He extended his hand.

"So nice to meet you. I'm Amanda."

"Did I hear your daughter say she'd be going in the first grade too?" Nikki asked.

"You did. At Whelk's Elementary."

"That's wonderful," Nikki said. "I'm a teacher there."

What were the odds? "Well, it's a small world. I'll be teaching there this fall too. Fourth graders."

"Oh, fourth grade is so fun. I've got the second graders. This will be great. How old is your youngest?"

"Jesse is four. I'd hoped there'd be a pre-K session at the school, but I guess I'll need to find a day-care program for him. I've been putting it off."

"I did the same thing. It was so hard to let go of Matt at that age." She grimaced. "I don't envy that. I cried for a solid week."

Amanda wondered who the adjustment would be harder for: Her or Jesse?

"You know, we have an outstanding pre-K and day care right here at the church. Remind me next Sunday and I'll introduce you to Anna. She can tell you all about it. They are really wonderful. Plus, they do some evening activities for all the youth. It gives us a night off."

"We do love that." Matthew playfully bumped Nikki's shoulder.

Amanda ached for when she'd been part of a couple like that, with their teasing jabs and knowing looks. "Thank you. That would be really helpful."

"Do y'all live right around here too? We're over on Wake Forest Drive."

"Yes." Amanda recognized the name. "One street over. At the end of Bayberry Drive."

"Did you happen to buy the bungalow at the dune line?"

"We did."

"That place has so many possibilities." Nikki beamed. "That's great! We're neighbors. The kids can play."

"I'm sure I'll see you over on the beach." Although she was surprised she hadn't seen them yet. Not even once. She'd have remembered someone with a child Hailey's age. Maybe Nikki worked a summer job too. Many teachers did.

Matthew clapped his hands. "Okay, let's load up. We've got things to do."

Young Matt spun away from Hailey and ran to his dad's side. "Where are we going?"

"You'll see." He turned to Amanda. "Really nice meeting you, Amanda. We'll see you around, I'm sure."

"That would be nice." She stood there and watched them walk away before she loaded up Jesse and helped Hailey get buckled into her booster seat.

Okay. No questions. No lies. That worked out fine. Until next time anyway. She climbed into the car and breathed a sigh of relief as she started the engine. She'd planned to go check out Paws Town Square after church today, but right now she just needed to slide into home. *Safe.*

The short drive to their house wasn't even long enough to get her heart rate back down.

Hailey and Jesse unbuckled and were out of the car as soon as she parked. They ran ahead of her to let Denali out in the yard and start a whirling game of chase. As she passed them, she wasn't entirely sure who was chasing whom, they were all in such a clump, but the giggles made her happy.

She went inside and slipped off her dress. She hung it up, then slid the outfits she hadn't worn in a long while out from the corner of the closet. She pulled out her favorite blue shirt and shook out the wrinkles before putting it back on the rack. She'd wear it to teach. She'd have to start getting presentable for work, and the summer was moving quickly. They were already six weeks in.

Orientation at the school was only a month away. At least she'd know someone there now, and she had a lead on pre-K for Jesse too.

She changed into shorts and a T-shirt, then picked up the shell from her dresser. She held it to her ear just as Hailey had. The whooshing sound mutated as she changed the distance from her ear, getting louder as she pulled it farther away.

A chill chased down her spine.

She pictured Jack looking into her eyes, saying "I do" on their wedding day there on the beach.

Jack was in her heart. *Always. Forever.* Their love, as vast as the ocean, was tucked inside her soul for eternity.

The children ran and played in the yard, a mingling of pounding sneakers and squeals. Instead of turning on the radio or television for company, she purposefully let the quiet cloak her. She noticed that her heartbeat squelched the flurry of thoughts that usually assailed her. Concentrating on a deep eight-count breath, then letting it out, she repeated that until she felt more at peace.

She got up and walked into the kitchen, ready to embrace the rest of the day. She filled a stockpot with water and began working on a big batch of spaghetti. She had three burners going: one with the ground beef; another with a garden mixture of tomatoes, celery, and onion; and boiling water that was about ready for the noodles to be dropped in. The sizzling and bubbling water made its own melody.

I'm going to do better. I'll ask for help. I'm saying it. I need help. "I need help." Her voice sounded unrecognizable, and that caught her off guard.

"I need help." Pushing back the guilt and just saying it was somehow freeing. She turned to be sure the kids were still outside and couldn't overhear. "I need help with the kids. With . . . things around here." She lifted her hands as she looked around the kitchen. It was tidy, but there were some things that needed a skilled touch, like the leak around the faucet handle and the wobbly cabinet door next to the sink.

Why was it she hadn't asked for help all this time? "I'm being strong for you, Jack. For us. For the kids. Being strong doesn't mean having to do it alone, though, does it? I need help, and that's okay. Right?"

The wooden spoon that was balanced across the boiling spaghetti fell into the pot, sending her skittering backward.

Her hand on her heart, she laughed as she realized what had happened and fished the spoon out of the pot and set it aside.

The kids seemed happy enough playing in the sandbox in the backyard today, so she left them to their own imaginations while she cooked a family-size batch of baked spaghetti to split between them and Maeve. It wouldn't be right to have tempted her with the mention of it and never deliver on it. Who didn't love spaghetti? The best part was it got better each time it was reheated.

It was nice to have an excuse to use her fresh herbs. She pulled down an Italian blend she'd dried last week and sprinkled it over the pot of simmering vegetables. The herbs changed the aroma in the kitchen.

She lowered the temperature on the stove to let the sauce bubble and padded to the living room, where she sat at the end of the couch. Tucking her feet beneath her, she reached for the journal Maeve had given her. There was an ink pen inside. She pulled it from the leather loop and clicked it. With slow, intentional movements, she wrote her name at the top of the second page.

Amanda Whittier

She closed the journal and reached up to tuck it on top of the row of paperback novels on the shelf behind her. At the last moment, she pulled it back, opened it, and wrote:

I will not be afraid to ask for help.

15

Amanda lifted her hand to knock on Maeve's front door. Popping in on Maeve had seemed like a wonderful thing to do when she was cooking. Now as she stood there with the casserole dish—*a dreaded casserole dish*—with Jesse and Hailey at her side, she hoped the visit would play out like it had in her mind.

She knocked, hoping for the best but feeling more awkward the longer she stood there. A cheerful flip-flop wind sock rippled in the air. On a really breezy day, it probably looked like a giant ready to step on the awning of the huge house.

A wind chime made from shells hung by the handrail.

Jesse and Hailey played on the stairs. "You two be careful."

The door opened, and Maeve's face lit up. "What a wonderful surprise!" She clapped her hands.

"I made that spaghetti I was talking about." She waved the kids to hurry up.

"You are too sweet. Hello, Hailey and Jesse. Thanks for visiting."

"Don't kill me. I brought food, but I promise it's not a nine-by-thirteen casserole dish of it." She held it up in front of her. "See? Just an eight-inch. And you can freeze it if it's too much for this week."

"No worries. We know all about those, don't we?"

Amanda held out the pan wrapped in a dish towel.

Maeve took it and lifted the foil from the corner. "My favorite. Spaghetti. This smells good. And to think I was going to eat tuna and crackers tonight. Not anymore." She motioned Amanda and the kids inside.

"This is for you too," Hailey said, raising the muslin-wrapped lavender and salts to Maeve.

"Thank you. What a beautiful gift." Maeve balanced them on top of the covered dish. "Come on in."

"I would've called," Amanda explained, "but I never got your last name or asked for your phone number. I hope we didn't interrupt anything."

"Not a thing. My last name is Lindsay, by the way. Come meet Methuselah." The kids hurried to catch up with Maeve, who had disappeared into the kitchen with the spaghetti but was now sweeping through the living room toward the full wall of windows and doors.

Amanda stopped. "Wow! This is a million-dollar view."

Maeve paused, as if she'd never noticed. "Well, I guess it is. Thanks for reminding me. I should appreciate it more." She stepped outside and Methuselah leaped to his feet, his tail wagging against the rocking chair. His nose sniffed the air.

"He's friendly," she said, sitting down in the rocker.

The kids dropped to their knees to play with him.

"Isn't he cute?" Hailey said.

"He's a mess," said Maeve. "Needs his nails cut. Be careful. Don't let him scratch you."

"*Methuselah* is a weird name," Hailey said.

"I'm going to call him Lala." Jesse had a way of making things work to his liking with no apologies. "Come on, Lala." He walked up and down the balcony, and the dog followed. "Sit. Stay."

"I see your children are quite the dog trainers."

"We got Denali when he was eight weeks old."

"He took forever to train," Hailey said.

Methuselah got up and lapped from the big ceramic bowl next to Maeve's chair, then wiped his chin on her skirt as he turned. "He likes to pretend that's an accident. I know better." Maeve flipped her hand in the air as if it were nothing. "You look very pretty today, Hailey."

Hailey half curtsied, pulling her sundress up on one side as she did. "We went to church today. I made another friend."

Maeve tilted her head back to Amanda. "The church up the street here?"

Amanda nodded.

"I went there when I was Hailey's age. It's a beautiful church." Maeve reached over and squeezed Amanda's hand. "That's great. I'm glad you enjoyed it."

"I don't know how it all fell into place, but I'm pretty sure I have you to thank for it."

"Me?" She shook her head. "No."

"Yes. There's something special about you. I'm very thankful for whatever it is."

"I'm just an old lady living my life the best way I know how."

"Well, you've touched mine."

"Well . . ." Maeve took in a breath. "Then I suppose it's what you needed. That's how life works. The right things at the right time."

"I thought we'd do a ride by the Paws Town Square you were talking about. Would you like to come with us?"

Maeve's shoulders drooped. "As much as I've wanted to go, I'm feeling tired this afternoon. The man who owns the place is an absolute doll. Please let me have a rain check."

"Absolutely. Anytime. We love field trips, don't we, kids?"

"Yep." They both nodded.

"I'm hungry. It's time for spaghetti," Jesse announced.

"No, Jesse, we'll eat when we get home. That was for Maeve."

She chuckled. "Jesse was born hungry, but I guess it's time I get these two home and feed them."

"You won't stay and join me?"

"Can we, Mom?" Hailey rose on her toes.

Amanda hadn't even considered that more than the meal, the company might be better appreciated. *Where are my manners?* She hadn't meant to impose themselves on the old lady. "Are you sure? I didn't bring this over to take up your entire day."

Maeve got up and gestured toward the house. "Don't be silly. It'll be nice. Hailey, you can help me dish it up." Hailey raced to catch up with Maeve in the kitchen.

So it was decided. Amanda stood there for an awkward moment, unsure of how to help or stay out of the way, when Hailey came back with napkins and utensils in her hands.

"Miss Maeve said we can eat out here on the patio."

"That will be nice." Amanda held the door open for Hailey, then went in the kitchen to gather plates.

"I thought we could use these heavy-duty plastic plates. Nothing to clean up."

"Works for us. What can I do?"

"Not a thing. Hailey and I can handle this."

Hailey returned, ready to be of service.

Maeve handed her a plate of baked spaghetti. "Take this one out for your mom, and then come back for Jesse's. I'll get ours."

"Okay." Hailey delivered the plate and came right back.

Maeve handed her Jesse's spaghetti. "I've got the rest."

When all the plates were delivered, Amanda and the kids gathered around the table and sat. Maeve went back into the kitchen for drinks.

"I love spaghetti," Jesse said.

"Let's use our good manners, okay, you two?"

"Yes ma'am." Hailey's and Jesse's voices blended like a song that touched her heart, their sweet faces beaming.

Maeve stepped through the doorway, carrying a dated golden-colored glass pitcher and a stack of paper cups. The pitcher sloshed, ice tinkling against the sides as she set it down.

Amanda folded her hands, and Hailey and Jesse began singing the blessing.

She couldn't help but notice Maeve's eyes tearing as they sang. She knew that feeling. Their purity touched her in these moments.

What have I done keeping our life so small?

Amanda pulled her car out onto the old beach road. It was only a short distance to the new four-lane highway. Paws Town Square sat off to the left. She was glad to see something being revived. Maybe if it was a success, more people would start re-purposing the old places rather than starting from scratch.

Whatever the old store was before it became Paws Town Square wasn't recognizable now. It looked like an official town square, clock tower and all. The parking lot had been repurposed, too, which made sense. How much parking did a kennel need? Most was pickup and drop-off.

"Is it a carnival?" Hailey pressed her nose to the glass. "Look at the water fountains!"

"Oh my goodness. This place is really cool." Amanda took her time through the long stretch of outdoor activities available. Dogs ran and played, their tongues hanging out and tails wagging.

"Denali would love it here."

Jesse shouted, "Go-kart track!"

"No, that's just a walking path." Amanda could see where

he would get that idea, the way it swerved and curved around the patches of green. "Want to take a tour?"

Their cheers rang in her ears.

Amanda pulled into a parking spot near the front doors, which looked more like the stairs of a courthouse. They went inside and took one of the maps that outlined the entire facility. There was a walking tour that was open and free to the public. "This looks like fun."

The shops on this floor were retail specialty stores. The Barkery offered dog-friendly baked goods to share with your pet, purchased as onesies or in bulk. A store called the Yap that imitated America's favorite youth clothiers carried custom collars, leashes, and bandannas. Toy Town featured nontoxic unbreakable toys for dogs of all sizes, including dog Frisbees for the Frisbee park outside. The spa was so fancy with its marble floors and high-shine accessories she wondered if they might take her in to get her nails done. The Veterinarian and FarmAcy took up the far end of the building, and from the looks of things, they were already doing a booming business.

Signs led to the free walking tour. From there she could see other trails active with dogs and handlers.

Amanda caught the attention of one of the workers, easily identified by the Paws Town Square logo on his shirt. "So, are all of these dogs being boarded, or is there a program for residents to bring their dogs here for walks?"

"You can get a day pass or even sign up for year-round access. Lots of people bring their dogs a couple times a week to walk them when the weather's bad or too darn hot like it is right now. I was just outside like ten minutes. Look at me." Sweat glistened on his brow. "Can't blame them folks for wanting to escape the heat. There's a few different levels if you want to use the water park or agility areas. The dogs down on that trail are all being boarded. We schedule their walks and runs throughout the day."

"What a neat idea!" She mirrored his enthusiasm.

"Yes, most definitely. And it's more than just dog boarding. We have programs to help bring former soldiers with PTSD to our workforce. We've matched pets with people, and we do some in-house canine training for companion dogs. It's a great company to work for."

"Wow. Sounds like it!" Too bad she hadn't heard about this before she accepted her teaching job. "Who wouldn't love to get paid to play with dogs all day?"

"Tell me about it. And the benefits are good too." He glanced at his watch. "I need to catch up to an appointment. Can I answer anything else for you or connect you with someone?"

"No. We're just going to look around. I have the flyer."

"Great. Well, I hope we'll see you back around here with your dog one day."

"Maybe you will."

He darted off into a jog.

"He was nice, wasn't he?" Amanda said.

Hailey and Jesse nodded. They seemed mesmerized by the number of dogs.

The three of them followed the road signs and entered the large-dog area of the facility. They stopped and stood on the visitors' side of the big-dog park. The pace there was slower, but the breeds were huge. A Great Dane walked to the low fence that separated the walkway from the park and hung his head over the railing in front of Jesse.

He tentatively lifted his hand. "Horsey?"

"No, Jesse. That's a dog. A very big dog."

A woman wearing a Paws Town shirt came over. "This is Duke. He's very friendly." The shiny black dog lifted his chin in the air and tucked his nose under her armpit.

The woman wiggled away. "That tickles." She brushed him aside. "He knows it tickles. He does it all the time."

"Can I pet him?" Hailey asked.

"Sure. Call his name. He'll come right to you."

"Hi, Duke." She waved her hand, and the dog walked over for some attention. "Nice doggy." Hailey's fingers swooped across the top of Duke's head and down his ears.

"He's here on vacation with his family," the woman explained. "They drove all the way from New Jersey with this guy."

Hailey's nose wrinkled. "Is that far away?"

"It is a very long drive, but they didn't want to vacation without him, so they checked him in here since no pets are allowed at Plantations Resort. They come visit him every day."

"I bet he really likes that," Hailey said. "He's sweet."

"Yeah, he's part of their family. They said they'd had him since he was just six weeks old."

Amanda reached over and petted the dog too. "I thought our English bulldog was big. This makes him look like a Chihuahua."

At that moment a beautiful tricolor shepherd ran the perimeter of the fence and then lay down on a boat-shaped bench next to a small water feature.

Amanda was captivated by the dog's grace. "He's beautiful."

"That's Gunner. He's a retired officer." The woman swung around and whistled. The dog stood and ran to her side. "*Sedni.*"

He sat, ready for another command.

She placed her hand out flat and said, "*Lehni.*"

"What language is that?" Hailey's head cocked to the side. "Is it dog language?"

"It's *this* dog's language. He's a military working dog. Or was. He knows all the same commands as the other dogs, but in Czech." She leaned over the fence and whispered, "That way the bad guys don't know the commands. Pretty sneaky, huh?"

Hailey nodded. "Gunner must be smart."

"He'll be with us until his owner gets out of the hospital."

"He looks like he has some age on him. I should give him the name of my hairdresser. She does wonders," Amanda teased.

"Yeah, he's a good old boy."

"Well, this is quite a place. We've had a lot of fun just visiting."

"You should stop at the front desk and get a week pass. Next time bring your dog with you. We offer a free trial for Whelk's Island residents, and honestly, the price of the day passes are ridiculously cheap. I bet you and your dog would enjoy a day here. The outside areas are a lot of fun too."

"Thanks. We'll check that out." They waved to the handler, then followed the walking path back to the main entrance.

Amanda stopped at the front desk to get a pass. It would give her and the kids another thing to break up their routine, and it would be good for Denali.

With the pass in her hand, she and the kids walked back out to the car.

"Climb on in." She helped Jesse into his seat and then went to the other side to double-check Hailey's seat.

"Can we come back?" Jesse asked.

"And bring Maeve?" Hailey added.

"We sure can." Amanda wished her children held the same kind of regard for her parents. They'd taken so quickly to Maeve. Amanda's parents had been around so seldom since she married Jack that they didn't play a big role as grandparents. They sent the obligatory gifts at the holidays, but she was pretty sure that if Mom and Dad showed up right now, neither of her children would recognize them.

16

Monday morning rolled around and
Maeve dreaded going to the doctor, but the appointment had
been set a month ago, and it was too late to cancel. Same-day
cancellations were downright rude. The only excuse was death,
and she wasn't there yet.

It was a dreary Monday on top of it. The rain spit and spat-
tered against the deck, and of course here she was, dressed and
ready to go an hour early.

She pulled on her red rain jacket and stepped outside. The
rhythm of the waves soothed her as she leaned against the railing. The wood had long ago weathered to a silvery gray,
smooth from decades of nature's sandblasting from the beach
below. She tied her hood around her face to keep her hair, almost as silvered as the deck now, from getting tangled in the
weather. A gust of wind slapped her skirt against her matching red rain boots.

She gathered the skirt's fabric in her hand, holding it tight
to keep it from blowing as she watched the ocean's dance, delighted the waves were at work pushing new treasures from its
depths during these storms. Shells from the creatures who'd
outgrown them, and sea glass that had tumbled so long that
every sharp edge was polished smooth. Occasionally, rem-
nants of shipwrecks off the coast of North Carolina would
wash ashore—at least she liked to believe the shipwreck part.

She'd been known to make up a splendid story or two about the things she found along the shore, even if she kept most of those stories to herself.

Rainy days left her eager to get out on the beach.

Hopefully, she'd make it back from her doctor's appointment in time to collect shells before the tide stole them away. But sometimes her doctor visits took nearly all day.

She glanced at her watch. *If you're early, you're on time, but if you're on time, you're late.* She went back inside, fed Methuselah, gathered her wallet, and locked up.

Outside she carefully navigated the stairs to the ground level. Her baby sister, Judy, complained about her living alone in their childhood home, but she and Judy never lived here at the same time. There were so many years between them that Maeve had already married and moved out of the house when Judy was born. Maeve had always felt more like a mother to Judy. Now Judy thought she wanted to take care of Maeve. Funny how things came full circle.

Maeve gripped the handrail. With the added weight of her rain boots, the descent was tricky. Judy wasn't wrong about their old family home being too big for one person or that the stairs were dangerous. Maeve herself had tried to get Mom and Daddy to close in the bottom level of the house years ago for the same reason.

She was older now than her parents had been then. *They were so hardheaded.*

A big raindrop plopped against her hood. Her face twisted as she glared toward the heavens. *Okay, so I'm a little hardheaded too.*

She walked down the path from her house toward the beach road. Used to be from here she could see across the way to the houses on the sound side. Whelk's Island wasn't that wide. Just a narrow strip of land, the ocean on one side and the sound on the other. Who'd have thought someday they'd have a four-lane highway that ran for miles connecting all these small barrier islands together?

When Maeve reached the doctor's office, she removed her coat and shook it out before going inside.

"Please tell me you didn't walk down here in this rain." Courtney, the nurse at the front desk, tapped her pen on the counter.

"A little water never killed anyone." Maeve hung her wet coat on the rack and then walked over and wrote her name on the check-in sheet.

"You know we could have arranged for someone to come get you."

"I know, I know, but it's not that far. Walking is good. Keeps me young."

"But this weather—"

"Good enough for ducks, good enough for me. It makes me a bit achy, but that won't stop me."

"You won't be saying that if you catch pneumonia."

Maeve turned and leveled a stare at Courtney. "You know better. Can't catch a cold from walking in the rain. It's always caused by bacteria or a virus. Now quit giving me a hard time." She started toward one of the chairs, then shifted and asked, "Is Doc running late today?"

"Not too bad. Have a seat. We'll get you right in and out."

"Low tide is at 3:24 this afternoon." Maeve tapped the face of her watch. "You know I don't want to miss that."

Courtney tilted her head the way she always did when she was going to give Maeve unsolicited advice. "Yes ma'am. I'm well aware. We've got you covered."

Maeve sat in the waiting area. She smiled at the tall redhead sitting with an adolescent boy at her side. Next to them, a man slumped in a chair. He looked like he hadn't slept in a week. She rummaged through the magazines, picking up one she thought she might not have already read. No such luck. All of them were months old. She tossed the magazine back on the table, half tempted to steal the lot of them to force them to bring fresh ones in. Crossing her leg, she bobbed the toe of her red boot. Wearing them always cheered her.

She sat quietly, listening to the conversations beyond the counter. How could those nurses not realize everyone sitting out here could hear everything they said? A minute later, Courtney came to the door and called Maeve back.

"How've you been feeling, Miss Maeve?"

"Getting old isn't for sissies." She stepped on the scale without being asked. She knew the routine.

"Well, it'd be easier if you'd let us get you some help."

Maeve waved off the comment. They'd had this conversation over and over again.

"I only mention it because we care about you."

"Thank you, but I'm fine," Maeve said, doing her best not to scowl. "I've made it this far alone."

"Room B," Courtney said.

Maeve walked down the hall and got comfortable. There was always a wait.

After a while, the doctor knocked at the door and entered. "Good to see you today, Maeve. How're you feeling?"

"Do we really have to go through the pleasantries? I'm dying. We both are keenly aware of it."

"Need more pain medicine?"

Her lip trembled. "Yes. I'm getting low."

"Thought you might be. The tests came back." He leaned against the cabinet, her file resting on his leg. "I'm sorry, Maeve. You're declining. I'm guessing you can probably feel the changes. Am I right?"

She nodded.

"We can still try some treatments if you've changed your mind."

"No. We won't be doing that."

"I didn't think so, but I had to ask. You've fought a good long fight." He flipped the folder against his leg. "You might really think about getting a Senior Helper, Maeve. Someone to lighten the load, help you prepare meals and clean up. Keep you company, even."

She stared at him for a long moment. "I promised Judy I'd go live with her when the time came."

"She's left me plenty of messages in that regard." The doctor clucked his tongue.

She shook her head. "I'm good to my word. It's time, isn't it?"

"You're an amazing lady, Maeve. I sure wish there was more I could do."

"I'll be with Jarvis sooner rather than later." A strange assurance came over her. "It's all I've really wanted for more years than you probably care to remember."

"More than I can count," Doc said without remorse. "You've been a handful at times."

"Don't I know it," Maeve conceded.

"Let me know how we can make you comfortable or if the medicine doesn't help with the pain anymore. I've got some numbers here for you. Courtney will make the calls if you need—"

"I'll handle things." She stood and gave him a hug. "You've been a wonderful doctor and a dear friend all these years. To me. To Mom and Daddy. Thank you."

She got up, grabbed her things, and walked straight out of the office. There was no reason to make another appointment to follow up. Everything from here forward was just a matter of time. She'd make the best of what she had left. What else could she do?

Outside the rain had stopped and a beautiful rainbow soared over the buildings in front of her. From here it looked like one end led straight to her house. She walked slower going home. Not from the news, but more to savor every step, every memory, along the way.

She stopped and took a seat on one of the benches around the flagpole in front of the post office. Someone had come and switched out the flowers since the last time she was here. Soon they'd be trading out all the red, white, and blue for fall-colored mums and pumpkins.

A clump of small shells, mostly bivalves, lay near the outer edge of the planter in the fresh potting soil. She scattered them with her hand, then sat there with her fingers still hovering as she noticed the words carefully scrawled inside one of them.

Say goodbye to the past,
because it's time to move on.

She picked up the shell and squeezed it in her palm. Her heart raced. It was possible she'd written the message in this shell at some point. She'd penned so many over the years she couldn't really say for sure, but this message, at this time?

She swallowed hard. The shell was small, but those few words held so much power.

It didn't matter where the shell had come from. This message was meant for her.

"Well, what do you know? I guess it really is time to call you, Judy." She looked up the street, then back up at the rainbow, thinking of Jarvis.

* * *

Amanda couldn't believe the amount of foam on the beach.

"It snowed!" Jesse leaped in the air. "Can I go see?"

"Take your sister with you."

They didn't have to get all the way down to the water to see it. The tide was receding, and mounds of foam covered the sand. Some of it blew across the beach and into the air, almost like snow.

"Wow! It's like Christmas!" Hailey chased Jesse through the foam.

Amanda set their things down and jogged down to join them. "Is it fun?"

Jesse picked up dissolving handfuls and flung them in the air.

Hailey cupped her hands, blowing the foam like it was a fluffy dandelion.

"What a surprise! I've never seen anything like this." Amanda chased and played with them at the edge of the surf line until they were all out of breath.

"Snow is good anywhere and any day." Hailey sat in the sand, sweeping her hands through it. "Too bad you can't make a snowman out of this kind."

"You could make one out of sand and cover it in the sea foam."

Hailey's mouth dropped open. "Yeah. Jesse, come help."

Jesse came over and flopped down next to Hailey and started to dig. Amanda watched the two of them pile and slap together the sand into something that looked more like a bowling pin than a snowman, but she gave them an A for effort. Getting the foam to stay on their creation was another story. The more they patted it, the quicker it dissolved. Finally, Hailey added shells for eyes. "I think he's done."

"This is Frank." Jesse put his hands on his hips. "Frank Beach Snow."

"Hi, Frank." Amanda loved how much happiness they found on this beach each day, and it was free for the taking. "Come on, kids. Let's get some sunscreen on before we get sunburned." The rain that had come through this morning had given way to bright sunshine.

They followed her and stood like soldiers, spinning as she sprayed them.

"Ready to roll," she said, spreading the excess over her own face and arms.

Jesse picked up his toy bag and dumped three small trucks and a tractor out into the sand. "Let's make a race."

Hailey took the big lime-green tire truck and carried it off to the side, where she made long sweeping movements. "I'm making the big turns."

With a truck in one hand and a tractor in the other, Jesse rushed to her side and started creating a mound of dirt.

Amanda sat and closed her eyes, satisfied with their purring motor noises and collaboration nearby. Every time Jesse made the beeping sound imitating the backup alarm on his truck, she shook her head. How did he even know that?

"Back it up, bub." His voice was gruff and insistent. "Hurry along."

Amanda loved how creative they were. They could entertain themselves for hours.

She was just beginning to exhale when a scream pulled Amanda out of her zone.

Hailey? Her eyes popped open. Her heart pounded as she scanned the water. She'd only taken her eyes off them for a moment. The ocean was dangerous. Frantic, she jumped to her feet.

Another scream. Another high-pitched pulsing sound.

Jesse stood at the water's edge with his trucks in his hands, staring back toward the beach. His tummy poked out as he watched, stunned.

Hailey ran, her feet pushing sand with each step, her arms out and fingers splayed as she moved.

Amanda raised her hand over her eyes. The silhouette of a man in an easy jog down the beach made her heart catch in her throat.

"Hailey!" Amanda spun, tripping in the twisting sheet beneath her. "Wait!" She struggled to her feet, trying to get traction in the deep sand. "What happened, Jesse?"

His mouth was in a soft O.

Amanda realized that it was Hailey screaming, and then it registered. She was screaming "Daddy" and running toward a man on the beach.

"Hailey!" The harder Amanda tried to hotfoot it down to the water's edge, the farther Hailey seemed to slip away from her. Amanda's chest burned, her eyes stung. *Daddy?* "No. It's not . . ." She ran harder. "Hailey, stop."

The sun beat down in long streaming rays, hot and bright. Her breath caught. If she didn't know better . . . but it couldn't be. Jack was gone. "It's not him." She slowed, trying to catch her breath.

Hailey screamed for him again. "Daddy!" Not a panicked scream, but a squeal of delight.

"No! Hailey, stop. Please stop." She watched as Hailey flung herself at the stranger. Her arms wrapped around his waist, her face against him as if she were clinging for life.

"I'm so sorry." Amanda uttered the words, but her brain couldn't keep up.

"Daddy, I've been waiting," Hailey said.

The man squatted down, his knees dipping into the water as he put his hands on her daughter's shoulders. "Hailey?"

Hailey wrapped her arms around his neck. "I knew you would come back."

He placed his large hand across her back, raising the other with his palm up.

Don't you touch my daughter. Her breath seemed to solidify in her chest.

The man's eyes locked with hers.

She stumbled to a stop as the familiar face registered. She took a step back.

"Amanda." He stood, with Hailey still hanging on him. "It's you?"

She stood there, confused and trying to grasp what just happened. She knew it wasn't Jack, but she clung to his name, his familiar face.

Just then Maeve came up to them, her hand tightly holding Jesse's. "What's happening?" Alarm etched her face. "I was coming up the beach from the house when—"

"I don't . . ." Amanda closed her eyes. Tears streamed down her face as she huffed, trying to catch her breath. She stepped back, shaking her head.

Paul Grant stood there looking at her.

"Oh my gosh." They were the only words she could string together. He looked the same. The hair, the tan. Wasn't like she hadn't seen him in just shorts and sweaty hundreds of times before. They'd been inseparable: her, Paul, and Jack.

"Amanda, I didn't know—"

Amanda snatched Hailey from him. She wrapped her arms around her, rocking her. "You scared me to death. Hailey, that's not Daddy." She breathed in the familiar scent of her baby's hair. "Don't ever run from me again. You're okay. Shh."

Hailey cried quiet tears. "I thought . . ." Her body lay against Amanda, soft like a rag doll.

"I know, baby. It's okay."

She could feel him still watching them. "You're okay. It's Paul. Do you remember? You were so little."

"What is going on?" Maeve demanded an answer.

"I was a friend. Am a friend of theirs . . . hers—"

"He was the best man in our wedding." Amanda stared at him, still hardly able to blink.

"Thank goodness." Maeve let go of Jesse's hand. "What a small world. You can't be too careful these days. Are we okay here?"

"Yeah." Amanda nodded, swallowing hard. "Hailey, honey, it's Paul. See?"

Her daughter slid off her and stood, facing Paul. "I thought it was Daddy. I've been praying so hard for him to come home so we can be happy again."

Amanda's heart froze right there. In that moment, it seemed to fall into a thousand shards around her. Hailey wasn't doing okay. She felt Jack's absence, her sorrow. For all the efforts to protect them from the grief she was trying to survive herself, they still had to go through it too.

"Hailey, I'm sorry. I didn't mean to get you all excited . . ." He held his hand to his heart. "Amanda, I had no idea. I didn't know you were . . ."

"How could you? I didn't tell anyone." She inhaled and then threw her arms around his neck. "Paul, I can't believe it's you."

He looked confused. "I didn't think I'd ever see you again."

"I live here now."

"It's so good to see you," he said.

"It's really you." She'd wondered what she'd say to him if she ever saw him again, how she could apologize for her behavior. "I'm so sorry I was unkind. It wasn't your fault."

"I wanted to call you a hundred times."

"I don't blame you for not calling. I told you not to. How can you ever forgive me?"

"Please don't push me away again." He held his arms out to Hailey. "Hailey, do you remember me? You were my little Lightning Bug. Remember?"

Hailey nodded slowly but inched over and clung to Amanda's legs.

"I can't believe how big Jesse has gotten. He's the spitting image of Jack."

"He is." Amanda looked at Jesse standing there next to Maeve. "I'm sorry. Paul, this is my friend Maeve. She lives up the beach from here." Amanda gestured between the two. "Maeve. Paul."

Maeve gave him a nod. "I know Paul. That was quite an entrance."

"Not intentional. I promise."

Amanda shook her head, then explained to Maeve. "Between the two of them, Paul and Jack, Paul was always the quiet one. They were best friends when I met them."

Paul looked concerned. "Hailey, are you okay? Jesse, do you remember me?"

Jesse shook his head.

Amanda held out her hand. "Come here, Jesse." She took her son's hand in her own, then turned back to Maeve. "There was a time when the three of us—Paul, Jack, and me—were always together. We've shared a lot of memories."

"We have."

"You looked like Jack jogging up that beach." She lifted her other hand, gracefully outlining the shape she could still see so vividly in her mind. "The silhouette. The way you move. I mean, the sun was behind you, but yeah. I thought . . . I mean, for a second . . ." She stood there blinking, not a single word coming to her, just that image. So much like Jack.

Maeve broke the silence. "Would you two like to catch up? I could take the kids back to my house or sit with them at yours. I'd be happy to do that. Hailey and Jesse, would you like to spend some time with me so your momma can visit with Paul?"

Hailey walked from Amanda to Maeve, never turning her back on Paul, as if she thought he might disappear. "Yes ma'am." She took Maeve's hand and then grabbed Jesse's with her other.

"Thank you, Maeve." She let go of Jesse's grip. "Take them to our house. It's closer. They can show you where everything is. I promise we won't be long."

"You take what time you need. We'll make do. I bet they have a thousand things to show me."

Amanda watched Maeve walk Hailey and Jesse over the dune. As soon as they cleared it, she sobbed. "I don't know what I'd have done if something happened to Hailey."

Paul lifted her into his arms. "It's okay. Everyone is all right. Come on. I'm sorry. I had no idea. Wow. You were the last person I ever expected to see again."

His shoulder bore the same tattoo that had been on Jack's shoulder. She'd always hated that he'd marked his body like that, but it was a Marine thing. Something she'd never understand or be a part of, but it made Jack the man he was, and she had loved every single thing about him. And he and Paul had done it all together. Two of a kind.

He guided her to the sand. "Sit down." His voice was so calming.

"No, I have some water and a beach blanket over here." She led him to their pile of stuff and sat. She took out two bottles and handed him one. "I can't believe you're here."

"I'm sorry I'm not Jack."

"Stop." It was hard to look at him again. They'd once been so close. He was like the other half of Jack. "Don't say that."

"I've asked a million times why I came back and he didn't. He had you, the kids, so much to come home to. I had nothing. It wasn't fair."

"No one ever promised us fair. There's not an answer to why. It took me a long time to accept that."

"Poor Hailey."

"We know he's not coming back. It was high hopes or dreams, adrenaline that got the best of us in the shadows. It's nothing you did."

He sat next to her and pulled his sunglasses from his face. He ran his hand over his eyes and then set his glasses on his knee. "When I found out that Jack died over there . . ." A glazed look of despair shadowed his expression. "If I hadn't taken the opportunity to work with the MP dogs, I'd have been there with him. That was the plan when we went in. That we'd be together." He clenched his fist.

"You couldn't have known what would happen."

He wore the pain in his blue eyes.

"It was a promise. I promised you on your wedding day I wouldn't let anything happen to him."

"Stop. He made his own decisions, and he could take care of himself. He could've taken a different assignment too. But he decided a six-month deployment was best. And if you'd been there with him, you'd have probably not come back either."

"Better than being back without him." He dropped his chin to his chest. "I regret it every day."

"I feel that too. It's hard to shake." Her lips trembled, making the words feel awkward. "Grief is so powerful. It'll drag you under."

"I'm still in shock that I'm sitting here with you." His eyes scanned hers. "You look like you're doing well."

She shook her head.

"How are you?"

"Surprised. Kind of wondering if I'm going to wake up." She pulled her legs underneath her. "I'm doing good now. Amazing in comparison to how I was two years ago. Last year was the worst." She pressed her hands together. "But now, most days I'm pretty good."

"We've been through a lot."

"Yeah. How are *you*, Paul?"

"Healing. Still kind of a work in progress."

She chuckled. "You always were."

"Ha. True."

"Sorry. Just playing."

"No. It's nice. Yeah, I just take it a day at a time. I struggled for a while. Really struggled. Got some help."

"That's hard to picture. You've always been so together. Controlled. Just like Jack."

"Thank you. I wasn't as tough as I thought I was, though. I shifted my focus from my loss to a way to help others. That's when I finally found some relief."

"That's good."

"My sadness kind of turned out to be a gift."

There's that talk of gifts again. Why is it so easy for everyone else to realize theirs?

She rubbed her hands together. She wondered if he'd noticed she didn't wear her ring anymore. "I don't know how I'd have gotten through it if I hadn't had Hailey and Jesse. They were the only thing that kept me getting out of bed every morning and putting my feet on the ground."

"So you live here now?"

"We moved here a couple months ago. I bought the house right on the other side of the dune."

His eyebrow lifted. "The tiny one tucked in the trees, next to the mega-mansion?"

"That's the one."

He shook his head. "You're not going to believe this. I put an offer on that house too."

"You're kidding."

"Nope. They told me there were other offers coming, so I made a full-offer bid, but they accepted another one. I guess it was you."

"That's so crazy that we were trying to buy the same house. What do you think the odds are of that happening?"

"About a million to one. Especially since neither of us ever lived in this town before. But that place felt so right."

"You felt it too?" She'd thought she'd been grasping at straws.

"Did you notice the Marine sticker on the surfboard?"

"Saw it. Yep." She laughed. "There was a postcard with Denali on it too. It was so strange."

"I didn't see that, but I did feel a connection when I walked inside. It wasn't the decor."

"No. Heavens, no. The place was a dump. But even so, I knew we could be okay there. I mean, it was at the top of my budget and still needs a ton of work. Upgrades have to wait, but I like it. It's turned into a cozy home for the three of us, and Denali, of course."

"I bet Denali has gotten big," said Paul.

"Oh yeah, and a handful, but Jack was right. We needed him. As much as I hated the idea of a dog, it turned out to be the best thing he could've left us with. Especially, well, you know . . ."

"All he ever wanted was for you to be happy."

"I know. I let him down for a while, but the kids and I are doing better now. We spend a lot of time out here on the beach. Maeve has been a great friend. We even went back to church."

"I'm glad to hear that."

"So, I bought this house from under you. Are you living nearby?"

"Yes, I am. I rented a house on the sound side." He twisted his sunglasses between his fingers. The silence lengthened between them. Finally he looked up. "Amanda, you mean the world to me. I want to be there for you, and the kids. Please let me."

"It's really good to see you again. I've missed you." She placed her hands over her heart. "I'd like to be friends again."

"I can't wait to catch up. I want to know everything." He pulled her into his arms.

She rested her head on his shoulder, smiling toward the heavens.

When I asked for help, I never expected this.

17

Paul walked with Maeve back down to her house. "I can't believe you know Amanda," he said.

"I could say the same thing." Maeve nodded, her eyes twinkling. "Incredibly tiny world we live in. Everything is so connected if you look close enough."

Thoughts were bumping through his mind. Amanda was here. He thought any hope of ever seeing her again was gone. "How'd you meet her?"

"Met her on the beach, through Hailey and Jesse a few weeks ago. Such sweet children."

"I was with Jack when I met her." Paul looked out toward the water. "I remember it as clear as if it were today."

"How long ago was that?" Maeve asked.

"Gosh, eleven years ago. They would've been married seven years now. You know her husband died about two years ago, right?"

"I do."

"We were best friends, Jack and I." He slowed his long stride for Maeve. "We were together when we met Amanda. One of my favorite Skynyrd songs was playing. I asked her to dance. She was just so lighthearted and happy. Not like anyone I'd ever met."

"What was the song? Do you remember?" Maeve asked.

"I do. It was 'What's Your Name,' and we were singing along

as it played. She reached up and whispered her name in my ear." He inhaled, remembering the zing that had rolled him that night. "Then I spun her around." Paul remembered every move, even the way she lowered her lashes when she politely laughed at his cornball jokes. "The three of us were together all the time after that."

"Kindred spirits." Maeve smiled gently. "She's a delight."

"I'd never met anyone so truly happy to just breathe the air." They turned up the beach toward Maeve's house. "You seriously walk this every day?"

"Sure do."

"I'm impressed."

"Well, I am impressed with you too, Paul. Amanda doesn't know about Paws Town Square?"

"No. She assumed I'm working with the MP dogs in the same capacity as when she last saw me, and I didn't correct her. I'm not sure how to tell her. I'm afraid she'll be disappointed in me for leaving the Marines."

"Why would she be? You're doing quite well."

"Her husband . . . he gave his life for this country. We were Marines together. It should have been me. He had a family. He had her." Paul took in a long breath. "After Jack died, and Amanda pushed me away, my whole life changed. It wasn't good for a while."

"Tell her." Her jaw set. "Don't leave a thing out. She'll understand."

He walked Maeve to the gate at the bottom of her stairs. "Thanks for inviting me to use your beach access. I had no idea it was about to change my life. I thought I'd never see Amanda again."

She nodded, making him feel like he needed to explain.

"Before Jack died . . . I'd promised her that I wouldn't let anything ever happen to him. I was the best man at their wedding. I'll never forgive myself for taking the new assignment that separated us. If I'd been there—"

"It wouldn't have done diddly." She pressed her finger against his chest. "You are not responsible for what happens in this world. There's only one Man who has that power." She pointed straight into the sky. "He knows what He's doing."

"But I—"

"No. No buts." The words were stern, but she lowered her hand, her expression softening. "You were in love with her, weren't you?"

He looked away.

"You can't deny it. It was in every tiny detail you described."

"It sounds so corny, but it was truly love at first sight, and it grew every day."

"Then how is it she married Jack?"

"I never told her. I've asked myself a million times why I didn't say something to her. It was timing. Bad timing on my part. I left to take care of my parents' estate when they died in a car accident. When I came back, I thought we'd just pick right back up, but the two of them had become more than friends."

"You never said anything? Not to either of them?"

"Of course not. I was Jack's best friend. One of us would be devastated if I said anything. I didn't want any of us to get hurt."

"So you took on that burden yourself."

"Maeve, you are an intuitive woman. Why am I telling you all of this?"

"Because you can. I'm an excellent listener. It's my thing."

"I can see that. Well, I will continue to use your little slice of heaven here at the beach if you don't mind. And one day I will run all the way down to the pier and back."

"I hope that's soon." She started for the gate. "Paul?"

"Yes ma'am."

"It's none of my business, but I think you should tell her the truth. You owe that to yourself, and to her. And mind your p's and q's." She leaned in and said with all intents of a warning, "She's still on unsteady ground. If you break that girl's heart, I'm personally coming after you. Do you understand?"

"Yes ma'am."

"Are you headed back over there now?"

"Yes."

"Good. Don't waste a moment. You never know how long your timeline is. Make every single day count and you'll have no regrets." She pressed her palms together. "I think you might be exactly what she needs in her life. I have a very high regard for you both."

She started up the steps but stopped and turned. "Another thing. She was supposed to start a home-based business when she moved here, but there was a snag and she's going to have to teach instead. Be a good listener. I bet you can figure something out together."

"Thank you." He headed to his truck, flattered and empowered by Maeve's words. Was there actually a chance that he and Amanda could be together? When Jack was alive, she was off-limits. Back then, he didn't care how broken his heart was—he loved them both and he wouldn't put Amanda and Jack's marriage at risk. But now . . . No one would sweep in and take her away from him this time.

He jumped into his truck and sat there and cried. Not tears for Jack. Not tears of anger. Tears of hope.

He'd thought the location here on Whelk's Island had been perfect because of its proximity to Camp Lejeune, but was it meant to bring him back into Amanda's life all the time? He'd never been one to believe in coincidences, but now faced with one, he could only hope.

The little voice in the back of his mind told him not to get ahead of himself. *If nothing else, I have fences to mend. I'm grateful for that second chance.*

As he steered the truck back onto the road, his heart beat so hard that he hoped he didn't wreck on the short drive over to Amanda's. That would be his luck. *I've got to see her again. Second chances like this don't happen . . . Not to me.*

He pulled in front of the house. That little shanty looked like a home now.

The message on that shell still sitting in his glove box popped into his mind. *Can there still be a chance?*

He hadn't specifically said he was coming right back, but by the time he opened his truck door, she was already heading out the front door with a huge smile on her face.

"This is us." She spread her arms wide as he approached the gate. The hinge creaked as she pushed it open. "I've used a whole can of WD-40 on that thing. There's no hope." She swatted at it.

"Redneck burglar alarm. Consider it an upgrade." He followed her into the yard. "And there's *always* hope."

They walked past Hailey and Jesse seated at a kid-size plastic table under a tree in the shade. Hailey sat at the head with two teddy bears and a baby doll, and Jesse was sipping from teensy pink plastic teacups. Hailey wore a tiara and held her pinkie extended. No surprise there. It's why he'd always called her Lightning Bug. She had a sparkle to her, that kid. Always had, just like her momma.

"Do you feel like this is a dream?" He tried to keep his tone from sounding too wistful.

"Sort of. I keep thinking about how mean I was to you."

"Stop. Don't apologize. It was a terrible time for everyone. I'm just pleased to see you looking so happy. You look just like I remembered." He followed her to the picnic table and they both sat down. "Hailey has gotten so big. She's losing that little-girl look."

He still remembered the day he and Jack stood at the nursery window at the hospital, looking at that little pink face peeking out from under the blanket. Her hands were so tiny. When Jack laid Hailey in Paul's arms, Paul was afraid her fingers might break if he touched them.

He and Jack had passed out pink-label cigars for days. By the time Jesse was born, they didn't bother with the cigars. Instead they filled the entire bed of Jack's pickup truck with boxes of Krispy Kreme "It's a Boy" doughnuts with blue filling. They'd even taken a picture of Jesse holding one of them. Well, not holding it, exactly. More like it dangling from his arm like a giant inner tube. He wondered if Jesse's favorite color was still blue.

"Wow, you've been busy with this place. What a difference." He glanced around the yard.

Pride perked at the edge of her smile. "Yeah, I paid my real estate agent's son to mow down everything that wasn't a tree so I could start from scratch. It made a huge difference."

"I like what you did with all the planter boxes. Your herbs?"

"Of course."

Hailey kept staring at him, and he wasn't sure what to say after this afternoon. Amanda noticed it too.

"Hailey and Jesse, Paul was Daddy's and my best friend. He was even there when you were each born."

Hailey got up and walked to their end of the table. "I've missed you."

"I've missed you too, Lightning Bug." When Hailey giggled, all those peekaboos, goodbye waves, and memories of carrying her from the car to the house came crashing in on him. "I'm sorry I've been away."

She reached out and touched his hand. "I'm glad you got to come back."

Unlike Jack. Those unspoken words hung on his heart. "Yeah."

"Don't ever leave us again." Hailey's lips pulled into a tight line.

"Hailey, that's not polite." Amanda looked mortified.

"That's fair," he said. "I don't want to leave again, Hailey. And, Jesse, do you know how big you were the last time I saw you?"

Jesse was a pint-size version of his best friend. Paul held his hand down at about the midpoint of his thigh. "Not much bigger than this high."

"I was little."

"You're a big boy now."

Jesse lifted his arms and made muscles. His body quivered as he struck the pose.

Paul reached over and squeezed his bicep. "Wow. You are strong."

"From digging moats. I'm a really fast digger. It makes your arms burn."

"I taught him everything he knows." Hailey stepped in front of her brother to vie for Paul's attention.

"I bet you two are a good team," he said.

"The best. Come on, Jesse. Let's finish the tea party." She sat back down, and Amanda and Paul watched them in an awkwardly weird but wonderful quiet.

Amanda spoke softly. "I hate that Jesse doesn't really remember Jack. I'm not sure how to keep all the memories alive without keeping the hurt around too. And Hailey . . . oh my gosh, if she doesn't end up a psychologist, I'll be shocked. That kid is so in tune with my moods. She can sense when I'm struggling. I hate that." Pain danced in her eyes.

"Perhaps Jack's working through them to make sure you're okay," Paul offered.

Her lips parted softly. "Hadn't really thought of that."

"You're a wonderful mother. If anyone can lead them through this, it's you. You know the way."

"Yes. I sure do," she said, pressing her hands together.

"I thought you might have gone back to Ohio. Your mom—"

She flipped a hand in the air to stop him. "That's a sore subject. She's been so determined to get me home that she's been no help at all."

"I'm sure she means well."

"You know how she can be," Amanda said.

It was true. Amanda and her mom had had their challenges over the years, but Paul knew after burying his parents that those matters didn't seem worth fighting over when they were no longer around to love.

She held her head high. "Our life is here now. It's a good place to be."

His whole life was here, too, although explaining that meant telling her that he'd left the Marines. She'd only ever known him as a soldier. Jack had died for this country. He'd wanted to fight for Jack's honor, but no matter what, he couldn't bring him back.

He wanted to tell her—Maeve seemed to think he should too—but it was too much to lay on top of the already emotional day. Instead, he rested his forearms on the table and leaned in.

"I'm so glad I saw you today. Thank you for letting me back in."

"I needed someone to blame, and your big shoulders were right there. You didn't deserve it, but I guess even that served a purpose. It made me figure it out by myself, and I needed that."

"My big shoulders are always here for you. For them. Please

let me help." He thrummed his fingers against the wooden picnic table. "I don't want to overstay my welcome, and actually I have some things to take care of this afternoon, but can I call you? Can we get together and keep . . . talking . . . pick up where we . . ."

"Sure." She stood up, a half smile on her face. "Oh, I guess you need my number, right?"

"Yeah." He stood, too, and handed her his phone.

She typed in her number and handed it back.

He pressed a button, and her phone rang from somewhere inside.

"I'll find that later," she said. "Thanks for coming by." She walked him to the gate and then, on tiptoe, hugged him around the neck. "Gosh, it feels good to get a real hug again. You always were the best hugger."

As much as he wished he could hug her all night, he let her go. "I'll call you." He backed up. "I'd better go." He opened the squeaky gate, his insides whirling. When he looked back, they were all waving.

Did this really happen?

He got in his truck, almost afraid to check his rearview mirror in case that cute house had turned back into the little abandoned shack that he'd try to buy a few months ago.

He started the engine.

His nostrils flared, trying to get air. Through Amanda and those children, his best friend lived on. His head and his heart were crossing swords over what this all meant and what he should do about it.

Bravely, he glanced back.

She stood there, her hand on the top of the gate.

He pressed his foot on the accelerator. Before he even realized it, he was pulling into his parking spot at Paws Town Square, thankful for second chances.

18

Maeve wanted to shepherd Amanda through to the other side of her loss, but she was comforted in knowing Paul would be there for Amanda too.

Time wasn't her own. The shell she'd found reminded her of that. She would call Judy. How crazy was this world that messages in shells found the right people and people's paths crossed at just the right time too?

It had been a hard call to make, but it couldn't be put off.

After talking to Judy, Maeve didn't have the energy to do anything but rest. She'd given herself permission to stay in bed all day if she needed to, but the ocean still called to her.

She set off on her walk a little later than usual.

Her heart lifted when she looked up and saw Amanda and the kids at the water's edge. Yesterday had been unsettling, even if it had ended well. It did her heart good to see their smiles.

"I thought you'd be exhausted after yesterday," Maeve said. "Didn't expect to see you out here today."

"It was definitely an emotional day." Amanda kicked the water in front of her with her toes. "Thank you for your help. That was so—"

Maeve raised her hand. "What friends do. I'm glad I happened along when I did. I don't think my heart has pounded that hard in years."

"Mine either." She patted her chest. "You have impeccable timing. You are a treasure."

Maeve made a delighted face for the kids. "Think that means I'm extra special?" She bent her knees, getting down to their level.

"Totally," Hailey said, and Jesse echoed her, as he did eighty percent of the time.

"Where are you going?" Jesse asked. "You don't have your bag for treasures."

"I'm going to walk down and say hello to Tug and The Wife."

"The bird!"

"Yes."

"I like that bird." Jesse flapped his arms like wings, stomping in the water, creating his own vortex.

"I like Denali," Maeve shared. "We had fun with him yesterday, didn't we?"

Jesse's head bobbed.

"He looks quite menacing, though," Maeve admitted to Amanda. "I was a little nervous at first."

"He looks burly and serious, but he's so good with the kids."

"How'd you come up with the name? Because he's more like a stump than a mountain?"

"Actually, Denali was somewhere Jack and I had always dreamed of going. To Alaska to see the highest peak in North America. The closest place to heaven. We'd been saving for it. Then the kids came. Then time just ran out."

"I've never been, but I've heard Alaska is lovely."

"Absolutely jaw-dropping landscapes. Undisturbed nature and the northern lights." She took in a breath. "I've been told you can hear them sizzle."

"You can still get there one day."

Amanda shook her head. "I think that ship has sailed."

"No. Not if it was in your heart. And he'll be there with you. It will always be, should be, a special place. You don't have to abandon everything because he's gone. You know that, right?"

"It would still be the trip of a lifetime," she agreed.

"And you've got a long life ahead of you."

"Did you and Jarvis have something you had always planned to do but didn't get the chance?"

"Gosh, no one has ever asked me that in all these years."

"I'm askin' now."

A thoughtful woman. So special. "Thank you for doing so. We did. We'd talked about spending a weekend in Charleston."

"That's not even five hours away."

"It may as well have been five days away because we never had the time to do it. We'd daydream about it, how it would be to walk under the grand trees with the Spanish moss hanging from the branches." She waved her hands in the air, as if she were envisioning it now. "Maybe I did more of that musing than he did. I don't know, but we enjoyed talking about it."

"That's half the fun."

"Dreams are good." When had she quit longing to see Charleston? She hadn't thought about that in years, although still now she could see the silvery moss in her mind. "I always thought some Spanish moss would look pretty hanging from the huge water oak in my backyard. Or maybe it would just look out of place."

"It probably would look pretty."

"Have you seen Spanish moss before?"

"Only in pictures."

"Me too. I've always wondered what it would feel like in my hand. Soft or stiff? Does it have a smell? Would it grow if you brought some home? I bet it would match the weathered gray of my house." When had she become such a talker? "Enough about me. What about Paws Town Square? Was it as neat as everyone says?"

"Yes. It was so much more than I expected. Walking trails. Dogs everywhere. Some playing together, some doing their own thing. And there were tons of handlers. They have indoor and outdoor trails too."

"I've heard most of those handlers start as volunteers. Some kind of coordinated effort between PTSD patients and the facility. I think they subsidize therapy for the veterans. I'm not really certain how it all works, but it's really neat. Takes a special man to build something like that." Maeve was pressing, wondering if Paul had told Amanda that he owned it. Knowing he and Jack had been friends filled in some blanks around the personal suffering that had driven him to do these good things. Lives touching lives.

"Even the facility design was an elaborate undertaking. I picked up a pass to give it a try. Denali doesn't do well in the heat, but he needs the exercise. The indoor trails are really beautiful. It's like walking in a park. You should come with us."

"I'd love to see it."

"You could even bring Lala," Jesse said.

"Only if they have a wagon." Maeve laughed. "That dog will be much happier left to his own routines. He's sort of a creature of habit, like me. I think I'll just tag along with y'all, if you don't mind."

"That works too," Amanda said.

"We're hungry, Mom." Jesse and Hailey stood at Amanda's side, looking like a couple of threatening seagulls begging for french fries.

"Aren't you always? I better get these guys fed."

"Why don't y'all come up to the house and have lunch with

me?" Maeve asked. "I made a big tub of tuna salad last night. Not the canned stuff. Tug gave me fresh tuna that he'd grilled. It's such a treat. I'd love to share it with y'all."

"Can we, please, Mom?"

"That's very nice. Thank you, Maeve. You said you were headed down to see Tug. We hate to ruin your plans."

"Don't be silly. Tug didn't even know I was coming."

"Great! Our things will be fine until we get back. Come on, kids. We're going to picnic at Maeve's house."

They got to Maeve's and hosed off their sandy feet before going inside. "Amanda and Jesse, you make yourselves comfortable on the deck. Hailey and I will bring the sandwiches out to you," Maeve said.

As Maeve made the sandwiches, Hailey hung at her hip. "Hailey, I'm going to go grab a platter. I'll be right back, okay?"

"Yes ma'am."

Maeve went across the hall into the sunroom, her favorite room of the house. When she was a child, it had been off-limits. The furniture had never even been sat on, not once that she'd ever seen. She'd cleared the room out and made it her own the first day she'd moved back in. It had been a work in progress ever since, growing and changing with Maeve's every trip to the beach.

The platter she'd been looking for was right there where she'd left it on the desk by the window.

She turned back to the door. Startled, she stopped. "Hailey? I didn't hear you come in."

"I got lonely waiting." Her head swiveled from one side of the three-windowed walls to the other. Not floor-to-ceiling windows like you might see in newer homes, but small individual panels, one framed above the other, each one a perfect three foot wide by two foot tall. Maeve knew because she'd used the deep wooden frames as shelves for her treasures.

At that moment, light hung around the child as though an angel had dropped her from the heavens. Hailey stood there mesmerized. "This is the prettiest room in the whole wide world."

The discovery of beauty from a child's eyes overwhelmed Maeve. She turned and looked at the treasures she'd collected. Her life's work.

"This is my sunroom," Maeve explained. "I like to come in here and relax while enjoying all the special things I've found."

Hailey's blond brows set in a straight line. "This isn't a sunroom. This is a shell room. Look at 'em all." She pointed her finger, air-tracing her way around each window. Taking it all in, and in no hurry at all. "They are everywhere." The last statement was barely above a whisper.

"Yes, they most certainly are." Maeve smiled at this little one. "Maybe more than my fair share."

"It's sparkly in here." Hailey blinked, then started toward the window that Maeve treasured the most. The one full of her most precious pieces of sea glass. "Look at these. They are like Christmas lights." She reached out and touched the outside of a tall apothecary jar filled with pieces of sea glass in shades of red, and she placed her finger over a brilliant orange piece. "Wow! That's the prettiest one."

"You have excellent taste. That's my most treasured piece."

Her eyes lifted.

"You can touch it. It's okay."

"Can I hold it?"

"Sure." Maeve walked closer and watched Hailey dip her hand into the jar to reach the dazzling nugget. She knelt down next to her. "It's the rarest color of all sea glass. My second favorite is this one." In a separate glass canning jar, Maeve picked up a cobalt-blue piece. "Look, it's the exact color of your eyes."

Hailey's eyes opened wide, and she pressed her face next to Maeve's hand as she held the sea glass, offering her the chance to compare the two. "I love this room."

"I do too. It's my happy place." The overstuffed white chair in the middle looked lonely now, but she'd never been lonely in this room. There was one other chair—a smaller one that she'd put a slipcover over—and then her momma's old Queen Anne ladies' writing desk.

For the first time, she pictured herself in this room differently: not alone but rather with Hailey and Jesse at her feet. It would be so much more colorful with their light in the room. Like shimmering curtains of sun with their energy and innocence in here.

Hailey leaned forward and whispered, "I can keep a secret. You're my new best friend." Hailey zipped her lips and threw away the key.

"You are my most special friend." Maeve took her by the hand and went back to the kitchen to gather lunch and take it outside.

Amanda and Jesse sang, "Row, row, row your boat gently down the stream."

Maeve carried the tray of sandwiches and drinks. Hailey opened the door, and the two of them joined in for the finale. "Life is but a dream."

"To dreams," Maeve said.

They ate lunch, and the afternoon offered a few puffy clouds that were a welcome relief on the scorching day. The conversation was easy, and the laughter made Maeve feel ten years younger. *Thank goodness I lived long enough to experience this.*

They finished eating and then Hailey got up. "Me and Jesse will take all the dishes to the kitchen." She collected plates, and Jesse gathered what he could. "We know how."

"Well, thank you." Maeve sat back in her chair, letting the two fuss around her. "That's quite wonderful. I feel like a queen for a day."

"Queen mermaid," Jesse said.

"That's our secret." As the two youngsters walked through the door toward the kitchen, Maeve sat there enjoying their delight. "Oh, Amanda. Remember when we were talking before and you said you had no gifts?"

"Yes. And I still don't have any." She took a sip of water and set her glass down with a bump.

"I beg your pardon. You, my dear, are a gift. Seriously, just the pure joy of being in your presence is a gift."

Amanda sputtered. "Oh right."

"No, I'm being serious. There's a sincere and gentle nature about you. Your honesty comes through, and it's . . . refreshing. Yes, you're refreshing." She understood exactly what Paul had seen in her the first time he and Amanda had met.

"Refreshing? Like a lemon-lime soda?"

"Ah, with effervescent bubbles. No, wait. Hailey and Jesse would be the effervescent bubbles." She reached over and took Amanda's hand into her own and gave it a squeeze. "I'm not trying to flatter you, and this isn't just some old lady spewing random thoughts."

Amanda sat back, looking a little uncomfortable.

"Listen to me. You bring light with you. You're bringing this old lady joy right now, and trust me, people who come into your path feel it too. I saw it when you were at the diner. The waitress. Tug. And even your friend Paul. I saw it in him. You think it has to be more, but what we get is enough. It's always enough. You just need to be yourself and listen to those brief whispers. Don't hesitate. Things are changing for you."

"Oh goodie." Amanda clearly thought she was joking.

"I'm serious. You wait. There is good change on your path.

I feel it." Maeve sat forward. "I saw you help that woman on the beach that day. The one with the husband who'd left with his cooler while she had to get everything else. That made a difference to her. It wasn't a craft or art or singing; it was you being you. You bolstered her when she needed help. You didn't think twice about taking action."

"Of course not. She needed a hand."

"The awe you inspire in your children as you share nature's bounty with them, at the ocean or anywhere—that's a gift. You have gifts you don't even recognize yet."

Amanda's laughter slowed to a thoughtful smile. "Thank you, Maeve. I hope you're right, but I will say this. Your friendship, you being on my path, has already touched my life in a very beautiful way, and for that I am grateful."

19

The next morning, Amanda read another passage from the book Ginny had given her. *I should have read it sooner.* She picked up the phone and dialed her. "Hey, gal. How are you? Did I catch you on your commute to work?" Amanda asked.

"Yes, lady of leisure, lounging on the beach. Some of us do have to work."

That was the nice thing about Ginny. No matter how much time passed between their chats, they were always easy. "I'll be doing it come fall. Of course, my commute is like two miles. I could ride my bike if it weren't for Hailey needing to get there too."

"You could get her a bike with a basket and a cute little pink helmet. You two would be adorable. Pink streamers on the handlebars, and playing cards clothespinned to the spokes."

"Yeah, that went out with our parents' generation."

"My dad put them on my bike," Ginny said. "I thought it was cool."

"Well, you always were a trendsetter."

"Thanks. So, what's new?"

"Settling in. Good routines. We love it here. The kids seem so happy. We spend a lot of time on the beach. It's heavenly."

"What's not to love?" Ginny teased. "Playing on the beach every day? I could suffer through it."

Amanda had thought to keep it to herself about Paul show-ing up, but she couldn't hold it in. "Guess who I ran into on the beach right in front of my house? You'll never guess. It was so unexpected."

"Don't tell me your parents finally came down."

"No. Not in a million years. Paul."

"Paul Grant, Paul?"

"Yep. Almost jogged right by us near the water one day. I was shocked." She didn't go into the whole we-thought-he-was-Jack part. That just made it sound a little too weird, even in her own head.

"You didn't bury him in the sand, did you? Is this the hey-best-friend-we-need-to-hide-the-body call? I've heard of those."

"No. I apologized for the way I acted."

"Thank goodness," Ginny said. "You needed to apologize. You were horrible to that man. I really felt bad for him."

"Misplaced anger. I know."

"I was just thankful it wasn't me you were shouting at. I'd never seen you like that."

"I can't believe he even wanted to talk to me."

"Especially after you told him he was just as dead to you as Jack was." Ginny sighed. "He knew you were hurting. I'm more surprised he never tried to contact you."

"No, he promised, and one thing about Paul—that man doesn't break promises."

"Even the promise to keep Jack alive?"

"Jack made that decision. Paul begged him to move over to another division with him, but Jack thought getting deployed for a shorter stint was a better trade-off. If he'd gone, maybe they'd both be here today, or maybe I'd have lost them both. I've made peace with that now. I knew it then, but I needed to blame someone."

"Honey, you've been through so much. I'm glad he's around. Paul's a great guy, and he was always a good friend to you."

"It's been really nice to see him." The words came out a little more wistful than she'd meant.

"Amanda, you deserve something nice. Something fun and happy. You're okay, right?"

"Yeah. I'm great. A little cautious maybe, but I'm fine."

"How'd he look?"

Like Jack. "Amazing. Better even, if that's possible."

"That's just wrong. How can a man be that good looking, and nice? And single?"

"He's just the same ol' Paul. Fun, sweet, thoughtful Paul." *And I can't wait to see him again, even though that feels so wrong.*

"Oh, sweetie. This is good. A big step. I'm really proud of you, although I feel slightly threatened about losing my position as best friend. I always thought he was sweet on you. This could be your second chance."

"Ginny! Stop that. I'm not looking for someone to fill a gap. I have the children to think of. Paul is a friend, but you'll always be my best friend. No one can take that from you."

"I'm holding you to that promise."

"You can. As long as you promise to come stay at the beach with me this year. Even if it's off-season and only two days."

"I will do that. I promise. Look, I've got to run. I'm in the parking lot. I can call you back when I get home from work if you need me to."

"No, no, I'm fine. I just wanted to tell you, and to thank you for always being there for me. I also wanted to thank you for the book you sent me."

"I didn't send you anything."

"Yeah, you did. Not recently, but back when Jack died. Honestly, I couldn't even bring myself to get through the whole inscription then."

"Girl, that was two years ago. I can't even tell you what the title of that book was if my life depended on it. I just didn't know what else to do."

"Yeah, well I couldn't bear to read it then, but it has been helpful lately. I've been reading a page a day. Thank you. It's been a long time coming. Might've been helpful if I'd read it when you gave it to me."

"You probably weren't ready then. Books are funny like that. If it doesn't seem right, set it aside and it'll be there when you're ready to hear the message."

"Thank you for the sweet words inside. They really mean a lot."

"I love you, Amanda. I'm so glad it helped, even if it did take two years to kick in."

Amanda disconnected the call and sat there curled at the end of the couch. She was lucky to have such good people in her life.

Hailey walked into the living room, wearing her polka-dot bathing suit and a pair of star-shaped sunglasses she'd begged for at the pharmacy checkout.

"Hey, glamour girl."

"Hello, dahling," Hailey said, dragging out the words in the most Southern of drawls.

"Oh my. Is it like *that*?" Amanda pretended to blow on drying nails. "I see. What can I do for you, Ms. Hailey Whittier?"

"I'm here to see if we shall go to the sandy beach today."

"Why, sugar, I do think that would be lovely. As soon as my nails dry."

"Your nails aren't wet," she said.

"Oh. So they aren't."

"Can we take our nail polish off like Miss Maeve's?"

"Sure. Go get the polish remover. It's under the bathroom sink. And some cotton balls."

Hailey went down the hall and came running back with the items. At the same time, Jesse came into the living room and lay on the couch beside her.

Amanda removed all the color from Hailey's nails and did Jesse's toes even though they were naked already. His feet were so ticklish he could hardly stand it. She cleared the polish from her own nails and then put the remover away.

"Beach?"

"Finally!" Jesse hopped to his feet.

They'd been on the beach about an hour when Paul showed up carrying a big bag.

"What are you up to?" she asked. "I didn't know you were going to be around today."

"I hope that's okay. How are you?" His smile reminded her of better days.

She raised her hand over her eyes, straining against the sun. "We're good."

"Mister Paul!"

Hailey and Jesse danced around him. "What do you have?" Jesse tugged on his hand. "Is it for me?"

"Jesse! Manners, please." She gave him her serious look.

"Please?" Jesse uttered.

"Still not buying it, but I'm working on it," she said to Paul.

"I should've called first, but this was kind of a last-minute idea. I was in Kitty Hawk for something yesterday and found this kite. It made me think of Hailey and Jesse."

"Us?" Hailey pressed her hands together and her face brightened.

"I knew it!" Jesse smacked Paul's hand in a very low high five.

"It's a surprise for both of you." He dropped to his knees. "Want to know why?"

"Yes."

"Because there are two monkeys on it. Like you two."

"We're not monkeys." Jesse pursed his lips. "Nope."

"You seem like silly monkeys to me."

"No, I'm a boy." Jesse cocked his hip out, propping his hand on it. "And she's a sister."

"Hmm. Do you like to climb?" Paul began the inquisition.

"Yep."

"And laugh?"

"Uh-huh."

"And most importantly, do you like bananas?"

"Mmm." They both licked their lips. "We love bananas."

"Well, there you go. And lucky, too, because I brought you frozen bananas for a snack, along with this super-special acrobatic surprise."

"Frozen?"

"They are so yummy!" Paul doled out the frozen bananas. "First, one for Mommy. Then Hailey, because ladies first."

"And Jesse!"

"And Jesse. There you go." Paul crumpled the bag and tossed it into the bigger bag, then pulled out a long something or other.

"What on earth is that?" Amanda asked.

"This bright-green—"

"Green's my favorite color!" Hailey screamed. "If it's not pink."

". . . kite has two monkeys eating bananas on it, and look, their tails hang super long from each side of it. We are going to fly this in the air."

The kids' eyes widened, but they looked to Amanda for confirmation.

"When your dad and I were young, we used to fly kites on the beach."

"How do you make a kite fly?" Hailey asked.

"I'll show you."

They gnawed on the frozen bananas while Paul wound up the kite string. He had a fancy plastic contraption way nicer than the stick Amanda had used when she was a kid in the neighborhood park trying to fly a diamond-shaped paper kite.

By the time Paul had rigged up the huge kite, the kids had devoured the bananas and run down to the water to rinse away the stickiness. This wasn't your average dollar-store kite. It was as wide as Amanda was long.

As Hailey and Jesse ran up, Paul turned to her. "I hope you're ready to be impressed."

She rolled her eyes. He and Jack had always been in a race to one-up each other, only now Paul seemed to be mastering it alone. He took off his shirt and dropped it to the sheet, then lifted the kite into the air and started running. "Come on, kids. You have to run with me or it won't take off!"

The very air around him seemed electrified. She found herself fixated on his bare chest. The enthusiasm with which he lived pulled at her senses. Would she ever feel that way again?

The kids ran at breakneck speed to catch up with him, although he was just taking long, languid strides. It took him no time to get the kite in the air, and as it lifted higher and higher, the squeals coming from Hailey and Jesse did too.

She jumped to her feet, clapping. The kite with the playful monkeys soared above them.

"I'm impressed!" Amanda shouted.

Paul and the kids made their way back and forth along their little stretch of beach. Occasionally, he'd tug on the strings and make the kite swing through the air, even accomplishing a pretty artful loop the loop at one point, which she had a feeling was complete and utter luck. Not that he'd admit it.

"You must have been pretty sure you'd get that kite up in the air to bring along that much string."

"I did spring for the premier line reel. Go big or go home."

No surprise there. "Once a Marine, always a Marine," Amanda said, but there were the intangible things about a Marine that had always impressed her the most: their uprightness of character and sound moral compass.

"Yeah, worse things to be." He winked and handed the kite line to Hailey. "Your turn, Hailey."

She clutched with a white-knuckled grip. "Here we go." She skittered off-balance for a moment, the kite dipping lower.

Paul uttered a few encouraging words and reeled in the line to urge the kite back in the air.

"You got it," he said.

Hailey stood there with pride. "I'm doing it, Mommy!"

Amanda loved how gentle Paul was with Hailey and Jesse.

Jesse jumped in the air, then squatted with his hands on his knees and his head tilted straight back, watching the kite hang in the sky.

Paul stepped over next to Amanda. "I thought it would be fun. Jack and I spent most of our childhood on the beach. There's so much to do."

"I know. He'd have enjoyed this so much."

"Yeah, he would've. Of course, we'd have had two kites."

"And it would be a competition." They both said it at the exact same time, which made them laugh.

"Because everything always was," she said, searching his expression. There seemed to be something he wasn't saying.

"Yeah." A lazy grin spread to his lips. His gaze touched her a second too long.

It was so quick that she almost wasn't sure it happened.

"Except over you," he said. "We never competed over you." His brow arched.

Is he flirting? The realization sent her mind reeling.

"This is hard work," Hailey called out, breaking the moment.

Paul jogged over to help Hailey. "Your arms are getting tired. Let's give Jesse a turn to fly it for a little while." He grabbed the line and did a few tricks with the kite.

Hailey let go and dropped her arms to her sides. "Exhausting."

"Come over here, you." Amanda held her arms out. "Was it fun?"

"Yes. So much fun."

Amanda rubbed Hailey's arms.

"Very hard work, though," her daughter added.

"You got it, Jesse. There you go." Paul sat in the sand with Jesse standing in front of him. "You're rocking it." Paul reached up and tugged the string, making the kite dip in the sky, then pop up even higher. They shouted hooray so loud that Hailey raced over to be part of the excitement.

While Amanda unpacked lunch, she watched Paul pull in the kite and fold it down.

He and the kids walked over still all abuzz about the kite antics.

"That was so much fun!" Amanda said to Paul. "An amazing time. Thank you."

"I'm glad I happened to see it in the store window. It was cooler than I remembered."

"It's hard to come up with new and different things to do with the kids every day. This is great."

"I'd like to do it again one afternoon."

"Sure. They really enjoyed it. They'd love that," she said.

"What about you?" He sat down next to her on the sheet. "Would you love it?"

The way his eyes were fixed on her made her heart pick up its pace. Joking, she said, "I'd probably like it more if you'd just come fix the toilet that won't quit running."

He laughed, then with a straight face asked, "You're not serious about the toilet?"

"Oh yeah. It runs and runs and runs. But not continually. No, it happens on its own merry timeline so that it wakes me up. Scares me every time." She picked up some sand and swirled it in her palm. "No big deal. If that's my biggest problem, I can deal with it."

"I can fix the toilet."

"I wasn't really asking you to fix it." She shrugged. "I was kidding around."

"I know that, but it's usually an easy fix. It could be the twist of a screw or a twenty-dollar part and save you more than that on your water bill. At least let me look at it. If it's a bigger problem, then you'll know what you're facing."

She hesitated. *Why am I making this a big deal? Just say thank you and let him do it.* "Fine. Take a look, but don't do anything."

"Thank you."

"No, thank *you*," she said. "I appreciate it. Really."

"No problem. I'm just that kind of guy, or have you forgotten?"

It was true. Between him and Jack, he'd been the handier one. Whenever there was something to fix, Jack waited until Paul could come over and help with it. "I guess I had kind of forgotten that. Well, then at least let me fix you dinner."

"I'd love that. You always were a great cook."

"You remember?"

"How could I forget? Your meat loaf and mashed potatoes are still in my dreams."

"Comfort food."

"Yeah. And what was the thing you did with chicken nuggets and sesame seeds? Do you still remember how to make that?"

"Yep. It's the kids' favorite, but I don't make it that often, even though it's easy."

"And stuffed wontons. You'd make that dipping sauce for them." He closed his eyes for a moment. "Okay, now I'm starving."

She reached in her cooler and handed him a PB&J.

"No." He pushed it back toward her. "I'm fine. Besides, the kids will be hungry."

"Eat it. We can walk over the hill for more provisions. You look fit enough to make it."

He snagged the sandwich and took a bite, then handed her the other half.

"Thanks." They ate in silence and watched Hailey and Jesse play. They'd come over and inhaled a sandwich between them so they could hurry back to what they were doing.

It was nice to have company and not feel like she had to fill every second with conversation. It was even nicer that it was with Paul. She'd missed him, but in an odd way like he had to be gone, too, because Jack was. It was strange having half the duo. She snuck a glance his direction. He and Jack looked less similar than she'd remembered. Paul's face was less angular than Jack's.

Paul pushed his sunglasses on top of his head and lay back, propped on his elbows. "It's peaceful out here."

"It is. I feel like I can breathe easier." She turned and looked at him as he rested there with his eyes closed, enjoying the sun. "You're welcome to join us anytime. Or don't join us. Just come out here."

"Be careful what you ask for. I might be here every day."

Strangely flattered, she peeked at him again, watching him relax. "I can think of worse problems."

His eyes opened and he sat up. Something passed between them, and then—thank goodness—he made a joke. "Like that running toilet."

"Even that." She drank in the comfort of his familiarness.

"Mom!" Hailey skidded to a stop in front of her, holding her hand as if she were in agony.

"It was an accident," Jesse insisted. "I didn't mean to step on her hand."

"Let me see," Amanda said, taking her daughter's hand into her own. And like that the moment was gone. "You're fine, sweetie. It was an accident."

She turned to Paul. "I think someone's tuckered out," she whispered as she stood and started gathering things to leave.

Tired and sweaty, they all walked back over the dune with not much to say. The kids hosed off outside, and then Jesse announced he was sleepy.

"I know how you feel, little man," Amanda sympathized. "The sun really saps it out of you, doesn't it?"

"Why don't y'all take naps," Paul suggested. "I'm going to look at that toilet and see if we need any parts."

"You promised to just evaluate. Don't you be spending money I don't have."

"I know, I know." He walked toward the back door. "Do you have a screwdriver?"

"I do. Drawer next to the fridge."

She heard the back door slam against the frame. After brushing the sand from their things, she joined them inside.

Paul was already walking back into the kitchen. "It's better than it was, but we can fix it right for less than twenty bucks."

"I've got twenty bucks," she said. "Let me get my purse."

"No, I've got it. I have a couple errands to run anyway. I'll stop by the hardware store and come back for dinner. A home-cooked meal has got to be worth twenty bucks."

"You don't have to do that. I'm not broke."

"It's a fair trade," Paul said. "I'll see you in a little while. Text me if you think of anything you need while I'm gone."

"Okay." Her heart hitched as he walked out. "Come on," she whispered to the kids. "We can all take a catnap on the bunk beds. Go grab my pillow, Hailey."

They piled onto the lower bunk in a heap. She programmed her alarm on her phone, then set it to vibrate. With any luck the kids would nap longer and she could start dinner without them underfoot.

20

Amanda lay there unable to nap. Instead, all she could think about was Paul. She slid out from under Hailey's leg and Jesse's arm, wincing with every tiny movement and hoping she wouldn't wake them. When her foot finally reached the floor, she let out the breath she'd been holding and tiptoed to the door. The loud hum of the AC helped cover the sounds from the creaking floor.

She closed the door behind her, then gave an enthusiastic fist pump. The quite time had refreshed her, and now she had a few minutes to herself.

In the kitchen, she gathered everything to get dinner started. Chopping, slicing, and mixing, she found that she was smiling for no reason at all.

She made the meat loaf extra large to ensure there was plenty for Paul and some leftover for sandwiches. The best part, in her opinion.

With a bowl of washed potatoes, she stepped out into the backyard and sat at the picnic table to peel them. Nothing like homemade mashed potatoes. They were always worth the extra effort.

Peeling and dicing them, she hadn't even heard Paul until he was right next to her, at which time she screamed like a girl. *The kids are probably awake now.*

"Sorry, didn't mean to scare you."

"You didn't. Just caught me off guard. I guess I was in my potato-peeling zone."

He raised his hand. "Don't let me interrupt that."

"Kids are still asleep, unless I just woke them up with my girlie scream."

"I'll be quiet." He carried his bag inside.

She watched after him for a minute. It was nice of him to take care of the toilet, but surely he had better things to do. She cut up the last of the potatoes and then went back inside to boil them.

She heard Jesse and Hailey talking to Paul in the bathroom. Clearly, her scream had done the trick. Too bad for Paul. It made her think of the sign at the service station that had different rates, like "Fifty bucks extra if you stick around to chat." Daddy would have said they were being an "awful help." It hadn't occurred to her that it wasn't a compliment until she was in her midtwenties. It was funnier now.

The kitchen smelled of meat loaf, barbecue sauce, and fresh herbs. She poured glasses of sweet tea and set the table while the meat loaf cooled on the counter.

Paul, Hailey, and Jesse walked back into the kitchen. "Toilet's good as new."

"Thank you." She drained the water from the potatoes and began whipping them. "That's great news."

"We helped." Jesse propped his hands on his hips.

She offered Paul a sheepish grin. "I bet you did." She booped Jesse's nose. "My favorite helpers."

"They were better help than Jack would've been." Paul looked like he wanted to swallow the words. "I'm sorry," he mouthed from across the counter.

The words stabbed, threatening to take her voice. "No." She tried to act like she'd barely noticed. "It's fine. Probably true." She set the meat loaf and the bowl of mashed potatoes on the table next to the gravy boat and broccoli. "Umm, yeah, you were always handier. But let's eat before the food gets cold."

She grabbed for the spoon in the mashed potatoes at the same time he did.

They stopped, a hot second hanging between them until he pulled his hand back. "Let me serve this up while it's still warm. You can slice the meat loaf." Her heart hammered as she portioned the food for the kids, then let Paul make his own plate.

They sat down at the dining room table. The kids sang the blessing, which always filled her heart with happiness. Their pure voices lifting praise and trusting in the Lord was a good footing, and that was important especially after what they'd been through. Life had a way of shaking you off your footing when you least expected, and that foundation was the only way to survive it. She peeked across the table and noticed Paul watching Hailey and Jesse with a grin on his face.

"Amen," they all said.

"They are too much," he said to Amanda. "Man, I've missed y'all."

"I'm sorry about everything." She placed her napkin in her lap. "My anger was misplaced. I was—"

"Don't." He raised his hand. "You were right. I let you down. I promised you I'd protect Jack. I shouldn't have been so arrogant to have made that promise. If you give me another chance, I will never let you down again. I can promise you that."

All those awful things she'd said—he'd been living with them while she'd mentally whisked him aside. Maeve had articulated it best: Her misplaced anger had been a release. The only way she could cope. It was easy to see that now, although the emotions had seemed real at the time.

He placed his hand on top of hers. "We're okay, right?"

"Yes. Thank you." She watched the smile return to his face.

He turned his fork on its side and cut a bite-size piece of meat loaf. He followed with a spoonful of mashed potatoes and gravy and a satisfying moan. "You still got the cooking chops. Aw, man, this is good."

"Eat up. You know me—I always make too much. Which is just enough when you're feeding Marines."

He took a big swallow of his tea and gave her a thumbs-up and a wink.

"Semper fi!" Jesse yelled.

"He hasn't said that in a while." Amanda placed her fork next to her plate. *Semper fi* had been Jesse's first words, the way Jack told it. She was pretty sure the first word he'd actually uttered was *mine*, although she'd tried hard to hear it as *Mom*.

Paul reached over and high-fived him.

The conversation over dinner was mostly between Paul and Hailey. Jesse was never one to chat during a meal. Fully focused on the food in front of him, he wore some of it on his chin. She handed him a napkin, and he wiped his face without missing a bite.

After dinner they cleared the table, and then Paul offered to help with the dishes.

Needing a moment to herself, she insisted on washing them while he and the kids went out back to play. Competing thoughts raced through her mind. Sometimes not having the luxury of a dishwasher was a good thing, like tonight, when she could stand there lost in her thoughts through the mindless task.

The chatter from outside was like music. Paul had bought bubble solution and was blowing bubbles faster than Hailey and Jesse could chase them down. Occasionally, a bubble would fly past, popping against the window frame. One was so big the bluish-yellow orb bounced against the screen before it burst in a soapy, firework-like spray. A mixture of giggles and squeals floated inside. Usually those sounds were joyful noise, but tonight she felt . . . flat.

She stacked the last of the dishes on the draining rack and walked back to her bedroom. After closing the door behind her, she sat on the edge of the bed. In her feminine bedroom, the only masculine touch left was Jack's shirt on the back of the chair. She moved it from its place of honor into her arms, hugging it in front of the mirror.

Is this okay? It's so nice to have Paul here, almost like you're back, but it feels like I'm betraying you.

She stood there, wishing for an answer, swaying slowly to the left and the right, ticktock. *Tell me what to do.*

In the reflection of her bureau mirror, the shell on the corner of her nightstand reminded her of what was important. She didn't have to pick it up to read the quote. It had been on her mind ever since they'd found it.

"All the art of living lies in a fine mingling of letting go and holding on."

She laughed at the memory of Hailey asking who Have Lots was.

Letting go.

Amanda held the shirt to her face, breathing in the fabric. Just the other day, she'd caught the scent of Jack from it again, but today there was nothing there. *I've been fooling myself.*

She carefully laid out the shirt on her bed, pressing her hands along the fabric as she made each fold, then rolled it down into a small envelope-size bundle. She'd thought redecorating in all the feminine colors would make a difference. She held the shirt. This draped across the back of the chair—it wasn't Jack. Jack was in her heart. In her children. He'd always be here. There was nothing to hold on to.

Thank You for watching over us. For bringing special people along my path. Always at the right time. In Your time. I'm listening. Don't let go of my hand.

She slid out her top dresser drawer, the one where she kept her most beloved jewelry and mementos, and tucked the shirt there. She then placed Jack's watch, the one she'd had engraved for him on their wedding day, right on top of it.

I love you, Jack.

She stepped outside into the dimly lit backyard. Paul sat on top of the picnic table in a flurry of bubbles. The kids hopped and jumped, chasing them across the yard.

"You two are going to sleep good," Paul said.

"You get extra credit for that, Paul Grant," Amanda teased. "Are y'all having fun?"

"More fun than hunting ghost crabs." Paul puffed out another spewing fountain of bubbles that Lawrence Welk would've been proud to call his own.

"Ghost crabs?" Hailey stopped in her tracks. She clocked a finger back and forth toward Paul. "There's no such thing as ghosts."

Paul grimaced but recovered quickly. "You're exactly right. However, there is such a thing as ghost crabs." He made pincher actions in the air with his fingers. "The little crabs hide in the sand all day, but at night they come out. If you flash a light on them, they freeze just long enough to grab them."

Hailey looked to Amanda for confirmation.

She shrugged.

"Don't tell me your mom hasn't taken you ghost-crab hunting." Paul glanced at Amanda, a surprised look on his face.

"We don't hunt." Hailey's lips pursed into a perfect tiny bow. "That's just horrible. Look what happened to Bambi's mom. I'll never hunt. Animals are precious."

He laughed out loud. "Oh my goodness. She really has thought this out."

"She knows her mind."

"Well, little miss, I don't go hunting, either, but I think you would love ghost-crab hunting, because no crabs are hurt in the process. It's an adventure." He blew a flurry of bubbles, then pulled in Hailey and tickled her until her face went pink. "Everyone comes out alive."

"Okay, stop before she spews." Amanda waved her hands above her head. "Whoa, it's bedtime for you and Jesse. Get those teeth brushed and get in your jammies."

"Mom?" Hailey had her puppy-dog eyes working overtime.

"Yes. You have to. There's always tomorrow. I'll be in there in a minute." Amanda watched them leave, then turned to Paul.

He rubbed his hands together. "What a day! Thanks for letting me be part of it."

"Are you kidding? You made it. Thank you for spending your time with us."

"Could I come over one night next week and take them ghost crabbing?"

"It's an actual thing?"

"Oh yeah. It's fun. I'll bring the headlamps, buckets, net, and shovels."

"That's quite an inventory. This sounds like an archaeological dig."

"Nah. Way easier than that. It'll be a blast."

"You're on." She motioned toward the back door. "Want to help me tuck them in?"

His eyes lit up. "I'd love to." He reached for her hand.

She peered at it with hesitation but placed hers in his. "Okay." They walked inside together. There was an awkward do-si-do of sorts at the door, but she let him hold it for her and he followed her back to Jesse's room.

"You two share bunk beds?" Paul walked over and pinched Hailey's nose. "I loved the top bunk when I was growing up."

"I have my own room," Hailey said. "I just like being in here with Jesse. He needs me."

"You are a very good sister."

"I know. We can say our prayers without help."

He nodded, crossing his arms in front of him. "Okay, let's do this."

Hailey started and Jesse stayed about a word behind her the whole time. "Now my lay me . . ."

Amanda had never had the heart to correct them. Hailey had always said it that way, and when Jesse learned it from her, it was too sweet to fix. Someday she'd tell them, when they had their own kids. Or maybe not.

"Sleep tight," Paul said while backing out of the room. Amanda walked over and kissed each of them on the forehead. "I love you both so much. Happy dreams."

She closed the door behind them.

"I will get out of your hair," Paul whispered over his shoulder as he moved down the hallway. "Thanks again."

"Anytime, Paul." She followed him to the front door so she could lock up once he left.

When they got there, he turned and dropped a kiss right in the part of her hair, then squeezed her shoulders. He pushed the door open and jogged off.

When he got to the front gate, she noticed that it didn't creak.

Did you fix that too?

"Thank you," she whispered into the night. She watched

him get into his truck, a great big four-wheel drive with a crew cab.

This was a different joy than she'd ever felt. With the house secured, she sat on the floor with Denali, absently stroking his thick skin. *Am I crazy?*

"What do you think?"

Denali lifted his head, snuffling and wheezing, then set his chin on her leg and groaned.

"I know. It's exhausting to think about it." She pushed the skin on his face forward, making all the wrinkles squish together, then placed her hands on both sides of his face like a face-lift. "You're an old soul, aren't you? You've been such a blessing to this family. Thank you for being such a good dog." She scratched his ears, then got up and walked toward her room, stopping halfway to slap her thigh for Denali to follow her.

He lumbered forward, his rolls shifting as he walked.

She climbed into bed and sat there hugging her pillow to her chest. Tonight as she said her prayers, she added a few things to her list: frozen bananas, kites, bubbles, and Paul. *Mostly Paul.*

21

Overnight, things had cooled off, making this morning feel more like a spring day than the middle of July. Amanda walked out to the mailbox to collect the mail. The rusty frame had seen better days. She'd have to come up with a way to spruce it up. It might be a good family paint project. She reached inside and grabbed the stack of envelopes.

She lowered the stack to flip through them when a shock of color caught her attention, glinting at her feet. A shell about the size of a silver dollar lay there. It was nothing special, just a regular old clam shell. They were everywhere, but this particular one was almost purple. A natural pinkish band ran horizontal around it, kind of like a cross on top. She picked it up and rolled it over in her hand. The inside simply read,

Interrupt worry with gratitude.

The tiny letters curled in an imperfect way. She cupped the shell in her palm. The Bible said something about casting her worries on God. But when it came to actually releasing the worry, she was a big fat failure. Maybe the shell would help remind her to release her worry to God.

She slipped it into her pocket with hope.

Flipping through the envelopes, she meandered back toward the house. When she pushed the gate open, it didn't make a sound. *Not so much as a squeak?* She remembered the absence of the creak last night when Paul left. She wiggled the gate back and forth. Sure enough, it was as quiet as if it were brand-new.

Hailey walked outside with Jesse in her wake. "Hey, Mom, what ya doing?"

"I was thinking." She set the stack of envelopes on the picnic table outside. "What if we walk down the beach and go in the back way to Tug's Diner today?"

Jesse marched around the picnic table. "We're ready."

"You two make me laugh." She got up and marched alongside Jesse. "Let's go, then."

Hailey grabbed her shell-collecting bag and ran to catch up.

"We are so grateful for this beautiful day," Amanda said, touching the shell in her pocket. "Right?" An attitude of gratitude was something she could help instill in their days while helping her stay positive too.

Instead of taking the beach road, they walked to Tug's by way of the shoreline. Hailey and Jesse didn't seem to mind the long walk, only stopping to add treasures to Hailey's bag. A wave washed in, sending a fine mist into the air. Amanda pushed her bangs from her face. The salty spray had left her ponytail sticky and stiff. *Who cares about bad hair when you feel good all the way to your soul?*

"Almost there. See it?" Amanda pointed to the building that hung over the dune. It was strange how the shore eroded a teensy bit each year from both sides. The Atlantic and Pacific. It seemed if it was pulling California into the water the way people talked, they'd be getting more and more coastline here on the East Coast. But Maeve said the shore was shrinking here, too, and if anyone knew, it would be Maeve.

By the time they reached the steps, Hailey was dragging her bag of shells.

"Oh goodness. I think you may have to leave those out here, Hailey-bug. They are so sandy." Amanda picked up the bag and shook it. A cloud of sand rained down in front of them.

"They got heavy."

"That's okay. They'll be safe out by the birdcage."

They traversed the steep wooden stairs up to the gazebo, where The Wife called out a greeting.

"Hello."

"Pretty bird," Hailey sang. "You're going to have to take care of my shells while we eat, okay?"

The Wife made a series of clicks and clucks followed by, "I'm okay. You okay, my pretty?"

Amanda set Hailey's bag on the railing next to the birdcage. "I'll go in and order while you two visit the bird."

"I love that bird." Jesse marched straight over, calling her name the whole way.

When Amanda pushed the back door open, balloons ricocheted precariously against it. *Please don't pop.* The whole place was filled with pink helium balloons in pairs. She scanned the room for a table.

"Kimmy had her babies. We're celebrating. Are you alone today?" Tug lumbered over, almost a wobble the way he shifted his weight from leg to leg as he moved.

"The kids are outside talking to The Wife."

"She's a talker." Tug grabbed menus and motioned for her to follow him.

"Amanda?" Maeve waved from the corner booth. "Come sit with me."

"Hey there! Tug, we'll join Maeve if that's okay."

"Okay by me." He handed Amanda the menus, and she slid into the booth across from Maeve.

"Bring more coffee, Tug, would you, please?" Maeve moved

her mug to the edge of the table, then caught Amanda's eye. "How are you doing?"

"Great. Look at all the pink!"

"There are so many wonderful things happening. They won't be home from the hospital for a few days, but we'll have to go visit as soon as they are."

"I'd love to join you. Two babies at once. Wow. I could barely keep up with one at a time."

"It won't be easy, but we'll offer a hand. That's how the locals are around here. Like one big family." Maeve smiled. "Speaking of one big family, I can't quit thinking about the odds of Paul jogging up on the beach. You two being old friends and all that. Isn't it wonderful how the world reconnects people?"

"I still can't believe it. I thought I'd never see him again. But it was good to reconnect." Heat flooded her cheeks. She hoped Maeve didn't notice. "He came over yesterday and flew a kite on the beach with the kids. They loved it!"

"I saw that big kite from my porch. I'm sure the kids did love it. How about you?"

It was like Maeve could see right into her heart. "I liked it too. It was a lot of fun."

Maeve's eyes narrowed. "He seems like a really good man."

"He is." The words had come out so breezy. Just thinking about him left her pulse racing. She put her hand on the bench, steadying herself.

"What's wrong, dear?"

"I don't know. Nothing." In an attempt to change the subject, she quickly added, "Just a lot going on. Must be all the excitement."

"Is Paul meeting y'all here for breakfast?" Maeve's head popped up, scanning the restaurant like a meerkat on alert.

"No. I'm sure he's working. It's a long ride to the base, but I guess it's worth the drive to live here. I wouldn't have understood that before. But now, after living here, I get it."

"I agree. Whelk's Island is a very special place." Maeve nodded slowly.

"Oh, I wanted to tell you. I found a shell this morning." Amanda took it from her pocket and placed it on the table. "This one has a message." She looked into Maeve's eyes. "It's not the first one I've found."

Maeve thrummed her fingers on the table. "I suppose it means you're extra special." She ran her thumb across the shell, then turned it over in her hand before looking back up at Amanda. "Interrupt worry with gratitude," she read. "Are you worried about something?"

"My future, I guess. How I'm going to take care of my children on my own. If I'll be a good teacher. If moving here was smart." She'd danced around the most important thing worrying her at the moment. "Paul showing up like he did. What will people think?"

"About the two of you spending time together?" She shrugged. "You're old friends."

"We were best friends. *Are,* I guess." She pressed her fingers to her temples. "Is it weird that it seems like time just rolled back? When Jack died, that whole situation tugged us apart, but it wasn't like Paul had done anything. It was the grief. I was angry and hurt. It was just too hard to be around Paul. He and Jack were inseparable."

"I can understand that. So then why would people think anything of it?"

"You know how people talk. It's been barely over two years."

"No one is counting anymore but you." Maeve set the shell

back down in front of Amanda. "It's self-explanatory. Don't worry about any of that. Just focus on making every single day a happy one. Live every moment to overflowing."

"Cast my worries. I know, I know. I was praying about that this morning. I'm great at saying I'm doing that, but then I worry too."

"Then you don't believe it." Maeve placed her hand on top of Amanda's, patting it with each word. "No backup plan. Trust in the journey."

"I'll try."

Just then the server came over, so Amanda placed their breakfast order, then handed the menus back to the waitress.

"Paul stayed for dinner with us last night," she blurted out.

"You say that like it's a bad thing. It's dinner."

"So you think it's okay? Really?"

"Yes, I absolutely do. He seems wonderful. It scared the puddin' out of me the way Hailey went screaming up to him on the beach. About gave me a heart attack, but no, I'm not worried about him one bit. He's a good one." Maeve paused, then lifted her shoulders in an impatient shrug. "Honey, Jack's never coming back. If there's something romantic or even just comfortable about being with Paul, enjoy it. Take a chance. The only people who need to be right with it is you and your children."

"He *is* great. I'm not going to lie. It's been nice having him around, even just a day or so. He fixed my toilet. I'd mentioned it randomly ran in the middle of the night, and he went straight to the hardware store to get the stuff to fix it." She snapped her fingers. "Like that. I didn't even mention the gate being creaky, but he fixed it too. Just did it. Didn't even tell me he did it."

"That's pretty nice. That was always my love language." Maeve tittered. "The little things. Take my garbage out and I feel so special. Other people are material. I don't remember what all five love languages are, but you get the idea."

"Oh yeah. I've heard of them. I'm the same way. Fixing my toilet was better than a nice piece of jewelry, any day of the week."

"Sounds like Paul knows that about you." Maeve seemed to be studying her reaction, making Amanda self-conscious.

"He should. We were all best friends for a long time."

Tug sat down at the table. He made a playful double cluck with his tongue and patted Maeve's hand. "How's my best girl this morning?"

"I'm fine, you old flirt."

"She loves it when I flirt with her," he said to Amanda. "Plays hard to get, but I know." He leaned sweetly over and nudged Maeve.

"Stop it." Maeve swatted his hand away. "You say that to all the girls."

Amanda had a feeling Tug wasn't kidding, though. There was a sparkle in his eyes, and kindness in his actions.

"What do you two have your heads together about this morning?" he asked.

"The shells with the messages," Amanda said to Tug. "Have you ever heard of anyone finding more than one?"

"Yes, I have. Remember, Maeve? There was that article in the paper a few years back. That woman had found what, two or three?"

Maeve didn't seem to remember. "Not sure."

"It's strange how the right message gets to each person," Amanda said. At least that was the case with the two she had found.

"I don't know," Tug said. "I liken it to how we can all sit in church and hear the same sermon, but each of us feels like that preacher was giving us a personal communication. We all hear what we need to hear." Tug got up. "More coffee for my best girl?"

"Thanks, Tug." Maeve's soft response was filled with appreciation. "That'd be great."

Amanda waited until he got out of earshot, and then she leaned in. "He likes you."

"No." Maeve shook it off. "We just have a million years of history."

"I wouldn't be so sure about that. I'm telling you, I can see it in his eyes." The door opened, and Hailey and Jesse zipped inside to a chorus of the *Gilligan's Island* theme song led by The Wife.

"We learned a song." Hailey scooted into the booth. "We love playing with that bird. She really likes us too. We're trying to teach her our names."

"She's very smart," Maeve said. "She'll be saying hello to you by name before you know it."

Hailey clapped her hands. "I can't wait."

"Hey, you two," Amanda said. "I was thinking about taking Denali over to Paws Town Square for a walk this afternoon. How does that sound?"

Jesse bounced in his seat. "That would be fun!"

"Maeve should come with us," Hailey said. "You *have* to see that place."

"Yes, Maeve," Jesse said. "Please?"

Maeve hesitated, but only for a moment. "Yes, I've been wanting to see how it turned out, and the time keeps slipping away."

"Slipping away? Is everything okay?" Amanda felt a note of panic in her voice.

"Oh, it's just an expression. I'm not getting any younger." Maeve seemed uncomfortable, shifting in the booth. "I could go around two. Would that work for you?"

"That sounds great," said Amanda.

The waitress brought their order to the table, and Maeve got up. "I'm going to let y'all eat. I need to get home and make some calls this morning so I can play later."

"I'd offer you a ride home, but we walked down today too. Besides, I know you prefer the beach route, and I'd never try to come between you and your treasures."

"Well, you are one of them, my dear. You and these two." Maeve pointed at the tops of Hailey's and Jesse's heads. "But I do need my daily dose of the ocean as well." She spread her arms wide and started to walk out the door. "The tide beckons me."

It was late in the afternoon when Amanda pulled into Maeve's driveway and tooted the horn. Denali lazed in the back between the car seats.

Maeve walked down the stairs. It was the first time Amanda had seen her in anything other than a skirt or dress. Dressed in blue jeans, she looked alarmingly thin.

"Hi, Maeve!" Jesse said.

"Hello, you two. Didn't I just see you this morning?"

Hailey blew her a kiss. "You did. And Denali's here too."

"I don't think he's very excited about going walking." Jesse's lips pulled to the side.

Maeve slid into the passenger seat.

Amanda glanced in the rearview mirror before backing out onto the street. "This may be the world's shortest walk."

"It'll be fine."

They drove over to Paws Town Square, and Maeve marveled at the surroundings as she got out of the car. "It's pretty enough to be a resort for people, not just pets."

Hailey tumbled out of the car, and Jesse raced around to

help her with Denali, who was standing at the edge of the seat, looking out but not budging. Hailey tugged on the leash, but that only made Denali lie down.

"Don't pull him too hard. Here, let me get that." Amanda walked over and commanded Denali to get out of the car, finally tapping him on his rear end to get him moving. He hit the ground with a hefty one-two snort.

"Let's go, Denali." Hailey started walking, and Denali moved in a languid lumber, picking up speed at a slow rate. Jesse skipped alongside.

"You'll love this." Amanda hung back with Maeve. "When we got home this morning after breakfast, someone had rolled my trash can out to the street for me. Had to be Paul."

"That was so thoughtful. Let the man do nice stuff for you. Quit being surprised. There's not a mourning period we have to complete before we're allowed to feel happy again. Besides, I like seeing you smile."

"It's taken you years to get there. Why are you rushing me?" Amanda tried to make it sound like a joke, but honestly, did she have a right to feel this way about Paul?

"I'm a hardheaded old fool, and I didn't have someone like me around to give me expert advice. Everyone is different. Some people find love again immediately."

"What if he's just feeling guilty?" Amanda lowered her voice. "Survivor's guilt or something?"

"I don't think he's that kind of guy. Enjoy it and keep living a good life. It will all fall into place."

They walked inside and Maeve let out a gasp. "A bakery for dogs? What will they think of next?"

They took to the walking trail. Air-conditioning and fans kept the air not only cool but dry, which was a relief from the humidity outside. They noticed that fun facts were posted among the plants along the route. Some were even multiple choice with electronic answer boards. The kids had fun guessing them, and as a team they'd scored pretty well.

Surprisingly, Denali enjoyed the walk once he got going. His tongue curled as he panted, but it looked like he was smiling.

A few people passed, walking their dogs.

"Amanda?"

The voice had come from behind them. She turned and so did Maeve.

It was Paul, jogging up with a German shepherd wearing a service vest.

"Paul? What are you doing here?" The dog's vest looked heavy. "I can see you're running, but does the base let y'all train here now?" As hot as it was, it would be a nice way to train, but then she never knew any Marine to worry about doing things the easy way. They were as tough as they came. "I take it this is your military working dog."

"Oh no. This guy's retired now. I'm just running him. Keeping us both in shape."

He'd always been committed to a healthy lifestyle as long as she'd known him.

"Hi!" Hailey waved to Paul. "Can I pet your dog?"

"Sure. His name is Gauge."

"Hi, Gauge." Hailey reached down to pet him.

Amanda watched her, proud that her little girl wasn't afraid, but then she caught Maeve looking Paul square in the eye for a long moment. Amanda watched them both but couldn't read either of them.

Maeve grabbed for Denali's leash from Amanda. "I'll take Denali and the kids over to feed the koi. I hear they'll come right up to the top of the water."

She was already racing away with Hailey and Jesse in her wake.

"Yeah. They will," Paul said. "Clap three times," he called after them. He shifted the shepherd's leash in his hand. "Don't think she even heard me," he said.

That was strange. Amanda couldn't help the feeling she was missing something between the two of them.

22

Paul regretted not telling Amanda he was no longer a Marine the first time she'd made mention of it. That would've been so much easier. The way her head was cocked now, he could tell she thought something was up. Maeve's stink eye hadn't been all that subtle either.

His mouth was as sticky as a tree toad's toes. "Amanda, I'm not in the Marine Corps anymore."

"What?"

"Haven't been for a while now." He watched her, waiting for that dash of disappointment in her eyes.

Her long lashes lifted. "That's the *last* thing I expected to hear."

"I should've told you sooner. When Jack died, I became reckless. Guilt took over my good judgment. I had to get out and redirect my attention before I got someone else killed. I was a mess." He lowered his head. "I'm sorry if I've disappointed you."

"What? Paul, you haven't disappointed me. Sure, I was proud that you and Jack were serving our country, but that's not what makes you special. It's who you are inside. In fact, it's a major relief." Her tongue flicked across her lips.

"I don't want you to think less of me. Jack gave his life for this country. He's a hero."

"Stop, Paul. I hate to even say this out loud, because I've

been trying to ignore the possibility of it, but if you were still in the Marines, I don't think I could risk that hurt again. I mean, I realize it's a long shot that anything would ever happen to you, but I—"

"There's more. I'm running Gauge here because I own this place. Well, not just this one, but the whole business. The location in Virginia, and three more underway."

He could almost hear her replaying what he'd just said in her head, but she didn't look offended or mad or even that surprised. *Please let this be okay.*

Her eyes darted from one side of the huge building to the other. "How did you achieve all this in such a short amount of time?"

"I was broken emotionally, but I had a plan. I wanted to still make a difference, and I got lucky. I tapped on the right doors. Got the right investors and supporters who also wanted to make a difference for our veterans. You see, it's not just the kennel or these retired military dogs. It's the veterans who need work while healing from PTSD. We are partnering closely with several organizations." He stopped and took a breath. "Sorry. I'm kind of passionate about it."

"Congratulations. This is amazing!" She looked around. "I'm . . . I don't know . . . impressed. Proud. Excited for you. All of that."

He sighed with relief. "I'm really proud of it. This company is so much more than a cool place to leave your dog. There's a lot of personal stuff that goes along with it. Ties back to my fellow military men and women. It's a long story."

"I want to hear it, no matter how long it takes. And, Paul . . . I could never think less of you. No matter what you did. You're not what you do. It's you." She tapped his shirt at his heart. "This is who you are. You have always been thoughtful and caring."

"I've been so blessed, and I'm passing it on, Amanda. There's so much more to this business that I can't wait to share with you. It touches lives in a way that I could have never dreamed of, and I don't do it alone. One heart touches another and the talents just flow."

"Gift. This is your gift." She nodded with a reassuring smile. "It sounds like it was meant to be. I'm so excited for you and so proud of you." Gauge sat at attention in front of them. She reached down and stroked his ear.

"I need to finish Gauge's run. Can I come over tonight?" *Please say yes.*

"I was hoping you would."

"Yes." The fist pump had been an automatic response. He pulled her into a friendly hug. "Thank you." He released her, looking into her smiling face. "We're going to run. He's on a strict exercise routine, but I'll be over tonight. I can bring pizza."

"No, I'll cook. Just show up. Whenever. We'll be there."

He took off running. His legs felt strong, probably from the adrenaline, and the dog geared up right with him too. He turned and waved a hand in the air. "See ya later."

Maeve stood on the bridge with the kids. Jesse was on tip-toe, peering over the rail.

The boards echoed as Gauge's feet double-timed across the planks over the exercise pond.

"See y'all later," he said as he jogged by.

"Bye." Hailey and Jesse were still waving when he transitioned from the bridge back to the Astroturf. In the reflection of the large round security mirror that hung between the trees, he could see them still standing there. When he spotted Amanda's bright-blue shirt, his pulse quickened.

She wasn't mad. Glee pumped through him.

He took Gauge for one more fast lap, and then they cooled

down with a game of catch and fetch in the water-park area outside. The two of them relaxed and dried in the sun. *Best job in the world.*

He'd honored Amanda's wishes to stay away, but when he saw her on the beach, those old feelings flooded back. A thousand what-ifs ran through his mind. He thought about his love for her all these years, impossible to act on while Jack was alive. He'd all but buried those feelings in finding a way to move on. Seeing her again awakened all of that hope.

He'd worried that Amanda wouldn't understand how he could leave the Corps after Jack had given his life for it. He'd dreaded telling her, but she seemed genuinely relieved by the information.

All that worry for nothing.

Now he just needed to win her heart.

That evening, Paul stood at the back door of Amanda's house with a paper grocery sack in one arm and a yellow plastic bag hanging from his other hand.

"Hi, Paul!" The kids raced from the living room to greet him.

"Hey!" He placed the bags on the floor, picked up Jesse, and slung him into the air. Then he twirled Hailey. "You ready for fun tonight?"

"What are we going to do?"

"It's a secret, but I promise you'll like it." He turned to Amanda. "How long until dinner?"

"About forty-five minutes. Do you need a snack?"

"Nope. That's perfect. I have a project for the three of us while you finish cooking. That is, unless you need our help." He reached down and tickled Jesse. "Because all the fun happens after dark."

"Nope. I have dinner under control. You are dismissed."

"Awesome." Paul moved the plastic bag to the corner, then unpacked the contents of the paper bag.

"What is all that?" Amanda asked.

"Well, the other night I fixed your squeaky gate."

"I noticed. Thank you, by the way."

"You're welcome. Although it occurred to me later that I'd also eliminated your redneck burglar alarm."

She snickered. "It wasn't intentional, but I guess it was a pretty good alarm."

"So I got you one of these systems where you can use an app to see who's at the door and the gate. It's safe here in town, but couldn't hurt, right?"

"That was thoughtful." She picked up one of the boxes. "Yeah. Great!"

"Won't take long to install, and then you can see what's going on here even if you're over on the beach."

"I do like that."

"Can I have your phone so I can set up the app?"

"Sure," she said. "It's on the charger over there by the door."

He picked up the phone and took it to her. "Can you type in your password for me?"

"You can probably guess it. My birthday. Do you remember it?"

"I do." He pecked at the keys and downloaded the app. All the while, Jesse shadowed him, picking up the boxes and wrappers as Paul installed the cameras at the gate and front and back doors. There were double-stick tape and Velcro options, but he went ahead and screwed the tiny cameras into place. No reason to do a job halfway.

A few more twists of the screwdriver and everything was working. He had the kids ring the doorbell and tested it, then gave Amanda a quick lesson.

"I love this. How handy! Especially if I'm waiting on packages. Thank you." She walked back over to the stove. "I need about ten more minutes. Then we'll be ready to eat."

"Anything I can do?" he asked.

"Not a thing."

"It smells great. We'll go outside and stay out of the way until you're ready."

She mouthed, "Thank you." He liked the feeling of being helpful.

"Let's go. All three of you." He ran behind Denali, giving the lazy dog a little encouragement to go outside.

The yard was small, but they still had a decent amount of space to play in. It was nice that the entire property was fenced in.

Hailey tugged on Paul's arm. "Paul?"

"Yeah, Lightning Bug?"

"I need to tell you something."

"Okay, sure." He stooped down to get to her level. "What's up?"

Her mouth moved from side to side. "I think this is going to make you really sad."

"Oh no."

"Are you ready?"

"Yes," he said. "I'm ready."

She wiggled a finger, begging him in closer. "Daddy is in heaven." She placed her hand on his shoulder.

Paul took in a quick breath.

"We don't talk about it much, but I know you love him too. He's not coming back. We miss him a lot." She placed her hand on his arm. "You're gonna be really sad for a while like us."

"I am." He patted his chest. "It breaks my heart, but thank you for telling me."

"It's okay. I'm here for you, and Jesse will make you laugh." She rolled her eyes. "He's really good at that."

"You are very grown-up. Anybody ever tell you that?"

"Mom says it all the time."

"I bet she does. You're extra special."

"You are too." She wrapped her arms around his neck so tight he had to lift his chin up to get a good breath, but he'd have given up breathing completely for this moment. He sucked back a sob that hung in his throat.

"It's okay to cry if you need to."

He pressed his fingers to his nose. "Thank you."

"Daddy told me to be a good girl when he left. I'm doin' my best, but it's not always easy."

"I bet you are. Guess what! I have a surprise for all of us tonight."

She let go of his neck. "I love surprises."

Amanda stepped out onto the stoop. "Come on. Dinner's ready."

Jesse led the way, with Denali on his heels. He was the first one in his chair, sitting high in his booster seat. Paul took the spot between Hailey and Amanda.

"Macaroni and cheese." Paul's head lolled back. "I'd forgotten until this second how much I used to love your homemade mac 'n' cheese."

"It's my favorite," Jesse said.

They enjoyed the panfried ham, macaroni and cheese, and fresh tomato-cucumber salad over silly conversations about cartoons, shells on the beach, and bugs they'd collected in the backyard.

"This dinner was great." Paul rubbed his belly. "Are you full too?" he asked Jesse, who rubbed his belly in response. "We better clean up the dishes and the kitchen so we can get ready for fun!"

"What are you up to, Paul Grant? You're keeping secrets from me now?" Amanda teased.

"Not really a secret. More like a surprise."

"Oh, well that's totally different." Amanda looked over at Hailey, who seemed to agree. "I love surprises."

"I need something from the store, though. Could we . . . all three of us . . . get *you* to run to the store? We have something else we need to do out here while you're gone."

"I see. Running me out of my own house?" She looked over at Hailey and Jesse, who were practically bouncing with excitement. "You sure you can handle these two?"

"Absolutely."

"Can y'all take care of Paul while I'm gone?" Amanda reached for her purse.

"Absolutely," Hailey said, so mature for her age.

"I'll help," Jesse added.

"Okay, okay," Amanda said, pretending to concede. "I'll play along."

Paul scanned the room, then clicked his fingers. "I need a pen and paper."

"Junk drawer, by the refrigerator," Amanda said, pointing toward the kitchen.

He opened the drawer and took out a pen and a tiny rectangular hot-pink notepad. "Um, couldn't spare something bigger than this to write on?"

"How long is your list?"

"Not long. I'll make it work." He turned around to write, then folded the sheet into a postage stamp size. "Don't open that until you're in the store."

"Why?"

"So it'll be a surprise for you too. Do I have to tell you everything?"

"Apparently." Amanda lifted her keys from the hook next to

the back door. "I'll be back in a jiff." She lifted a finger toward Jesse. "You be good for him, okay?"

Once Amanda had shut the door behind her, Paul grabbed Hailey and Jesse each by a hand and ran toward the front window, ducking down to peer over the windowsill. "Let's make sure she's gone, and then we'll get started. But we'll have to work fast."

He watched as she got into her car and pulled away from the front of the house onto the street.

"Move out," Paul said. "To my truck." Paul lifted a big bag over the bed of the truck, then handed an extension cord and white Christmas lights to Hailey and Jesse to carry.

He made quick work of putting up the tent. Not one you sleep in but more the party kind with netting to keep out the mosquitoes. Then he plugged in the extension cord and ran it over to drape twinkle lights around the edge.

In his truck, he also had nine blocks. He carried them over about six feet from the tent and put them in a circle. "You two, go collect twigs and place them inside the blocks here." He propped a couple of large branches in the middle to get them started.

"Are we having a campfire?"

"We are!"

Jesse's mouth dropped open. "I've wanted to do that my whole life!"

The kids were so excited you'd have thought Paul had put Santa inside the tent too.

"She's back! She's back!" Hailey yelled as she ran from the front gate, where she'd been posted on lookout.

"We're ready." He gathered them and they all three sat inside the tent. It was starting to get dark, so the twinkle lights were beginning to really show up.

"Would you look at this!" Amanda came around the corner

and stopped short of the tent. "This is beautiful. Look at how busy you were while I was gone. Wow!"

"Do you like it, Mommy?" Jesse danced at her side.

"I do. I think you're going to really like what Paul had me pick up too."

"What is it?" Hailey asked.

"Guess," she said.

Paul watched their interactions with pleasure.

"Turtles?" Jesse looked hopeful.

"Nope."

"More lights. Colored ones!" Hailey's guess should've been no surprise.

Amanda lifted up the shopping bag, then tugged out a giant bag of marshmallows. "S'mores!"

"No way!" Hailey clenched her hands into fists. "Oh my gosh. This is the best night ever."

"We collected sticks for a fire and everything," Jesse said.

"Okay, and there's still more." Paul went inside and brought the yellow bag out with him. "When it gets dark, we're going ghost crabbing." He handed out headlamps and buckets with matching shovels to everyone. "Amanda, you can be in charge of the net. It even has a light on it."

"My. This is quite an adventure."

The kids raced around the yard, wearing their headlamps, and Paul and Amanda sat in the tent.

"This is a lot of work. Thank you. It's really nice."

"You seem off. Did something happen while you were out?"

"Yeah. It's stupid."

"Tell me."

"I don't know why I'm letting it bother me." She let out a huff, then looked him square in the eye. "I ran into one of the wives from base at the store. She's here vacationing for the week. She made a comment about us spending time together."

Paul grimaced. "I mentioned it to Scottie when I saw him. He must have said something. That got around fast. I'm sorry."

She lifted her hand to stop him. "No. We're friends. It's fine. It's just the way she said it. I felt so . . ."

The look on her face weighed on him. Why did people have to be so judgy? And what if they *were* more than friends? It's what he wanted more than anything. *Please don't shut down on me now.* "She's a pot stirrer. It doesn't mean anything."

"Maybe." Amanda shrugged, but the mood still hung over her. "What would Jack think? I wonder."

"I think he'd be glad you're smiling. Or you were. I think he'd be glad we're renewing a friendship that meant the world to all three of us. He's not here to take care of you. I think he would trust me with this." He hated the fact that one little comment had made Amanda second-guess things.

"Is it duty? Honor? Is this some kind of secret Marine code, you being here?" Her jaw pulled taut. "You don't have to do that."

"No, no. You're my best friend. I want to be here. You make me happy. Don't let this ruin our night. Come on. We all need this. Life is good."

"It does feel good, but does that make it right?"

"Something brought us back together. I think this is meant to be."

"What is this?" She gestured between them.

"I don't know. I know what I want it to be, but I don't want to scare you away."

"I'm already scared."

"Don't be. Please don't overthink it." He took her hand. "Relax. It's time to ghost crab." He turned on his headlamp, then reached over and flipped on hers too. "Let's gather the troops."

Her smile sent an encouraging rush through him.

"Fall out, woman!"

Amanda scrambled out of the tent, and Hailey and Jesse ran over, almost out of breath. "Are you two ready to go?"

"Yes. Gather the pails. The net. Onward to the beach!" Paul bellowed.

They marched in single file over the dune to the beach. "Left, right, left."

For an hour they ran and danced in the damp sand, watching for the crabs to pop out so they could swoop them up and put them in the buckets. As it turned out, Hailey was better at it than any of them. Finally, they dumped all the buckets and watched the crabs scuttle sideways across the sand for safety.

"That was fun! I was the best!" Hailey cheered.

"You were very good. A natural." Amanda placed a pretend crown on Hailey's head. "Miss Ghost Crab."

Hailey curtsied. "Now what?"

"S'mores time," Paul said. "Back to headquarters."

After s'mores, the kids wanted to bring their pillows and blankets out and sleep in the tent.

He pointed at the fabric stretched overhead. "This is really more of a picnic tent to keep the mosquitoes off us while we play. I tell you what. I'll bring my sleeping tent over someday and we'll do a campout. Deal?"

"Okay."

Amanda tucked them in, and he waited outside by the fire.

She came out to sit with him. "Jesse was asleep before they finished the prayer. It was a pretty awesome day. Thanks for everything."

"You're welcome. I had fun too."

He put another marshmallow on the roasting stick, twisting it over the flames until it was golden brown, and offered it to her.

"Thanks." She pinched her fingers around it and bounced it in her hand. "It's hot." She blew on it, then nibbled at the crispy edges. "Some things are yummy no matter how old you get."

"I know." He puffed the flames off another marshmallow and ate that one himself. *I can't leave here with you second-guessing us. I want to be more than friends.* Fear knotted in his gut as he sat there staring into the fire, hoping for the right words. After a long silence, he put down his stick and grabbed Amanda gently by the hands. "I'm sure this seems abrupt, but we were so close before."

"We were."

"I'm so sorry I haven't been there for you all along. I wish I'd fought to stay and help even when you pushed me away, but I needed the time. I wouldn't have been useful no matter how good my intentions were at that point."

"I wasn't ready for it either."

"All I've thought about is you. This whole time what made me know I had to change . . ." He swept a hand through his hair. "I got reckless, Amanda. You are all that kept me from self-destructing. In my heart I knew I couldn't give up. It was always you and Hailey and Jesse."

"I'm glad you're safe, but that doesn't have anything to do with me. I mean, I'm selfishly happy you're not in the Marines anymore and are going to do something else now."

"Amanda, it has everything to do with you."

She stared at him. Obviously, none of what he said was making sense.

"I never thought about you as anything but my best friend's wife and my best friend as long as Jack was alive. I loved him like a brother, but, Amanda, you stole my heart the first night I met you. When you leaned in while we were dancing and told me your name, I thought to myself, *This woman is special.*"

"You're sweet, but—"

"No, no buts. Jack knew, but we had one priority back then: Marine Corps to the core."

Her mind reeled, replaying moments from the past. From before she'd married Jack.

"When I came home and you and Jack were a couple, I was torn apart, but he was my best friend. I looked high and low for a woman just like you. Like Jack's Amanda. There isn't another Amanda that I could ever find. Everyone I dated I compared to you. But you're the best, Amanda."

She laughed, and that hurt his feelings.

How could she think this was funny? But then he recognized the nervousness in her laugh. *For Pete's sake, this is coming out of the blue. Slow down.*

He laughed at himself. "I'm sorry. Okay, that was a lot to throw on you, and it sounds crazy and might even be. I'm not here expecting a declaration of love or anything, but I do want to be in your life. I want to be there for you and the kids." He stopped and took a breath. "Sorry. Let's not get ahead of ourselves. Not us. I mean me. I know you need time, but please let me be there for you."

He sat there baring his soul. "Please give me a chance. We can take it as slow as you need to. Let's see what happens."

Her eyes lowered and she bowed her head.

Afraid she was going to say something he didn't want to hear, he filled the silence. "Amanda, if there's one thing I've learned, it's that there are no coincidences. We ended up in the same town. That has to mean something."

She raised her chin, hope in her eyes, a smile on her lips.

He sighed. "I probably should let you get to bed too." The last thing he wanted was to rush her or mess it up.

"I am bushed. It was a lot of fun, though." She stood, chuckling. "Thanks so much, and thanks for not letting me allow that old gossip to get the best of me. You're right, she always did like to stir the pot."

"Let's trust the right things will happen. Enjoy every day and then do it again."

"That sounds really good."

He extinguished the fire and rolled up the extension cord to be sure no one would trip on it. "Do you mind if I leave up the tent? I thought it might be nice for y'all to enjoy over the summer."

"Yeah, I can put a couple of chairs in there. We can stargaze. You always liked that."

"That would be really nice." He walked over to the gate.

He could hear her phone ping, just as it should when the gate opened. He turned and she gave him a delighted thumbs-up.

"Sweet dreams," he said.

Her arresting smile tempted him. She'd be in his tonight. He looked up into the sky.

I love this woman. Please let her be mine . . . forever.

23

Amanda pulled in front of Maeve's house. She leaned over to the back seat. "You two, stay put. I'll just be a minute," she said to Hailey and Jesse, then got out of the car.

She had been pleasantly surprised by the phone call from Maeve this morning. It was nice to be able to do something for her. She'd been such a sweetheart to Amanda since they'd moved here.

Dressed in a flowing pink sundress, Maeve looked like Mother Earth coming down the stairs.

"You look so pretty," Amanda said.

"Well, it's a very special occasion. I can't wait to meet the two newest residents of Whelk's Island."

"It's so exciting." Amanda helped Maeve into the car.

The trip to Kimmy and Nate's house was shorter than she'd anticipated. Apparently, Becky had been expecting them, because she was already on the front porch, waving when they pulled into the driveway.

Maeve jumped out of the car and went up the stairs. She and Becky hugged and celebrated.

Amanda gathered Hailey and Jesse. "Be on your best behavior. Promise?"

"Yes ma'am." They were eager to see the twins too. The idea

of two people who looked exactly the same seemed like magic to them.

"Come on in," Becky called from the porch. "I have some treats for you two kids." She nudged Amanda when she reached the top step. "I'm going to practice my grandmother spoiling on your two. I hope you don't mind."

"I'm sure they'll love that." Amanda watched Hailey and Jesse light up, but her heart sank as she thought about how little time they'd ever spent with her parents. Their own grandmother and grandfather.

Once Amanda was inside, she hung back while Maeve walked over to the chair next to Kimmy and the twins. "Kimmy, you and Amanda will become close friends. You both have that spirit of teaching. Kind souls."

"Amanda, it is so nice to meet you." Kimmy, an athletic strawberry-blonde who only favored her mother by way of their jade-green eyes, stage-whispered, "Maeve is the kind one in this town. I aspire to be her someday."

"Oh, I can understand that," Amanda said.

"This is my husband, Nate. I don't think he's realized how much work is ahead of us yet." Kimmy sounded overwhelmed herself.

"Hi, Nate. Congratulations to you both. I love babies, and mine are growing up so fast. I have one starting school this year. You have your hands full, so please let me help out."

Hailey and Jesse popped into the room, both sucking on cherry-red popsicles. "Someday I can babysit for you," Hailey said.

Kimmy jumped right on that suggestion, speaking to Hailey as though she were an adult. "That'll be perfect," Kimmy said. "Until then, you can all learn to play in the ocean together. I can teach you to surf."

Hailey and Jesse exchanged an unsure glance. Amanda was pretty sure they didn't understand what surfing even was. They still had a lot of beach life to learn. Whelk's Island was the perfect place for that.

Maeve turned to the matching bassinets in the middle of the room. "Your babies are beautiful, Kimmy."

"Thank you. I can't believe how tiny they are. They don't even seem real."

"Which one is which? Tug told me their names, but I'm not sure he even got them right." Maeve leaned forward, touching one of the bundled twins.

Kimmy laughed. "Well, he probably got the names right. They aren't identical."

Nate placed a loving arm across Kimmy's shoulder. They made a sweet couple, both with light hair and tan as could be. "Nixie is on the left. It's a German name that means 'little water sprite.'"

"Oh my gosh, how perfect is that, and she looks just like you, Nate. I bet she's going to be a blondie." Maeve reached for and held Nixie's petite hand. "You are a beauty. Tell me about the angels." She looked over to Kimmy and Nate, smiling as she hunched her shoulders playfully. "I always ask babies that. They light up. I wish they could tell us what it's like to be with the angels before they come to us. I can tell she understands what I'm saying." Maeve stepped back, looking at Kimmy. "They look so much alike."

"I was so afraid we wouldn't be able to tell them apart. I'd read that people write with Sharpies on their feet or put colored wristbands on them, but that seems so weird." Kimmy shook her head. "I'm glad I won't have to resort to that. Brenna has a slight reddish tint to her hair, like mine. For now, anyway."

"I think they both look just like their mother," Nate said. "Thank goodness."

"Oh, stop." Kimmy wrinkled her nose at him. "He's always saying that. You know you're good looking. Stop that."

"Oh, Kimmy. I'm so happy for y'all." Maeve took a bag out of her purse. "I didn't wrap this all pretty or anything, but I have something for the girls." She pulled tissue paper from the bag, untangling delicate wires before finally holding a beautiful mobile between her fingers in the air for them to see. Small pieces of sea glass hung on short silver wires, and larger pieces from long wire. The mobile twisted, casting colorful light from the sea glass.

"Maeve, that's beautiful. Did you—"

"I made it for you. So there's a story here."

"Isn't there always," Kimmy teased. "Right, Momma?"

Becky nodded with a grin.

"Well, the day I heard you were in the hospital on bed rest, I was at Tug's Diner for breakfast. When I walked down on the beach, I found these two perfect pieces of pink sea glass." She pointed to two rosy pieces at the top. "Now, I don't know how much you remember about sea glass, but pink is very rare. To find two pink pieces so nicely matched on the same day at the same place . . . that's no coincidence. At that moment, I knew your twins were both going to be girls. I just knew it."

"Maeve, thank you for this. It will be perfect in the nursery."

"I hope so."

Nate took the mobile from Maeve and hung it from the window frame. As the artfully coiled wire moved, each brilliant piece of sea glass cast rainbow hues of color around the room.

Nate stared at it. "That is art. Quite fascinating, really, even for an adult. I want it over *our* bed."

"Thank you, Maeve," Kimmy said.

Hailey's mouth, red from the popsicle, formed a perfect O. "Look at all the colors!"

Maeve looked pleased. "I'm glad you like it. I've always heard that color and movement is good for babies. It gets them looking around and wondering."

"Well, there's nothing more wonderful than the sea. You and I have that in common. I love this mobile so much." Kimmy teared up. "I'm sorry. I'm doing a lot of crying right now, but you're so sweet and talented and wonderful. Maeve, we love you. Thank you for doing something so special for our girls."

Maeve pulled Kimmy into a hug. "Oh, honey, I'm so proud of you. You're a strong, beautiful woman. You're going to be a wonderful mother."

"I hope so. I was terrified to have even just one baby. I don't know why the Big Guy upstairs thought I should get a double dose, but I'm trying to remind myself it's a blessing."

"It most certainly is." Nate returned to Kimmy's side. "I'll do my part, baby. Don't you worry."

Amanda fanned her tears from the tender moment. "Well, my gift is not handmade or colorful like Maeve's, but I promise you it is practical." She carried a stack of gifts over to Kimmy.

"You didn't need to bring a thing."

"I've got two children, remember? They are two years apart and that was hard enough. I'm tickled pink to help you in any way that I can. Any friend of Maeve's is most definitely a friend of mine."

"Thank you." Kimmy opened each item carefully. "They are wrapped so pretty I hate to mess up the paper."

"Oh good grief." Nate took one of the boxes from her and ripped into it. "No offense, but I went through this with her at our wedding shower. She takes a year to open each one, and then it's not like she does anything with the paper."

"What do you want me to make from it?"

"I don't care, but if you're going to painstakingly protect the paper as you open the gift, you ought to do something with it afterward other than throw it away."

Kimmy made a funny face. Nate kissed her on the nose, to which she crossed her eyes. "It's the only bad habit she has. Totally fine with it, as long as she lets me open half the presents so I don't fall asleep."

"We have an understanding." Kimmy lifted matching dresses into the air. "Oh my gosh, these are too cute."

"I couldn't resist. I promise everything else is practical."

Nate picked up the big box of preemie diapers with one hand. "Oh great. I guess I'm going to be a pro at these soon." He put his other hand on his hip. "I wouldn't admit this to just anyone, but I had no idea how many diapers newborns went through in a day. No wonder they are in boxes of eighty to a hundred."

"Hopefully, you'll be a pro by tomorrow," Kimmy said, rolling her eyes. "These babies are pooping machines."

Amanda remembered bringing Hailey home and all the things she had to learn as a new mom. Jack never really mastered the diaper thing until Jesse came along. Paul gave Jack a hard time about it. Come to think of it, Paul probably changed as many diapers as Jack did on their kids.

"She's not exaggerating," said Nate. "I told her we could save enough to send these girls to college just by raising them in the ocean like mermaids. The cost of these diapers is outrageous, and we're going through them like soapsuds."

"Yeah, we're not doing that!" Kimmy shook her finger at Nate. "I'm never going to be able to leave my girls alone with you for fear of your shortcuts. I can see it now. They'll each be on one side of the kitchen sink so he doesn't have to change a diaper."

"Are you going to let me hold one of these babies?" Maeve looked like she wasn't willing to wait one more second.

"Yes ma'am. I'm sorry. You could've been holding them all along. Go for it."

Maeve walked over and scooped Brenna right out of her bassinet. "I know we're not supposed to have favorites, but this one looks exactly like you did when you were born, Kimmy."

Becky sat proudly at the end of the couch. "I told her the same thing. Nixie's already sassy just like Kimmy was, though."

Nate scooped up Nixie. "Hey, girl." She wiggled her arms and looked completely content with him. "She's so light." Nate lifted her up and down, then cradled and rocked her.

The rest of the room seemed to fall away as Amanda focused on Nate holding the baby. When Hailey first came home from the hospital, she wouldn't stop crying. It was Paul that finally got her to quiet down, although Amanda had told herself at the time it was more like a round of hot potato and he got the lucky handoff. It struck her that Paul had been there through all the big moments: before she'd married Jack and then as part of their family at the birth of each child. Their first words, birthdays, and first steps. Most recently their first kite. First ghost crabbing too.

Amanda put her hand out, steadying herself on the back of the chair she was standing next to.

Maeve and Nate walked closer to each other with the babies, holding them at an angle to see each other. Then Nate turned to Amanda. "Do you want to hold her?"

Amanda snapped out of it and took Nixie. The innocent life in her arms was half the size of Jesse the first time she held him, and Nate was right. She was as light as a feather. Her movements didn't even look real. Tears blurred Amanda's vision. "She's beautiful." Amanda pressed her thumb to the baby's hand. "You are so special," she whispered.

Memories of her own children filled her heart. Being a new mother and that first feeling of reassurance at the thump of their heartbeat. She carried the baby over to Hailey and Jesse. "Come meet your new friends."

They walked over, peering at the fragile life in her arms.

"She's little," Jesse said.

Hailey pressed her finger against Nixie's soft arm. "I'll save all my pretty dresses for you. I'm growing so fast that Mom just bought me new ones. You'll look so pretty."

"Awww," Kimmy said, tears slipping down her cheeks. "She is the sweetest."

"And you are the most emotional," Nate said, hugging her shoulder, then pressing his cheek against her head.

Maeve put Brenna back in the bassinet.

Kimmy reached toward Nixie. "I'll take her. It's about time to feed them."

"Again?" Nate shook his head. "I wish I could get her to feed me and give me snacks this often. Sometimes she forgets to eat at all and it'll be eight o'clock and I'm praying for a PB&J."

Kimmy rolled her eyes. "You are so mistreated."

"On that pitiful note, we are going to leave," Maeve said. "Thank you for letting us join in your celebration. I'm so happy for you two. And for you, Becky. Being a grandmother is going to be exhausting but the best part of your life. I wouldn't have missed this for the world."

Hailey and Jesse hugged Becky. "You can be our grandma, too, if you want."

Becky clutched her heart. "I'd love that." She turned to Amanda. "These two are absolutely the sweetest."

They walked back outside feeling the joyful light of those fresh new lives. Amanda watched Hailey and Jesse run to the car and climb into their car seats. They were growing up so fast.

24

Amanda had been busy getting ready for school orientation night, and she'd tried a couple of practice runs taking Jesse to the pre-K at church to be sure he wouldn't have a meltdown when she had to start working.

Not to worry. Jesse loved going, so much so that it had almost hurt her feelings. But the week had flown by and they'd all survived it. Thankfully, the school offered day care for the kids while she worked half days getting her classroom ready, so Hailey and Jesse spent those days together, and both had made some new friends. Matt, who they'd met at church, and Hailey were both excited about the first day of school and had been practicing their alphabet together. Jesse could almost recite it too.

It had been a long time since she'd worked outside the home, and all the additional preparations were keeping her extra busy. So busy that she hadn't been on the beach much. It was possible she'd just missed Maeve on the new schedule, but she was suddenly worried about her.

Thank goodness the weekend gave her a little breathing room. She picked up her phone and dialed Maeve's house, but there was no answer.

Amanda checked the timing of the tides, since Maeve's walks usually coincided with low tide whenever possible, so she planned to catch her in the morning on the beach. She'd get the kids up early, just after sunrise, to walk down to Tug's Diner. They were sure to run into Maeve there.

"We'll take the beach walk to the diner this morning. Sound like a plan?" The three of them jogged over the dune to the packed sand, where it was easier to walk closer to the water.

Jesse carried the picture he'd drawn for Maeve. Amanda had rolled it into a tube and put a rubber band around it to keep it from getting caught in the wind and blown out to sea. Jesse liked the scroll, holding it up to his face and looking out at the horizon like a pirate the whole way.

"Well, if it isn't my favorite friends," Tug said when they walked in. "Where have y'all been? I thought maybe you found a new favorite place to get octopus for breakfast."

"No sir. We only come here. You're our favorite too," Jesse said.

"Mommy's working, so we have to go to camp at the school when she's there," Hailey explained.

"Well, as long as I'm still your favorite," Tug said, "then that's okay."

"You are," Hailey and Jesse agreed.

The kids slid into the booth, and Amanda sat facing them.

Tug brought Amanda a large cup of coffee and milk for the kids. "What can I get you, Amanda? I know what these two squirts want."

"I'd love a cheese omelet."

"Your wish is my command," Tug said.

The Wife echoed Tug's phrase from outside. "Your wish is my command."

"She's always stealing my lines." Tug started to walk away.

"Hey, Tug, have you talked to Maeve? I've been missing her on the beach since I've been working. It's been a week, and when I called last night, I didn't get an answer."

Tug returned to the table. "I spoke to her at the end of last week. Frankly, I'm worried about her this time. She's never done a disappearing act for this long before, and she won't let me come see her. Won't even let me drop off breakfast on the porch for her. I'm not sure what's going on."

"That's odd."

"She's had some health problems over the years, you know, but she's never one to complain or talk much about it."

"I'll go by there when we leave. Thanks for sharing that with me, Tug." She kept one eye on the back door, hoping Maeve would gracefully float in like they'd never missed a visit.

They finished breakfast and Amanda let the kids hang out with The Wife before leading them back down the beach to go home. Even though the tide was now coming in, there was still no sign of Maeve.

Amanda stopped at the mailbox on their way back to the house. Hailey held the door open for her as she juggled the stack of mail. She pulled the magazine and sales catalogs from the pile and set them aside, then started sorting the trash and the real mail into two separate piles on the table.

"Coupons," Hailey sang. "For ice cream! That should be in the good pile."

Amanda let Hailey stack them with the bills, which were mostly what she had left in her hands.

Paul's voice came from the back door. "Hello?"

"Come on in." Amanda walked down the hall toward the kitchen. "Hey there."

"Hey, yourself." He gave her a hug and then twirled her.

"Twirl me like a dancer too." Hailey raced over with her hand over her head.

Paul spun her and then grabbed both her hands and stepped back before twirling her again.

"That was like a whole routine." Hailey curtsied. "Mom, can I take dance this year?"

"I don't see why not. I'll check into it and figure out when we can work it in." The thought of her daughter in pink tights, a black leotard, and ballet slippers made her heart do a pirouette of its own. She'd make her tutus in every color of the rainbow.

"She'd be the most adorable ballerina. There's a dance academy over near Paws. I could help with the shuffling back and forth when you decide which nights you want to take her. Or Jesse could hang out with me at work while you two go."

"Wow, that would be great! Are you sure? You aren't too busy with the new stores and all?"

"Absolutely sure."

Jesse marched over to Paul and slung his arm around Paul's waist. "Me and Paul can do boy stuff while Hailey does ballet." Jesse put his finger on top of his head and did a ditzy spin. "Girl stuff."

"Oh, I see. Is that how it is?"

Jesse nodded. "We have to do boy stuff, Mom. You can't do boy stuff. You're still a girl."

"Oh. I always forget about that."

"Yeah, Mom," Paul teased. "You're totally all girl. A very, very, very pretty one."

"Well, thank you, sir." She felt heat rush into her cheeks.

"I had an idea," Paul said. "I thought you might want to get out and do something tonight since you've been working so hard."

"I'd love to, but I planned to try out a new herb-salt recipe tonight." *That sounds like a lame excuse. Worse than I'm washing my hair tonight.* She really did want to spend time with him. "It won't take all night, though. Can you keep these two monkeys busy for an hour or so? Then we could do something. Would that work?"

"Yes, please!" Jesse said.

Hailey ran over to the kitchen table. "Look! I can buy ice cream for us. I have coupon money."

Paul seemed to like that idea too. "Yeah. We could do that. Let's leave so Mommy can do her thing." On their way out the door, Hailey continued to talk nonstop about ice cream and what flavors everyone should get.

Amanda took a moment to enjoy the quiet in the house. Just like that, Paul had rescued her again.

She stood, relishing the idea of a little solitude with her herbs. It wasn't often she had quiet time to do whatever she wanted. A peace fell over her as she collected jars and ingredients to work on the new blend she'd thought of while watering her plants yesterday. Nothing compared to the aroma and taste of fresh herbs.

Washing them, she removed any discolored leaves and coarse stems. There was something about handling the still living plants like this that nurtured her.

She tamped a clean flour-sack towel over them to remove the moisture, then spread the variety across her favorite cutting board. Rosemary, parsley, sage, garlic, and thyme—all special in their own right, but adjusting them brought altogether new scents that were vital and fresh.

Chopping, she found a rhythm in the process. It only took about a half cup of salt for every three cups of loosely chopped herbs to get the right consistency. Some people used a food processor, but she preferred to use a knife. It took longer, but she had control of the size of the pieces and got to enjoy the wonderful smell while she worked.

With her eyes closed, she inhaled the aroma of the new recipe. Reducing the garlic and adding some sweetness from the pineapple sage she'd started growing changed the mix completely.

She spread the herbal mixture out in a shallow pan. Later

tonight when the kids were tucked in bed, she'd give it another stir, then cover and refrigerate for a few days to let the flavors really marry.

The dream of spending her days creating like this reignited. She promised herself she'd be sure to give these herbs and this dream a priority, if only for a short time, each week.

Outside, the party lights on the tent came on. She went to see what Paul and the kids were doing.

Paul pulled back the mosquito netting, letting it drape from the corner. "Surprise!"

"What are y'all up to?" Amanda stepped closer to the tent.

"We've got a secret plan," Jesse said. His dimple showed up the most when he was trying to keep a secret.

Paul walked over and placed his hands under her elbows. "Did you get everything done that you wanted to? We're fine out here if you need more time."

"No, I got more done than I thought I would. Thank you for giving me that time. It may not seem like much to you, but to me . . ." Her nose tickled. "It means a lot."

"Happy to do it." He slapped his hands together. "So, while you were busy, we came up with a plan."

"Uh-oh." Amanda made a frightened face.

"Don't be scared, Mom. It's a good plan," Hailey reassured her.

"Whew."

"Tug has agreed to stay with Hailey and Jesse while I whisk you away," Paul said. "Just an hour or so. Two, tops. If you say yes, I'll take them down there right now. What do you think?"

"I'm not sure," she said, looking to Hailey. "What do you think?"

Hailey looked at her like she was crazy. "I think it's the best idea ever."

"Then I do too." She turned to Paul. "Do I have time for a quick shower?"

"Sure. No hurry. I'll take these guys to Tug's. When you get done, I'll be right here waiting."

Waiting. Butterflies fluttered in her belly. "Okay. I'll be quick."

She showered and changed into a casual sundress, then pulled her hair into an easy side braid. She twisted in the mirror and fussed with her dress, then froze.

Am I primping? Her insides swirled. *Stop overthinking it.*

She slipped on her shoes and walked outside.

"You look beautiful tonight." Paul came over and slid his arm around her waist. "Are you ready?"

The compliment chased a blush to her cheeks. She lifted her hand to her heart, hoping he hadn't noticed.

Paul escorted Amanda to the truck and helped her in.

"Where are we going?" she asked as she buckled her seat belt.

"It's a surprise."

She grunted. "I hate it when you do that." Only he hadn't done that in years. It was like time had stopped, rewound, and dropped her back into an old scene. But this time, Jack wasn't with them.

"It's not far." He drove up the road and crossed the highway. He pulled into the back parking lot of Paws Town Square.

"This is the big secret?"

"Yep. I wanted to show you my office, and I have a picnic for us."

"Oh, that sounds fun!" She started for the handle, but he put his hand on her arm. "I'll get that." She sat back while he came around and opened the door for her. She was enjoying being treated like a lady.

Inside the building, a few people were still working, taking care of the animals and cleaning the grounds. Paul took her up to his office. Decorated in warm colors and lots of leather and wood, it was masculine. Paul turned on music and then opened the blinds of the second-floor windows overlooking the massive space. "This is the best view."

He walked over to the window and she joined him.

She stood there, looking out over everything. Paws Town Square was impressive at ground level, but from here she realized just how big it was. "This really is an awesome view. It's got to boggle your mind that you designed this. It's beautiful. The landscaping, the flowers. The way you've put every space to good use. You've got to be so proud." She turned and looked at him. "*I'm* so proud of you."

"It's been a labor of love. I get so much satisfaction from the help we're able to give through this company."

She walked over to his desk and sat in his chair, spinning around in a circle. "What's all this?" She pointed to the different colors on the sheets printed out on his desk.

"My meeting schedule. The colors are the different cities where new stores will be located. All are at different phases of the project."

"Wow! That's a huge responsibility."

"It's worth it." Paul lit two candles on the table, then opened a cooler holding some of the biggest shrimp Amanda had ever seen. "I made the cocktail sauce myself. I hope you like it."

"I'm sure I will. This is so nice. You really went to a lot of trouble."

"Amanda, I'd do anything for you."

The words washed over her.

Paul set out the shrimp and a tray of crunchy fresh vegetables. They noshed and laughed about old times until they couldn't eat another thing. "You spoil me. This has been so nice."

The first three chords of "What's Your Name" played, and they both recognized them immediately.

"I love this song," she said.

"It was playing the first time we met."

He pulled her to her feet and spun her around. As they danced around the room, they belted out the words. She laughed so hard she could barely breathe. She hadn't danced in years, probably not since Jesse was born at least. Paul whipped her around, and the old moves came right back. He crossed hands and she skidded to a stop. "Don't flip me!"

"Come on. We've done it a hundred times."

It was true. They did that move all the time, and they were good at it, but that was then. "That was two babies ago. No, I'll fall on my head."

He laughed and they moved back to safer steps to the rhythm of the song. After he spun her twice in a row, she fell into his arms and he dipped her, holding her there.

"Don't drop me," she whispered.

"You're always safe with me." He leaned and kissed her, and she kissed him back. There was nothing in her heart or mind but that very moment.

She traced her finger across his chest, then laid her cheek against it. His heartbeat was strong. Comforting.

He wrapped his arms around her and brought them both back to standing. They stood that way, face to face, arms around each other.

Then he leaned close and kissed her again. On the forehead.

Something clicked inside her. She pushed away and stepped back, plopping down into his desk chair. "Paul, this is moving so fast."

"It might seem like that, but, Amanda, I've always loved you."

She shook her head. "You said that. I love having you back in my life, but this is hard for me to wrap my head around. I've got two kids." She got up and walked to the window. "And you have all this. You're building new locations, and you have so much responsibility. Paul, you don't have to stretch your time thin for me. I'm doing okay."

"Amanda, this isn't some kind of guilt mission. My feelings for you are genuine. How can I prove that?"

She turned to him. "There's more than just my heart at stake here. Hailey and Jesse are finally getting their feet beneath them. What if you wake up and realize it's a mistake?"

"I won't."

"How do you know? What if it's too much? A family is a lot of work. You've got all those meetings set up across the country, and this work . . . it's important. Meaningful."

"Okay, I don't have any firsthand experience, but I was there with you and Jack. I remember how that was. I'll make the family work. I want that with you . . . more than anything."

"When I meet Jack in heaven, what will he think? I loved him. One hundred percent loved him. I don't want to take anything from that."

"Me neither." Paul dropped his head. "I wish you'd trust me. Tell me what to do. I'll do it."

"I need time. I need to know that if we need you, you'll be there. That we'd be the priority."

"We'll slow down." He brushed a tear from her cheek. "Oh, Amanda, I never want to be the reason for your tears. Never."

Amanda's chest tightened. "You don't understand. I promised myself I'd find a way to take care of us. I already messed up once."

"Messed up? What do you mean?"

"My plan had been to start the salt business. You know about that."

"So why didn't you?"

"I thought I'd do it from the house, but apparently you can't if a dog is on the property. Not even if you keep him completely out of the kitchen. I should've made sure before I pulled the trigger on the house."

"No. Then I'd have bought that house and we might never have found each other again."

He was right. "So many little things, all connected. One change and it all tumbles."

"Or it all comes together," Paul said. "I can set you up with space here. Heck, in every Paws Town Square location if you want it. Problem solved."

"No, Jack, it's not, because *you* solved it, not me."

He flinched, then stood there with a somber look on his face.

"Paul? What's wrong?"

His jaw pulsed. "You called me Jack."

She sucked in a breath. "I'm sorry." She turned away from him. *How could I have done that? Why?* "Would you please take me home?"

She couldn't even look at him the whole ride home. She'd been so worried that he was with her because of misplaced guilt, and maybe he never was the problem. Was she the one with misplaced feelings? *Am I trying to recreate the past with Jack through Paul?*

25

The next morning, Hailey and Jesse crawled into bed with Amanda. She couldn't make herself get up. There were too many things going through her mind, and as much as she didn't want to worry the kids, she felt unsteady and unable today.

"We're hungry, Mom." Hailey laid a hand on Amanda's back. "Can we have yogurt?"

"Yes, baby." Self-pity practically drowned her. *I can't do this.* "Hang on, Hailey. Come on. I'm going to take you guys to breakfast."

Wearing sweatpants and a tank top, she drove to Tug's Diner. She went inside and straight to the counter. "Tug, I need a favor. Can I leave these guys with you? I wouldn't ask if it wasn't important."

"You can leave them with me anytime. They aren't an ounce of trouble." He came around the counter. "You two, get up on these very special stools." They climbed up and he spun them around. "Are you ready for breakfast?"

"We're starving," said Hailey.

Jesse groaned melodramatically.

"Not for long." He turned them toward the counter and waved Amanda out.

"Thank you!" She ran outside and drove straight over to Maeve's. She meant to stop by yesterday, but then Paul came over. Now she couldn't put it off another minute. Upstairs, she knocked on the door and waited.

The television was on. Footsteps inside plodded, too heavy to be Methuselah. As if on cue, he barked from the backyard.

Finally a middle-aged woman wearing royal-blue hospital scrubs answered the door.

That set Amanda back on her heels. "Um, I'm here to see Maeve."

"May I tell her who is here?"

"Amanda. Is everything okay?"

"Just a second," the woman said without answering the question. A moment later, she was back at the door and leading Amanda into the sunroom.

Maeve sat in a white chair, looking out toward the water. She looked pale dressed in a soft-blue bathrobe. Amanda had never seen Maeve wearing anything other than gem tones.

"Maeve, I was worried. I haven't seen you, and Tug said you hadn't been feeling well. What's going on?" Amanda glanced over her shoulder. The woman in the scrubs was nowhere in sight. "And who is that?"

A pang of jealousy hit Amanda because the stranger knew more about what was going on with her new best friend. "You can always call on me for anything."

"Now, Amanda, don't be silly. You're busy. You have Hailey and Jesse, and school is getting ready to start." She motioned to the only other chair in the room. "Sit."

Maeve's speech rang oddly similar to the one Amanda had given Paul last night. She balanced at the front edge of the cushion of the small chair.

Maeve's color seemed off, and she was quieter than usual.

"I'm worried about you." Amanda folded her hands in her lap.

Maeve leaned in. "I'll be fine until I'm not."

Sounded just like something Maeve would say. "What does that even mean?"

"When Jarvis first died, I felt lifeless, and then I became so mad at him. But it all changed except the love. The love is always there. I've missed him for so many years, but my life has been very good. I'm not complaining. You've heard all this."

She gripped Amanda's hand. "My sweet friend, when I met you and saw that pain in your eyes . . . When I learned your story, it was like I was rescuing myself all over again. I didn't handle losing my husband with the grace that you did."

"I didn't," Amanda said, feeling ashamed. "I was a mess, but knowing you has helped—"

"You have managed this horrible hand with the ultimate grace, honey, and now you are beginning to live again." Maeve's head bobbed. "I once shut out the world. I really didn't even know what to do with myself. My life was void of meaning without Jarvis."

"I know that feeling." Amanda fought back the tears. She knew the sentiment too well. How helpless it made her feel. How broken she'd been. Even just this morning.

"Meeting you has been so wonderful. It's like a big finale with fireworks. You've brought real joy to my heart. And your children . . . oh gosh, they've filled a void I'd forgotten was there."

"I feel the same way. I love our friendship, and you've reached that special spot that my mom doesn't." Amanda recalled a missed message from her mom this morning. If only Mom were as comforting as Maeve.

"That works both ways, Amanda. You have a part in fixing that relationship with your mother. I stand firm on that advice. I hope you'll act on it."

Amanda laughed. "I hear you."

"Sweetie, I'm dying."

It was like a sucker punch, leaving her off-balance. Amanda never saw it coming.

"I've been sick for a very long time. Fought for years, treatments and all that, and now the fighting is over."

"How? What?"

"Does it matter? Cancer takes us all. Even old age is usually tattered with some cancer in the mix along the way, unless a fool doesn't go to the doctor and just isn't aware of it. I promised my sister, Judy, I'd come to her house when I got to this point. It's time."

"How can you be so sure?"

"I found one of those shells with a message," Maeve responded matter-of-factly.

"You did?"

"Yes. It said, '*Say goodbye to the past, because it's time to move on.*' My doctor had already told me it was time to get some help. I knew he was right. The shell just confirmed it."

Amanda looked to heaven. *Why do You have to take everything I love?*

"Is Paul with the children?"

"No, I left them with Tug."

"Paul's a very good man. Just let things happen, honey. It'll all work out as it should. You're not driving this party bus." She looked up to the sky. "He knows what He's doing."

"I know, but things are starting to get back to normal for me. I know it's selfish, but what if he changes his mind? What if he realizes it's guilt? He has that huge company to run, and we'll keep him from that good work."

"Amanda, he has capacity for you and those lovely children along with his good works. He's sincere."

"He wants to fix everything for me. That sounds like guilt.

When I told him about the hiccup with getting my business started, he said he'd give me space in Paws Town Square to do it. Just hand it to me. That's nuts."

"Or love." Maeve patted Amanda's hand. "If I let you live here so you can run your business from the cottage, is that any different?"

She stopped. "Yes, it would be totally different."

"How? I want to fix a problem for you, because I love you and want to help."

"I don't know." She closed her eyes.

"You are very special, Amanda. Paul's gesture is from the same place as mine. From the heart. Please allow me this one pleasure."

Amanda sat quietly, tears falling down her face. "I will really miss you."

"I feel the same way. You know," Maeve said, looking around the sunroom, "this is Hailey's favorite room in the house. She wandered in here that afternoon we made lunch together. I told her the room would be our secret. You should've seen her shine in here." Maeve pointed to the beautiful apothecary jar of sea glass on the windowsill. "She was so drawn to the sea glass in that jar. I'd like to be sure she gets that. I'm tying up loose ends this week."

"I can see why she loved it in here. It's almost . . . unreal the way the colors and textures fill the space."

"We had such a sweet talk. She's a brilliant child. You've been a dear friend, Amanda. You've had an impact on the way I live, and I've loved having you to talk to."

Amanda could feel the winds of change in the air.

Maeve's voice softened. "Don't be too hard on Paul. He wants to be there for you for the right reasons."

"And if it turns out to be guilt?"

Maeve sputtered, "That man has enough money to give you

a big fat check if that's all it is. Trust me, you don't go to the lengths that man has gone to for anything but love. His motives are genuine. Now, I don't know if that means you'll marry and live happily ever after, but I believe you two will be best friends again. The rest will fall into place. He's giving you his time, and together you're sharing the beauty in each day. You're breathing new joy in each other's lives."

"You think I should quit worrying."

"Which advice do you want? A good ol' island song?" Maeve sang in an island brogue, " 'Don't worry, be happy now.' " With a laugh she added, "Or John 14:27—'Peace I leave with you'? You know all the things I've shared. None of it is news. Why are you so afraid?"

"I don't think I could live through that kind of loss again."

"You'll drown in your own fear. It'll suck you down like a riptide and tear you apart if you let it. You can't live a joyful life if you're paralyzed by fear."

Amanda nodded.

"We might be an unlikely pair to anyone looking at us, but we've kind of rescued each other." Maeve's eyes glistened.

"You've definitely rescued me," Amanda said. "There are days when I stand at the waterline where the tide is bringing in the waves and lift my hands in front of me. It's like Jack is right there with me on our wedding day. I remember being there and the water almost getting to our feet with each wave. Jack held me so I didn't topple over and get wet. He had strong hands. I always felt so safe with him."

"There's a stillness in the house without your husband there," Maeve said.

"Yes. Some nights the kids are snuggled under their blankets, unaware of the weight of the world that I'm trying to carry for them, but I have to do it."

"You don't have to do it alone, though. Let Paul help. And,

Amanda, let your parents in. Even if you have to board Denali and go to them, you do it."

"I hear you. I do. But, Maeve, you don't have to leave Whelk's Island. I feel closer to you than I do to my own mother. I can take care of you."

"No. No ma'am. I want you to take care of you and your children and Paul. And Tug. Watch over that old fool for me."

"Maeve—"

"This isn't negotiable. I promised my baby sister I'd do this. I owe it to her. She'll worry herself to death if I don't. A promise is a promise, and it's time. We made the plan long ago with cool heads. It's the right thing to do. I'm not afraid."

Amanda could barely take in a real breath. "No. It can't be your time." She sucked in another gulp. "You're healthier than half the people under fifty around here."

"I'm tired." Maeve smiled, her teeth showing and her nose wrinkling as she lowered her lashes. "The trumpets will sound and there will be light, and no pain, and my Jarvis is going to be as handsome as he ever once was. I know exactly how it will feel to see him and to hold his hand again."

Amanda understood. It was the little things. Holding hands. The forehead kisses. The towel snap after cleaning the kitchen. That teary glance as they tucked their children into bed.

"Excuse me." The helper brought in two glasses of water. "I don't mean to disturb. I thought you could use these."

"Thank you." Maeve took them and handed one to Amanda. "Take a sip."

Amanda's hand shook, causing the ice to clink against the sides of the glass. "Thank you. When do you have to leave?"

"Next Friday. I've got some paperwork to get straight, and I need to make some arrangements for Methuselah at Paws

Town Square. I trust Paul will make sure he's taken care of. Poor thing is too old for another home."

"I can do whatever you need. Please let me help," Amanda pleaded with her. "Friday?" That was so soon. She already missed her. "Can I help you pack? I could pick up some boxes."

Maeve shook her head. "I'm taking two suitcases of things. You know what they say, 'You can't take it with you,' so I'll be leaving most everything behind. My sister is sending a car to pick me up. I'll just take my suitcases. Maybe a couple of my favorite shells for good measure."

"I'm stunned. You seem so healthy." She set the water glass down gently.

"Cancer doesn't have rules. It can be very sneaky." Maeve laughed. "It was hard for me to accept for a while, because for so many years after Jarvis passed on, I hoped I wouldn't wake up in the morning. Then finally when I started living again, I got the death sentence."

"I'm so sorry."

"No, don't be. I'm just being dramatic. I outlasted cancer for a lot longer than anyone expected. I did some treatments years ago, and I've bought a lot of time. But now there's nothing else to try and my organs are wearing out. I'm ready."

"You've certainly made the most of every day."

"And you should too. I've had a lot of wonderful years, but age is finally starting to take its toll, and that's okay. I met you and your family, and this summer has been one of my best yet. I'm so thankful I didn't miss out on that and grateful I was still here to see Kimmy start her family. Good stuff."

"You're special to us too."

"I wasn't sure how to broach this with you, but since you're here."

"Is there something I can do?"

"Well, I know you love your little beach cottage, but this place is bought and paid for many times over. All I pay is the insurance and taxes, and they aren't all that much. I'd like to offer you this house to raise your children in, or use it however you see fit. Start that business you dreamed of in the cottage. That could work."

"Maeve, that's so generous."

"Not really. Remember, I'm not packing anything up." She laughed. "It'll take you three years to dig out of all my junk."

"So a furnished house, even?" Amanda looked around. "I don't know what to say. If we did, at least Methuselah could stay here with us. This is home. He knows every inch of the place, and he has routines."

"Routines *are* important for the likes of us."

"I'll take care of him." Amanda looked at the wall of windows with the pretty colors streaming through. "We could really live here?"

"It's not much, but I'd be thrilled to know that a family who loves the beach is here. It's a good house to grow up in. I know. I did it. There's plenty of room. I don't even use the top floor anymore. You could host lots of guests. There are four more bedrooms upstairs. I used one as an office for a long time."

"Wow." Amanda's mind reeled. Things like this didn't happen to people like her.

"Or maybe instead of using your cottage for your business, you could rent it out and then use the income to continue to be a stay-at-home mom. Or not. Whatever your heart tells you to do. You're a smart lady. You'll figure it out. And if you let Paul come into your heart, I know he'll take wonderful care of you—and he can take care of you very comfortably—without my help. But let me do this for you."

"Maeve, you're too kind."

"If I'd ever had a daughter, I'd have loved her to be exactly like you." Maeve reached for her hands, taking them into hers. "You're a caring woman—kindhearted and strong. A wonderful mother. I always thought I'd have been a good mother."

"You would have. You're so great with my kids. And me. You're more of a mom than my own. You have been my redirection." She sniffled. Tears streamed down her face, but there was no use in brushing them away. There were too many to stop.

"Don't be sad, honey."

"You are nothing if not wise. You are going to be a tough act to follow. Hailey is going to live in this sunroom. I'm not ever changing a thing in here."

"I hope you'll continue to add your little treasures. It has been a very happy spot for me. I love this room."

"Are you sure we can't get a second opinion? More help? I could drive you anywhere."

"No, this has been a long time coming. I'm ready. I can feel my old body winding down. If I'm lucky, God will answer my prayers and let me go in my sleep. I'll wake up to Jarvis. He'll be holding my hand, there in the streaming light in heaven."

"You make it sound pretty wonderful."

"You know it will be."

"You're right. I do." She thought about the song that she played over and over, trying to soothe her pain when Jack died. *"Knowing what I know about heaven . . ."* Those lyrics reminded her why she shouldn't be praying him back: he was the one in the better place, and he'd be there for her when her time came.

"I think Hailey and Jesse need to know what's going on. Do you mind if I tell them?"

"Of course not. They've made this summer such a joy for me."

"What about Tug? He's worried about you. You've got to tell him, or do you want me to?"

Maeve sighed. "I think he knows, but will you ask him to come see me tomorrow morning between the breakfast and lunch crowd? I'll tell him. I owe him that."

Amanda stood and wrapped her arms around Maeve. "This sure isn't what I expected to find today."

Maeve's expression softened. "Life is rarely predictable if we're doing it right."

Amanda drove over to the diner. Hailey and Jesse were eating ice cream at the counter when she walked in. "No wonder they love you," she teased.

She nodded for Tug to follow her out to the deck.

"How is she?" he asked.

"I love Maeve," The Wife said.

"She wants you to come see her tomorrow between the breakfast and lunch crowd."

His head hung low. "It's not good. I sensed something was off. I've been noticing little differences."

"I'm sorry." Amanda wished she could tell him he was wrong. "You really love her, don't you?"

"More than anything in this world. Always have."

"Even before she married your best friend?" Amanda cocked her head.

"Definitely." His eyes glossed with tears. "It's not right to mess with another man's woman. I'd never do that. But even the Bible says it's okay for a widow to remarry. I never could get her to take me serious, though." He closed his eyes for a moment, then exhaled. "I love Maeve. I've lived my whole life trying to make her believe it."

"Tug, how can that be? You still loved her when she married someone else?"

"Love isn't simple. It's not convenient. It's in here." He tapped his chest. "In your heart. Your soul. It consumes you. You'd lay your life down for it. Step aside for their happiness. It's anything but easy, but it's true."

"Wow." *Oh my gosh. Paul.* She needed to fix things before she ruined them forever. The last thing she wanted was to punish Paul for loving her. "I've got to go. You check on Maeve tomorrow and let me know what I can do. Anything." Amanda pressed her hand to his cheek. "You're a good man, Tug." She turned and hurried back inside and rushed the children out the door.

She dialed Paul's number as they made the short trip home, unable to wait another second to correct the doubt that she'd caused.

Am I walking your same path, Maeve?

The call went straight to voice mail. "Paul, can you come over tonight? It doesn't matter what time it is. I don't want to do it over the phone, but I need to talk to you. Please? Thanks, Paul. I'll see you later."

26

Paul cursed himself for having missed Amanda's call. The last thing he wanted was for her to believe that anything came before her in his priorities. He'd been in meetings all day, but still he'd have had time for a quick text at least. The whole drive back to Whelk's Island, he wanted to call her, to hash out whatever she wanted to talk about, but her message had been adamant. He wanted to respect that.

He pulled in front of her cottage. The living room and kitchen lights were still on.

He walked up to the house and tapped on the screen door.

She jumped from the couch. "I'm so glad you came."

"Nothing could keep me away. Are you okay?" He walked inside and guided her back to her seat. She looked like she'd been crying. He swept his thumb beneath her eye.

She caught his hand, leaning her chin into it. "Sometimes life can be so confusing."

"It sure can." Worry etched his face. "Are Hailey and Jesse okay?"

"They're fine."

He let out a long breath. "Thank goodness. My mind has been reeling through a hundred scenarios."

"I'm sorry. I didn't mean to do that to you."

"Can I look in on them?"

"Yeah." She reached for his hand, and they walked to Jesse's room together. Paul twisted the doorknob and peeked into the room. Under the soft glow of the night-light, he saw the kids. They lay in tangles of sheets and limbs.

She put her hand on his arm, hugging his bicep. "My precious babies."

He patted her hand, then backed out of the room, almost holding his breath until the door clicked shut. "Remember that prayer you used to say when Hailey was just a baby? It was so sweet."

"Oh gosh, I haven't said that in a long time. Yeah, '*Two little eyes to look to God . . .*' is how it started."

"Yes, that's the one. I can still hear you saying it softly to her those first times you put her to bed."

"You were always there for the important moments."

"I could hear you over the baby monitor when you and Jack went to tuck her in. Your voice was like a melody."

"I didn't know you were listening. I'm surprised you remember."

"Like it was yesterday."

Amanda walked over to the couch and sat down.

"What's going on?" He took a seat next to her.

She leaned over and fell into his arms, crying.

"Hey there." *What in the world?* He put his arms around her, stroking her shoulders and neck. "What? Whatever it is, we can work it out. Tell me."

"It's Maeve." She sniffed back tears. "She's dying."

"Oh, I'm so sorry." *I can't fix that.* "What happened? She seemed fine."

"Apparently, she's been sick a long time. Her organs are beginning to fail. Her sister wants her to go to Macon, to let her take care of her until . . ."

"I'm here for you." He pulled her closer, caressing her back and planning to sit right there until morning if that's what she needed.

"The kids love Maeve so much too." Her tears dampened his shirt, each one a weight on his heart.

"Shh. I know. I hate this. She's great. Like a grandma."

"I'm going to have to tell them. She's leaving next Friday." She gobbled a sob. "They are going to be so heartbroken." The tears came with jagged breaths.

"So soon?"

She nodded. "I'm really going to miss her. Their hearts have scars already. What am I going to say to them?"

"We'll find the words. I'll help you. I'll be right here. I promise."

He held her until she fell asleep in his arms. He sat there looking at her, knowing where his heart was. He couldn't let her down. He wanted so badly to make all things right in her world. Desperately, he wanted to.

Paul's arm had gone numb hours ago, but he wasn't about to move. If Amanda woke, she might ask him to leave, and right here was where he wanted to be. With her. With Hailey and Jesse sleeping peacefully in the next room. All of them safe.

Rain began to fall, spattering against the porch and trees outside. He could feel that the hot air had cooled a bit, but it hung heavy and damp in the house.

Soon lightning snaked across the sky. The frenetic flashes strobed through the house. The heavy downpour gurgled down the gutters.

Just before morning, a roll of thunder shook the foundation. Amanda sprung up.

He stretched his arm, the prickly, tingly sensation almost

painful as the blood brought his arm back to life. He clenched his fist, then spread his fingers wide for relief.

"Oh my gosh. Did I sleep all that time?"

"It's okay."

"I'm so sorry."

"I'm not."

She pulled her feet underneath her. He could see the memories from yesterday filling in the dream spaces. "Maeve."

"It's life. She's lived a long one."

"She has, and she said she's ready." Amanda sat there sorting through conflicting emotions. "She's very peaceful about it. Why am I not?"

He ran his fingers along her arm. "Because we selfishly want to keep all the good people around us."

"We do." She nodded slowly.

"Exactly. It's why I'm still sitting here now, invited or not."

"Thank you, Paul. I know you didn't sign up for all this drama. Taking care of the kids and then me too."

"But that's exactly what I'm here for. For you, Amanda. For them too. This is what I want. More than anything. We're friends first always. I will always be here for you."

The moment was oddly quiet now that the rain had stopped, and he wondered what she was feeling. "The kids will be awake soon. I'm going to make you and the troops breakfast." He pressed his hands together. "Can I have free rein of your kitchen?"

"Only if I can have coffee first."

"You can. I'll bring you a cup. You hang right there."

"I won't turn that down."

He'd hoped she wouldn't. He went into the kitchen and made her coffee.

"For you, madam." He handed her the mug. "I'm going to

let you drink that while I rustle up some breakfast for all of us."

"An offer I can't refuse." She lifted her mug to her lips.

He went back into the kitchen and rummaged through the refrigerator and pantry, mentally making a plan. He wished he had the ingredients to make pancakes, but eggs and bacon would have to do this time.

He was taking the bacon out of the pan with a fork when Hailey and Jesse ran in and halted to a dead stop in front of him.

He turned, holding up the fork in one hand, with Amanda's pink butterfly apron wrapped around his waist.

"You're not Mommy." Jesse folded his arms across his chest, one eyebrow up in a peculiarly good impression of The Rock. Jack would have so loved that.

Paul knelt down. "Mommy is right behind you. In there."

They spun around and ran to the couch, hugging her. "Good morning, Mommy."

"Paul is cooking in your apron?" Hailey raised her arm in the air, palm up. "Is that crazy or what?"

"Hey now," Paul interjected. "Don't be talking about the chef behind his back. I happen to be quite the cook, and breakfast will be ready in a minute. Hailey, can you set the table for me?"

Hailey ran into the kitchen. "I can. I know how."

Paul dished the food onto the plates and carried them to the table. "Ding, ding, ding. Breakfast bell."

"It looks amazing," Amanda said as she sat down. Reaching for her napkin, she looked back up at Paul. "You picked this for me?" She twirled a dandelion between her fingers.

"I remember how much you love them."

"Did you know, Hailey, that when I married your daddy, he bought me this beautiful bouquet of white roses to carry but left them at his house? So I picked dandelions, five yellow ones and five fluffy seeded ones and made my own bouquet. I made Ginny drive slow to be sure I didn't lose any of the white fluffs on our ride to the beach that morning." She lifted the yellow dandelion and tucked it behind her ear.

"You look beautiful, Mommy." Jesse blew her a kiss.

"I couldn't have said it better." Paul moved around the table, still wearing her pink apron. "And after your mom and dad got married, we each blew one of those white fluffy dandelions and made wishes."

"That's right. We did."

"We do that all the time, don't we?" Hailey said.

"We sure do."

"We call them summer snowflakes," Hailey said to Paul. "And you can make horns out of them to make music, and Mom is an expert at daisy-chaining them into necklaces."

"And I bet you are too."

Hailey's long dark lashes fluttered. "Of course. She's my mom. She teaches me everything."

Paul bit down on his lip to not laugh out loud. That little Hailey was a firecracker.

"I can do the horn," Jesse said.

They told stories about dandelions and making wishes as they ate breakfast. By the time Paul and Amanda started clearing the dishes, Hailey and Jesse were anxious to get out in the yard to collect dandelions to show off their talents.

Amanda washed the dishes and he dried, making quick work of cleaning up the mess he'd made putting together breakfast.

He could see the burden she carried in her heart this morning. He could feel it too. It was nothing compared to losing Jack. She barely knew Maeve, but they had formed a tight bond. *At least I'm here this time to sail her through the loss.*

He put the last dish in the cabinet and shut it.

Amanda stood there with her back to him, wiped her hands on the dishcloth, and hung it over the front of the sink to dry.

What are you thinking? But he didn't press. He waited.

"She wants me to move into her house." Excitement tinged her words. "I mean, not just me. To raise the children there."

"It's an awesome location."

"She wants to let me live there. I'd have to pay the taxes and insurance. That's it."

"Wow!"

"It was so out of the blue." She turned around, leaning against the counter. "People will think she was crazy to let me live there."

"There's nothing crazy about Maeve. She's got her wits about her."

"Definitely. Oh, and she suggested I rent out this house or use it for my business. Someday I could hand this beach house down to them. Wouldn't that be amazing? To use the rental money to keep it up and improve it. Get some real air-conditioning."

"I could put central air in for you right now if you'd let me. You know I'd do that for you."

"Stop. No. You're missing the point. I could leave the house to them to vacation in and bring their kids here."

"That would be incredible."

"Do you think I should consider it? Moving to Maeve's?"

"If she wants you to live there, I think it's very nice. She doesn't have any other family except her sister, and apparently her sister has no desire to live on Whelk's Island."

"Yeah, I guess not. I wouldn't have to do anything about my house for a while, but maybe if we moved to Maeve's, I could use this for my herb business after all. I mean, Denali wouldn't be here."

"That's a great idea," he said. "Let her help you. Let me help you. I understand your desire for independence. I respect that, but don't cut me out. Please let me be a part of all this too. It's all I want. Do you believe that?"

"I do." She looked sincere. "Maeve was talking about paying you to put Methuselah in Paws Town Square for the rest of his life, but I told her if we stayed at her place, we'd take care of him. I think that'd be so much better. That poor old dog can't half see, but he knows his way around that house." Her eyebrows shot up. "Sorry. I didn't think about that taking business from you."

"It would be best for the dog to stay at the house if he can. I agree. My business is fine. Don't worry about that."

"Thanks."

"How is she getting to Georgia?"

"Her sister, Judy, is sending a car to pick her up. Maeve doesn't want to fly."

"Why don't we take her? I could drive. The kids could come."

"No, they'd hate a road trip that long. It needs to be a good experience for Maeve. It would be even better if she broke it up into two days. Even I don't like to sit in a car for more than five hours. I get all jammed up and achy."

"I could stay with the kids. They'd be fine with me. You go with her in the car, or drive. Whatever you think is best."

"You'd stay with Jesse and Hailey?"

"You know the answer to that. Of course."

"That's a really good idea." She pulled her hands to her heart. "I want to do that. I could make it something fun and relaxing instead of ominous." She smiled with excitement, despite the tears threatening to fall. "She always wanted to go to Charleston. She's never been. We could spend the night in Charleston. She could see those trees with the silvery Spanish moss." She clapped her hands. "Oh my gosh, it would be like the best girls' trip ever. Maeve said she's feeling pretty good, so why not?"

"I don't see why not. Talk to Maeve. More importantly, talk to Judy. Ask her if she minds if you hijack the transportation plan."

"Oh yeah. That would be the polite thing to do. Do you think she'd mind?"

"I have no idea. Maybe? I don't think like a woman, so I wouldn't dare assume." He shrugged. "Maeve knows what she's doing. But she might love the idea of seeing Charleston on the way. Maeve understands grief. Clearly, it's important to her to soothe her sister's grief. She has a lifetime's worth of memories of the ocean and its treasures in her mind. If she doesn't want to do it, don't be offended. You have to respect that."

"I know, but I don't have to like it."

27

Maeve, wearing her favorite summer dress, sat in the white chair in the sunroom. Her dress was more like a caftan, really, with fun little tassels along the bottom. The colors made her think of the stained-glass windows in the church where she grew up.

Tug walked in wearing his standard chef coat, unbuttoned part of the way, a plain old T-shirt underneath. He took off his hat as he entered the room. His hair was a mess. He was in need of a haircut.

"Thanks for coming."

Tug moved slowly, as if he thought she might dart off and run away. He sat in the other chair, his belly protruding forward like a modern-day chef Buddha. "Were you going to tell me?"

"I've been working up the courage to tell you for a week."

"So this is it. No more treatments this time?"

"No. I don't want to die sick and retching. I don't feel that bad. I think that's a much better way to go. Better than feeling horrible from massive amounts of chemicals in my body. Doc's been good to me through all this."

"I know. He's a straight shooter."

"He's a good man," she said softly.

"I'm a good man, too, Maeve. I'd do anything for you. All you had to do was ask."

She hadn't meant to make him feel slighted. She sat forward. "I do need your help on something, Tug."

"Anything, Maeve. You know that."

"I'm leaving this house to Amanda and the children. I don't think anyone will try to contest it, but if they do, I need you to make sure folks know I was in my right mind doing it. She's like the daughter I always wanted, and I know she's the one who should be here."

"I've seen how you've changed since she came along, and her kids adore you. You're not going to believe this, but I think they like you more than they like me, and you know all kids like me. All they talk about is Maeve and her shells." Tug mumbled, "Maeve, Maeve, Maeve."

"Well, don't hold it against me."

His belly rose as he laughed. "No one could ever question your state of mind, Maeve. There's not one loose marble in that head of yours."

"Thank you."

"My dearest friend." He leaned forward, cupping his hands in front of him. "I love you. I've always loved you. You know that, don't you?"

"Sure. I'm the one who got away. You've been telling me that for how many years? Way before Jarvis ever died." Maeve loved the ease of their friendship.

"It was kind of a joke in the beginning, but there was truth to it. I hope the few things you've let me do have made your life a little easier, or at least more enjoyable. Knowing you'll be coming down for breakfast has kept me getting up and going to the diner every day. You know they don't *really* need me down there."

"But you're so much fun, and The Wife would be sad not to spend the summers there."

"I'm better looking than all those young kids working for me too."

She pretended to completely agree. "I was getting ready to say that."

"I'm sure you were." He placed his hand on top of hers. "It's a very nice thing leaving your house to Amanda. I'll take care of her when you're gone."

Maeve sniffled. "I know you will."

"You tell my best friend that I've missed him." Tug squeezed her hand. "You tell him that I did my best to take care of you but you're just as stubborn and independent as you always were."

"You don't think he already knows all that? I know he's been watching over me. You too."

"I'm sure he has." Tug shook his head. "How can you leave Whelk's Island? This is your beach."

"It doesn't matter where I am, Tug. I'm ready to go, and this will bring Judy some peace of mind. She's my baby sister. I owe her that. Besides, wouldn't it be a little creepy for me to die here at home and then expect Amanda and her kids to love the place?" She shuddered.

"Oh yeah." His long, low whistle sounded like a missile. "That's kind of morbid."

"Exactly."

"Like I said. Not one loose marble in that beautiful mind of yours. This way everyone gets what they need and deserve out of all this." He slapped his chest. "I'm going to miss you so much. I love you, Maeve." Tug stood and reached for her hands. "Come here, you."

She stood and he hugged her, holding her tightly, both of them crying tears for more memories than anyone could remember anymore. He choked back a sob.

"Thank you for being the best best man in the whole world and for being the best friend." She tried to hold her voice steady. "Better than I deserved."

Whatever he'd just mumbled she couldn't make out.

He let go of her and stumbled back a step. "I need a minute."

She watched as he stepped out on the deck, leaning over it, his shoulders shaking. *He really did love me. It wasn't a joke.* "You silly old man. Why didn't you say that before now?" she said quietly.

He walked back inside a few minutes later, his eyes red and his nose swollen but his voice steady. "Will you let me at least pack some things for you to bring on your trip to Georgia?"

"That would be lovely, Tug. Judy is sending a car next Friday morning."

"Okay. Yeah, and anything else you need from me. I'll check your post-office box, help out around here. Whatever you need."

He walked back over and hugged her for a long time. So long that for a moment Maeve thought he'd dozed off.

"I gotta go before I get all sappy on you again," he said.

"Don't you grieve for me, Tug. I'll be with Jarvis. We'll get the fishing trip planned for when you make it to the pearly gates. There's got to be a good fishing spot. For sure Jarvis has already built a boat."

"I hope it's not an ark. I get a little antsy around a bunch of animals."

"You're so funny, but then again with Jarvis you never know. Thank you for being such a wonderful friend. I love you too." She pressed her lips to Tug's cheek, then slowly backed up, smudging her lipstick into his cheek. "You live that good life, Tug."

He nodded, then bolted out the door.

As the door closed behind him, she whispered, "Goodbye, my friend."

The Senior Helper was in the kitchen, listening. She was always listening.

Maeve walked down the hall and crawled into bed. She'd allowed Judy to work with the doctor's office to arrange the help here and for when Maeve got to Georgia, but she didn't have to like it. She was tired and thirsty. Didn't need a nurse for that. She took her pills and went to sleep.

When Maeve woke up, she remembered her dream. Jarvis was there. She could almost feel his presence. She looked at the clock on her nightstand. It hadn't been that long of a nap. Less than an hour, but she felt refreshed.

She got up and was headed to the kitchen to get some water when she remembered the aide was still there. She hesitated, but she wasn't about to hole up in this room all week either. She'd do her best just to ignore the woman.

"Miss Maeve, I made some soup. Can I get you a bowl and a sparkling fruit spritzer?"

Well, that didn't work so well. Maeve pasted a pleasant look on her face. "The fruit spritzer sounds wonderful. I guess I could eat something. I'll take it on the patio." She walked out on the deck, looking out over the water as she had for so many years.

The water perked and rippled when she saw the first dolphin crest. With delight, she reached for her binoculars. Sure enough, it was the dolphin with the notch out of its dorsal fin that made it look like a hook was among them. It was hard to count with so many coming out of the water alongside one another. At least twelve or more. Then she followed one specifically. *A calf.* So much smaller than the others. "Thank you for visiting me one last time." She watched until they were out of sight.

The helper came out and placed a bowl of soup with a lovely garnish on top and the drink on the table. "There you go. Amanda is at the door with her little girl. Should I ask them to join you or have her come back?"

"Please let them in, and if there's enough, it would be nice to share the meal with them. Thank you."

"There's plenty." The woman scurried off, seeming pleased to have something to do.

Maeve stood there at the rail. If Amanda had been a few minutes earlier, she might have seen the dolphin pod too. Hailey would have gone wild over the baby dolphin. She'd have to be sure to tell them to use these binoculars. No reason to take them with her.

Amanda, carrying a spritzer like the one the nurse had given Maeve, came outside. "Hi!"

Hailey carried hers with two hands.

"Hello, Amanda. What a nice surprise." Maeve locked eyes with Hailey. "It's marvelous to see you, my best friend."

Hailey giggled.

"Where's your brother today?" Maeve asked.

"He's with Paul. Mom and I are doing girl stuff with you," Hailey explained.

"I'm very happy that you are."

"Your helper is very nice," Amanda said. "She's going to bring us soup so we can join you."

Maeve rolled her eyes. "Soup isn't exactly summer food. I guess she thinks sick people eat soup. Whatever. Come, let's sit."

The chairs screeched against the slick worn wood beneath them as they sat down.

Amanda lifted the glass to her lips. "Oh, this is good. Apple, pomegranate? Maybe a dash of grape juice and seltzer water?"

"I have no idea. We don't talk much. I think she respects I like to be on my own. I like that she respects that."

"Well, that's good." Amanda took another sip, then set the glass back on the table. "You look well today."

"I feel well."

Amanda paused. "Maeve, I want to talk to you about our discussion yesterday. Were you serious about us moving here?"

"Very. I've got an appointment with my lawyer in the morning. I want to be sure no one can hassle you about it. I talked to Tug about it too."

Hailey clenched her fists, her feet swinging so much she practically wiggled out of her chair. "I'm going to be able to live in *this* house with the shell room?"

Maeve nodded. "Will you take care of all my treasures?"

"Forever!" She crossed her heart. "I promise."

Maeve leaned over and hugged Hailey. "You are as special as your mother. Don't let anything or anyone change you."

"Yes ma'am, and I'm going to love Methuselah for you too." Hailey straightened in her chair, glancing at Amanda in a way that told Maeve she'd been encouraged to be on her best behavior.

Amanda put her forearms on the table. "I thank you so much for the generous offer. I'd love to take you up on it. I promise we will take wonderful care of it and carry on the kindness you've shared in this town."

"I have no doubt that you will, and Hailey, too, as she grows up."

Amanda grabbed Hailey's hand. "I'm as excited as she is."

"Can I go tell Methuselah?" Hailey pointed to the scruffy dog lying in the shade in the backyard.

"Yes. He should definitely hear it from you," Maeve said.

Hailey raced down the ramps to the backyard. Her feet pounded on the boards.

"Maeve, how will I ever thank you?" Amanda lifted her hair off her neck. "There's so much room here, and air-conditioning too."

"Oh goodness, you don't have air-conditioning down there? Amanda, you all need to come stay immediately. It's so muggy this time of year."

"We're fine. I promise. I have a little window unit and fans. The kids haven't even complained. We're managing." She leaned back in her seat. "I do want to ask you a favor, though."

"Okay."

"I'd like for you to let me talk to your sister."

Maeve wasn't so sure about that. She took a deep breath in, but before she could respond, Amanda rattled on.

"I'd love to accompany you to Georgia, Maeve. Please? We could make a girls' trip out of it. I was thinking it would be a much nicer ride if we split it into two days."

Maeve agreed that two short days in the car would be easier than one marathon ride.

Amanda continued. "I want to leave here on Friday and take you to Charleston. I want you to see the trees and all the Spanish moss. We'll stay the night. I've already looked into it, and Paul will stay here with the kids. Then we'll drive the rest of the way the next day after a nice leisurely morning. Please. Please say yes. I promise it won't be a lot of walking, and if you're tired, you can just look out the window at them."

Maeve lifted her glass to her lips, then flopped back into her chair. "That might be the kindest thing anyone has ever thought of doing for me."

"Please. It will be wonderful. A memory I can cling to, and you too. Please?"

Maeve sat there, rubbing her finger along the condensation on the side of her glass. "Yes. Yes, we should do that. I feel good enough to do it, but frankly the long trip, sitting in a car all that time, did seem a bit daunting even if Judy was going to send a limo."

Amanda squealed, leaping to her feet and running around to the other side of the table. She wrapped her arms around Maeve, laying her head against her shoulder. "Thank you! You won't regret it. Thank you!"

The helper stepped outside with the soup.

"I'm so excited!" Amanda scurried back to her chair. "This is wonderful!"

The woman placed the soup in front of Amanda and another bowl on the table for when Hailey returned.

"Thank you." She watched the nurse leave and shut the sliding glass door behind her. "I can't eat. I'm too excited. My stomach is full of butterflies. Our trip is going to be so beautiful." Maeve smiled so wide she could feel her bottom lip tremble.

Amanda picked up her phone. "Can I call Judy now and discuss it with her?"

"Yes. Use my phone. She may not answer if she doesn't recognize the number. She's funny like that."

"Can't really blame her," Amanda said.

Maeve went inside and got her phone, then came back. She pecked the number on the screen. "Hey, Judy. Yes, it's me. Of course I'm fine. I will be until I'm not. Yes."

Maeve put her hand over the phone. "She's a worrier."

"Mm-hmm. No, we're set, but I need you to talk to my dear friend Amanda. We want to change something about the ride down. Yes, I'm still coming."

She handed Amanda the phone and watched her light up as she talked to Judy. Maeve almost wanted to pinch herself to make sure this moment was real. To see the beautiful moss-laden trees, in person, was the only thing that she'd never had the chance to do. She couldn't wait. She couldn't think of any-one else she'd want to do it with either.

"Yes ma'am," Amanda said. "I'll stay in touch the whole way. I'll text you my number as soon as we hang up. Thank you for allowing me to butt in on your plans. This is really important to me. Maeve has been a life changer for me, a real angel. I can't wait to share this with her."

Hailey marched back up the ramp at a much slower pace with Methuselah in her wake. "We had a really good talk. He's super excited. He asked if he could sleep in my room with me."

"I see." Maeve winked at Amanda.

"I don't know. What do you think, Maeve?"

Maeve pursed her lips, as if really considering it. "I think he would love it. He has a doggy bed that he sleeps in just outside the kitchen, but I bet you could teach him to sleep in it in your room too."

"Yes! Jesse can sleep with Denali, and I can sleep with Methuselah. We can each have our own dogs. The older one for me because I'm the oldest."

Amanda's head bobbed up and down. "That makes perfect sense to me."

They ate their soup, and it was actually quite good. Maeve felt a little bad for the snarky thoughts earlier. That poor woman was doing a fine job. It wasn't her fault she wasn't wanted, or even really needed at this point. There'd come a time when having a helper was necessary. May as well get used to it now.

When they finished eating, Amanda cleared the dishes, leaving Hailey sitting there with her. Maeve could see the ques-tions rolling through the young girl's mind.

"Mommy said you have to move away. That you're sick."

Hailey studied her. "You don't look sick. You're old, but you always look that way."

Maeve's belly shook as she swallowed back the laugh. "Well, it's not the kind of sick you see."

"Mom said you two are going on a road trip next weekend."

"That's right. I'm going to live with my sister in Georgia. I won't be coming back."

Hailey looked out toward the ocean. "Are you going to heaven?"

Bless her little heart. It saddened Maeve that these children, at such a young age, already understood this kind of loss and what going to heaven meant. A knot formed in her throat. "I most certainly am going to heaven. It's going to be so beautiful."

"The most beautiful place ever." Hailey's eyes widened. "No one hurts there, and all the animals are nice, even the wild ones, and the streets are gold. You might need sunglasses, because gold is really shiny."

"I hadn't thought of that. I'll pack my favorite ones."

"I'm not sure if they have shells there. I hope so." Hailey tilted her chin up. "Please tell my daddy I love him and will never forget him. I'll see him again one day. And you too. Will you look for me? You won't forget me, will you?"

"No ma'am. I will never forget you, Hailey. Your daddy won't either. I hope that every time you stand in my sunroom you think of me."

"Is it okay if I call it our shell room instead?"

Our? "I'd love that."

"I'm going to have you in my prayers every single day, and Jesse and I say prayers together with Mommy, so that's prayers times three."

Such big and loving promises from an innocent, sincere heart.

28

Friday morning got there so quickly that Amanda barely had a chance to worry about how much she'd miss Hailey and Jesse. But she wanted to do this for Maeve. The kids were in good hands with Paul, and he had Tug to call in a pinch.

She had to work fast to pull it all together. She'd never been to Charleston, either, but with a specific goal in mind, she had a good plan and couldn't wait to get started. Taking the trip would be bittersweet, but she treasured the opportunity to spend this time with Maeve uninterrupted, helping her fulfill her lifelong wish.

Judy had insisted they use the limo service she'd scheduled and offered to pay extra to allow them to break up the ride into two days for the side trip. Paul used his airline miles to book Amanda a flight back home. Everything had fallen into place without so much as a snag.

Amanda looked forward to meeting Maeve's sister. The age difference between Judy and Maeve was nearly twenty years. She could see why Judy might feel like she needed to take care of Maeve, since Maeve had taken care of her when she was young. She wondered how much Judy would be like Maeve, if at all.

Amanda and the children met up with Paul and Tug at the diner. The guys assured her everything would be fine and made her promise not to worry and to have the trip of a lifetime. That was a hard promise for her to make, but she'd try to keep it.

She hugged and kissed Hailey and Jesse, but they seemed almost eager to get rid of her since they were so excited to have a camping weekend with Paul. She tried not to take it personally.

The kids waved goodbye from the counter while Paul walked her back outside to her car.

"I trust you completely." She placed her hand on his cheek. "I can't thank you enough for doing this for me. I know it's a big favor to ask."

"It's not. I'm happy to do it. Now, you better get going." Paul stopped next to her car. "I'm not going to bother you, so you call if and when you need to, okay?"

She nodded and started to open the car door, then turned back and ran into Paul's arms. He held her tight. "You girls make these days the best possible, and then you and I are going to make memories here. I love you, Amanda. I always will. I've got this."

He kissed her, on the mouth this time.

"Thank you. I'll see y'all soon." Amanda let go of Paul and got in her car, throwing it in reverse and heading home before she changed her mind.

He loves me.

She drove to her house with those words teasing her brain. *Like love love? I can't process this right now. Focus on Maeve.*

The driver would be picking them up at Maeve's at ten o'clock.

Amanda had made some cookies and a casserole for Paul and the kids, but if she had to guess, they'd eat at Tug's the whole time she was gone. She wrote a good-night note for each of them and laid them on their pillows. A big heart on the front of each note. Paul's too.

She grabbed her luggage, then closed the door behind her, feeling blessed for the path she was on. She loved this little house and all the special moments Whelk's Island had given her so far.

She drove over to Maeve's house. She left her overnight bag in the car and climbed the stairs.

Maeve met her at the door. "Are you as excited as I am?"

"Yes. I couldn't sleep all night!"

"Come on in. I feel like ten o'clock will never get here." Maeve hurried her inside. It was a beautiful day. The Carolina blue sky was as clear as could be. There wasn't one cloud overhead, and the ocean was as calm as bathwater.

The nurse had finished up her short term last night, so Maeve and Amanda were alone.

"It was nice to have the place to myself this morning," Maeve said. "One last time."

"Are you sure about all this? You can change your mind. We can make it work. Me. Tug. Paul. We'll all do whatever you need us to."

"No. I'm sure of my plan."

"Do you have everything you want to take?"

"Yes."

The doorbell rang. "That's probably our driver." Amanda grabbed Maeve's hands, unable to hold in the little squeal of anticipation. "I'll let him in."

But it wasn't the driver. It was Tug. "Look what the cat dragged in, Maeve."

Maeve turned from where she stood at the deck's railing. "I thought we said our goodbyes."

"You said I could pack you some stuff for the trip."

"You're right, I did. Thank you." Maeve gave him an obvious look up and down that made Amanda laugh. "I don't see anything. What'd you bring me? A jelly bean?"

He lifted his empty hands. "Ha! No. It's downstairs. I put everything in two small coolers. One for hot stuff, and one for cold. Figured I'd load it in the limo for you."

"A limousine. Can you believe it? I've never ridden in a limo before," Maeve said. "Not even on prom or when we buried Mom and Daddy. They just had a Lincoln Town Car for the family, and that was expensive enough."

"We'll be traveling in style." Amanda struck a playful pose, one she thought would give her that socialite appearance, flinging an imaginary scarf over her shoulder.

A double honk came from outside.

"I bet that's him this time." Amanda left Tug and Maeve and went to the front porch to check.

"Holy cow!" Amanda shouted. The limousine looked like it stretched clear across the driveway. She waved to the driver. He stepped out of the car, wearing a blue suit and a hat. "We'll be right down."

He waved, then got back in the car.

"Oh. My. Goodness. Gracious. Wait until you see our ride!" Amanda called Maeve and Tug over. "Come on. You have to see it. And, Maeve, he's even wearing a hat!"

Maeve stepped onto the porch. "What in the world was Judy thinking?"

"I don't know, but you are in for a treat," Tug said. "You deserve it. Enjoy every moment of it."

"Oh, Tug. Goodbye, my dear, dear friend."

Amanda watched Tug hug Maeve gently, as if he thought she might break, and then he kissed her on the neck. Tug, having known Maeve his whole life, would surely feel an enormous loss when she was gone. Amanda's heart ached for him. Heaviness weighted her own heart, and she hadn't even known Maeve that long.

Amanda ran down to her car and grabbed her bag while the

driver went upstairs to get Maeve's things. When she looked up, she saw the driver carrying two small suitcases, and Tug was escorting Maeve down the stairs.

How does someone reduce a whole lifetime of belongings and memories down to two suitcases?

She watched Maeve stop and turn back, taking a last look at her home of so many years.

I still can't believe you've entrusted me with your home. I promise I will take care of your priceless treasures and love this place, this town, and its people as much as you have.

"Are you ready?" Amanda asked.

Maeve turned and kissed Tug. "*Now* I'm ready." She ducked her head and inched her way inside. "My. Would you look at this?" Her head swiveled, seeming to take in the rows of LED lighting, the beautiful accents, and the fine-crystal glasses next to the ice bucket.

"Let's do this." Amanda slid into the back of the limo. "Oh wow. The leather is like butter, Maeve. We are really in for a treat."

Blue bottles of water lined the shelf, almost too pretty to drink. Amanda opened one and poured them each a glass. Then she discovered the small refrigerated section with the fruit garnish. She put a slice of lemon and a cherry in each of their glasses. She handed a drink to Maeve, then raised hers.

"To road trips, and forever friends." Amanda tapped her glass to Maeve's.

"And adventures." Maeve took a sip, then set it in the indention on the console.

Tug carried two coolers from his truck and put them in the back of the limo. "Wooo! This is fancy, girls." He shook his head. "Don't worry about bringing the coolers back. I have a million of them. You just enjoy all this or give it away. Have a great time."

"Thank you, Tug." Amanda noted the sadness in Tug's eyes as he stepped away from the car and shut the door.

Maeve had tears in her eyes. "He's a good man."

The driver settled behind the wheel and lowered the privacy glass. "Ladies, we're in for about a five-hour ride down to Charleston. We've got beautiful weather, so you sit back and relax."

"I didn't catch your name," Amanda said.

"James," he said. "James Hall."

Maeve started laughing. "Home, James."

"Not the first time I've heard that. You just give me a heads-up if you'd like to stop, or we can plan to do so every hour where you can get up and stretch your legs."

"Yes, please," Amanda said. "We won't dawdle, but it would be good to take a break and move around."

"We could practically line dance back here!" Maeve shouted toward the driver. "How about we stop at around two hours and then an hour after that, then just two more hours and we'll be there?"

"You got it. Push that button if the situation changes or you need to break for snacks or anything else. I'm at your service. You have your own access to the radio and movies back there."

Amanda started pushing buttons. "Movies too? Check this out."

"I'm truly delighted to experience such grandeur. And more than the limo, I'm glad to be with you," Maeve said.

"Well, here we go." Amanda took Maeve's hand in hers.

The limousine backed out of Maeve's driveway. Tug raised his hand in the air, waving as they left.

"This town looks different from this vantage point," Maeve said. "It's grown so much since I was a little girl."

"I'd loved to have seen it back then."

The ride was so comfortable that time flew by, but getting out to stretch did make it an easier day.

Maeve told Amanda all the town secrets. Who she could count on and which people to watch out for.

As they crossed into South Carolina, the landscape changed.

"I wonder if Jarvis and I would've ever made this trip had he not died so unexpectedly."

"I wonder. I think about things like that too. Like our trip to Denali."

"You know what I've missed most about Jarvis?"

"What?"

"The way he held my hand." She put her own hands to-gether. "There was something about the way he held my hand. Not too tight, but firm, and I could feel his love in that simple gesture."

Amanda's heart pinched. "Jack always gave me forehead kisses. I loved them." She closed her eyes. She could almost feel him kissing her on the forehead now. The way he pressed his lips to that spot. She blinked away tears.

"It's the little things." Maeve pointed her finger toward Amanda. "Always the little things that make the difference." She clicked her tongue against her teeth. "The funny thing is, I can't pinpoint what might've been the little thing he would have loved about me. I bet he had no idea how much the way he held my hand meant to me."

"Interesting. Jack always told me forehead kisses were the most honest and complete showing of love. For that reason alone, they meant the world to me. I wonder what he would've missed about me."

"I hope I remember to ask Jarvis when I see him again." She patted Amanda's leg. "When I see Jack, I'll ask him too."

"Good. Let me know."

"I'll see if that's allowed. Listen to the ocean, because if at all possible, that's where I'll be."

Amanda had no doubt that would be the case. "I'll do that. Did Jarvis love shells like you do?"

"No, and I didn't collect them like I do now when he was alive. But back then, I had a few special pieces. Doesn't everyone? You know, the obligatory jar of shells, and the one on the back of the toilet in the bathroom. I found comfort in collecting them after he was gone."

"You'll have so much to tell him."

"So much to share."

"I hope there are shells for you in heaven. Whatever is there, it will be enough."

"You're so right."

When they pulled in front of the hotel, James went inside to check them in. Amanda had already prepaid for the room, but she wanted to get the key before they took their drive to see the trees Maeve had dreamed about all these years.

James came back and gave Amanda the key. "Here you go. Are we ready for the main event?"

"So ready," Maeve said.

The driver headed through town. It wasn't long before the privacy window lowered again. "Almost there."

"I've got my camera so we can take some pictures," Amanda said.

"I'm not taking any," Maeve said. "You take all the photos you want. I want to experience it and be present in the moment."

"We're now entering Boone Hall Plantation," the driver announced. "Almost three-quarters of a mile of these trees and Spanish moss." He opened the sunroof and slowed the car to a crawl.

Maeve rolled down the window, marveling at the site. "It's more beautiful than I dreamed."

"Can you pull over and stop the car?" Amanda asked.

"Sure."

When James pulled over and put the car in park, Amanda took Maeve's hand. "Come. Stand up with me."

Maeve climbed to her feet, and they stood with their heads out the top of the limo. Maeve reached up, her fingers grazing the dripping moss hanging like an old man's beard. "It's amazing."

They spent an hour enjoying the lane leading to the plantation, all from the comfort of the limousine. Amanda took a ton of pictures. Just as much for her as for Maeve, though.

"This is the neatest place I didn't know I wanted to see," Amanda said.

"Thank you," Maeve said. "It's even better than I dreamed."

"Would you like to see the plantation?" Amanda asked. "They have a butterfly garden and all kinds of historical things here."

"No, I really don't." Maeve shook her head thoughtfully. "This is the one thing I wanted to see, and I don't want anything else to land on top of this memory."

"Fair enough." She looked at Maeve. "Do you want to say it?"

Maeve looked questioningly at her, then started to laugh. "Oh, I do! Home, James!"

James announced a couple of other landmarks as they headed back, such as a tree that was estimated to be more than four hundred years old, and he also offered a colorful history lesson as they cruised down Rainbow Row on their way back to the hotel.

"The houses here on Rainbow Row were built in the seventeen hundreds. Originally, all of them were painted pink, but there are many rumors about how the rainbow of pastel houses came to be. One story—my personal favorite—is that the different colors helped drunken sailors identify which house they were to bunk in," James explained. "It's the longest cluster of Georgian row houses in the country and said to be the most photographed spot in the fair city of Charleston."

"My goodness. And people think the beach houses on Whelk's Island are colorful. We have nothing on these folks!" Maeve exclaimed.

"It's cheerful. I kind of like it." Amanda snapped a picture to share with Hailey. This would be right up her alley.

James pulled in front of the inn and got a cart so Amanda and Maeve could take the coolers and their overnight cases upstairs. He had the room across the hall, and the plan was to be ready at eight in the morning to head to Macon. "I'll take this up for you rather than calling the bellhop."

"Thank you, James."

Amanda was grateful she didn't have to navigate the luggage cart, as James himself seemed to be having trouble with it, and he was a big guy. She opened the door to their room and let Maeve go in first. She couldn't wait to hear her reaction. "Amanda!"

She stepped in behind Maeve.

"I've never stayed anywhere so opulent. This was not necessary. We could have spent the night at a little beach inn and I'd have been fine."

"No way. This is a girls' road trip. We have to do girlie, fun things. We deserve some pampering."

Maeve walked over to the huge oak armoire against the wall and opened one of the doors. "Look at these robes." She squeezed the fabric between her hands. "They're so soft."

"Those are for us."

"If it's okay with you, I'd rather eat whatever Tug sent along for us, put on our nightgowns, and call it an early night."

"Works for me." Amanda went to the bathroom to wash her face. When she finished, Maeve already had dinner set out for them. The aroma of home cooking filled the room. "That smells good."

"It's still warm too." Maeve picked up a fork and knife. "He even sent us real silverware."

"Nice touch." She sat in the chair across from Maeve.

"Fried pork tenderloin, one of his specialties. My absolute favorite. Mashed potatoes and gravy. Green beans—the good fat ones." Maeve unwrapped a square pan covered in foil.

"What is it? Rolls?"

"Nope. Corn bread."

They ate, nibbling on everything and not saying much. Amanda got up and looked outside. "It's starting to get dark. There's another reason I picked this hotel, besides the fact that it looked really pretty online." She pulled back the curtain. "In about thirty minutes, all of these beautiful trees out here are going to light up."

"You're kidding."

"Nope. We can sit out on the balcony and watch it all come to light."

"You've really thought of everything. I definitely don't want to miss that." Maeve grabbed her overnighter and headed into the bathroom.

A few minutes later, they stood out on the balcony in their nightgowns and fluffy white robes. They weren't the only ones doing that. To the left and right, Amanda noticed couples in their robes too. They stood waiting for something to happen. People meandered along the road below, anticipating the event. A nervous energy filled the air.

"Even if they didn't light them up, the trees are lovely

here," Maeve said. "Almost as beautiful as those at the plantation."

"I'm glad you're enjoying it. I'm loving it."

Suddenly everything lit up and the town went silent. Seconds ticked by, peacefulness cloaking them. White twinkle lights lit every single tree for as far as they could see. The moss blurred the lights, making it appear like a misty haze.

And just as quickly as the lights came on, voices rose and chatter started filling the air. The perfect moment had passed.

Maeve went back inside. "This has been a perfect day." She sat down on the bed. "I'm going to have amazing dreams tonight."

Amanda had followed her inside, locking the french doors behind her and pulling the curtains. "Me too. I'm going to sleep like a baby." Amanda picked up a small box from the nightstand and peeked inside. Thank goodness the hotel had been able to do this for her.

"This is for you." She handed the small box to Maeve.

"What is it?"

"Open and see."

Maeve opened the box, then put the top back on it. "You did this?" She lifted the lid again. "Spanish moss of my very own."

"Yes. I had them freeze it to be sure we weren't delivering you to Judy with a bunch of bugs, but I wanted you to have something to help you remember this trip every day."

"Oh my. Judy would've gone crazy at the thought of bugs. Almost worth the look on her face, but I wouldn't dare do that to her."

"Not exactly the way you want to be remembered."

Maeve shook her head. "Could shorten the grieving process. She wouldn't miss me as much when I'm gone. It could be considered a favor."

Amanda couldn't hide the shock. "I can't believe you just said that."

"You're right. That wasn't nice." Maeve covered her mouth. "That was really bad. Thank you. Very thoughtful." She scooched down on the bed, laying her head on the pillow. "I can't believe you've done all this for me. We've known each other such a short time, but it feels like longer, doesn't it?"

"You feel like forever family to me." Amanda turned off the lights over the beds, then went back over and opened the drapes. "The lights will be nice to fall asleep to, don't you think?"

"Yes." Maeve pulled her covers up under her chin.

"Honestly, I'm not sure if it's pretty or spooky at night," Amanda said.

"I guess that's a matter of perspective, but I still think it's gorgeous. I wish I'd been able to put some of this moss in my tree in the backyard. It would've been so beautifully out of place on that live oak. I would've . . ."

Amanda turned toward Maeve, who had fallen asleep midsentence. She wondered if she was dreaming of the moss in the trees tonight. She hoped experiencing it firsthand had lived up to Maeve's dreams.

She missed Hailey and Jesse, but she treasured this time with Maeve. She was so glad she'd been able to take this trip with her. It seemed like such a small thing compared to the gifts Maeve had given her. Not just friendship, but the strength to move forward. The trust Maeve placed in her buoyed her faith. Amanda and her children would be better people for having known her.

She thought of that first shell she found with the quote by Havelock Ellis: *"All the art of living lies in a fine mingling of letting go and holding on." I'll miss you so, Maeve. I'll let you go, but I'm holding tight to these memories forever.*

29

Amanda woke to the gurgling coffeepot in the hotel room.

Maeve grabbed a towel, trying to smother the noisy pot. "I'm so sorry. I didn't mean to wake you. I was trying to do something nice and have coffee ready, but this is a whole lot noisier than my old drip coffeepot."

"No, it's fine. I'm ready for coffee too."

"Coming right up." Maeve poured a cup for them both.

Amanda took one of the mugs. "How are you feeling today?"

"I'm still flying high after yesterday. It was a perfect day." Maeve's eyes glistened. "It was so beautiful. I dreamed of Spanish moss and starlit nights."

She'd seen Maeve get up in the middle of the night for medication. She wondered how she really felt. She hoped the trip wasn't too much for her, but she pushed the worry away, instead concentrating on enjoying another wonderful day together. That was her priority. "I'm going to have to bring Hailey and Jesse back to see this someday when they're a little older. I'm so glad we got to do this."

"Me too."

They both changed out of their nightclothes and packed so they'd be ready before enjoying a second cup of coffee out on the balcony.

A double knock came at their door. "That must be James."

Amanda walked over to the door and opened it. "Good morning."

"I'm here to collect your luggage."

"We've got everything ready," she said.

James rolled in the cart and piled their bags on it. "You ladies take your time. We're in no hurry. I'll be parked right out front."

"Thanks, James." Amanda walked through the room to be sure neither of them had left anything behind. "I think we're all set."

"Okay, then let's get this show on the road." Maeve clapped her hands together.

"I hate for this trip to end," Amanda said. She walked over and hugged Maeve. "I'm going to try so hard not to blubber. I keep reminding myself that you're the lucky one."

"That's right. Don't forget that."

They checked out of their room and, as promised, James was parked just outside the door. It looked like he took up the space of three cars with the limo. Well, three little ones, anyway.

Maeve giggled. "I feel so important."

"Like a star traveling incognito. I'll be your assistant." Amanda did a suspicious double take, pretending to clear the way for her. "This way, Ms. Maeve. We've got the paparazzi at bay."

"You know how I love the bay," she teased.

Amanda laughed all the way to the car.

James closed the door behind them. Then, as he pulled away, he raised the partition.

Amanda stretched out. "Want to watch a movie? Or maybe listen to some music? We've got a little less than five hours to get there."

"No movies. I'll just fall asleep. Music would be nice. Although none of that loud stuff."

Amanda fiddled with the radio, finally landing on an oldies station. "This will be fun. I love the oldies." Amanda thought James was worried something was wrong with the car because he kept rolling down the windows as if he were listening for something, but then she realized he might be trying to drown out their bad singing. Not that she cared.

When James stopped for fuel, the two women sat quietly for a while, until Amanda spoke up.

"Maeve, can I ask you something?"

"Anything, dear."

"I wanted to ask you if you had anything to do with the message in the shell for Kimmy. The one Becky found."

Maeve inhaled deeply, as if she were getting ready to go underwater. "I didn't even know she'd stumbled upon it until someone mentioned it in the diner. But no, I didn't write that for Kimmy." She sat there staring at Amanda for a long moment. "However, I did write the message in that shell." She looked away, then back at her hands folded in her lap. "I have no idea how that same shell showed back up again."

"But you did write the message?"

"Yes, I did. Twenty-five years ago."

Amanda thought she'd heard wrong at first. "Twenty-five years ago?"

Maeve nodded. "After Jarvis died. That shell was special to me. I still remember so vividly every moment from the day I found it. Jarvis had taken me over to Sand Dollar Cove to collect sand dollars. There's not a dock there, so Jarvis anchored out in the water. The water isn't deep there when the tide is out, so we walked to shore. It never got up to our hips."

She went on to tell her she'd collected several flawless sand dollars. "Jarvis didn't care about that stuff, but he knew it was a perfect day for me. Excited with my bounty, I waded back to the boat but stepped on the sharp edge of that shell."

She removed her shoe, showing Amanda the scar in the middle of her foot. "It bled like a shark had bitten me, blood pooling in the water around my calves."

"That sounds so painful."

"It was. Jarvis picked me up and carried me to the boat. He took off his shirt and wrapped my foot to slow the bleeding. Then he grabbed a roll of silver duct tape and slapped it on the gash to hold it together until he got me to the hospital."

"Oh. My. Gosh."

"I bet you're wondering if I dropped my sand dollars."

Amanda laughed. "Actually, knowing you, I'd be surprised if you *did*."

"You'd be right. I didn't drop any, but a few ended up with bloodstains that I never could get out. They're in the window in my special room."

"*That's* a story."

"Jarvis was so sweet, sitting with me for hours in the emergency room, holding my hand and getting me cups of water. He was good about things like that. That shell was a symbol of how much he loved me. How he'd take care of me. I knew if I fell ill, I'd be in excellent hands with him. Never had crossed my mind that he'd be the first to go, or that it would be with no notice."

Amanda waited while Maeve seemed to gather her thoughts.

"I hate that we didn't get to say proper goodbyes, but I know it was better for him that way. I hope for the same for myself—to just not wake up one morning."

"I can see why that shell was so special to you. But what made you write that message, and how did Becky end up with it?"

"Do you remember I told you about taking out the boat in the rain? After Jarvis died?" She cast a questioning glance at Amanda. "Out of the thin air that night—the night I couldn't go on—I took action. I took that shell down from the mantel, where it had been since the weekend we found it. I sat at the table on our sunporch under the light of a single bulb and carefully wrote a note to Jarvis."

"That's so sweet."

"I can still feel the marker in my hand that night. My skin was so dehydrated from having laid in bed, trying to die—no food or water—that my skin sort of hung to the marker. That's when I wrote, 'I can't wait to be with you, but until then know I'm gathering treasures and stories to share.'"

"So how did Becky get that shell?" Amanda leaned in.

"I honestly can't say. I dropped it in the water. I watched it sink. But that one—for Jarvis and the first shell I ever deposited—like so many of them, came back. Not directly to me, but it was a sign of some sort. Maybe that all of our lives are intertwined."

"Maeve, my life intertwining with yours has been a gift."

"And you and Hailey and Jesse are gifts to me."

Amanda let the story soak in. She held her hand to her heart. She ached for Maeve, and for her own loss. *It is her. It's always been Maeve.* "The other shells? Were you behind them all?"

Maeve smiled gently and nodded. "Even the ones that you found. On the dune and by your mailbox."

Amanda recalled the words from the shell that had been by the mailbox: *"Interrupt worry with gratitude."*

"But, Amanda, not every shell I wrote landed where I thought it would. I did find that shell the day I made the decision to go to Judy's; however, I didn't write that one for me. I don't really remember who I'd written it for or where I'd left it, but I think it was my handwriting. And I needed that message at that time."

"Your advice has helped so many."

Maeve shook her head. "No, Amanda, I wasn't the messenger. I was just the shell collector. I found the treasures and shared them when I thought someone needed to be reminded of hope, but when and where those shells were found was out of my hands."

"Those shells were your gift. It is truly amazing, Maeve. The note in Becky's shell was so perfect for you to Jarvis—and Kimmy and her new twins. Does that make you wonder if it may have even had another stop somewhere along the way?"

"I'd never thought of that, but perhaps." Maeve seemed intrigued by the possibility.

"The Havelock Ellis quote. The one in the shell we found. It's become my favorite."

Maeve nodded. "A lot of the shells have been specific to a situation. Something I wanted to say without being a busybody old lady, and never just my opinion. I used quotes and scriptures or a simple word or two. 'Believe.' 'Have faith.' 'Hope.' Just something to make people pause for that split second it takes to get back to the reality of a situation and find hope. It's all about hope." Maeve looked at her. "I did leave those shells for you."

"I'm so glad you did."

"I only hand delivered a few compared to the probably thousands I've cast into the ocean or left in flowerpots or along the dunes. And somehow they seem to land in the hands of people who need the message."

"Did you ever hope that's what would happen?"

"I never really thought about it until it started becoming a thing. Honestly, the ones I didn't plant seemed to help as much as the ones I did. Like the one that Becky found."

Amanda pressed her hand to Maeve's arm. "Your wonderful gifts to so many. It's going to be sad to think no one might ever find another."

"Unless they keep recirculating. They could keep popping up for years. I kind of hope they do." Maeve looked out the window with a smile on her face, rather quiet for the rest of the ride.

James must've been ready to be back in Macon, because it took less than four hours to get there.

"I think James may have sped." Maeve flashed her a knowing look.

For some reason, that struck Amanda's funny bone. "Are you planning to wage a citizen's arrest on our driver?"

"That would be a first for me." She giggled with a wicked look in her eye that made Amanda wonder if she might actually do it.

When they got to Judy's neighborhood, Amanda worried about Maeve living in a subdivision like this. Not that it wasn't nice. It was. Huge houses on big sloped lots. Old-timey lamp-posts lining the walking paths dotted by professionally land-scaped beds, but it was nothing like Whelk's Island.

"I guess this ride was a warm-up for the style in which you're about to get accustomed to," Amanda teased.

"I've never even seen a picture of her house. It's more grand than I'd imagined, but that doesn't impress me."

"Maeve, call me every day if you want. Or not at all. Please call if you need me or want to talk to the kids. Anytime day or night. And if you want us here, we will be here. I promise."

"Oh, Amanda, you are so special. I will remember that, and thank you for this trip. It's meant the world to me. There's not one thing that I want for now."

Maeve held Amanda's hand the rest of the ride.

They turned into a long driveway lined with crape myrtle.

The road curved, making a large circle in front of the house. In the middle of that circle, a large fountain sprayed water into the air.

"Very pretty." Amanda noticed Maeve's lips tightening. "Are you okay? You can come back home with me. Whatever makes you happy."

"I'll be fine. It won't be for very long. It's the right thing to do, and I'm at peace with this."

Amanda nodded, unable to respond, else she might start crying and never stop.

"Amanda, some people only come into our lives for a season. I'm glad our paths crossed. I needed you in this phase of my life, and I pray that my experience has somehow brought you some peace with your recent past and possibly given you a nudge toward a happy forever after with Paul. This summer has been so eye opening for me. I'm definitely going out on a high note. Don't you mourn for me. I want you to celebrate. Hang colorful lights across the yard and throw a wonderful party. Be brave and enjoy everything you deserve in this lifetime. Do not waste a single day."

"Yes ma'am. I promise I am listening to your every word. I will make you proud."

"Oh, Amanda. I already am."

James opened the door and helped Maeve out of the car. Amanda also got out, feeling protective of her new friend as Judy and her husband made their way toward them.

Amanda hung back, not wanting to interfere with Judy and Maeve's reunion. There were hugs and introductions, and it was all a blur to Amanda. She was thankful when James interrupted the chatter to offer to take her to the airport if she wanted him to since they made such good time.

Judy didn't hesitate. "Absolutely. Amanda, thank you for getting my sister to me safe and sound. You are a good friend."

"It was my pleasure. Can you hang on one second?" Amanda dipped into the back seat of the limo and pulled out a small bag. She reached in and grabbed a card, which she handed to Judy. Then she presented a photo album to Maeve. "The kids and I made this for you. It's just pictures from home."

"Thank you." Maeve hugged her, holding her a long time. "I love you, Amanda. Kiss my little angels in the palm of their hands for me. Tell them I'll always watch over them. And you—you are going to be fine. Go ahead and get moved into the house. You don't have to wait until the papers come, but they are on the way. Reinvest in your new reality. Live. Love. Laugh. And keep that sand under your feet."

"Yes ma'am."

They both cried, not even bothering to sweep the tears to the side. Amanda choked back a sob as she slid back into the limo.

At the airport, Amanda bought a paperback novel and settled in at her gate. She resisted the urge to call Paul. If things were going well, she sure didn't need to disturb them or make the kids antsy for her return.

When she did the calculation, she could've driven by the time she added the wait at the airport and the flight time. But at least it gave her time to be alone with her feelings.

When she got off the plane, her hands were sweating. She was ready to get home. She went straight to baggage claim and retrieved her suitcase. When she turned around to go outside and get a taxi, she spotted Paul, Hailey, and Jesse all holding signs. Hailey and Jesse each had eighteen-inch poster boards with **Mom** colored on them. Paul held a big yellow cardboard with **The Most Beautiful Girl I Know** written across it in big black balloon letters. Underneath in red were the words "We missed you."

She ran over to them, throwing her arms out, wanting to hug them all at the same time. "I love you all."

She knelt down and Jesse clung to her while Hailey draped herself across her back, kissing her ear. "We love you, Mommy."

Paul hovered above them.

"Things went well?" She looked at her two children. Good as new, like nothing had happened. Their big smiles cheered her heart.

"It was so much fun. We did a lot of stuff. We even slept in the backyard. Like camping."

"Wow, that is very cool!" Amanda stood, reaching for Paul's hands.

He took her hands in his. "Welcome home."

"I'm so happy to be back. Thank you. Please tell me the kids behaved for you."

"They were great. I was horrible. Hailey had to put me in time-out."

Hailey laughed hysterically. "He was good. Plus, he made us the best pancakes in the whole world."

The thought of Paul, in her apron, cooking for Hailey and Jesse filled her heart. He never looked happier. "You really had fun with them, didn't you?"

"I did, but I've been counting the minutes until I'd see you again."

"Oh my gosh. I'm the luckiest girl in the world."

"I hope you feel that way every day." Paul took the handle of her suitcase. "We're parked just across the way. Line up, kids." He took Jesse's hand, and Jesse took Amanda's. Hailey ran to Paul's other side, holding his hand that was on the suitcase. "We've got a system."

"Very nice."

When they got to the parking garage, they all piled into Paul's truck. Amanda loved that he had moved the car seats to his truck. "Wait. Did you buy new car seats?"

"Yeah. We should both be ready to transport whenever necessary, don't you think?"

"Sure, I guess so." She hadn't meant for it to sound so hesitant.

"Is it okay? Did I overstep?"

"No. No, you didn't. Thank you, Paul."

"Mine has a cupholder," Jesse said.

"I bet you like that." Amanda looked over her shoulder at her two sweet children. *We're all going to be fine.*

Paul started his truck and set the navigation system for home. He took his eyes off the road for a quick second and smiled in her direction.

Her mood, which had been reflective just a little while ago, seemed lighter now.

"I almost forgot. I told Kimmy and Nate that I'd watch the twins for a couple hours tomorrow morning," Paul said. "They are going on a surfing date. Do you want to come along? I mean, no pressure. If you can't, I understand."

"I'd love to help."

"And those meetings that you saw on my calendar—"

"I know you're busy." She dreaded his being gone so much, afraid that she'd find herself filled with fear that he might not return, as silly as it sounded even in her own head.

He reached for her hand. "It's not as busy as it was. I've delegated some duties. My focus is still on achieving the goals I set for Paws Town Square, but I've promoted a few people to take on more responsibility. I should've done it a long time ago, but it was all I had to focus on." He looked into her eyes. "That's no longer the case. I have more in my life now: you." He glanced in the rearview mirror. "And them. I'll be here for all three of you. No matter what."

"I don't know what to say." Amanda stared at him. Thank

you didn't begin to explain the feelings of being loved and protected. Grateful for that, she said, "We'll find a balance together. What you're doing is very important. I want to be part of that too."

"Then you will." He grinned, his arms flexing as he gripped the steering wheel. "You have no idea how happy I am."

"I feel it too."

30

Over the course of two weeks, Amanda had packed a few boxes each day to move to Maeve's. She'd decided how she would set up her little bungalow for her business. Even dreamed of a pretty sign out front by the gate. No one would ever see it but the mailman and her, but it would give it even more of a cottagey feel.

She was finally going to start her herbal-salts business after all. But with so many things changing, she'd decided to still teach this year and take the time to make a strong business plan. Plus, she still wanted to refine her product line and processes.

They spent most days at Maeve's already, and there was joy when she and the kids spoke of her. It was therapeutic to be among her things and strive to live like she had: joyful, hopeful, and in balance with the ocean. The air-conditioning was a great relief, and the kids loved running up and down the stairs. It was just the motivation she needed to hurry up and finish moving out of the cottage.

Paul came in the back door as she was packing up all her herbal salts. She already had a few boxes filled. It was as if the stuff in the cabinet was never ending.

"Good morning," Paul said. "Starting in here now, huh?"

"Yep."

"What's all this?" He looked inside the top of the full box, then lifted out one of the containers. "Inventory?"

"Sure is."

He opened the jar and inhaled. "This smells great. I'm so happy that you're able to chase this dream. Without any help."

"Well, technically Maeve helped, but I do feel more independent about it. I'm sorry. I hope you appreciate why I can't let you give me a space."

He returned the jar to the box and raised his hands. "Not another word. I like you being strong enough to do your own things. I completely understand."

She was so much busier these days, but she didn't mind one bit. "I am, but I need to also keep my priorities straight."

"Kids first."

"I want to put God first. And you and the kids first. Everything else second."

"We need to work on your math," he teased. "But seriously, I have people who can help you set up a website and everything. I hope you'll let me make that connection for you. They're amazing, and it wouldn't cost much. You have plenty of room for inventory here, so why move all this to Maeve's? Which, by the way, we need to quit calling it Maeve's house."

"What should we call it?"

"The Shell Collector?"

She laughed, but it wasn't a half-bad idea. "I kind of like that. Yeah, I really like that. A nod to Maeve. She will always be a special part of this town. Plus, it's catchy."

Paul said, "I was kidding, but it does kind of work."

"I'm going to give these salts away until I can get a business going. I'll get some feedback and start a customer base at the same time. I'm going to build a very strong business plan, just like you did. Baby steps. I can do it."

"I know you can do it on your own, but if you want to bounce ideas off me or whatever, I'm here for you."

"I'd love that kind of help. I'm really excited about this. Salt of the Earth is going to be a real thing." She pushed the jars back onto the counter. "And you're right. No reason I can't leave the inventory here."

He lifted his hand and high-fived her.

She slapped his hand. "To Salt of the Earth," she said, then hugged him.

"We could set you up a little kiosk at Paws Town Square on the weekends if you want," Paul said. "We've been talking about letting vendors rotate through to give the regulars something new and fresh."

She squeezed her hands together. "This is pretty exciting. Wait, do you think it's smart for us to mix business and our relationship?"

"That depends. I'd like us to mix everything. I don't have any plans to be anywhere but where you are. I was hoping you were feeling it too."

"What if things don't work out?"

"Then we'll still be friends."

"If I lost your friendship, I'd—"

"You are the most important friend in my life. That will never change. I can promise you that." He placed his hands on her hips. "Amanda, if we didn't at least try, we could miss out on something really amazing. I know you're not ready right now. We don't have to rush things, but can't we at least try? Then someday we could get married and all live together in The Shell Collector. I hear there's plenty of room."

She sucked in a breath. "You know I'm afraid."

"That's okay. We'll work on it. Together."

I want to believe that. "Losing Jack left a hole in both our lives, but now it's like he's bringing us together."

"It's a strange place to be. I get it."

"I wonder if we're just filling the gaping wounds and these might not be real feelings that we're experiencing."

He looked like he was holding his breath. "But you are feeling something, right?"

"Something. Yes. For sure."

"That's all we need for now."

Her breath quickened. "Definitely." She reached out and placed her hand on his chest. His heart was beating as hard as hers was. He was afraid too.

Amanda had brought home only one small bag of Spanish moss, but once she realized what she should be doing to honor Maeve, she'd contacted the inn, and the woman there was more than happy to help her out. When the box arrived on Saturday morning, she gathered the children and Paul and Tug and they all worked tirelessly to get it done, putting any other plans on hold.

They laced the Spanish moss throughout the tree, spreading it far enough apart that hopefully it would love its host and not only grow but thrive there. Amanda handed strands of white lights to Paul, who used a rake and a tall ladder to get them as high as they could be on the old live oak in Maeve's backyard.

It had been a long, hot job, but they'd made it fun by letting the kids separate the moss into pieces and hand them up like they were an assembly line. Hailey named each bunch. Hopefully, she would remember which was which. To her they looked like bearded old men, so they had names like Bart, George, Frank, Gary, Rick, Larry, and Bob.

Afterward, Paul made barbecued chicken on the grill, and

the kids anxiously awaited nightfall so they could see the live oak all lit up.

They had a countdown to the big event, and against the dark night sky, the lights really did make the backyard look special. Especially from the second-level deck.

Amanda took pictures. She couldn't wait to call and tell Maeve about the lights. She'd order copies of the photos and send them to her. Maeve would love it. Amanda could imagine the twinkle in her eye when she saw them.

Paul moved closer to Amanda. "Let's all join hands in honor of Maeve tonight. How's that sound?"

Amanda's heart warmed. "It's a beautiful idea." She looked at Hailey and Jesse. They were both nodding. "Yes, we all miss her," Amanda said.

"Okay, then," Paul said quietly.

They all joined hands, standing there on the balcony overlooking the glowing tree full of Spanish moss and lights.

Paul started, "Thank You, heavenly Father, for another day to be with You, to learn and grow and work according to Your will. Today has been a special day for our family." He squeezed Amanda's hand. "We are so blessed to know You, to walk with You, and we are so grateful for all the things and people You've put before us. Tonight we're here together thinking of our dear friend Maeve. Please hear us and be with her in this time of transition. Amen."

Paul then shifted his tone and seemed to be speaking directly to Maeve. "Maeve, you stood up for me, for my dreams, and helped me gain the support of this town. For that I thank you, but most of all I thank you for letting me use your beach access, where I was reunited with the most important person in my life. I'm forever indebted to you. You are most definitely an angel here on earth. I bet the Big Guy has extra-special plans for you."

Jesse followed Paul's lead and in his little-boy voice said, "I love you, Miss Maeve. Will you ask Jesus if we can make drip sandcastles in heaven? Tell Him I can dig Him a moat too. See you soon."

"Miss Maeve, it's me, Hailey. Thank you for being my friend and teaching me so many things. We're in your house, and I'm taking very good care of our secret shell room for you. I think of you every time I look at the shells and beautiful sparkly sea glass because those sparkles remind me of you." Hailey lifted her head. "Is that good, Mom?"

"It's perfect."

"I bet her ears are tickling," said Hailey. "We said very nice things." Hailey clapped her hands. "We love you, Maeve."

Paul and Amanda exchanged a glance. The kids were so precious and kindhearted.

Amanda looked at her phone. "Oh goodness! I need you two to go brush your teeth and get into your pajamas. It's way past bedtime. It's ten after nine."

They didn't argue, just ran straight up the stairs to their rooms.

The next morning as they got ready for church, Amanda couldn't resist any longer. She sat at the desk in the shell room, waiting for Maeve to answer her cell phone. When she didn't, Amanda left a message, letting her know they were thinking of her and wanted to see how she was doing.

Amanda gathered Hailey and Jesse and went to church. Paul met them there, and for the first time, both of the kids went to children's church, having fun meeting new friends. It was good they were getting some socializing in. Not only at school, but here too. She'd kept them close for so long, and she was glad to see them adjusting.

As they pulled out of the parking lot, Amanda waved to Matthew, Nikki, and Matt. No one asked any questions about Paul. They were accepted just as they were.

When they all got back to the beach house, the kids went upstairs to change clothes. Amanda picked up her phone and saw that she'd missed three calls from Judy.

But before Amanda could call her back, Hailey came in dressed in her purple bathing suit, next to Jesse, who was wearing American-flag trunks. "We're ready to go to the beach."

"I just have to return this call first."

"I'll take them on down," Paul said.

"Okay, I'll be there in a hurry."

"Awesome." They took off down the stairs, and Amanda watched all three of them run through the sand toward the water.

She stared at her phone, almost a little nervous to dial, but then she punched in the number.

"Hello?"

"Hi, Judy, this is Amanda Whittier. I'm sorry to bother you, but I was hoping I could speak to Maeve."

"I'm sorry . . ." Judy's voice dropped. "She passed in her sleep last night a little after nine o'clock. I was going to call you."

Amanda's throat tightened, making it hard to breathe. "Oh no."

"She was so peaceful, Amanda. You gave her such a gift by making that special drive here. She went on and on about the moss in those trees."

"It was beautiful." Amanda thought of how gorgeous the live oak looked as they turned on the lights for the kids . . . just about that same time last night.

"She was holding the moss you had given her, clutching it,

reaching out. Then she closed her eyes and smiled. She had her hand curled—"

"Like someone was holding it?"

"Yes. How did you know?"

"She said that's what she missed most about Jarvis. The way he held her hand." Amanda struggled to swallow. Maeve would never get to see the pictures of the moss they'd put in her special tree. Her heart squeezed. She'd like to believe she already knew, though.

"I'm so sorry you called before I had a chance to let you know." Judy sighed.

"No, that's fine. I understand." She would miss Maeve, but believing that at long last she'd be reunited with Jarvis, it was hard to feel sad for her. "Judy, your sister was special. Thank you again for allowing me to have that sweet time with her. Please let me know what I can do to help."

"Well, thank *you* too. I'm not sure why she finally gave in and came, but we treasured our time together. It was too short, but she wasn't in any pain."

"I'd love to go to the service if you'll send me the details."

"I surely will."

Amanda hung up the phone and walked over to the over-stuffed chair in Maeve's sunroom, or secret shell room, as Hailey called it. She sank into the chair, praying for Maeve. She must have passed as they lit up the moss in her tree. She hoped somehow their thoughts of her last night had comforted her all the way to heaven and that Jarvis greeted her as though they hadn't missed a single day together.

A tiny bit of her wished she could see Jack, to tell him they were okay. To tell him herself that although her life was changing and growing, her love for him would always be there.

Amanda took a photo album from the bottom shelf and carried it back over to the chair. It was Maeve and Jarvis's wedding pictures. Maeve had been stunning—a model-like beauty. Her gown had been simple, but that's all she needed. Jarvis's love for her was undeniable in the way he looked at her.

"You're with Jarvis now. I can picture you two holding hands." She let out a small cry, tears dripping from her chin. "Please tell Jack I love him and that he will always own a corner of my heart."

31

At the end of the week, Judy called to inform Amanda she was following Maeve's wishes to be cremated and have a funeral on Whelk's Island at the church Maeve had gone to as a child, where their parents were buried. The same one that Amanda, Paul, and the kids attended now.

Thank you. It was as if Maeve had reached out and hugged her.

Amanda couldn't wait to tell Tug. He'd been so quiet. He was hurting, and this would most definitely help him feel like he could say goodbye, with the service being right here.

She invited Judy to stay at the house, offering to let the family have it and she'd use her cottage during the funeral, but Judy refused. She'd already booked a condo on the marina, and she was coming by herself.

"May I take care of the obituary here locally, or have you handled that?" Amanda asked.

"Already done," Judy said. "Don't be impressed. Maeve had all this outlined and finalized. All I have to do is show up."

"I'm not surprised."

"Me neither," Judy said with a laugh.

Maeve's obituary ran in the paper the following morning.

On the day of the funeral, cars were parked down the main beach road for as far as Amanda could see. Throngs of people came to say goodbye to Maeve.

The service was beautifully done. On a large easel at the front of the church was a large portrait of Maeve on the beach, facing the water, her skirt flowing in the breeze and her arms open wide. A gorgeous carved wooden box with a golden seashell on top contained her ashes.

The pastor did a lovely job outlining Maeve's life, then opened the microphone for anyone who cared to share their memories.

Amanda, Paul, Hailey, Jesse, and Tug sat in the front row with Judy. Becky, Kimmy, and Nate sat behind them. The rest of the pews were filled with people from town.

A few folks got up and shared stories about their relationship with Maeve, and then Tug rose to his feet and walked to the front. He seemed shaken, but his voice was loud and strong. He looked across the room, then closed his eyes. "Maeve, my girl, I'll never stop loving you. You've been the light in my heart for as long as I've known you. You've been the life of this town. If you can see all of us here today, then you can see that you're already missed."

Tug's message was short, but from the nodding heads and tears, it was obvious it landed on every heart in the church.

He sat down next to Amanda. She squeezed his hand as she watched people line the aisle. They walked up front and placed a single shell in the sandy tray under the box holding Maeve's ashes.

The choir sang a song, and a local country band performed two other songs that Maeve had requested, including "Go Rest High on That Mountain" and "Don't Cry for Me."

As they sang, Amanda walked up and knelt beside Maeve's picture.

Thank you for being at my side through every wobbly step I've made since I hit these sandy beaches. Thank you, Maeve, for being a true friend and sharing your most precious memories and experiences with me. You gave all your gifts in such an unselfish way and challenged me to find mine. I hope I can learn and live by that. Methuselah is acting like a puppy, and he is having daily playtime with Denali. You wouldn't even recognize him. It's so sweet. We love you.

Tears blurred her line of sight, but Paul reached for her hand and led her back to gather the children and leave.

They walked with Tug to the parking lot.

"It was really lovely." Tug wiped his eyes. "I miss that gal."

"We all do." Amanda reached for Tug's hand. "You two were friends forever. I only had the privilege to know her for a short time, but she was an angel to me. She really changed my perspective. She cleared the murky sadness from my heart and reminded me to live." Amanda squeezed Tug's fingers. "I will always love her for that."

"I miss Maeve, Mommy," Hailey said.

"Me too." She gave her daughter's hand a gentle squeeze. "It's okay to miss her."

Jesse stood wide eyed, clinging to Paul.

"But Maeve promised me she'd tell Daddy I love and miss him," Hailey said. "So I'm okay. She said she was excited to be going to the streets of gold. I told her to take her sunglasses. I hope she remembered."

"I bet she did." Amanda looked at all the cars in the parking lot. Maeve touched so many lives, and they didn't even know the half of it.

Judy walked up behind Amanda. "Thank you again for all you did for my sister."

"Of course. Won't you come over?"

"No, I'm headed straight home." Judy rushed off to a waiting car. Amanda wasn't sure if she had driven or was catching a flight. Amanda was so thankful Judy had honored Maeve's wishes for the service.

Paul led Amanda and the kids to the truck and drove them

back to the beach house. When they pulled into the driveway, there was already a car parked there.

Paul looked at Amanda with a question in his eyes. "You sit tight for a minute." Paul got out and spoke with the man in the car, then motioned for them to come on.

He introduced the man to Amanda. "This is Mark Ledger, Maeve's lawyer. He has some papers for you."

"Oh, okay. That's fine." She examined the tall man. He didn't have that lawyer look. No, he looked more like he could catch a wave with his longish hair and sun-kissed skin, despite his advanced age and the high-dollar suit. She'd seen him at the service.

The kids went to the backyard to play with the dogs while Paul and Amanda met with Mr. Ledger in the living room.

"I thought it would be best to get this over to you today. It's pretty cut and dried." He set a folder in the center of the table. "Her sister, Judy, left me some things from Maeve to you. Before she moved, Maeve and I had a couple of meetings to get everything taken care of."

Amanda sat with her hands in her lap. She thought it odd that Judy wouldn't have just given them to her herself.

"Maeve signed the deed to this house and property over to you. You'll be responsible for taxes and insurance beginning two years from now. She's left the funds to take care of it until then and to board her dog if you choose to do so."

"We'll take care of Methuselah," Amanda said.

Paul dipped his head. "Absolutely. We've got that covered."

"All I need is your signature here and here and we'll get the deed transfer done."

Amanda leaned forward and signed the papers. "That seems too easy."

"The house was paid for. No liens or anything, although I did have a title search done for Maeve as good practice."

"Thank you."

"All the details are in this package." He slid it over to Amanda. "That's all I need from you."

Next to the papers, he placed a simple blue box.

Before she could ask what it was, Mr. Ledger reached into his jacket. "And this is from Judy." He handed Amanda an envelope as he stood. "I'll leave you to go through everything. If you have any questions at all, call me. There's no charge, and I'll take care of whatever queries or problems you encounter."

"Thank you, Mr. Ledger."

"You're welcome. I'm really sorry for your loss."

"Thank you."

"I can let myself out." He stood, straightened his jacket, and left.

"This is a lot to take in," Amanda said. She turned and laid her head on Paul's shoulder.

"She was very generous."

Amanda opened the card from Judy first.

Dear Amanda,

You and your children made my sister's life so full at the end. She cherished the days since she met you. You made her last days happy, and she was then ready to meet her one true love in heaven. I know because she told me so, and she also told me she hoped she would die in her sleep, which is exactly what she did. I pray you can find comfort in that. Carry on and treasure your life with those precious children and recognize your gifts. Give them away. God will keep giving you more.

Maeve's loving sister,
Judy

She passed the letter to Paul.

He held her hand while he read it. "She was something," he said. "You two have the same heart."

She picked up the blue box that Mr. Ledger left on the table. It had some weight to it. She lifted the lid. Inside, there was an envelope on top.

Amanda opened it, then looked up at Paul. "It's information about Denali, the mountain in Alaska." A glossy brochure highlighted a two-week cruise and rail trip along with a stay to see the northern lights. "Doesn't this look beautiful?"

"Jack really wanted to take you there. I'm sure if he had one regret about not coming back, it was that you two never got to make that trip."

She looked at the pictures. "I still want to see it. All of it. The summit. The northern lights. Those small Alaskan communities."

She swept back tissue paper and lifted out a blob of Bubble Wrap secured by packing tape. "This is really taped up tight."

"Here, let me get that." Paul took the knife from his pocket and sliced the tape. He pulled the Bubble Wrap from the outside. "It's a shell."

"Oh? I should've known." She breathed a happy sigh. "It's a conch. She loved them." She turned it over in her hand. "It has a message. Like the other ones."

"What's it say?"

"Trust the journey." She handed him the shell. "Paul, I believe you are on this journey with me."

He squeezed her hand.

"There's a card." She opened the envelope and read it out loud.

Dearest Amanda,
You are stronger than you can imagine. It has been my
honor to call you my friend. Thank you for sharing your time

and allowing me to be a small part of Hailey's and Jesse's lives. Grief is a tricky monster. I pray that you and the children will not grieve my departure but rather take joy in knowing that I am with Jarvis on those streets of gold. Tell Hailey I have my sunglasses and I will find Jack. I bet he's waiting on me with Jarvis.

Embrace your life. I want you to. We all want you to. Be brave, my friend. You have a wonderful life ahead of you. I hope you love Denali and that it's everything you've dreamed of. You made my dream come true. I had no idea that our girls' trip would be as wonderful as it was. Hopefully this Denali trip will be just as special. If you want to know what I'm thinking, it's that you and Paul and the children will all take this trip together and make memories that will last a lifetime. I believe you can trust Paul, but don't listen to this old lady. You trust your heart. I'll be watching, and if I get to ask for an assignment, you'll be hearing my voice in your ear every time you walk that beach.

I love you, my dear. Raise your children strong like you. Let Him show you your gifts and He will lead you.

Until we meet again.

> *Your friend,*
> *Maeve*

She looked into Paul's eyes. "Would you want to go?"

"I would walk on hot coals for you. Whatever you want, I'll be there. But if you need to do it alone—for Jack—honey, I get it."

Of course you'd say that. Paul was never selfish. His joy came from the things he did for others. She looked into his eyes, which seemed to lead straight to his heart. "I am so thankful and grateful you are in my life. Our lives. I want you to go to Denali with us." Yes, she did. That was a memory she wanted to make with him.

His smile brightened. "I can't wait."

Amanda let out a breath. "I'm so lucky to have known her. I will never be as amazing as she was, but I hope I can make her proud."

"You already are. You two were meant to meet and lift each other."

"It would seem so, wouldn't it?" Amanda looked around at the lovely home she was now living in.

"You are a strong and remarkable woman. I am so grateful for the love that is growing between us."

"Paul, for the first time, right this minute, I truly feel worthy of love again."

"I will never let you down." He shook his head, his eyes glistening.

"Thank you for being patient with me."

"I will wait as long as you need." He took a knee in front of her. "Don't freak out. I'm not asking you to marry me today."

She cried, hugging her arms to her chest.

"I want to put it out there that when you're ready, I do want you to marry me. I'll wait as long as it takes. I want to be your husband. To love, honor, and obey you. To help you raise your and Jack's children the way you'd have wanted it."

She hugged his neck.

"Interrupt worry with gratitude."

The next morning, it took a moment for Amanda to realize where she was. It would take some getting used to living here in Maeve's house. She heard voices from outside. She pushed the covers back and walked into the hall. She followed the sound toward the front door and stepped out onto the porch. Paul, Hailey, and Jesse looked as guilty as three pirates standing there at the bottom of the steps.

"What is going on?"

"A couple things, actually," Paul said. "One planned, one unplanned. Which do you want first?"

"Hmm. Planned?"

"It's such a good surprise," Hailey said.

"Come on, Hailey. You can help me carry it." Paul and Hailey disappeared under the carport area and stepped back out with something under a big sheet. Jesse danced around, giggling. Keeping the secret was probably about to kill him.

She stood there trying to figure out what they were up to.

Hailey raised her hands in the air. "Three. Two. One!"

Paul let Jesse pull the sheet back. Paul held a four-foot wide sandblasted sign that read, **The Shell Collector.**

"Oh my goodness. For the house?" Amanda ran over. "I love it!" She traced her fingers across the textured wooden sign. The raised letters were charming, and in each of the O's there was a shell. It was perfect.

Hailey and Jesse jumped up and down. "Paul let us pick out the colors," Hailey said.

She reached up and kissed Paul on the lips. She caught herself, then glanced down, hoping it hadn't upset Hailey or Jesse, but they didn't seem to have even noticed.

"What was the unplanned?" she asked. "It can't be better than this."

"It's a really close second," Paul said. "Might even be better. Close your eyes."

She closed her eyes.

"Hold out your hand."

She extended her hands.

He placed something in them.

She opened her eyes and looked at the simple shell in her hands. "Where did this come from?"

Paul pointed to the house near the flower bed. "It was tucked right there."

She read the short sentiment in the shell: "*In His Time. Trust there is a time for every event under heaven.*"

Maeve was certainly still here, guiding her.

"Shall we hang this sign?" Paul pulled a ladder out of the back of his truck.

"Absolutely."

It only took about five minutes because Paul had already placed the screws. All he had to do was climb up and hang the sign there on the house. "What do you think?"

The colorful sign brightened the front of the house. The kids whooped and hollered so loud it was very likely both Maeve and Jack heard them.

Amanda walked out to the edge of the driveway. "It looks great!"

"I'm glad you like it."

"I do."

"Ready to go inside?"

"I have one more thing to do," Amanda said. "You and the kids go on up. I'll be there in a minute."

"Sure, babe. Take your time."

She watched until all three of them had gone inside. Then she took the phone out of her back pocket, scrolled through her contacts, and clicked on her mother's phone number. It went straight to voice mail, but she took a breath and left a message.

"Hey, Mom. It's me, Amanda. It's been too long since I told you I love you. I'd like to bring the kids up to visit."

Acknowledgments

People often say writing is a solitary job, but I could never do this alone. It truly takes a village to take an idea through the process of turning it into a novel. This book is no exception.

Thank you to the many people who helped me along the way.

Steve Laube for opening up doors to find the right home for this novel. *The Shell Collector* has a special place in my heart, and Steve understood that. I love working with the team at WaterBrook. Thank you, Steve. This is only the beginning. I can't wait to see where this journey takes us.

Becky Nesbitt for seeing the potential of this story. From the moment we met, I felt like I had a new friend, and I appreciate the mentorship she shared with me through this story. Becky, you made this book sparkle as brilliantly as sea glass.

Andrew, my sweet husband, thank you for being patient through the process, especially the part where I'm struggling with the story and tired from staying up all night. You are always there to pray with me and remind me where to place my worries when I falter.

My dear friends Missy and Pam. Missy for the real estate details I needed in the research phase. It's so wonderful to have smart people ready with answers faster—and more reliable—than the internet. The same goes for Pam for helping me build out the fun Paws Town Square. She's had a dream of running a dog camp. I don't think it'll be in an old ghost box in a city, but boy, wouldn't that be a hoot.

Hidden Haven in Tobaccoville, North Carolina, for hosting my getaways to bring this book to completion and inspiring a new story too. I love staying there.

Special thoughts for the friends and family of Mike Wiles, who passed away during the developmental edits of this book. I'd promised to make him a character one day, so I wove him into this story as Paul's right-hand man, Chase. Mike had said he'd always liked that name. Mike played a special role in my husband's business start-up, and he'll be greatly missed. Like Chase, he had his struggles, but he'd found his place. I'm sorry he won't ever get to read this.

Kitty Hawk Kites for being around as long as I can remember and still carrying the coolest stuff. I hope ghost crabbing and flying kites never go out of style.

My cousin Diane Pyatt Hartman passed away just a month after my husband died in 2014. The previous year she shared a touching story with me that a friend of her family had experienced involving a mysterious shell. We shared many emails and phone calls about it, and it was nice to having something to talk about besides the cancer that was making her so sick at the time. I wish you were here for this book launch, Diane. I treasure feeling so close to you while writing this novel.